Return of the Fae

S. M. SAVOY

Published by
Ace Lyon Books
January
2018

Books by S. M Savoy

Valor

A Warrior's Fury

A Sun Priest's Magic

Beyond Valor

Published by
Ace Lyon Books
Cover Design by S. M. Savoy
S. M. Savoy Return of the Fae
ISBN 978-1-947122-16-1

Contents

Return of the Fae

Time to Grow Up

Sam flopped onto Jen's bed, knocking a pile of shirts to the floor. The shirts scattered, covering a heap of shoes and discarded pants.

"Going a little overboard, aren't you?" Sam lifted a perfectly shaped eyebrow as she examined the mess in Jen's small room.

Jen huffed and held a black, lacey blouse across her chest, then threw it on the bed. Eyes narrowed, she examined the few remaining shirts in her closet.

Sam sorted through a pile of discarded clothing and laid a few pieces aside. "What if he's ugly, or old, or a creep or something?"

"He isn't a creep. And so what if he isn't Mister Universe? I'm not exactly a supermodel either."

Sam made an unhappy sound and stood to

root through the pile of clothing on the bed.

"Try this" – she handed Jen a bright-red long-sleeved shirt with a scalloped hemline and dark-blue skinny jeans— "and don't be stupid; you could get any guy you wanted if you'd talk to one."

The blue eyes Jen met in the mirror were full of concern. Even concerned and wearing a frown, Sam was effortlessly beautiful. Her golden-blond hair curled naturally and picked up glittering highlights from the sun without a salon. Long and thick, it reached the middle of her back in loose, rolling waves.

Jen had given up trying to mimic the look an hour ago and scraped back her straight brown hair into its usual ponytail. Jen's shirt, which Sam held against her chest, would swim on Sam's petite full-busted frame.

For the billionth time, Jen felt like a geek beside her best friend. A tall, plain, flat-chested geek. She took the makeup kit Sam handed her and stuffed it into her carry-on bag. No eyeshadow on Earth would give her Sam's sparkly baby-blues. Thick, black lashes framed Sam's sky-blue eyes, shadowing her delicate cheekbones. The best she could say about her own face was it wasn't ugly.

Resigned, Jen put on the clothes Sam handed her.

Sam smiled as she continued speaking. "No, Ethan Lance isn't a creep; he seems nice, but what do we really know about him? And really, even if he's amazing, what's the point of all this? He lives in Ireland, and we live here, in Bristol. You can't have a real relationship online. Someday, you'll actually have to date a real boy."

Jen snorted. "He is a real boy. And it's just a short flight away…" She gave Sam a hug and crammed the clothes she'd picked into her suitcase. "Stop worrying. I realize he's a fantasy guy."

"You just love his accent."

Jen giggled. "That and his mad skills. I tried to recruit him to replace Miguel, but he won't leave Jon. You know how rare that is? I think that's the first time anyone ever turned down a chance to join our guild."

Sam shrugged lightly, grimacing apologetically. "Not very. Jon's guild is the second-best guild on this server. Frankly, Genesis is falling apart a bit. I hate when they add legendary items to the game. All of a sudden no one wants me along."

Jen winced and turned away. Sam got invited to raids because of her. Mostly the guild didn't mind when Sam tagged along, and in fact treated her nicely. The pictures Jen had posted on her website of Sam wearing a bikini on their vacation in Mexico saw to that. But Genesis was made up of serious gamers and carrying Sam through a hard dungeon meant no one got the loot.

Sam gave her a rueful smile. "It doesn't bother me unless they're dicks about it." She folded the black lace shirt and tucked it into Jen's bag. "I'll never be good at the game, and I don't care."

Jen turned back to pack her laptop and mouse. "As long as you keep playing with me when you're famous."

Pink crept across Sam's cheeks. "It's just a small production company." She jumped to her feet and twirled. "I'm going to be Clara in a real ballet in three weeks. Can you believe it?"

Jen laughed as Sam continued to pirouette around her bedroom, leaping over the piled clothes.

"I believe it. You're amazing. Thanks for taking the week off and coming with me. We're going to have a great time in Japan."

Sam flopped on the bed again and grinned. "It'll be fun, and I'm bringing my practice clothes. Besides, if you win, you're paying for my ticket, and you've got a great shot. If Philip and Miguel can get along for five minutes, that is." She winked and batted her lashes. "And, if you can keep your mind off Ethan."

Reminded, Jen turned back to the mirror and frowned. "I hope he isn't too good-looking."

"You better hope he isn't gay or married." Sam jumped up to answer a knock on the door.

"I hope he's interested in me too," Jen said, but too softly for Sam to hear over Randy's boisterous greeting.

She finished packing and brought her bags into the tiny main room. The all-in-one kitchen and living space barely fit a couch and small table.

She and Sam had shared this apartment for three years now, but she didn't think that would last much longer. Sam and Randy were in love and serious.

"You've got thirty minutes to say goodbye!" Jen called after them as they headed to Sam's room which was separated from hers by a bathroom. "I'll be downstairs." She stifled her giggle, doubting they heard her, and locked the door behind her.

Neither she nor Sam made much money. Their small apartment was in a crappy section of town above a Vietnamese restaurant. She loved the apartment and her neighbors though. When Sam moved out to live with Randy, she'd miss this.

Soon, she'd have to decide what she was going to do with her life. In six months, she'd graduate from college, and she couldn't count on winnings or her parents to support her. Without her to worry about Sam would've moved in with Randy a year ago. Jen's neediness was straining her friendship with Randy, and she couldn't blame him. It was time to grow up.

For a moment she paused, clearing her head before banging on Kuan's door. Kuan was surprisingly sensitive to moods for someone so out of touch with reality.

She banged again before he answered, but she'd expected that. Real world interruptions from his gaming came hard.

She was struck again by his beauty as he answered the door. Unusual genes had produced high cheekbones and brilliant, periwinkle-blue eyes. When they'd first met, she'd assumed he'd gotten his blue eyes from his American father, but his Vietnamese mother had the same startlingly gorgeous eyes. His height and the shape of his face were from his dad, smooth cheeks and silky black hair from his mother.

To Jen's surprise, he answered the door freshly showered with a bag packed. Wet, black hair held back in a tight ponytail left a damp spot on his clean, black sweatshirt. Baggy jeans slid from his hips, exposing blue boxers. Neither the hairstyle nor the jeans were a fashion choice, he just couldn't be bothered with eating or grooming.

"Did you eat yet?" Without waiting for his reply she pulled him from the apartment. "Let's go get your mom to feed us."

Downstairs in the restaurant, his mother greeted her with a smile and prepared two plates, which she and Kuan ate standing in the back of the busy kitchen. Kuan's older brother handed her a soda and Kuan a bottled water.

"Good luck, Bro. I really hope you win the money." He gave Jen an anxious glance. "You'll take care of him, right?"

"Sam and I will take care of him, and he'll be staying with Kirk. Besides, we all know he won't leave the tourney grounds." She had to glance away to hide her guilty wince about Kirk. If Kuan's parents knew Kirk was a drug dealer they'd never approve of the association.

Jen didn't like it either, but Kirk kept his private life out of the game. His crush on Sam was growing wearisome, but he was, hands down, the best warlock in the game. She was willing to overlook his marijuana sales for a chance at a half-million-dollar prize.

Kuan snorted. "Why would I? that's the entire point of going."

"True." She exchanged smiles with Kuan's brother. His brother didn't understand Kuan's gaming obsession but did his best to support him anyway.

His mother wiped her hands on a dishtowel and brought Jen an envelope containing Kuan's passport, plane tickets and spending money.

"Genevieve, I can't thank you enough. His father and I worry so, but if he can support himself like this…" She kissed Kuan's cheek and fussed with his clothes. Tears filled her eyes, and she hugged him hard a moment before stepping back. "Go be the best druid you can."

"Don't worry about me," Kuan said, then kissed her cheek. "I love you guys, but I was meant to be a druid."

His mother winced and turned to Jen again. She kissed her cheek and whispered, "Take care of him."

When Jen had first moved in, Kuan had really struggled with the realities of life, having heated arguments with his family about his gaming and refusal to do anything else. Loud arguments she and Sam heard through the floor. To get any studying done, Jen had looked Kuan up online. Finding his screen name was easy. That was all he ever talked about.

Until that time she'd been a casual gamer, but she'd been inspired to get him tournament ready. And it worked. His parents had stopped complaining once he began making money. By the time he graduated high school, he made enough to support himself, and she made enough to pay her half of the bills.

She and Sam made sure Kuan ate, showered, exercised and slept in real life, and kept him focused in the game, making sure he spent time getting good gear, not just attractive gear, and attending raids, not just wandering through the forests being a 'druid.'

Twice a week she dragged him to a karate class with her. And twice a week, Sam took him jogging. Grateful that Jen took care of their son, his parents lowered their rent and gave them free meals.

She and Kuan ran their guild together. He had a real knack for finding so-so players and teaching them to be amazing players, leaving the planning to her.

With his help she'd developed ideas for a video game of her own. When she graduated this spring with a computer science degree, she'd have time to work on them. And if they won the tourney, she could afford to stay in the apartment alone and do it.

Kuan paused at the door and glanced back. "They don't see it, Jen. To them, it's just a game. But that's who we are." Before Jen could decide if she should try to break his delusion, he bounded up the stairs to her apartment. A twinge of guilt slowed her pace. Normally, she took every opportunity to convince Kuan he wasn't really a druid, but now she needed him to be the best druid he could be.

"Let's pry Sam from Randy and get to the plane. This is going to be amazing!" he called over his shoulder.

"Would you relax?" Sam plucked Jen's hand from her arm and placed it on the plastic seat rest.

Jen absently apologized, her anxious gaze scanning the crowded airport waiting room for Jon.

"Oh, there he is. Should I go say hi or wait and let him come here? Or—"

"Chill." Sam pulled Jen's hand away from her mouth to keep from biting her thumb nail. "Let him gather his team, and we can check Ethan out from here. And stop biting your nails."

An excited tingle built to a knee jitter as Jen stared at Jon. She knew his entire team from prior tourneys— except Ethan. Maria, Ascendant's druid, entered the waiting room and hugged Jon, then Josh their team's shaman entered, followed by

Lindsey the team's sun-priest, trailed by her family. Jen let her breath out in a whoosh as Maria hugged a tall black man.

"Ethan's black," Sam said and giggled as she smacked Jen's jittering knee.

"He's beautiful," Jen said and frowned and slumped back in her seat. Broad shouldered and clean-shaven, Ethan's tight white T-shirt showed off muscled arms and a narrow waist.

"He sure is," Sam said, sounding impressed. "Go say hi."

"What's the point... look at him. He's way out of my league."

"Don't be stupid; go say hi." Sam stood.

Jen snatched at her and missed. She debated following or hiding. The thought of Sam catching Ethan's interest first decided her.

"Watch our stuff," she said to Kuan who didn't glance up from his laptop, and ran after Sam. By the time she reached her, her palms sweat. Butterflies danced in her stomach, turning to flip-flopping fish when Ethan turned to them and smiled, revealing perfect, white teeth.

"Jen, Sam, I looked forward to meeting you guys in person."

She shook his hand, the contact sending a tingle straight to her loins.

"You too; hey guys." Sam hugged Jon and his team, then elbowed Jen hard.

A hot blush covered Jen's cheeks as she realized she'd stood gaping like an idiot for minutes. "I'm glad you came back to the game. We missed you." She gave Jon a sickly smile. "Did he tell you I tried to poach him?"

Jon winked at her. "Yep, try all you want; it won't work. Ethan and I have been friends for years. I even went to his wedding."

Jen's gaze flicked to Ethan's hands, and sure enough, he wore a wedding ring. *Of course he's taken,* she thought to herself and stood stupidly, not knowing what to say. A hot blush burned across her cheeks. Sam jumped in, making small talk and plans to meet for lunch.

Jen heard none of it. Her wits felt frozen along with her smile. She managed to mumble goodbye and followed Sam back to their seats without tripping.

"Well, crap." She grabbed a magazine to fan her burning cheeks.

"Sorry, Jen, but I warned you," Sam said, smiling but looking concerned.

"Warned her about what?" Kirk asked as he dropped his carry-on by his feet and kissed Sam's cheek.

He slapped Kuan's shoulder and nodded to Jen. He too wore his hair long and pants loose, but his scruffiness was a fashion statement. So was the five o'clock shadow, dark sunglasses and gold jewelry. Jen spent a second admiring the large diamond in his ear, sure it was real.

She wondered how Kirk always managed to show the same exact extent of scruffy. His facial hair always seemed like he needed a shave. He never grew a full beard, yet she'd never seen his cheeks clean-shaven. The look suited him, giving him a sexy, dangerous air.

She answered him while speculating on how much he made a year selling drugs to afford such expensive jewelry. "Nothing. You get the email I sent about chipping in to buy the locate spell for Philip?"

"I'll lend him the gold, but I'm not giving it to him." Kirk sat beside them and peered over Kuan's shoulder to view his screen.

Kuan glanced up. "Sorry, Jen; I don't have much at the moment. I just bought new vanity spells— look." Kuan turned his screen to show her.

Jen admired the pictures Kuan showed her as she said, "I like the black bird best too."

Sam giggled.

"Stop," Jen hissed. "Black Raven form is dramatic. I love how the designers made the feathers shimmer with that hint of blue," she said to Kuan.

"Too much gold and way too much time spent farming for a vanity spell." Kirk patted Kuan's shoulder. "It's pretty though."

Sam put an arm around Kuan's shoulder. "I think making them hard to get makes them special. If everyone had the black panther and bear it wouldn't be as cool."

Kuan tapped the keys that transformed his

character into a bear. "Look how awesome I am now. This is how I'm meant to be. It was totally worth all those quests and gold."

"Sure, it was." Sam leaned over to admire the bear.

Kuan grinned at her. "Did you check your mail? I sent you a tamer spell I found yesterday. Thought you might like to have ten lesser animal pets at once."

"Really," Sam said, sounding thrilled. She opened her laptop and logged in.

A frown furrowed Kirk's brow. "I'd have got you one if I knew you'd like it. I didn't realize…" He sighed and watched glumly as Sam oohed and ahhed over the spell.

Jen bit back her laugh. Sam would've gushed over anything Kuan gave her, but she did love the vanity spells. Her armor was crap because she spent all her gold on special effects for her spells and pets.

"I can't help either. I spent all my gold on Improved Scare Beast," Sam said.

"Seriously?" Kirk's eyes widened and he took Sam's laptop. "Holy crap, you did! I think there are only two guys on this entire server with that."

"Because it costs a ridiculous amount of gold for a spell that does nothing except change your form and scare beasts," Jen said as she leaned over Kuan to see the screen in Kirk's lap. "If they'd let you use it to fly beyond six hundred yards, then I'd be interested."

Jen grinned at the dragon on Sam's screen. "Sweet, you picked the blue one. You're enormous…"

"Look." Sam leaned over and tapped a key. A gout of flame shot from the dragon's mouth. "Wouldn't it be cool if you could use the dragon indoors? I'd totally raid like that, breathing fire and clawing my enemies."

Kirk and Kuan continued to admire Sam's dragon. Jen flipped open a magazine and pretended to read it while staring at Ethan.

Sam was right, meeting someone in a game was stupid. She'd gotten her hopes up for nothing. So what if he was super nice if he was married? If she'd met him in person, she'd have known not to waste a second thought on him, his looks alone would've dissuaded her. No one that good looking would go for the plain girl.

She pasted a fake smile on her face and stood to greet Philip and his girlfriend. Sam glanced up, then turned to Kirk, pretending great absorption in the game. Jen wished she could do the same. Philip's girlfriend, Sue, was a real bitch, and she'd hope they'd have broken up by now, but she should've known better.

Sue wouldn't leave Philip until after the tourney and then only if he lost. Already she eyed the members of Ascendants, Genesis' toughest rivals, planning her next conquest. How Philip could miss her contemplative stares Jen didn't know. Sue ogled Jon as if he were a side of meat she was considering buying for dinner.

"Let's get a snack. Save our seats, Jen." Philip pulled Sue with him to the nearby food court.

"Maybe he isn't as oblivious as he seems," Sam said, making Jen laugh.

Sam always knew what she was thinking.

"This is going to be a nightmare," Jen said as Sue hugged Josh, Ascendant's shaman while Philip glowered.

Still Be Friends

Ethan handed Jen a soda, then offered the tray to Kuan and Sam. "Team Valor is playing amazingly well."

Jen nodded her thanks. "I ran into them in the hall yesterday as they were leaving. They were very ill, sweaty and pale. Can you imagine their times in the games if they weren't?"

"They'll for sure be the team to beat next year when they're old enough to play in the majors."

Ethan sat beside her and crossed his legs over the empty seat in front of them.

"Hah, you don't have this tourney sown up yet."

He grinned and winked at her. "No shame in second place."

"Glad you think so." Jen smirked and smoothed her hair, then wanted to smack herself for forgetting he was married. So what if her ponytail was a mess or her mascara smudged. All the worry and effort to look good was wasted when a simple question could've saved her weeks of angst.

He threw his head back and laughed, completely oblivious to how he flustered her.

Jon sat behind them and leaned forward. "I've been thinking. Team Valor is going to be hard to beat. Maybe we should merge our guilds."

Jen frowned. "What would we do for tourneys? Two tanks and two druids. You just want Kuan and Kirk."

"True…" Jon grinned and slapped Kuan's shoulder. "Think about it though. You could have an all-girl team. You as the tank, Maria as an elemental druid, Lindsey as a sun-priest—"

Jen eyed Maria and Lindsey speculatively. Both were very good players. "That would be kind of cool. I'm not saying yes, but let's plan a raid together and a few PVP matches. You can bring three of my top five-man teams with three of yours. We likely have enough skilled players to do three complete thirty-man assaults on Higard Castle, which is one extra then if we stuck to our own guilds. And we'd need some way to disperse gear fairly between the two guilds, although we'd get more and better gear working together."

Jen pursed her lips and eyed Jon thoughtfully wondering how long he'd been planning this and if he had ulterior motives. Cooperation in the game would get them farther than competition, but there were sure to be problems from her guild members who'd see a merge as losing their raid position or competing against Jon's guild for the limited gear.

Video game raiders took such things very seriously. Especially as until this year, Genesis was the undisputed, top ranking guild on her realm until Jon's guild, Ascendants, had nudged them out. Maybe her guild would welcome fresh new players of equal skill?

Jen's gaze traveled to the corner of the room where Philip and Miguel argued.

Ethan nodded toward them. "Both talented players, but ego's the size of the Atlantic. They're really going to bring your score down if they bicker the entire time."

"I know." Jen heaved a sigh and went to break them up.

"I really like that about you, Genevieve Frey, how hard you work to keep your team happy," he called after her.

Despite herself, she felt a little tingle from his compliment. A bubble of happiness surrounded her until she reached Philip.

"Don't even talk to her," Philip was shouting in a furious whisper as she approached.

Damn it. Miguel was a horn dog, always flirting. The bigger the wedge he could drive, the happier he was. Thin and wiry, he wore his black hair short and spiked. *His entire personality was spiky,* she thought as she stepped between them.

She'd invited him to the guild, and to the team, against Kuan's wishes when Eric had backed out and had been regretting it ever since. Her greed was going to ruin her guild, but this one win would support her and Kuan for five years, and despite his major personality flaws, Miguel was a skilled rogue.

"Hey, guys, come watch the matches. We can argue three days from now." Jen took Philip's arm and tried to lead him away.

Other gamers watching the bouts on the big screens lining the convention hall while waiting for their turns glanced over but Team Valor confronting a red dragon on the screen drew their attention away.

"This asshole thinks he can make a move on my girl—" Philip pulled away and turned back to Miguel. "I don't give a shit what's at stake. You think I won't bug out and leave you stranded for a fifth player, you're fucking wrong." Hands on his hips, he leaned forward and glared at Miguel.

Jen forced a smile and stepped between them. "Miguel, just apologize already. And leave Sue alone." She wanted to smack him and yank Philip away. Hell, she wanted to smack them both for fighting over a skank like Sue.

A half-smile on his face, Miguel leaned against the wall with his arms crossed. "I'm willing to call his bluff. And can I help it if she digs me?"

Jen's shoulders relaxed when Sam appeared.

Sam took Miguel's arm, leaning really close.

"If you aren't going to watch the matches, how about taking me for lunch?"

'You owe me,' Sam mouthed over her shoulder as she led a grinning Miguel away.

Jen rubbed her temples where a headache throbbed. "Where's Sue now?"

"Getting us sandwiches. He's such a dick, Jen. We really need to replace his ass."

"Can we talk about this after the tournament? Whatever else he is, he's a good rogue, and we need one if we're going to win. And I don't know about you, but I could sure use the money. Think of the vacation you could bring Sue on."

She felt like a heel, manipulating him like this. He was crazy about Sue and Sue took advantage, making him nuts by flirting with everyone. Sue was pretty in a cold, overdone way, and Philip a classic geek, a chubby nerd with acne, glasses, and no fashion sense. He was trying way too hard to keep her interest. Jen pulled him back to her seat and pushed him down in Sam's vacated chair.

"Where'd Sam go?" Kirk asked.

"Lunch."

"With Miguel, that fucker." Philip slouched in his seat and glared at the big screen showing the dragon convulsing on the ground while Team Valor huddled under a priest shield.

Jen wanted to smack him. Now Kirk was angry too, and she'd missed the last bout.

Ethan snickered.

Jen said, "Sam is keeping Miguel occupied

instead of letting him incite Philip to leave. Let's all thank her when she gets back. And where the hell is Josh?"

Ethan shook his head and glanced at Philip.

Jen closed her eyes and rubbed her temples hard. Of course, he was with Sue. This was going to be a long three days. Next time Kuan could pick the team.

Jon strode onto the plane at the head of his team. Jen whistled and clapped despite her disappointment. Beside her, Sam clapped too, then Kuan and Kirk joined in.

In moments, most of the returning gamers clapped for team Ascendants. Gamers filled two-thirds of the economy section of the plane. Almost all the European players were on this flight because of the discounted ticket prices the tourney had arranged. A few from other places were taking advantage of the cheaper fare to travel to England before returning to their homes.

A flight attendant holding a mic stepped beside Jon. "Hello, I'm Ramiro one of the stewards for this trip. For those passengers who are wondering what's going on, we have the winners of the Ultimate Battle Magic tourney onboard. Although I see most of you have attended the tourney by your sweatshirts."

Loud cheers from the other players were joined by a polite scattering of applause from the passengers.

Jon grinned and held up both hands in a victory sign.

The steward smiled and handed him the mic.

"Thanks, guys. It means a lot to me that we can all play so hard for our teams and still be friends at the end of the day."

"Oh, barf," someone called out.

"You got lucky," someone else shouted.

"Yeah, lucky Genesis couldn't get along to save their lives— literally."

Loud laughs and jests greeted that, making Jen's ears burn. The constant bickering had gotten them killed more times than she liked to think about. Every second spent resurrecting had lowered their score. They'd even had to redo scenarios completely because they couldn't cooperate enough to get a resurrection off. The memory burned like acid because it was all her fault for inviting Miguel to the team in the first place.

A few more people called teasing comments, at least most sounded teasing to Jen. Her twinge of disappointment morphed to a wave of anger, turning her face red. Philip and Miguel had continued to fight and pulled Kirk into their arguments until she had to scream at them and watch every damned thing in their bouts. If they'd kept their heads in the game, they might've won.

She felt like she and Kuan had pulled their team through their PVP matches by sheer force of will. She spared an angry glare for Sue who encouraged the bickering by flirting ruthlessly. Sue sat between Philip and Josh, ignoring Philip with her hand on Josh's arm. If Jen never saw her again, it would be too soon.

Jon thanked them again, then waved for silence. "I spoke with Mrs. Hayes this morning. Team Valor isn't expected to last the day. Whatever the lightening was that irradiated them and caused their plane to crash is killing them. I know some of you were friends and all of us knew them. Let's take a moment to pray and send our good wishes to them and their families."

Sam squeezed her hand. "Those poor kids," she whispered.

A minute passed in silence. The plane engines built in noise, easy to hear in the quiet. Even the passengers who had no idea who Team Valor were or what had happened to them respected their moment and kept still.

Jon crossed himself, then cleared his throat. "I had an idea I want everyone to consider. Jen and I spoke about joining forces, but what if we all did? Let's face it, we're the best Ultimate Battle Magic players in Europe.

"By joining forces, we could take down any dungeon or castle and really gear our characters out. I realize we'll have too many tanks, but most of us have off-specs we can play just as well. We could take turns tanking and leading. Not only would we learn by watching but keeping up with each other will inspire us."

He waited a moment for the excited response to die down. "We all have valued raid members and others who aren't so great. With the five guilds represented here, I'm sure we could do enough runs to keep everyone happy. Some dungeons are better than others loot wise for certain classes. With this number of talented players to choose from, we can easily set up runs for everyone to try for the piece they're interested in."

"Who would be in charge?" Cass Lopez, the leader of Graveyard Shift, called.

"Overall, me, but we'd all get a say. My job as a systems analyst puts me in an ideal position to set up runs which would benefit the most players."

"You mean benefit you," Miguel hollered.

"No, I mean all of us. I have the equipment at work to write spreadsheets comparing loot to manpower. If you guys send me lists of ranked players, who you have available on what days, I'll set up a few runs and we'll see how it goes."

"Genesis is in," Jen shouted.

"Ether is in too," Tony reached over his seat to high-five her.

The plane jerked and began to move. Jon held up a hand. "This is awesome, guys, and I look forward to playing with all of you. The steward needs his mic back for this plane to lift off, so we can talk more in the game. Let's aim to hold our first mixed raid this weekend."

An excited ripple of talk traveled the plane.

"Thanks again, and thank you, Ramiro." Jon handed back the mic.

"It's almost how it's supposed to be," Kuan said in a dreamy voice.

Jen glanced at him concerned by the tone. He'd taken their loss in stride with no sign of upset. Now he sat staring out the window across the aisle from them as if he expected Santa Clause to appear.

She peered through the window but saw nothing at all. The interior lights glared on the night-dark glass, hiding the airport and other airplanes as if they were alone in the world. A shiver traveled her spine and she hurriedly turned away.

Yes, All Of them

"Jen." Kuan grabbed her arm and said her name in an odd tone, sounding both excited and nervous.

She removed her headphones and glanced at him. His eyes sparkled so brightly she thought he might be feverish and she lifted a hand to feel his brow.

He wasn't looking at her, but out the small window across the aisle. She sat beside him in the center aisle surrounded on all sides by other players from the tourney. Passengers she didn't know sat across the aisle from Kuan.

Kuan half rose in his chair now. She turned to see what had captured his attention just in time to see the window blow out in twinkling shards. The woman in the window seat screamed and threw up her hands. An alarm sounded, and oxygen masks dropped from the ceiling, but Jen's attention remained on the white lightning that flowed through the window.

The lightning arced over the people nearest the window without touching them and before she could turn back or blink, it hit Kuan.

"Yes," Kuan said on a gasping moan. "All of them."

She'd turned partway back to Kuan but couldn't complete the turn or any movement. The lightning jumped and hit her with stunning force, freezing her in place and knocking the wind from her lungs. Pain built rapidly as if she burned from the inside out. With no breath to scream, she sat and watched helplessly as the lightning struck Sam, then leaped the aisle to Josh.

The pain grew in intensity until blackness took her.

When the window blew out, Ramiro ran to the phone that connected him to the pilot.

"Lightning is loose inside the cabin. Turn us around and bring us back."

"How bad?" the co-pilot asked.

"Worse than flight Two-Twelve. Lightning is bouncing all over. About half the people are struck so far." Ramiro had to yell over the screams of the passengers. He dropped the phone and grabbed his microphone. "Remain seated and buckle your seatbelts! Apply your oxygen mask, then your neighbors or children's! Assume the crash position with your hands over your heads!"

With a trembling hand he snatched up the phone again.

"Get us lower. Quite a few tendrils are pulsing against the ceiling. We aren't going to end up with one small hole."

"Jesus Christ," the co-pilot said, sounding horrified.

Ramiro grabbed Shelia, the other flight attendant, and pushed her into the jump seat where he buckled her in. Wide, shocked brown eyes fixed on him.

"What is that?" Her gaze returned to the main cabin as she frantically began tightening her seatbelt.

"Looks like lightning, but we can expect it to rip its way out." As he spoke, he grabbed the first-aid kit and slung it over his shoulder, then yanked the portable defibrillator from the shelf beneath the microwaves and turned it on to let it warm up. He stuffed a pair of scissors and roll of duct-tape into his back pocket and grabbed the cabin mic again.

"Clear the aisle and buckle up!"

A wave of blue fire tipped with golden-purple edges sprang up in the center of the cabin. It flowed across the passengers and up the walls until the entire cabin was lit with an eerie, blue glow. The passengers shrieked and prayed. Lightning pulsed and lingered. White phosphorescent strands crisscrossed the cabin, connecting passengers in a random pattern sometimes skipping a block of seats completely and then hitting ten people in a row. Brilliant white tendrils drifted to the ceiling, growing brighter by the second.

"Everyone, return to your seats!" Ramiro bellowed into the mic. "When that lightning blows through the ceiling, it's going to leave a big hole! If you aren't firmly buckled in, you'll be sucked out! Please, do your best to secure items in the pouches on the seat backs! Beneath your seats, you'll find life vests! Get them on, but don't inflate them!"

Hysterical yelling continued, and the people huddled in the aisles began to push and shove each other as some tried to return to their seats while others refused to move. The distant echo of Josie yelling directions in the first-class cabin came to Ramiro over the muted roar of the engines and screams.

Ramiro buckled himself in tightly and clutched his supplies. Beside him, Shelia prayed, a half-hysterical plea for deliverance.

"I've declared an air emergency and have turned back to Japan," the pilot said over the cabin intercom. "Please remain calm and in your seats. I'm dropping speed and altitude—"

A ripping metallic squeal cut him off as the lightning blew through the cabin ceiling. The cabin lights died, and the plane shuddered. Another squeal followed. Loose debris flew about the cabin. Wind whistled so loudly Ramiro knew it must be a big hole despite the fact he couldn't see it.

Sparks drifted from the ceiling, and the smell of burnt rubber permeated the air. The plane continued to shudder and jitter. Ramiro snatched the pilot phone where it dangled from its cord beside him.

"We have a big hole back here."

"We've lost our left engine and have a fire in the right-hand side engine. Comms are down, and emergency power isn't responding. Our right rudder is locked. This plane is going down. Prepare the passengers as best you can. I called in our position but received no—"

The pilot cut off abruptly.

Another squeal of ripping metal was met by loud screams. Ramiro's eyes had adjusted to the lower lighting given off by the floor and ceiling strips, so he saw the passengers still in the aisle get sucked from the plane. Wind shrieked through the gaping hole in the ceiling, masking the passenger's screams.

"Mother of God," Shelia whimpered.

Ramiro placed his hands on Shelia's cheek, forcing her to look at him, not the lightning and screaming passengers. "Shelia, when we land, we'll only have a short window to get everyone off this plane safely. I want you to man the front, right exit. Get rows H, J, K, forty-four to thirty-five on board and detach when the raft is full."

He leaned across the aisle to the other two flight attendants. "Jasmine, you take the left exit and get rows A, B, C, from forty-four to thirty-five. Annie, you stay and make sure no one gets left behind in those aisles. The lightning seems confined to this center section. We'll likely have casualties. Leave the dead but take the wounded."

Annie nodded. She'd bit her bottom lip so hard it bled.

"I'll see if I can get two passengers to help us man the back exits. If not, once the front section is emptied, you and I will man the back and empty the remainder in our sections. But don't release the rafts until we're sure no one alive remains."

The lightning disappeared as suddenly as it had come. The plane fell at a steep angle tilted hard to the left. Loose luggage and unsecured items tumbled about the plane. Passengers screamed and cursed as debris hit them before it was sucked out the gaping hole in the ceiling.

The fiberglass roof continued to break off in chunks, the metal frame squealing as it twisted from air pressure. A large chunk broke off and fell inside, bouncing around the cabin before being sucked back out. Piercing shrieks and screams followed it as it left a trail of injured in its wake.

Ramiro cupped his hands around his mouth. "Stay seated when we land until we get the doors open!"

No one paid him the slightest bit of attention. He was certain his voice hadn't carried to anyone at all. Beside him, the other three flight attendants began to chant the standard 'Brace, Brace! Assume the crash position with your hands over your heads— brace-brace!' He couldn't hear the other attendants seated in the back of the plane over the screams of the passengers, shrieking wind, and tearing of metal, although he knew they too would be calling out the same instructions.

Sheila loosened her seatbelt to reach the backup mic attached to the wall behind her seat and handed it to him. This one worked off batteries that he hoped someone had checked recently.

"Remain in your seats when the plane lands!"

A wave of relief made his palms sweat as people quieted to hear him. "We'll be exiting from the front doors first. If you're seated in the middle aisle, please wait. The life-rafts can hold approximately thirty-five people each. There's no use pushing and shoving to board one. We have enough room for everyone if we cooperate. If the person seated next to you needs help, assist them to the exit."

The rising shriek of wind through the growing hole in the ceiling competed with his yelled instructions. He continued as his training had taught him, hoping desperately he could quell the panicked passengers enough to get them all out safely. The plane shook so hard he doubted it would land at all, but he firmly pushed his fear away and continued yelling directions.

"Assume a braced position for landing with your feet together flat on the floor and head resting on the seat in front of you. Keep both hands atop your head, avoid interlocking your fingers, and keep your elbows in." He called out what rows should go to which exits, but most people stared uncomprehendingly or hunkered in their seats.

The plane shuddered and jerked hard as it leveled out. Ramiro's ears popped painfully. A few people used their cellphones as flashlights as Ramiro repeated the brace instructions. The light revealed gruesome injuries caused by jagged metal. About half the passengers seemed to hang limply in their seats unconscious or dead already. Broken wires and jagged metal lined the hole above their heads.

A metallic grinding noise grew in volume until it drowned the renewed screams. The floor shuddered so hard Ramiro was afraid it would tear away and suck them all out with it. A heavy jolt bounced him in his seat. Sheila handed him a flashlight and a life vest. He shoved the mic in his pocket and leaned forward, covering his head with his arms.

"Thanks," he said, doubting she heard him.

For what felt like hours, but was probably less than five minutes, the plane swayed from side-to-side in steep oscillations as the pilot attempted to bring it to an even keel with a frozen rudder, a gaping hole in the roof, and one engine. The screams died down the better to hear the shouted instructions from the flight attendants.

Engine roar and a chilling crackling noise masked the mumbled prayers and moans of pain from the passengers.

The plane hit the ocean with a jarring crash and a metallic ripping of metal, and again the passengers screamed. Water gushed through the hole in the ceiling and sloshed against his feet in moments. His head hit Sheila's knee hard, dazing him. Loud crunching noises beneath them were accompanied by a noxious odor. Before the plane came to a complete stop Ramiro had released his seatbelt and ran down the aisle to the rear doors, using seat backs to balance against the uneven floor.

"Can you man these doors?" he asked two men sitting in the closest seats.

An older man glanced at the white-faced woman beside him and began undoing his seat belt. "Yes, I – yes, what do I need to do?"

The younger man nodded and release his seat belt. Both followed him.

"Don't let too many aboard the raft. I'll pull the lever that will inflate the emergency slide. Get about thirty-five aboard then pull this red lever again. It'll be stiff; you'll have to really yank it. If you overload, you'll sink, but if you go too soon…"

The men nodded they understood.

The plane rolled on the waves. The screaming stopped, changing to hysterical sobbing. Cries of pain mixed with calls to friends and family members. Passengers began to curse and argue as they pushed into the aisles.

Thick, black smoke crept into the cabin. Ramiro pulled the lever to open the rear door, and the two men helped him push it to the side. He yanked the cords that inflated the emergency debarkation slides. The younger man followed him to the emergency exit across the aisle where they did the same. Already people elbowed their way to the back.

Ramiro grabbed his mic from his front pocket.

"Please help those who can't help themselves! If you're in the front section, go to the front! Don't push and shove! If a raft is full, wait for the next!" He turned to the man who stood beside him. "What's your name?

"Warren."

Warren leaned out the opening and scanned the water, absently brushing his shoulder length brown hair from his face. When he turned back, water droplets had already soaked the front of his shirt and jeans and dripped from his hair.

"Okay, Warren, remember, not more than thirty-five, but wait for them."

Warren nodded and gestured for people to slide into the raft.

"Please leave all belongings behind. No luggage will be allowed aboard," Ramiro said as he pulled a man away from an overhead bin and pushed him toward the exit. "Don't hold up others to save things. Keep the lines moving."

He continued to yell advice and direction as the passengers boarded the rafts. Some dragged unconscious people with them but most rushed past the unmoving passengers without sparing them a glance.

Ramiro climbed over a seat back and felt for a pulse in the first unresponsive man he came to. He grabbed a man's arm as he passed in the aisle. "He's alive, take him with you." While he spoke, he unstrapped the man in the seat.

The man he gripped scowled and shrugged him off. The man behind him stopped to help. Ramiro checked the next passenger, then the next. Finding another one alive, he grabbed a random passenger again. He used the defibrillator twice for the dead passenger, seeing no result, he climbed to the next unconscious woman. He continued this way the length of the plane, handing off the unconscious passengers to others waiting to exit. Annie was checking the right side, handing off the unconscious passengers the same way. By the time he'd checked the left side, the aisle was almost empty.

"Annie, gimme a hand here. These three are just unconscious."

"There's room on this raft," Warren hollered. "I'm afraid to leave the doorway and help though. These assholes are being fucking selfish and will leave without us.

"Stay there!" Ramiro called.

Warren turned his head and yelled out the door, "Sit the fuck down, we're waiting! I fucking see it's sinking, but we have time!"

Ramiro grabbed a blond girl under her arms and dragged her down the aisle to Warren who handed her to someone aboard the raft as Ramiro ran back for another. Water splashed around his ankles by the time he'd gotten the next girl out.

"Hurry the fuck up!" Warren called.

Annie passed him in the other aisle, dragging another unconscious woman.

"I'm hurrying," Ramiro mumbled as he checked the center aisle. The girl bleeding from her severed arm and deep lacerations across her face was still alive. He used scissors to cut a seatbelt loose and ragged strips from the seat to bind it, holding the makeshift bandage in place with duct tape, and carried her to the boat.

"Fuck waiting on the corpses. Let's just go!" someone in the boat yelled as Ramiro ran back down the aisle.

"She isn't dead, just hurt," Warren said.

The plane began to list, sinking fast from the front. Ramiro grabbed the unconscious boy without checking for a pulse and hauled him to the boat. "Take him and go."

"You come too," Warren said as he yanked the lever to release the raft.

The emergency inflatable exit ramp detached from the plane and fell into the ocean. Cold spray doused him. Ramiro turned to head back for another. Warren grabbed him by the arm and jumped into the raft, pulling Ramiro with him. A man swore as they landed atop him.

The plane slid below the waves in a froth of air and bubbles. In moments, all that remained was a tip of a rear rudder poking from the water.

"Jesus, how many were still aboard?" someone asked in a shaking voice.

"About seven. I'd just started checking the center aisle." Tears filled Ramiro's eyes. " I hope they were dead already."

A woman aboard the raft was doing CPR on the last boy.

"You could've fucking killed us all," the man who hadn't wanted to wait shouted.

Ramiro ignored him, smoothing his wet hair back with both hands as he scanned the horizon. Moonlight illuminated the gently rolling waves with a silvery glow. "See if we can paddle over to the other boats. Look," he gestured to the closest boat where the passengers leaned over the side using their hands to paddle. "They seem to be trying to head somewhere."

He bent over the edge and began paddling, ignoring the complaints and sarcastic comments from the passenger.

"What's your name, sir?" he finally asked.

"Stan Bosko; what difference does it make?"

"I want to be able to tell the reporters how fucking helpful you're being."

Stan shut up. He didn't try to help paddle, but at least he was quiet, Ramiro thought gratefully.

"Look— land!" a woman yelled.

It's Our Fate

Jen woke with a raging thirst and a throbbing headache. Something rough poked her back, and she ached everywhere.

"Just throw them into the water," someone said behind her.

"Take their clothes first."

"Stop it. We can't just throw them away," a woman said, sounding outraged.

The argument continued as Jen forced her eyes open and struggled to sit, raising both hands to cradle the pounding in her head.

"What happened?" Her voice emerged scratchy and weak. Someone lay beside her. Sam, she realized in horror. Kirk lay beside Sam with a blackening eye vivid on his white face.

"Oh my God, Sam!" Terrified now, she leaned over her friend to see if she breathed.

The argument penetrated, and a shiver shook her as she realized strangers spoke of throwing dead bodies into the sea.

A man knelt beside her and smoothed her hair back. "Good, you're awake. Do you remember me from the plane?" Without waiting for an answer, he continued, "I'm Ramiro, one of the flight attendants. Your friend will likely wake in a few minutes." He stood and rose his voice. "They're coming around. If we stick together, we'll be fine."

He squatted again beside Jen and felt for the pulse in Sam's neck. A gasping moan behind her made him turn. Jen turned to see too.

"Philip, oh God." Tears sprang to her eyes.

Beyond Philip, a line of unmoving people lay on the water's edge. Waves crashed onto a rock outcrop, sending droplets of spray into the air and she realized she was soaked. The rock she laid on rose to a point behind her where bedraggled people huddled together in tight groups. Strained faces stared out over the sea.

Beside her, Sam moaned. She turned back to her.

"Sam, please be okay."

"Man, my head," Sam croaked and pushed herself up with hands that shook. "Where the hell are we?"

"I think our plane crashed." Jen turned to Ramiro. "We crashed?"

"Yeah, but I'm sure the pilot got a message out. We just need to hang tight and help each other until rescue workers arrive."

His worried brown eyes scanned her, then he peered over his shoulder.

The arguing over the corpses had escalated to name calling.

"I better see if I can settle that down." Using his hands to balance against the uneven footing, he crawled up the rock and over the pointed peak.

"Wait here, I'm going to see if I can find Kuan." Jen gave Sam a quick hug and smoothed the wet hair from Kirk's brow before scrambling to her feet.

Sam gasped and cried out, seeming to notice Kirk for the first time. Blond hair swung forward to cover her face as she leaned over Kirk.

Barnacles cut into Jen's palms as she followed Ramiro, using her hands to balance on the slippery slope. The peak of the rock dipped sharply to a thirty-foot flatter section before angling into the sea.

Waves crashed against the edges of the rock, sending glittering arcs of spray into the air. As far as she could see, gray water surrounded them. The wing of the plane stuck from the water about half a mile away. The entire rock outcropping was smaller than a football field.

Overhead, black storm clouds blocked the sun, casting deep shadows. Before her, a group of men argued beside corpses laid in rows. Beside them, so close there wasn't room to lay, the rest of the passengers from flight Four Fourteen huddled under the yellow, plastic emergency slides, crying and moaning.

"Wait, please don't!" Jen yelled to the arguing men as she scrambled over the rough rock. "Who are they? I have friends missing, please!"

Blood rushed from her head so hard she thought she might faint or vomit. Three members of team Ether lay before her. Two with not a mark on them. Carry was so mangled Jen almost didn't recognize her. A jagged cut crossed her face, continuing across her shoulder, ending where her arm used to be. Someone had tried to bind the wound with cloth strips.

"Carry!" Sobbing she fell to her knees. Her horrified gaze landed on Everett and skittered to Josh. "The others? Did you throw some away already? Kuan!" she screamed and pushed herself to her feet.

Ramiro grabbed her arm. "We left the dead on the plane. The boy sitting with you is under the far boat. He needed to be resuscitated and has been unconscious since we got here."

"You wasted our fucking time-saving corpses when we should have grabbed food!" a man yelled.

"Idiot, this is a sea; there's plenty of food," another shouted back.

"Mr. Bosko—" Ramiro said in a tone of forced politeness.

"Fuck, you!" another man snarled, interrupting Ramiro.

A fight broke out, which she ignored, as she

scrabbled over the slick rock to the farthest upside-down boat. Ramiro followed and helped her lift it. Half deflated from long gouges running the length it was hard to shift.

"We have nothing else to keep them warm with. The escape slides worked to get us here but make crappy boats." He lowered his voice and stepped closer. "Without medical care soon, most of these people will die."

Blood leaked from rough bandages made from scraps of clothing wrapped around arms, legs, and torsos. Bruised faces and crooked limbs met Jen's horrified gaze.

Ramiro laid a hand on her shoulder. "Most haven't woken, and I hope they don't until help arrives."

He squatted and felt pulses. Jen grasped Kuan by the shoulders and pulled him from beneath the boat. "Help me bring him to Sam, please."

"I'll help you, Jen."

"Ethan." Relieved to see him, she didn't think, she grabbed him in a hard hug, which he returned.

"Jon?"

"Just woke." Ethan gestured with his chin to the far side of their tiny island where Jon stood arguing with the heavyset man with sandy-blond hair who Ramiro had called Mr. Bosko. "He's stopping those ghouls from throwing the dead into the sea. We'll move them to the steeper side to give the living more room to spread out, but there's no need to toss them like garbage."

As he spoke, he lifted Kuan in a firefighter carry. Jen offered an arm to balance against as they crossed the peak of the rock together.

In the minutes she'd been gone more unconscious passengers had woken and now sat staring about in horror. She was glad to see only a few sported bloody wounds.

Ethan placed Kuan beside Sam and sat beside her. Sam leaned over Kuan, her blond hair hiding her face. Jen couldn't tell if she were crying or not. She picked Kuan up again and sat with his upper body across her lap.

"Miguel— Philip?" Sam asked.

"Philip and Miguel are here." Jen gestured to the still unconscious people to their left. "Sue is with the other passengers."

Jen curled her lip. In her opinion, Sue was a complete bitch.

"What a bitch," Ethan murmured.

A semi-hysterical giggle burst from Jen, and she slapped her hands over her mouth.

Thunder rumbled. Jen glanced at the sky, noting the dark scudding clouds with dread. A cool breeze kicked up, fluttering Jen's drying hair

"How long have we been here?" Sam asked.

"I'm not sure. My watch broke." Ethan held up his wrist to display his broken watch. His gaze lit on something behind her and he stood. "Maria's awake. Be right back."

"We'll be here," Sam said in a falsely cheerful tone, making Jen laugh again.

A soft rain began to fall and was soon a sleeting downpour.

"Awesome," Jen said as she leaned further, trying to block the rain from Kuan's face. Chilled to the bone in moments, she began to shiver.

Sam leaned back and cupped her hands to capture the water. A second later, she shrugged out of her bra and held it up to the rain.

"Mine won't do a speck of good," Jen said.

"Even a B-cup is better than no cup." Sam grinned and winked at her.

"Ha- no, I meant it's lace."

Ethan returned with Cami, Maria, and Miguel. "Philip's awake and went for Sue. Lindsey woke too and is with her family. That's a great idea, Sam. Huddle up to conserve body heat, everyone. Those clouds look like a serious storm. This won't be a quick shower."

The other women removed their bras, rung them out, then spread them to catch rain water.

Jen's cheeks flushed when Ethan eyed her doubtfully.

"Mine's lace," she mumbled.

Ethan chuckled, then stood again. "I'm going to make sure they thought to flip the boats to collect the water. Who knows how long we'll be stuck here." He scrabbled over the rock.

Within thirty minutes everybody had woken and gathered in a miserable clump. After sharing their slightly salty water, they joined the rest of the passengers.

"I liked our side of the rock better," Sam whispered.

Jen had to agree. The moans and complaints on this side were hard to listen too. Night fell, and the rain continued. Kuan hadn't spoken since he'd woke. He sat behind Sam with his arms around her, a faraway look on his face. He felt feverishly hot to the touch.

Sam and Kuan's body heat warmed her despite the rain that fell. Ethan sat behind Jen with his back against hers and his arms around Cami. Jon pressed against her left arm, holding Maria. Lindsey clutched her two boys. All three sat in her husband's lap.

Someone beneath the nearest boat whined in pain interspersed with deep moans.

"Shut the fuck up!" Mr. Bosko bellowed.

"You shut up!" a woman snapped back.

Jen cringed as the yelling escalated.

"Put him out of his fucking misery. The fuckers going to die; why let him suffer?"

"No!" Ramiro hollered. "Anyone kills anyone else here, for any damn reason, and it'll be reported as murder. We help each other. Instead of complaining, help him. Make him as comfortable as you can."

Jen closed her eyes and leaned on Jon's shoulder. He put an arm around her. To her surprise, she dozed off. When she woke, golden rays of dawn light streaked the sky. Most of the survivors still slept although a few stirred. A baby's cry woke others. Jon stretched and stood.

"I need a bathroom. Girl's room to the left, boys to the right." Jon stepped to the right, then halted and knelt. He cupped his hands around his mouth to holler, "We can eat the mussels and oysters lining this rock. Gather the seaweed, and we can spread it to dry and make a fire to open them." He clambered over the peak and disappeared from sight.

Jen rose and offered Sam a hand. She wasn't hungry. Her head still hurt, and she felt queasy. The other girls followed her. The corpses gave her pause. She averted her eyes and climbed down the steeper rock to the edge.

Sam stood with her hands on her hips, eyeing the edge of the rock with disapproval. "This is gross. I'm going to need toilet paper. My stomach is seriously gurgling."

"Me too. Guess I'll just wade in and use the water." Jen stepped forward then lowered herself to her butt to test for footing under the water. One slow step at a time she eased into the water. "The rock drops sharply about three feet out," she warned as her foot met nothing except water.

"We're going to get covered in our own shit by the waves." Maria stood ankle deep in the water, frowning at Jen.

"Got another suggestion?" Jen asked, hoping she did.

"Go on shore, then go in and, um, wipe? We can rip up our underwear or something."

"There's over two hundred people on this rock. If we all go on the shore…" She lifted her hands to shade her eyes and peered out to sea. Nothing except gray clouds and dark water met her searching gaze.

Sam sat and pulled her sneakers and socks off, then wiggled out of her jeans and removed her underwear. "Go as close to the edge as you can and hope the waves clean it off. I figure with my socks and underwear I can wipe at least five times and we're sure to be rescued way before then."

Everyone else followed suit and relieved themselves at the water's edge. More women passengers joined them. Jen was glad they'd arrived first as complaints and cursing rent the air over having to squat where others had gone.

Back on the other side, she accompanied Ramiro to check on the injured. Two had died in the night. Jon and Ethan carried them to the steeper side to lay with the others.

"Can you help me out of here?" A woman asked Jen and gestured to the boat above them. She lifted a hand to her forehead and winced. "I'm Arden Long.

"Jen Frey. And yes, we can move you. How bad are you hurt?"

"Broken leg and maybe the hip too. Is there any water?"

Cami leaned over Jen's shoulder. "Are you Double-D thirst or B-cup thirsty?"

Arden smiled, then winced and grabbed her

head again. "B-cup. We have anything to make a splint?"

"No, sorry. We have no supplies at all."

"I should stay still under here, but it's freaking me out. I'm a bit claustrophobic. I'll likely pass out when you move me, and maybe vomit, so wait on that water." Arden lowered her voice to a whisper. "The woman next to me has serious internal injuries. If you move her, she'll die. Don't move her even to clean her."

Tears filled her eyes, and she covered her face with her hands. "She'll likely die anyway. The swelling is massive. I'm sure she has an internal hemorrhage."

"Are you a doctor?" Cami asked.

"Yeah, an OB-GYN, but I did a stint in emergency. Fat lot of good I can do though when I can barely move."

Jen turned her head to call, "Jon, Ethan!" before turning back to the doctor. "They can move you, and we'll do our best to help. Maybe we can be your hands and eyes if we describe the injuries?"

Arden nodded and lifted a shaking hand to brush back her hair.

Sam dug into her pocket and withdrew an elastic, then gathered the doctor's long, brown hair and made a quick braid.

"You called?" Jon squatted beside them.

"Can you carry Arden to the first boat?"

"Yep."

"Don't freak and drop me if I scream or pass

out." Arden lifted her arms to Jon who bent and lifted her, grunting with effort.

Arden screamed shrilly. The blood rushed from Jon's face, but he continued with slow, careful steps. Ethan hovered beside him with his hands out as if ready to catch her if Jon tripped.

"Almost there," he said in a kind voice.

Jen followed, then scrambled ahead to search for the flattest spot she could. Rough and uneven, no such spot existed. No room remained under any of the boats. Although calling them boats was an injustice. Most had deflated and would never float again. The rough rock had seen to that.

Jon laid Arden as close as he could and stepped back. Arden clenched her teeth into a grimace and panted hard at his feet.

Ethan knelt on one knee beside her and took her hand. "Hang in there. Help will be coming."

"Tell me about the other injuries, maybe I can help."

Still holding her hand, Ethan began to describe the injured.

Jen stared at Jon in horror, then peered over her shoulder. No one except those struck by lightning on the plane sat on the steep side of the rock. Them and the corpses. The sickly, sweet smell of decay had been replaced by the foul odors of sickness, keeping everyone else on the other side of the rock. The stench did nothing to calm her gurgling stomach.

Jon faced them with a grim expression. "For their sake, we should stay on this side. If this sickness progresses like I think it will, within ten hours we'll be too weak to move."

"This can't be happening." Sam sounded terrified.

Jen pulled her closer. Her entire body shook. Kuan stood behind them with a hand on each of their shoulders.

"It's our fate," he whispered, speaking for the first time, and kissed Jen's temple. "Don't be afraid, Jen."

"We're dying?" Maria began to cry, then leaned over and dry heaved. A wave of retching followed.

Everybody struck by lightning had been ill for the last day, vomiting with diarrhea, growing progressively worse.

"I'm so sorry, but I really think we are. Team Valor lasted four days, but they had medical care. When I spoke to Mrs. Hayes, she told me they'd been unconscious for two, but their vitals were so low she didn't expect them to last more than a few more hours. From what she said, we can expect to become delirious until we fade into complete unconsciousness."

"Someone shot our plane with the same weapon?" one of the people Jen barely knew asked.

"Who knows what caused it. We have the

same symptoms of radiation poisoning as Team Valor did and were also struck by lightning on a plane. It seems reasonable we can expect the same fate." Jon shrugged and pulled Maria into an embrace, and then grabbed Lindsey who cried with her hands over her face.

"Will it hurt?" Kendra asked.

Jon ran his hand over Kendra's bowed head. "Yes. Team Valor was on a morphine drip and complained of severe aches and pains while they could speak."

"We don't have morphine." Kendra began to cry too. "We should kill ourselves."

"Maybe he's wrong." Miguel smiled as if he was having the time of his life. "Besides, how would you kill yourself? I guess I could strangle you or something if you want?"

Kendra cried harder, and Miguel laughed, cutting it off abruptly. "Sorry, I didn't mean that, just…"

Jon kissed Maria's forehead, then Lindsey's. "Give Arden or Ramiro messages for your families. They promised to pass them on."

"If they don't die on this rock too," Philip said bitterly.

"Make your goodbyes and return to this side. We could infect them."

"Maybe the radiation washed off in the rain and we won't die, just be sick awhile," Tony said hopefully.

Jen glanced at him, then examined everyone.

All appeared ill and pale with dark circles under their eyes and chapped lips. Ethan rose and headed back to the other side. Lindsey stood and followed.

Jen closed her eyes against the loss in Lindsey's face. Her family would sit by helplessly while she died. "Those poor kids," she murmured.

Sam began to cry. "Want to go leave a message?" she whispered through her tears.

"No. My parents know I love them, and you and Kuan are here. Arden will tell my family I sent my love without me having to say a thing."

"I wish I could say goodbye to Randy."

"Go leave a message."

Sam laughed bitterly and sagged against Jen's shoulder.

"I don't have the energy to climb this stupid rock, and what would I say?"

Jen laid back against the rough, slanted surface and closed her eyes. "Tell him you loved him and wish him to be happy." Guilt threatened to smother her. Sam wouldn't be here if not for her.

Sam sobbed, her warm breath fluttering Jen's hair. Kuan picked her up and sat beside Jen, tucking Sam against his side.

Kirk sat beside Kuan and rested a hand on Sam's back. The sadness in his eyes when he looked at Sam made the tears fall from Jen's. Her beautiful friend was going to die in horrible pain. With all her soul she prayed for Sam to be spared suffering.

"I'm here. Don't be afraid, Sam," Kuan kissed Sam's forehead and ran a hand over Jen's head. His palm felt hot and dry against her face. Fever-bright blue eyes met hers. To her surprise, he appeared neither afraid nor worried but calm, almost eager.

A wave of grief passed over Jen for this gentle boy's death.

"You can't fight destiny. A new adventure awaits." He sat with them, stroking their hair and offering comfort as they vomited bile and dry heaved.

Lost in misery she barely noticed the loud yells and screams from the other side of the rock. The day progressed to night and increased pain. Kendra cried and moaned. Her begging for help got on Jen's nerves until she wanted to scream for her to shut up— that they were all suffering. By morning she knew she was dying and hoped it came quickly. Fire traveled her bones in increasingly painful waves. Every touch and movement was agonizing. Kendra quieted to hissing moans of pain.

Loud voices above her brought her back from the comforting dark. Pain like she'd never experienced scalded her in hot waves. She tried to shriek and couldn't make more than a hissing moan.

"Take one more step, and I'll see you're charged with murder. We can't help them, but we don't need to hurt them either. And return his fucking earring."

Ramiro sounded furious, Jen thought in the part of her mind that wasn't begging for help.

"Unless you think you can kill everyone on this island, back the fuck up right now."

She faded into black again, wishing she could tell Ramiro to let them kill her.

When next Jen woke, Kuan sat beside her with his hand still resting on her shoulder. Sam's fingertips brushed hers. The rock beneath her gouged into her skin in a million points of agony. She drifted in a sea of pain. Moments of clarity came farther apart as the day progressed. If she'd possessed the energy, she'd have shrieked with pain or thrown herself into the sea to end it, but her limbs wouldn't obey her. The night passed with glacial slowness.

Morning sun seared her skin as if each ray were a sword. She managed a low moan.

"Soon, Jen," Kuan murmured.

Poor beautiful Kuan, she thought before darkness took her.

Become Your True Self

An indeterminate time later, Jen woke. Kuan pressed her shoulder hard, sending ripples of agony through her body.

"I am myself," he said wonderingly.

The pressure left her arm and a brilliant, white light engulfed her. Kuan's delighted laugh made her smile, and she realized the pain had ended as if switched off, leaving her feeling weak and tired.

"Jen, embrace your true nature. Be who you're meant to be!"

Dark clouds dimmed the sunlight, only small shafts of light drifted down to pierce the gloom. Kuan stood staring into the sky with a rapturous expression and transformed into a raven with feathers so black that blue-tinted the edges. Larger than any natural bird, his spread wings shadowed her, ruffling in the breeze.

"You're beautiful," she said in awe.

He fixed a glowing blue eye on her, then became a man again. "Join me, Jen. Be your true self."

Green sparks traveled from his fingertips and landed on the unmoving people beside him. Blue mist between his hands became a glowing green ball that he threw at Sam. Jen recognized his Greater Heal. Bemused with this fever dream, she sat and casted Sanctuary. A glowing, yellow circle of light appeared beneath her.

He laughed and spun away, becoming a black panther and leaping forward, landing twenty-five feet away. A golden-green glow infused the ground he stood on. The people lying there stirred.

Jen rose shakily to her feet. Sam turned on her side, lifting herself on an elbow. Golden strands of hair remained on the rock beneath her.

"Did we die?"

"Yes, I think so. I'm just happy the pain ended. This is a good dream; look how happy he is." Jen gestured to Kuan who grinned while throwing green balls of light at the unconscious people lying on the rock.

Sam sat and laughed. "He was meant to be a druid. Even in my dream I see him that way."

"This is my dream." Jen frowned. "Here, I'll prove it."

Both hands held before her, she typed on the air to cast her group heal. Blue mist gathered about her fingertips and she made the motions to cast like she did in the game. Small, golden-yellow, glowing balls flitted from her fingertips. Each ball swelled until they reached baseball size and bounced between the people still lying unmoving on the ground. Those the light touched glowed for a moment, then stirred.

"See— my dream."

A scowl furrowed Sam's brow as she stood and glanced down at her filthy jeans. "Well, dream me up some new clothes because these are disgusting."

Jen had to agree. Vomit and feces splattered her clothing. Patches of dry, flaky skin covered Sam's face and what she could see of her hands. A sour, putrid smell filled the air as more people stirred. Jen turned and casted another heal. "I wish I could, but I don't have a spell for that."

"This dream is starting to suck."

"You're still the most beautiful woman I've ever seen," Kirk said as he stood and hugged her.

Kuan bounded to Sam in panther form and resumed his natural shape. "This isn't a dream, Sam." A delighted smile on his face, he hugged her and kissed her cheek. "We've become our true selves. This is our destiny." He pulled her to the ocean at the edge of the rock. "Jump in and clean off. You'll feel better."

He released her hand and began removing his clothes.

"What the hell," Philip said as he stood and took a staggering step forward.

Jen turned from the now naked Kuan and inspected the rest of them. Everyone stared in Kuan's direction with amazed expressions. Blistered skin had left loose patches and discolored circles, giving them a gruesome appearance except for their amazed smiles. She turned back in time to see Kuan leap into the ocean and become a dolphin.

Sam began to remove her clothes.

"Stop!" Jen called and hurried forward. A tremble shook her hands and her breath came hard. Stunned amazement shifted to denial and back. Her brain couldn't accept the evidence of her eyes.

"Aww, it was just getting good," Miguel said. "Leave them alone and maybe they'll have sex right there."

"Eww— perv." Maria rose and brushed at a small crab climbing over her leg, knocking it away. With a grimace of distaste and disgusted sniff, she flicked another small crustacean from Lindsey's shoulder.

Jen glanced at Maria as she reached Sam's side. "We aren't dreaming."

"Of course, I am. He's a fish," Sam said.

"Trust me, Sam, we aren't. Maybe we went crazy or something, but..."

"Well... crazy— a dream— whatever— I want out of these filthy clothes." Sam began unbuttoning her clothes again.

"Okay, guys, let's give the ladies some

privacy." Jon waved the men to him and led them around the curve of the rock. "The corpses are gone."

"Probably the smell. We fucking stink," someone said.

Sam giggled and kicked off her sneakers to remove her pants.

Jen undressed, grabbed her clothes, casted Valorous Leap and leapt forward, splashing twenty-five-feet away into the ocean. Sam shrieked and followed, leaving her clothes on shore.

"This feels amazing, but I wish I had soap. This is the weirdest dream I've ever had." On her back, Sam kicked her feet and waved her arms to stay afloat.

Jen submerged and ran her hands through her hair. Her heart pounded hard when clumps of hair came away, tangled in her fingers. Her head broke the surface, and she gasped for air still brushing hanks of loosened hair from her fingers.

Sam screamed and thrashed to reach her. Long strands of brown hair caught in her fingers as she ran her hands over Jen's head.

"I want to wake up now," Sam said.

Jen said nothing. The hair caught in her fingers horrified her. The women began to wail as they touched their heads and their hair fell out in clumps.

"Don't freak out." Jen reached to Sam and combed her hair with her fingers, removing thick hanks and letting them drift away on the current.

"Radiation makes you lose your hair. We'll be okay now though, and it'll grow back."

"Your dream sucks," Sam said and began to cry.

Jen didn't try to convince her again. She did her best to scrub herself with her bare hands and a clump of seaweed then tried to clean her filthy clothes.

None of the women spoke much. Short bursts of conversation faded to bewildered silence or soft crying.

"What happened?" Maria trod water beside Jen, peering at her with narrowed eyes. "How did you and Kuan cast those spells?"

"No idea. Can you do it too?" Jen lifted her hands and pretended to type. Blue mist coalesced around her fingertips, and she threw the ball of light at Maria.

"I recognize the heal spell, but that's crazy." Maria flicked her fingers and became a dolphin. A second later she was clinging to Jen and crying.

Jen patted her back. Wide-eyed, Sam stared at them. She pursed her lips, then submerged. The water remained undisturbed, Sam nowhere in sight. Before Jen could panic, Sam resurfaced. An antique diving helm now seemed to be covering her head. The helmet faded before Jen had time to examine it.

"Underwater Breathing works," Sam said

Crouched in the water on the edge of the rocky shore, fourteen women stared at them. Jen swam closer, towing Maria. "We seem to have been changed somehow by the lightning. Try your spells. Pretend to cast like you did in the game."

Jen laughed in delight and clapped her hand as Lindsey casted a heal then levitated and floated atop the water.

A ball of orange fire flew into the air. Bright orange with glowing white edges, it expanded as it traveled. Jen followed its progress as it arced thirty feet in the air before impacting the water with a sizzling crash. Another ball of yellow fire shot into the air from where the men had gone. A glowing orange rock spun over Jen's head, leaving a flaming trail. Spray shot up from the impact, cascading warm droplets over her. Awe filled Jen as she recognized a warlock meteor spell. Chills rippled her skin. I'm really seeing magic, she thought in wonder and again wondered if she were dead.

Loud exclamations and laughter interspersed the casting. Jen's gaze landed on the silent people lining the rock ridge, staring at them.

Lindsey jumped to her feet and rushed to her husband. She grabbed both her children and kissed him.

Sam giggled and turned away, crossing both arms over her naked breasts.

The women continued to cast and exclaim. Jen joined them. Awe flickered to disbelief and back. Jen wondered if she were dreaming, dead, or maybe crazy. Kuan's head broke the surface, causing the women to laugh and cover themselves.

"I'm not peeking," he said as he handed Sam her suitcase. "Maria, Cami, we can get more suitcases if you'll bring someone to carry them."

"Can we get a radio?" Lindsey called.

Kuan swam closer and began to leave the water. The giggles seemed to make him change his mind. He hunkered low enough in the water for modesty. "I wouldn't know what to get. Can you cast water breathing on Ramiro or something?"

Jen clapped her hands. All eyes turned to her. "First, we're going to use all the soap and shampoo in Sam's case, then clean our clothes as best we can and dress. Kuan remained dressed when he shifted back from raven form." She grinned as her voice carried with magical clarity to the people standing atop the ridge. Just like in the game Valiant Shout amplified her voice so all within her line-of-sight could hear her and all she'd had to do was think of being louder. "Then he can bring us to the wreck, and we can scavenge it for food, a radio, and retrieve luggage."

She made a shooing gesture at the crowd staring from the ridge. "Go back to your side while we clean up. We don't know what happened either."

Sam lugged her suitcase through the water and up the rough slope of the rock. Bright pink stickers decorated the side, spelling her name. She handed Jen a bottle of shampoo and a women's razor. "Do me a favor and cut off the remaining strands. It's got to look better than this scary mess." She tugged lightly on a hank of Jen's hair and grimaced as half came off in her hand.

"Me too," Maria said.

"Line up if you want a shave." Jen waved the razor. "Get a haircut and a handful of soap."

By the third woman, the razor was too dull to give a close shave. Jen eyed the rough clumps remaining on Lindsey's head and frowned. "We need a straight razor. Maybe one of the men brought one."

Lindsey said, "Try your sword. No way do I want Billy to see me like this."

Jen's eyes widened. It hadn't occurred to her she could summon her sword. She pictured the steps she'd have taken in the game to summon it and a sword appeared in her hand. The women clapped. Another thought and she wore her righteous armor. She bowed with a dramatic flourish.

Kendra donned her summoned armor for a few seconds, dismissing it instantly.

Jen bit back her laughter and turned away, the stifled giggles of the other women making her wince. Kendra's stomach almost covered her armor, making her appear naked with splashes of red showing beneath the rolls of fat. Skimpy red leather that looked good on a curvaceous video game figure looked ridiculous on an overweight, balding woman. Jen was thrilled she'd chosen a more modest white halter for her everyday wear instead of one of the many racier outfits available.

"Cool." Sam ran a hand over Jen's silver cape and white miniskirt. "Can you do the prot set too?"

A second of visualization changed Jen's armor to her black protection set, leaving her standing before them in a black, leather bikini formed of black straps and silver buckles. She blushed so hard she thought she might faint and changed it back to the white set. Sam giggled, then joined by the other women, laughed until tears streamed down her cheeks.

"Sorry, Jen, but your expression."

Still laughing, Lindsey gestured for Jen to continue her haircut.

"Here's hoping I don't cut your head off." She bit her bottom lip as she scraped Lindsey's head as carefully as she could with her sword.

Lindsey shrugged and said, "Don't think you could. I'm an ally. You couldn't hurt me with your sword. Try it and see. I can always heal myself if you can."

Jen considered, then tried to stab Lindsey's big toe. The sword passed through her foot and stuck into the rock beneath. Jen yanked it out and tried again.

"It responds to your will, Jen. As long as you don't mean me harm, you won't harm me." Lindsey ran her hand along the edge of the blade. "Feels dull to me. I bet if you swung it at me, it'd pass right through me. Shauna's fire didn't hurt me at all although it warmed the water."

Jen ran her hand over Lindsey's shaved scalp.

"Cuts hair though."

"Because you will it to."

Jen shrugged and beckoned Shauna forward. "Whatever, as long as it works."

No hair or dirt stuck to her summoned clothing as she shaved their heads. She tried to dirty it, but the armor remained magically pristine.

By the time everyone had shaved and washed, Jen was exhausted and wanted nothing more than to sleep. Dressed in their wet clothes, the women rejoined the rest of the passengers. Ethan handed her a can of soda and packet of pretzels. His laughing gaze traveled her righteous armor.

A hot blush scalded her cheeks.

"Ramiro is with Kuan, Jon, Tony, Rob, and Cass, retrieving what they can from the wreck."

"Where are the rest of the boats?" Jen asked.

"While we were sick, a bunch of people took off. I heard the fight, and it sounded like a doozy. All the boats that could float are gone. They only left the ruined ones behind."

Arden approached, carrying a case of soda. "Drink another. You'll need the sugar and calories. You all look like you lost fifty pounds." She ran her hand over Sam's head. "The men feel fine. No more illness, just tired. How are the women?"

"Same." Jen grinned at her. "Kuan healed you?"

"Yes. You should've seen him; he glows with power. People were freaking out, but he healed every single one of us. I keep pinching myself to make sure I'm not dreaming. The woman with the internal bleeding is perfectly fine now."

"I wish they hadn't dumped the corpses; maybe we could have resurrected them."

"It was days, Jen. The spirit releases after three hours." Ethan turned and waved a hand at the broad expanse of ocean. "Even with magic we're still stuck. If they'd left the boats, we could've got everyone on them and out of here with the druids help, but now…Well, the druids might be okay, but… See that black line in the distance?"

He waited until she nodded to continue.

"That's one hell of a storm, and it surrounds us on all sides. We're in the eye. When it reaches here, we're in trouble. This rock is normally underwater except for the tip. Kuan says there's a bunch of tips sticking from the sea and it's shallow in spots for about a mile around us. The coral is sharp and close to the surface. It's what shredded the bottom of the boats. Man, I wish they hadn't left us, they'll likely sink without a druid to scout for them. This is either a sinking or emerging island, but the storm will raise the water height. If we're still here, we'll need to swim.

"Any luck with the radio?" Jen asked.

"No." Ethan shook his head, nodding toward the men grouped around a dismantled radio. "This sunken isle is good and bad news. The bad news is shipping will be avoiding this area, and I doubt planes are going through that storm. Lightning flickers in it."

Fear skittered along her spine at the mention of lightning.

While Ethan spoke, Kirk approached and summoned a cauldron with a flick of his conjured wand. Blue mist solidified into thick, black metal. Green fire flickered beneath the cauldron while glowing blue runes raced around the edge. Loaves of white bread formed, poking crusty brown edges over the top, filling the air with the aroma of freshly baked bread.

"Take one." He pulled Sam to the cauldron and pointed.

She obediently took one.

"What are you saying? We're going to die here anyway?" Kendra's voice rose shrilly and echoed. A paladin tank like Jen, Kendra could project her voice too.

"We need to portal out."

Jen held up a hand to stop the exclamations. "What's the good news about the island?"

"Because it's so big, it can likely be found on maps. Brent already left through his portal with thirty volunteers. We'll wait as long as we can for rescue."

"Why not just go?" Arden asked as she grabbed a loaf of bread.

"One each. Only the recipient can eat it," Kirk said as a man took two.

Jen grabbed a loaf. "Portals in the game didn't work well. They could trap you in the earth or even put you so high up you went into orbit unable to fall."

"That doesn't sound good," Arden muttered, then louder. "Did the volunteers know that?"

Ethan took a loaf and nodded his thanks as he spoke. "Yes. It's going to take them time to convince people and get us help."

"If they don't just lock Brent up and kill the rest of them," Miguel said. He laughed at their horrified silence. "What— you don't think the Americans will freak when they see what Brent can do? All our governments are going to freak. You can bet your ass they try to control us."

Ethan laid a hand on his arm. "They have to come get us if they want to control us and once they do, it'll be impossible to hold us. Let's worry about the problems we have— not future ones."

Jen ate her bread and drank her soda, letting the talk wash over her. Ethan sat beside her answering questions about the different abilities the casters had.

Sam nudged her with an elbow and gestured to Philip with her chin. "I almost feel sorry for him. How is he that gullible?"

Jen followed Sam's gaze. Sue hung on Philip's arm with such overacted devotion Jen giggled.

"Serves him right if he's dumb enough to fall for her. She's going to have her work cut out to keep him now though. A man with real magic is sure to impress the ladies."

Sam snorted.

Jen didn't remember falling asleep. She woke when raindrops hit her face and found herself laying with her head on Ethan's chest. He sat as she did and stretched.

Red climbed her neck, settling into her cheeks when he caught her staring at his rippling muscles. She scrambled to her feet, shaded her eyes with her hands, and peered into the distance. Less than a mile away, the storm approached with a dazzling display of lightning. Three-foot waves crashed against the rock. The water had already risen about six feet. Their island was rapidly shrinking.

"Time to get up, everyone." Ethan strode forward and grasped Jon's arm. The two men conferred a moment before Jon waved his hands in the air.

"We're going to form six raid groups of thirty people each. Each group will have at least three magic wielders in it. Philip and Shauna will form portals. Once you're in a bedroom, exit as fast as you can to make room for the others. Please memorize your raid leaders name and be prepared to listen to directions addressed to your group."

"What difference does all that make?" someone yelled.

"A huge difference! If you miss your portal, you'll be stuck here. The mages will have to accept a raid invite for each group so you can use the portals."

Thunder rumbled, making Jen jump. Lightning flickered so brightly it made her eyes water. She wanted off this island before that lightning got here. The rain arrived, falling in slanted sheets across them.

"Jen, help me get this organized!" Jon called.

By willing it, her voice gained volume. "Okay, people, group up with your friends and families! We'll do our best to keep you together to go through at the same time! Louis, Cole and Tony Ellis are group one's leaders. Line up before them and tell them your names. Lou, invite them all by full name and go through last in your group. Tony goes first."

Jen gave Sam's shoulder a squeeze. "Kirk, Sam, you're the leaders of group two." She continued to set the groups, her voice carrying easily over the growing wind and thunder. Jon and Ethan assigned people to their groups and double-checked each one while the survivors of flight Four-Fourteen lined up in rows.

Waves almost reached the flat stretch of rock they stood on now. Thunder crashed overhead, and a woman screamed as lightning struck the water twenty feet away. The wing of the plane barely poked from the water and acted as a lightning rod. Streak after streak of lightning struck it, but soon it would be out of range of the fast-moving storm, and they were the next highest object.

"Okay people, one last check," Jen called.

"Group one, holler out your names one at a time in the order you'll be passing into the portal."

Jen turned to Jon after the last group called out their names. "We're as ready as we can be, I guess. Philip is going last. Dave will go right before him. If he see's anyone else here, he'll invite them and form a new portal." She flinched from the lightning that hit the rock peak behind her.

Jon clapped her on the shoulder." See ya on the other side. Okay, Philip, we're ready."

The Fall into the Past

Wind whistled past Jen's face, billowing her silver cape. She realized she was falling before her eyes adjusted to the faint starlight. Screams dwindled in the distance and grew above her as the rest of her raid followed her through the portal. She spread her arms and craned her head back.

Above her, the edge of the portals glowed blue. Bright flashes of lightning spilled from the centers, illuminating her friends as they stumbled through. In seconds, she was too far to hear them scream as they learned the portals had malfunctioned, dropping them out in mid-air instead of solid ground.

We knew something went wrong when no one in Brent's group returned with help, Jen thought in a corner of her mind.

Most of her attention was focused on her

current predicament.

How high were they? she wondered as she tried to spread herself out to face downward. Judging by the fading screams, they were pretty far up. Not a survivable fall. As her eyes adjusted to the darkness, she was able to make out darker shapes plummeting to earth near her. She typed the keys to cast Valorous Leap on an imaginary keyboard and leapt forward to grasp the nearest person.

"Hold on to me!" She didn't hear the reply if any. A suitcase hit her left shoulder, the impact jarred but didn't hurt.

Wind whipped the man's words away. Valiant Shout made her words clear, a passive ability that let her be heard across a battlefield if she willed it so. For a moment, the surrealness of her situation gripped her, and she fought back a hysterical giggle. She'd casted a magic spell— and it had worked.

An enormous bird dove past her, a darker outline in the dark night. She recognized Kuan in bird form but couldn't take the time to stare after him. She leapt again and grabbed a screaming woman clutching a toddler.

"Don't let me go," Jen bellowed.

Far below her, a glimmer appeared. Unable to spread herself out for more air resistance she fell faster now. She debated her options. Did she have twelve seconds before impact? Another leap might use the cooldown, making it unavailable to land gently. While she could shield herself from harm, she wasn't sure it would work for the people she carried. While she debated, she realized it wasn't ground beneath her, but water. She leaped again and missed. The man clinging to her back wrapped his hand in her cloak and stretched for the screaming man above him.

He yanked hard, spinning her sideways in his effort to reach the man flailing above him. Jen was afraid her cloak would rip from her shoulders. Only small decorative silver latches held it on. Then she wanted to smack herself. It wasn't a real cloak, but a magical one and only she could remove it. Her cloak neither stained nor ripped, always appearing pristine no matter what she did to it. The sudden clutching hands of another person relieved her.

Two giant birds swooped beneath her, catching, slowing, and releasing people pinwheeling through the air, letting them splash into the ocean without the fatal momentum. A few people fell slowly, appearing to float.

They must be levitated by priests, Jen thought.

Kuan reappeared from the darkness; his black raven wings blending into the dark night. He grabbed a screaming man and dropped him on one of the levitated men, banking hard and folding his wings, he disappeared into the dark. Jen yanked her gaze from the thrashing arms and legs of the people nearest her and stared down. The water rushed up to her; she didn't dare leap again.

The woman clinging to her neck repeated the

first few lines of a Hail Mary over and over right in Jen's ear. With a flick of Jen's fingers, she casted a Greater Shield. Wind no longer ruffled her cape, and the whistle of air past her face stopped. Unable to see her shield, she sighed in relief at the evidence it had worked.

"We're okay. I'm going to leap into the water," she said in a normal voice, not trying to project the sound. "The druids will be able to help you, just stay afloat. Tony can levitate us, and the druids can search for land. Please, if you can swim, search for the dead." While she spoke, she casted another Lesser Shield on a man falling above her. Very few people still fell. Most had passed through the portal before them.

A spot of neon-green luminescence appeared on the surface of the water. *Kirk*, Jen thought, relieved he'd managed to portal to the surface. She wished they'd thought to have Kirk make summoning stones. *Too late now though.* The water took on texture. Small waves became visible dotted with darker squares she assumed was luggage and people flailing and ducking from the hail of bodies and suitcases. In the dark, it was hard to tell distance. She waited until the ocean appeared to be mere feet away and leapt.

Water closed over her head. She kicked hard for the surface, grateful when her passengers released her. A dark shadow— she realized in horror was a body sinking— caught her eye. She swam toward it, tangling her hand in long hair and yanking.

Weak from lightning induced illness and lack of sleep, she struggled to pull the woman to the surface. She wasn't a strong enough swimmer. The body pulled her down. Black spots danced before her straining eyes. *Think, damn it,* she screamed at herself. *You have magic now!*

A litany of spells crossed her mind, but nothing she thought of would do a lick a good. She leapt upward, her chest aching to take a breath. Ten more seconds until she could cast Valorous Leap again and she sank like a stone. To survive she'd have to drop the woman or resurrect her, but it took twenty seconds to cast Resurrect the Dead, and another three to heal her and what if she couldn't swim either? She summoned her steed, hoping it would work, but was still amazed when it did.

A white war horse appeared beside her. Brilliant blue eyes fixed on her. The long, white mane rippled in the water. She grabbed the blue leather reins, laying herself across the saddle. The horse kicked for the surface. Just like in the game water slowed her. The magical horse appeared to be able to breathe. Its chest rose and fell as if it strained, and bubbles trailed from its nose.

Her head broke the surface, and she gasped, drawing in a lungful of air and spitting out a mouthful of saltwater. For a moment, she laid across her horse's neck, breathing deeply before sitting straighter and casting resurrection.

A golden-yellow light surrounded the corpse laying across the saddle before her. The light appeared to sink into the body until the body glowed translucently. When the light dimmed, the woman stirred and sat, a deep moan changing to a cry of pain. Awed amazement made Jen shiver. She casted a heal while staring about her.

Screams ended in splashes as passengers of flight Four Fourteen fell from the sky. The sudden abrupt ending of the screams horrified her. Jen nudged her horse's side and headed to the nearest sinking corpse. She grasped a leg and yanked a body from the depths.

The woman with her crowded and slowed her.

"Can you swim?" Jen asked.

"Oh my God; oh my God."

"Shut up! Can you swim?"

"Yes; Jesus, this can't be happening."

"Great, get off and hold this guy." She pushed the woman into the water. "If you can grab anyone, do it."

"I can't hold him, he'll drown." She sounded panicked.

"Yes, you can. He's already dead, just don't let him sink. I'll rez him in a minute."

As Jen spoke, she guided her horse to another man who slammed into the water and began to sink. She grabbed him by the hair and tugged him across the saddle behind her. A shrieking woman above her flailed at the air. Jen casted Valorous

Leap and grabbed her. She recognized the woman as someone wh'd entered the portal before her and wondered how she'd emerged so much later than her but put the thought aside to cast another shield. They fell together, her Greater Shield absorbed the impact. She released the woman in the water and kicked back to the surface.

"Samantha?" Her yell echoed across the water.

"Jen?" Kendra screamed. "I can't swim." Her desperate cry boomed over the water with magical clarity.

"Summon your charger. Grab the horses, people. Rangers, if you can hear me, please cast air-bubbles on people and let them sink. The druids can retrieve them. Find the corpses.

A yellow glow appeared, illuminating a small circle of light and a running figure.

"Tony!" Jen called.

The glow approached her. Damp to the knees, Tony ran along the top of the water, his glowing Hands-of-Sun casting shadows about him.

Jen resurrected the man on her horse while Tony ran up.

"Do we have a ranger anywhere? Kuan, I need you!" Jen screamed, her yell echoing and silencing everyone around her. She cursed herself for not sending Kuan through the portal with Sam.

"Sam is with Kirk, floating near his portal." Tony flicked his fingers, and suddenly it was no effort to stay afloat.

She almost sobbed with relief as she braced her hands on the water and pulled herself out as if climbing from dirt. On top of the water, she ran back to her horse and grabbed its reins, pulling it with her as she headed for the green neon glow in the distance.

"Kuan!" She screamed again and summoned her Sword-of-Truth into her hand, raising it aloft, hoping he'd spot the blue glow.

Kuan's black raven-shape plummeted from the sky. A loud screech cut off abruptly as he switched shapes mid-dive becoming a dolphin and falling into the water. A second later his human head broke the surface.

"Come with us and get Sam. Find as many corpses as you can."

No more bodies appeared to be falling from the sky. The screams had been replaced with calls for help and crying. Men and woman both called for friends and loved ones.

A large group of people floated beside Kirk's portal. Two men ran atop the water, dragging bodies through the water behind them.

Kendra sat astride her charger, casting resurrection and crying.

"Don't grab my horse, you'll sink us. Hold each other." Her voice echoed.

"Cass?" Jen called.

"Here! I'm casting Underwater Breathing on the ones who can't swim.

"Okay, keep doing that. Jamal?" In the corner of her mind, she took a moment to be grateful Underwater Breathing was an ally spell, not a party only spell. The confusion would make it impossible for the rangers to invite and cast. Now all they had to do was point and cast.

"Haven't seen him," Cass said.

"Maria?"

A giant eagle soared over Jen, transforming into a woman. Maria splashed into the water beside her.

Jen grabbed her in a quick hug before speaking. "We need to find land. Too many can't swim. Head east. If we landed near Philip's home, we should be off the coast of England. Get a summoning stone from Kirk before you go. If you find land" –she grabbed the first person she saw swimming— " You, what's your name?"

"Fred Merrithew. My wife is missing— "

Jen interrupted, "Summon Fred Merrithew. Fred, we need you to hold it together. Trust us, we're going to search. Go with Maria and get a summon stone from Kirk. Kirk will need help organizing. Help him while we search."

Another enormous bird arrived, her brown wings ruffling the water. Unlike a real bird, she could hover with small strokes of her wings.

"Cami, go with Cass and find the people under the water, dead or alive." While Jen spoke, she casted Sanctuary on top of the water. The soft, yellow glow of her spell gave enough light to show the scared expressions on the people swimming nearby." Kirk, summon your cauldron; we need summon stones!" Jen blessed her passive ability to project her voice at will.

Cami transformed into a dolphin, dove, and disappeared.

"Everyone who can swim, please help someone who can't! Group up on the yellow circle! There are too many of you for Tony to cast Ascension on everyone. Form a circle, use the levitated people to keep yourselves above water! Raid leaders, get yourselves organized; find out who's missing and if we have injured!"

Philip hollered for Sue, then Jen. Jen released the reins of her horse and ran toward his desperate shouts.

"Philip?"

"Sue didn't come through the portal! We were holding hands and stepped through together! Oh God, where the fuck is she?"

Jen reached into the water and took his hands. His weight pulled her feet into the water. To her, the water and air felt room temperature. In her armor temperature had no effect on her. Not so Philip. He shivered, and his lips were blue.

"Put Sam in group four!" she hollered, hoping Brandon, the leader of group four, would hear and comply. The rangers Endure Elements buff would protect their groups from the cold water. She was kicking herself for dashing through the portal so unprepared.

Philip was frantic. "I have to go back!"

"How? You can't reach the portal above us."

"Then I'll recast." A slight blue glow solidified into a doorway hanging inches above the water. Through the doorway, a room appeared. A blue comforter lay on the floor beside an unmade bed. Dirty clothes covered the floor, and the corner of an empty pizza box peeked from beneath the bed. Philip's room, just as it had appeared on the island when he'd first casted the spell.

"Philip, you don't know where it will take you. Look around—"

Her words were wasted. Philip disappeared as she spoke. A man swimming nearby reached out and touched the shimmering vision of a room. He disappeared too.

"No! You could fall again. God, you could end up anywhere. Where's Dave? Dave!" No one answered Jen's shout. "Stop, we'll find Dave and try his portal! We know this one doesn't work!"

"Invite me, please! I want to go home!" another man yelled.

Beside Jen, two people argued.

"No, we aren't trying that again. We could fall to our deaths twice. I won't do it."

The woman sounded hysterical, and Jen didn't blame her. She recognized her as the woman she'd just resurrected.

"Nina, we have to. Do you want to drown here?"

"Stop it!" Nina shrieked.

Her husband ignored her and yanked her toward the portal. Jen hesitated, not liking the man-handling, but not wanting to waste time on a domestic dispute either. And you couldn't force someone through a portal. It took an act of will just like in the game where you had to click the icon yourself. Even throwing someone through the doorway wouldn't work, they'd just end up on the other side of it.

"I'm going! Stay and drown if you like!" Nina's husband snapped.

"You'd leave me here..." Nina sounded amazed and heartbroken.

He didn't answer. He turned his back and grabbed the portal. Nina screamed as he disappeared.

Jen didn't know what to do, encourage her to follow, stop her? Either way could be death. Nina lifted a trembling hand to the portal, then snatched it back, paddling backward.

"I'm so sorry," Jen said.

"He left me. He fucking left me." She turned to Jen, her wide eyes changing to an angry glower. "He floated down. I crashed like a ton of bricks. How could he be so insensitive?"

Jen shrugged, helpless to answer her.

"Are we going to die here?"

Jen craned her neck to peer over her shoulder at Kendra who called for people to return to the Sanctuary.

"Don't let the non-swimmers go, they'll

drown!" Kendra screamed. "Jen, stop them!"

Jen didn't know how to stop them. Survivors in Philip's group splashed and pushed in their haste to reach the portal. For a moment, she was tempted. She could survive another fall, and maybe this time she'd end up in Philip's bedroom safe and sound in London, but these people needed her. She'd be beyond cruel to abandon them. And holy hell, she didn't want to be the one who had to convince the authorities magic was possible. For a minute the thought of her future as a magic wielder among normal people almost overwhelmed her.

"I'll deal with it later," she mumbled. "No, we aren't going to die here," Jen said firmly and ran back to her glowing circle of light.

Tony floated atop the water in the center of the circle, holding his brightly glowing hands aloft and casting Ascension as fast as he could between casting group heals. Sparks of light flitted from his fingertips and bounced around the swimmers, arcing into the air to impact the floaters in a dazzling display.

Jon called out, "Tony, cancel your Hands-of-Sun. Conserve magic. I want everyone to link arms. I figure we have about one more minute before the horses disappear from fatigued swim." A babble of cries and moans greeted that. "We need to float here until the druids find land. Kirk, how's the summoning stones coming?"

"Cauldron is ready, but it's taking two people

to hold it up."

"Tony, keep them levitated and Kendra, and any other magic wielder who can't swim. Get the children out of the water if we can. Do we have a count of missing yet?"

People hollered their missing friends and loved one's name.

"Quiet!' Jen yelled, willing her voice to be loud. "Now, one at a time. Tony, raid team one, how many?

"Sixteen."

"Kirk?"

"Three."

"Terri!" Terri didn't reply. "Shit, anyone see her?"

"No, I think we're missing twelve," Matt said.

"And we're missing nine, but the druids are still finding people," Ethan added.

The other raid leaders called out their missing and injured until the numbers jumbled in Jen's head.

Search for Survivors

"Give me a second here." Jen rubbed her eyes hard with the heels of her hands, then ran her palm over her skull, wincing when she remembered she was bald.

"Matt, take over Terri's group until we find her. Cass, can you cast air-bubble on everyone? We need to conserve energy here, people. Group one, invite Kirk and get a stone. One stone per person! Kendra, stay with Kirk and call for an invite to group two when he's ready."

"Let's switch the rangers around every ten minutes to give everybody some respite from the cold," Cass said.

Jen glanced over at Cass. Small movements of his hands stirred the dark water he floated in. A barely discernable yellow glow lit his fingertips every time he casted. In daylight, the light wouldn't be noticeable at all. A group of people surrounded him, helping children remain afloat. His passive calming aura seemed to be working. Instead of thrashing about and crying, his group huddled close to him, helping each other. Jen wished they had enough rangers for every group, not only for their Endure Elements buff that made anyone in a ranger group able to ignore hot or cold, but their innate ability to calm people. A skill that in the game let rangers pass very close to enemies without being attacked and could calm rage and fear effects on friendly players and enemies.

"Great idea, Cass," Jen said. "Did anyone count how many people passed through the second portal?"

"I can't believe Philip left us here!" a woman called out.

"I saw six go, but there might've been more," Jon said. "Kirk, once you give everyone a stone, reform the groups to give the casters and druids water. Hopefully, drinking water works like in the game to replenish our magic."

"People are still missing!" a man cried out, his voice breaking in a sob. "My son is missing."

Jen squatted atop the water before him and tried to sound reassuring. "I know, and we'll do all we can. The druids will continue to search. Right now, we need to organize. Kirk will have to summon us out of here."

Another wave of questions and yells traveled over the water.

"Listen up if you don't want to get left behind! Fred will summon Sam. Sam will summon Cass. I want every single person sure of who they're summoning. We can't screw this up. We'll wait until everyone has at least two summon stones."

"We can't just leave the missing!" a woman yelled angrily.

"We won't. It'll take Kirk two hours to make us all two stones because of the timer to form a cauldron. We'll wait for the druids but after three hours the spirit releases. I'm not saying a resurrection won't work then, but—"

"You shouldn't have sent Maria away!" a man shouted.

A grumble of assent followed.

Jen stood to face her accuser. "I sent her to find land. How long do you think we can keep all of you afloat? How long until hypothermia sets in? The magic wielders have to sleep sometime. We can't survive out here. We need land, it's as simple as that. If Maria finds land, she'll summon Fred. Fred will begin the chain, summoning Sam. Everyone, memorize the full name and face of the person you're assigned to summon! Make sure they have a summon stone on them!"

Jon strode atop the water to Jen's side. "Fred, if Maria summons you soon, wait a half hour to start the summon chain, giving Kirk enough time to make us all stones. Anyone have a working watch?"

The yellow glow of a resurrection spell,

followed by a softer glow of a heal, lit the night. The druids had found another body. Jen prayed they'd find them all before it was too late.

"Me. It's four fifteen, assuming we're in England's time zone."

Jen didn't recognize the voice, and it was too dark to make out the speaker. "Remind me to resummon my horse in thirty minutes for the swimmers to rest on. Please, everyone lay back in the water and float. We might be out here a long time."

Jen left Jon reassuring the floaters and ran atop the water to Kirk.

"How's it going?" Without will behind it, Jen's voice was soft and didn't carry far. Sam stood atop the water beside Kirk. She grabbed Jen in a tight hug.

"Fine," Kirk said. "I'll need a break after forming the third cauldron though."

"Okay, do the water cauldron next and drink some. You summoned your wand, right?"

"Duh." Kirk snorted in derision and huffed.

Jen released Sam and laughed, glad the darkness hid her blush. "Sorry."

"Relax, Kirk," Sam said. "This is new to all of us. Jen's doing a great job."

"You're right, she is. Is the next group ready?"

Jen rolled her eyes; again glad the dark hid her expression. Kirk always agreed instantly with anything Sam said. Sam never received sarcastic or rude comments. *Although, to be fair, Kirk was always super nice to Kuan too. For different reasons, but…* Jen pulled her thoughts away from Kirk, and turned back to the circle of light emanating from her Sanctuary. Reminded, she recast.

Jon was organizing everyone into groups small enough to fit inside Sanctuary. His deep voice carried across the water and reassured Jen. It seemed to do the same for everyone as the yells quieted to hear him.

"Anyone can use a paladin's sanctuary, but it will only work for fifteen people at a time, so we need to take turns," he said to his attentive audience.

Three more resurrections went off almost simultaneously.

Kuan jumped from the water in dolphin form, changing to a bird mid-leap. He hovered above her, then fell to the water in human shape. "Get an air-bubble and come with me. We could use the light from your sword."

"Go," Sam said needlessly.

From the corner of her eye, Jen saw the bronze ring encircling her neck. Sam had bought the special effect that made her Underwater Breathing spell appear as an antique diving helm instead of working invisibly.

Jen closed her eyes and pictured the steps she'd have taken to remove Ascension in the game. She sank into the water. Kuan shapeshifted into a dolphin. Feeling ridiculous, she climbed onto his back and grabbed his fin with one hand, holding her sword up with the other.

Kuan dove, slicing through the water with ease. The light from her sword made his skin appear blue. Jen peered over her shoulder and could barely see the tip of his tail. The sword lit only a narrow swath around her. What they needed was Tony's Hand-of-Sun. She smacked herself in the head with the hand holding the sword.

"Take us back. We can get wizard light."

Kuan turned and surged toward the surface, returning to the center of the lit spot of her Sanctuary.

"Rob, Matt, can you make us light-balls and get the kids on your floating disks?"

A minute later, she once again clung to the back of the dolphin. This time she held aloft a baseball-sized orb that gave off a soft, white light. She'd released her sword, letting it return to mist. Another light-ball dangled from a nylon stocking tied around Kuan's neck.

Yellow radiance from the light-balls attracted fish and lit about fifteen feet in every direction. Jen had no idea where they were going, but Kuan seemed to know. He swam strongly without hesitation.

An edge of a white sneaker caught her eye.

"There— to your left."

A young boy drifted in the water. Jen grabbed Dillion, Lindsey's youngest son, tucking his small, lifeless body tight against her. Horror over his condition warred with relief that she'd found him.

The way his body bent informed her he had more broken bones than not. She hoped he'd felt nothing.

Her body shook with tears she couldn't feel amidst the ocean waves. *Stop*, she told herself firmly. *Keep your eyes open and mind calm. The others need you alert, and Dillion can be resurrected.*

The thought still awed her, and again she pondered if this was all a fever dream, but the fear for the passengers relying on her help felt all too real.

They'd found three more corpses before Kuan surfaced. She handed the dead to willing volunteers, and they dove again.

They searched for thirty minutes and found four more. Jen recast War Charger, leaving her horse behind for the swimmers to rest on until it disappeared again from Fatigued Swim.

Exhausted by the days spent on the bare rock after the plane crash with neither food or water, the survivors of flight Four-Fourteen clung to her horse and stared at her with desperate eyes.

Despite increased stamina from her newfound magic Jen felt tired herself, and she'd barely casted anything. Kirk would be tiring, and they needed him. Soon they'd all be tiring, unable to keep casting, and those without magic would begin dying with no hope of a resurrection. Uneasy from her thoughts, she held Kuan tighter as they returned to the hunt.

If the search weren't so desperate, the ocean

would've been pretty. Brightly colored fish swam alongside them. Large patches of sandy bottom interspersed with clumps of coral and barnacle encrusted rocks housed larger fish, most of which swam away from them. Small orange and yellow fish darted amongst the coral.

Cami had gotten a light-ball from a wizard, making the ball Jen kept in the nylon vanish away. Jen held out the remaining glowing orb and peered through the dark for any sign of the missing. The two dolphins crisscrossed the ocean floor, Cami, with Steve astride her back, seen as a glimmer of light in the distance.

As a fury warrior, Steve was immune to harm from hot or cold. Cass was needed to help keep the weak swimmers stay afloat and cast Underwater Breathing. Jen and Steve gathered the luggage they came across and dropped it beside Brandon who stood atop the pile with his Sanctuary beneath him, holding his glowing Sword-of-Truth aloft— a beacon for those who couldn't swim and had sunk to the bottom.

If the land they found was another deserted island, they could retrieve the luggage.

People gathered beside the luggage, staring upward through the dark water with terrified eyes. Unable to swim either, Jamal, a ranger, stood with them, ready to cast Underwater Breathing when the first cast wore off. Jen hoped they'd be safely on dry land by then.

Jon called her when she surfaced next. Dillion

clutched him, his tear-streaked face pressed against Jon's chest.

"My mommy?"

"Sorry, sweetheart, we'll keep looking for all of them." A hot sick feeling filled Jen's stomach.

The little boy sobbed. Jon patted his back, his face grim. "We can't hold out like this much longer. Despite Sanctuary and ranger buffs, Kendra's had to resurrect two deaths from hypothermia so far. As soon as we move a group out of the sanctuaries to let another warm up..." Jon sighed and rubbed the back of his neck with one hand.

"The water and air are just too cold to survive in long. Even the levitated are cold. I've put all the children in with Sam, gave her lead, and told Fred to start the summoning chain with Kendra. She can place Sanctuary and rez and heal on shore as needed."

Jon lowered his voice. "Brandon and Jamal are keeping the people who sank warm enough for now. Group three, magic wielders who have no resistance to cold, are with Cass. We can't afford to lose any. People will start dying very soon, and while we can rez them, they'll just die again until we hit diminishing returns. We'll soon have to pick which ones to sacrifice."

Jen bit her lip. Thirty-six people were under the water with Jamal and Brandon. Nothing could harm you while standing on the glowing ground of a paladin's Sanctuary, but it only worked for fifteen people at a time— half a raid.

"Leave Jamal underwater and recall Brandon to the surface. Another Sanctuary can keep fifteen more people from feeling the cold and Jamal can keep thirty warm by himself."

"Can we help six more stay afloat up here to give them a chance to warm up?"

Jon sighed hard and peered over his shoulder at the wizards casting fireballs into the water. "Jen, no matter what we do, if we don't find land soon, people will start dying. Stay here and cast Sanctuary. The search will have to wait. The living need us. Let Kendra rest thirty minutes."

Kuan bobbed his dolphin head in acknowledgment. Jen frowned, worried about him now. He must be even more tired than she thought if he wasn't bothering to change back to human form to speak with them.

Jon laid a hand on her shoulder and squeezed. "I'm sending Cami east and Kuan north to look for land. We'll save as many as we can as long as we can. I'll speak to everyone and ask for volunteers before making a choice on who lives and dies. Three rangers and three paladins can keep everyone warm until we need to rest.

"Once the summons start, we'll recall all three druids and they can search for the missing again with you, Steve, and Brandon. I told Ethan we'd summon him back here to tell us where they are. He's number five in the chain. Number six has two stones. I was thinking if Maria finds another island, maybe we could retrieve some luggage?"

"Yeah, the druids are collecting it," Jen said. "But have the first people summoned try to bring the few floating pieces with them and make sure it works before we waste our time retrieving it. Maria's been gone almost an hour. This spot will be impossible for the druids to find again. Where do you think we are?"

Jon's expression tightened. "Who the hell knows. We could be a mile off shore. Maybe they shot her down or something."

"Gee, that's a cheery thought."

Jon gave her an apologetic grimace. "I keep hoping a boat will appear, but no one's seen anything."

"I like that thought better. Keep looking."

"The wizards are shooting fireballs in the air every ten minutes or so, and the rest in the water. Maybe someone will see and come investigate. It helps, it's warming the water, but it grows cold quick. They can't keep it up very much longer; it's a big ocean…"

Jen gave Jon a quick hug. "Just hang in there. Does everyone have a summoning stone?"

Jon held out a red orb for her to examine. "Yes, and some have two, but will they even work?"

"Seems likely, and what else can we do?"

"Only our best." Jon slapped Jen's shoulder. "You guys go get Brandon.

She and Kuan dove again to retrieve Brandon.

They glided through dark water now, maybe fifty feet down with nothing to see except the occasional fish. Kuan swam much slower than earlier. Below them, Cami swam further south, a barely seen glow in the dark water. Forty people were still missing, and they hadn't spotted a corpse in over thirty minutes.

"They might not be here at all. Maybe the portal worked for them," she said, willing it to be true.

Kuan paused his slow swimming, then continued.

The thought eased Jen's heart. Maybe the missing waited in safety and comfort, worried for their loved ones. It would take a while for an authority to believe them. And they'd have no idea where to send help. Likely Lindsey and the rest would send rescue workers to the island, thinking they got trapped there. *Not that they knew where the island was either...*her thoughts depressed her.

Kuan swam unerringly to Brandon, the glow of Sanctuary a faint glimmer in the inky dark. She explained quickly, avoiding meeting the eyes of the people she'd be leaving alone in the dark ocean. Heartsick, Jen clung to Brandon's broad back as Kuan towed them to the surface.

Jon hailed her. "Fred disappeared seven minutes ago."

Jen heaved a relieved sigh that Jon echoed. Tightness eased in her shoulders as a man disappeared before her eyes. Three seconds later, the woman who swam beside him disappeared along with the suitcase she clutched. It was working. Jon glanced at his borrowed wristwatch and held up a red orb.

"Ethan Lance," he said.

Ethan appeared before them and sank into the sea where he threw an arm around Kuan to stay afloat. "Maria found another deserted island, a big one. She saw forests but no lights. I asked them to pause when they hit group three to give us time to retrieve the luggage. The missing... some didn't make it through the portal. We've had numerous reports of people entering together and falling alone.

Rob handed Jen a new wizard light. A bird with brilliant pink and gold plumage that appeared to drip sparks sat on his shoulder. The bird cocked its head, fixing her with a glowing blue eye.

"A real firebird..." Her awed gaze followed the bird as it soared into the sky. Brilliant blood-red feathers shaded to orange and gold on the underside of its wings. It left a trail of sparks as it flew.

"So beautiful," she said as she stared after it. She turned back to Jon, her gaze landing on Dillion who slept on his shoulder. "When we leave here, we won't be able to find this spot again."

Ethan released Kuan and gave her a quick hug. "Jen, we did all we could. It's been two hours and twelve minutes. Continue searching. A fresh air-bubble will take you safely to hour three, then we'll summon you."

"We need extra stones in case we find anyone."

"Yeah, he's waiting beside his cauldron. He saved all our lives with that," Jon said.

Jen nodded tiredly and headed to the cauldron. Red glowing runes, the familiar pattern from a video game, traced the surface and she couldn't help smiling. She took a stone.

"Take two. There better be enough for all six of you to take two. I caught one asshole taking extra earlier. We moved him to the last summon group. I think we should leave his ass here to drown."

Sam laid a hand on Kirk's arm.

"It isn't harsh," Kirk said angrily. "Taking two stones meant someone else didn't get one. He was willing to let someone die here."

"He has a family, Kirk. He just wanted to make sure they both got called," Sam said.

"Still..." Kirk turned away.

The green glow of his cauldron made Kirk's exposed skin look sickly. What Jen could see of it anyway. He now wore black chitinous armor that covered him completely, except for his face. The matching helm was nowhere in sight. Unlike her armor, Kirk's armor had rounded curves and no visible seams. There was something organic and sinister about it. Diaphanous, black, bat-shaped wings with glowing red veins fluttered behind him occasionally as he moved, appearing and disappearing in random intervals.

Levitated to hold the cauldron up, Nina wore Kirk's cloak draped around her shoulders. Made of shiny, slick material, the cloak trailed into the water. Midnight-black with a border of neon green, Genesis's guild symbol on the back, a bright lightning bolt slashed across a world triad, glowed the same eerie green. The same symbol as her cloak. Her cloak… she wanted to slap herself again; it hadn't occurred to her to let someone else use it.

As if reading her mind, Sam said, "It wouldn't work. Brandon tried, but when he got out of range, the cloak disappeared."

Jen smiled crookedly. Sam returned the smile. For a moment Jen let herself be grateful for her best friend's presence.

"You think Kuan summoned that lightning somehow?" Jen traced a finger along the glowing white edge of lightning on her cloak. The material appeared to be very fine silver chainmail with the symbol picked out in white, but it slipped through her fingers like silk.

"Discuss it later," Jon said. His thoughtful gaze traveled the green symbol on the cloak wrapped around Nina.

Jen nodded and saluted, letting herself sink into the depths, clutching a fresh wizard light in her hand.

Landfall

Jen grasped Kuan's slick dolphin fin with one hand as he glided through the depths. The ball of light she held illuminated fifteen square feet of dark water around her to daylight brightness.

Sam called her name. Jen just knew if she answered yes, she'd join her. She'd wondered what a summons would feel like. If she'd have a choice or just be dragged away.

"I'm being summoned," she said before releasing Kuan and thinking yes. She appeared before Sam who hugged her tightly.

"Thank God. The wait was killing me. Did you find any more?" Sam asked.

"No."

Sam pulled her to a bonfire and handed her a roasted piece of meat. The smell made Jen's mouth water. Wolves howled in the distance. Jen's shoulders tightened at the eerie noise. Everyone turned to face the forest until the sound faded.

"What's this from?" Jen sniffed the meat before gingerly taking a bite.

People huddled around fires dotting the beach. Some lay in the sand, apparently sleeping, while others sat holding their hands to the blaze.

"Maria caught a deer. She's out hunting with Cass now. Miguel knew how to butcher it. This is a big island. I can't believe no one is on it. That's a real forest, not a jungle. Fuel for the fires is plentiful. Where the hell are we?" Sam gestured to the towering pine trees on the edge of the beach.

"No idea. How many are still missing?"

Sam took a deep breath. "Sixty-six. Twelve for sure followed Philip. Thirty-two almost certainly never came through the portal. Twenty-two... we don't know."

"Jesus, so many."

"One hundred and twelve saved," Sam offered in a hopeful tone.

Tears filled Jen's eyes and she clutched her friend. Sam rubbed her back a moment before stepping back and wiping her face on her sleeve.

"Eat and rest." She tugged Jen to the fire and pushed her down beside Kirk. "Stay here." She ran off to greet Kuan.

Ramiro sat beside her. "Didn't find any more?"

"No." She pressed her hands against her eyes unable to meet his sad gaze.

"Not your fault, Jen. None of this is your fault. Maybe some will wash up, and you can try to resurrect them." He chuckled suddenly. "I can't believe I'm saying that. What you can do is so amazing. I'm kind of worried about that. That the government will make you disappear or something."

She glanced down at the white armor she wore and shrugged. "No one can hold me if I'm wearing my righteous armor."

"True, but you aren't immortal. You can be killed. Not easily, but still. And I hate to say this, but your family could be used against you."

Ethan plopped down on the sand behind them. "If they try that shit, they'll be very, very, sorry. You're right though, we need a plan. When the sun rises, and the druids can see farther, they're bound to find people. We need to be ready. God, my wife must be freaking out. I bet everyone thinks we're dead."

Jen closed her eyes, letting the meat fall to her cloak. Her mom and dad would be frantic, her little brother hurt and confused.

Sam returned and stood behind her.

"What about Valor?" Miguel said as he reached past Kirk's shoulder to rip a piece of meat from the deer on the wooden spit.

"What about them?"

"They got hit too and were sick as hell when we left. You think they changed too?"

"Who knows? Guess we'll find out," Kirk

said.

"No— I mean, we should contact them if we can, to get our story straight. Maybe the government doesn't need to know about us?"

"How the fuck could we keep it secret?" Kirk gestured with his chin at the men and women milling around the campfire. "You think they aren't going to mention falling through a portal, or Kuan, or this?" He rapped the cauldron beside him with his knuckles, making a sharp metallic clunk. He rose his hand to examine his fist and smiled. "Not a mark on it."

"Maybe we were the only survivors?" Miguel said.

"Jesus," Sam said and scooted away from him.

"Just kidding. Don't get your knickers in a twist." Miguel smiled at her.

Sam stared at her feet, rubbing her palms on her jeans.

Miguel eyed her a moment, then examined the crowded beach before turning to Kirk.

"You really summoned a demon?"

"Yes, and it was terrifying," Sam said.

Jen glanced behind her. Cami and Brandon stood beside Kuan, dripping seawater.

Sam shivered and pushed between Jen and Ramiro. Kuan sat and folded his legs gracefully. Jen put an arm around him and handed him her hunk of meat.

Sam shivered again and leaned closer. "He opened a pit up beneath the cauldron and black smoke poured out. It stunk like rotten eggs, and purple and yellow flames crawled from the cauldron. I looked inside, and it appeared endless, just a deep, bottomless pit of nothing."

Jen put her other arm around her.

"It was easy." Kirk sounded smug. "Just like in the game. I called, and it formed the same way. The smoke turned to a man-shaped cloud. I didn't try to make it do anything, just cast Demon Armor, and here I am."

"Have you tried to take it off yet? I imagine you need too, to pee." Miguel snickered when Kirk made a soft sound of distress.

Jen wanted to smack him. Even after all they'd been through together Miguel could still be a real asshole.

She turned to Kirk. "Just picture how you do it in the game. It worked for removing Ascension. We have so much to learn. We should've made the summon stones before we left and the light, food, and water."

"It's not like we had a lot of time…" Kirk crossed his arms and glared.

"We need rest. None of us are at our best." Jen leaned her head on Kuan's shoulder.

Kirk stood and his black armor disappeared, leaving him in ripped jeans and a black hoody, the same sweatshirt Jen wore beneath her armor. The sweatshirt the tourney had given her with UBM written on the back and left sleeve and her character's name on the front in cursive script above her heart.

"Easy," Kirk said, sounding relieved. He spread his arms and waved them. "That's amazing— how well the armor blocks cold and heat. I can feel the chill in the air and the heat from the flames now."

Sam leaned forward, her eyes intent. "Maybe you could send your demon to retrieve the dead bodies?"

"Wait," Jon said as Kirk turned to the cauldron. "Rest first. They're dead; a few more hours won't hurt, and you're tired. Let's not take a chance a demon runs amok here."

Sam bit her lip. "Yeah, you better wait."

Jen shivered, imagining the destruction a freed demon could cause before they could defeat it. And what if they couldn't? Would it run away and rampage in cities and towns like in the game?

The thought horrified her and by Jon's expression scared him too. In the game, players created and released demons in the hopes of killing them later for loot. Sometimes, the creation was a mistake that wiped an entire raid. Summoning a demon while too injured or tired could release it. Generally, demons that were killed quickly carried no loot and were relatively easy to kill, but occasionally a rare, epic demon would spawn, and it could take sixty or more players to kill it.

The computer-generated guards would fight the demons, which grew stronger the longer they remained free, and players would help defeat them, but the towns were always damaged and players killed. Here, real people would be killed and cities destroyed if they couldn't find it in time.

"Never risk a demon getting away," Jon said forcefully, and Kirk nodded.

Miguel laughed and rose, dusting off his jeans before sauntering to the fire closer to the water where Cass was skinning a rabbit and showing giggling children.

Kirk glared at him, shaking his head.

Jen relaxed and removed her armor with a thought. Kirk wasn't stupid; he'd be careful. The conjured bread she'd placed in the front pocket of her hoody appeared exactly as it had when she'd placed it there.

"This is amazing. Where does it go when I put my armor on? How come the water doesn't affect it, or mold?"

Sam shrugged.

Jen replaced the bread, resummoned her armor and leaned back in the sand, using her cloak to cover herself, not from the cold but because it still embarrassed her to be seen in her armor.

Sam snickered and lay beside her. Jen sighed hard and used her cloak to cover her friend.

"Your armor is pretty."

"Don't go there."

Sam snickered again.

Jen had spent way more time than she liked to admit acquiring attractive armor for her character. Vanity pieces were rare drops and required long hours of farming, a lot of gold, or both.

Her righteous armor wasn't too bad, a white mini-skirt and white halter top with silver trim. Knee-high, white boots with short, silver heels covered her feet and lower legs, and thin, silver bracers connected to silver, fingerless gauntlets on her hands. An inch-wide, bright band of silver studded with bright-blue gems circled her bald head. Shiny silver scrolled pauldrons magically stuck to her upper arms, barely covering the curve of her shoulder. A sparkly silver chain held her cape on. Her cape never moved. With no fastenings at all, the silver chain always fell across her collar bones, never choking her.

On her video game character, the pieces looked sexy, on her— not so much. Her character was tall and voluptuous with long, thick, golden hair always perfectly tousled. Jen sighed and ran a hand over her bald head. She was just tall.

"At least you can choose which one to wear," Sam whispered and giggled.

Jen glared. Her protective armor, the set she wore while tanking, was basically a black leather bikini with silver buckles and black straps— with her flat chest it looked ridiculous. The helm was worse. The long tail of shiny black feathers made her feel like a stripper, or maybe it was the thigh-high, black leather boots.

"At least the boots feel like sneakers," Sam said.

Jen laughed. Sam always knew what she was

thinking. "That's because they are sneakers. It's all an illusion."

Sam ran her hand along the cloak. "It feels pretty real to me." Tears filled her eyes and she squeezed them closed. "This all feels horribly real. I keep hoping I'll wake up. I bet Amy is comforting Randy right now, the ho."

Jen laughed sadly and took Sam's hand. "You've only been gone a week. He'll wait. And jeez, if he doesn't, do you want him?"

Sam said nothing, closing her eyes and feigning sleep.

Jen drifted off, thoughts of her family haunting her.

Loud voices woke her. She winced when Kendra bellowed for quiet. A golden sun shone above her in a mostly cloudless sky. Small waves lapped the sandy shore and dashed against the bigger rocks that dotted the edge. Seagulls wheeled and called in the distance. Behind her, the sand turned to gravel sprinkled with low bushes, then to towering forest.

She had to pee badly, but the angry voices warned her something big was afoot. Sam stirred as Jen scrambled to her feet. A shadow passed overhead. She rose her hands to shade her eyes and peered upwards. Kuan flew overhead.

"Beautiful," Jen whispered, admiring the sleek, black wings in sunlight.

Wings so black they appeared to have blue edges shaded her face as Kuan soared above them.

He'd retained his mass and made an impossibly huge bird. He folded his wings and dove. The call he loosed drew attention. He plummeted to earth, spreading his wings at the last second to slow his descent, and transformed into an equally large black panther. He landed lightly and became himself.

Jen sighed enviously, wishing she'd rolled a druid.

"As far as I can see there's no sign of civilization except smoke rising about twenty miles to our left."

"As far as you can see… what's that mean? Can you see the entire island?" Fred asked.

"No, the trees go the horizon. There are fields and hills, but I didn't see the sea behind us. The coast spreads and curves. Again, as far as I can see; I'm guessing at least a hundred miles."

"That can't be right. There's no island with these types of trees that big, not uninhabited at least," someone yelled.

Kuan shrugged. "I'm reporting what I saw. Maria went to check out the smoke. Cami went northwest. I can go look again if you like.

"No, stay here." Jen grabbed his arm. The thought of Kuan going off alone made her really uneasy. "One druid with the group at all times. A forest like that"— she pointed with her chin at the trees behind her – "will have predators. Cass, set a ward. No one enters the forest alone."

The woman Jen recognized as Nina from the

portal incident snickered. "What— you expect bears or tigers to attack?"

"I have no idea what's in the woods, and that's the point. Maybe what happened to us happened worldwide. What if that storm covered the entire world? Who the hell knows what happened? Maybe the reason no one came was because there's no one left."

"That's crazy!" a man shouted.

"This is crazy." Jen used will to project her voice. "Everything that's happened is impossible, yet here we are. Let's not argue about the impossibilities; let's take basic precautions." She jerked her thumb at the forest behind her. "That's a big, thick, deep woods with no sign of people, ergo it likely has animals. So, we should be cautious."

"Okay, everyone, listen up!" Jon waved his arms in the air, then rested a hand on Dillion's head who clutched his leg. "Cass and Maria brought back more game. Let's get that cooking. Jen, can you mount up and go look for water? Follow the coast, a stream is bound to connect. Meanwhile, we're going to reorganize again. I want all wielders and raid leaders to join me, and we can discuss the best way to split buffs and make sure everyone has someone looking out for them."

"Who put you in charge?" Mr. Bosko yelled and pushed himself to the front of the crowd.

"I put me in charge. I've had survival training, have you?" Jon scanned the gathered crowd through narrowed eyes. "We don't have time to vote all democratic-like. Decisions need to be made. The nights are cold and will get colder. Let's plan, and act, and not worry about where we are but about how we can help each other."

He turned to Kirk. "Can you make us more summon stones and water?"

"He needs the cauldron to summon a demon— Shut up!" Sam yelled when people began murmuring. "It isn't a real demon; don't be retarded. He needs one to send to look for the missing."

The murmuring quieted. Kirk grinned at Sam.

Jen summoned her steed. Blue mist solidified into an enormous white horse before she could blink three times.

"You need a name."

She rubbed the horse's white nose. The horse shook its head and snorted then bobbed it and tapped the ground. "Can you understand me?"

The horse bobbed its head again. A crowd surrounded the horse, reaching out to touch it.

"It feels warm and smells sort of horsey," Nina said.

Sam pursed her lips and crossed her arms. "It is a real horse, but I think it's you too," she said to Jen. "Try thinking directions at it."

Jen clapped her hands and laughed when the horse circled, then lay in the sand. It stood and shook, sending sand flying. Not a speck stuck to its gleaming, white coat.

"It's a magical construct, how you perceive a horse, but it isn't a real horse." Sam nodded as if in agreement with herself.

Jen shrugged. "He still needs a name." Warm breath wafted her cheeks as the horse exhaled noisily. A long, white tail swished, flicking the horse's sides. Silver hoofs stamped the ground, and it whinnied. "I'm not making it do any of that."

Sam shrugged. "Maybe not consciously."

"It doesn't matter. Jen's right, the pets need names. We can't go around saying 'Hey horse' or 'summon your bird,'" Rob said. He held up his arm, and his firebird appeared on it. Gold talons encircled his arm, and brilliant red and gold plumage spread to balance. "Meet Joash. I'm keeping his true name to myself for a while."

Jen nodded thoughtfully. In the game, calling a familiar's true name made it appear before you. If you were being attacked, it'd help you fight or could lead allies to you. Harming one harmed the wizard who conjured it, even if they were nowhere near it. If the wizard was already injured, killing the bird could kill them too, a tactic often used when dueling. The wizards would need to be sure only those they trusted knew their familiar's full names. She knew Matt's bird name from the game, but not Rob's.

Sam snorted and held a hand out to stroke the dark-gold breast. "So soft. You're beautiful, Joash."

The bird cocked its head, then preened.

Jen laughed. "He sure is. I need to think about what I'm going to call my horse." She vaulted into the saddle with effortless grace. It felt natural, as easy as breathing. "I'll go look for water."

Without her having to do a thing, her horse spun and headed down the beach at a gallop. A wide grin formed on her face, and she leaned forward, urging her horse on. Sand kicked up from the flashing, silver hooves. She wondered how fast they were going. It seemed very fast to her, but she had no way to judge.

"Whoa," she said unnecessarily ten minutes later. Her horse had already slowed and picked its way up the narrow brook. Trees overhung both sides, shading a shallow stream that barely covered her horse's fetlocks. The horse pranced up the middle, splashing water with each step. Jen slid to the ground and scooped up a mouthful.

"Tastes normal, not salty. Good as spot as any, I guess." She drank her fill and climbed back on her horse. "I think your name is Gallant. What do you think?" She laughed when the horse nodded agreement.

She straightened suddenly, Sam called her. She heard nothing but knew Sam summoned her. "Later, Gallant, Sam calls. Yes," she said aloud and found herself before Sam again.

"You aren't going to fucking believe this." Sam grabbed her arm and dragged her to the group surrounding Maria.

9

What Do You Mean When?

Jen stared at Sam's white face, shocked to hear her swear. Sam never swore unless seriously angry.

"I'm telling you, stone age." Maria was saying as Jen arrived. Maria jerked her chin in greeting but didn't stop speaking. "Not literally stone age. But real rough. Small huts, crude garments. The woman wore long skirts and leather vests, the men tunic things or leather leggings. What children I saw looked small and dirty, half-naked, and sickly. I'm sure of where we are just not when."

The words washed over Jen, their meaning eluding her.

"What do you mean when?" Tony sounded aggravated. "What the hell are you talking about?"

Jen began to tremble. She turned to peer into the woods, the impossible woods.

"We traveled through time?" she heard herself say.

"I think we did. For sure those were the white cliffs of Dover. This is England, just not our England. Maybe it's another dimension or something. Same date just different. Whatever it is, there are people, just not tech. No cars, no big buildings, no lights— nothing."

"Did they speak English?"

"I didn't linger." Tears filled Maria's eyes. "It scared me. I came right back. What if everyone here is like us. How will we get home?"

A wave of terrified silence passed over the crowd. People began arguing and yelling questions and suggestions in a confusing cacophony.

"Quiet," Jon bellowed and the crowd quieted. "Wherever we are, we're stuck here." He lifted Dillion and hugged him. The boy stared around at them clearly not understanding what was happening.

For a selfish moment Jen was glad Dillion didn't understand he was now an orphan and she wouldn't have to tell him.

"You don't know that," a man said.

"What's your name again?" Jon asked.

"Warren Reed."

"Mr. Reed, we traveled here by magic— a mage portal, and we have no mages left. So, no more portals. Even assuming there are other mages here, they won't have portals to our England, just theirs. We don't know what caused the lightning or who or what it affected besides us. What we do know is never in our recorded history has anyone arrived from the future, never mind someone like us." Jon jerked a thumb at his chest.

"Personally, I think the chances of a miracle occurring and returning me to my proper place is nil-zero-zilch. The portal malfunctioned, and here we sit."

"Couldn't Philip return for us?" Sam asked.

"How? Say he survived his return portal, finds Sue and they're safe in his room. So, he recasts. What are the chances the portal malfunctions and sends him to us? How does he know where we went? His portal only leads to his home and major cities. Cities that aren't here yet. If this is the past, how does he find this exact year?" Jon hugged Sam and grabbed Kendra who began to cry, pulling both women into a tight embrace.

"I'm sorry, but the odds just make it impossible, even assuming he was willing to go through a portal and risk losing Sue again."

"My mom and dad? Josh?"

The loss in Dillion's voice felt like a knife in Jen's soul. She collapsed to the ground, sitting in a heap with her head in her hands. Jon's words seemed unreal as if they couldn't apply to her. She'd been sure she'd get to see her family soon and put the last few nightmarish days behind her.

"You're sure it was Dover?" a man asked in a tight voice.

"I'm sure. God, I wish I wasn't, but I am.

Neither Saint Mary's nor Dover castle where there, which means we're before the eleventh century."

"Or you're wrong, and this isn't Dover."

"Maybe. I hope so." Maria rose her hands to cover her face.

Jen was reminded of her hairless state and ran a hand over her bald head. The metal circlet tipped. She removed it and ran it through her fingers. The reality of her situation stifled her for a moment, leaving her breathless.

"If this is possible, who's to say what isn't." She stood and waved the circlet. "We've seen true miracles, but Jon's right. We need to plan as if we're here for good. We need shelter and food. I found water a few miles away. Let's get there and make a plan. First, we need to find out if the natives have magic too."

"No, you're supposed to stay where you land so rescue workers can find you!" a man called.

"Don't be a fucking idiot. There won't be a rescue," Kirk snapped.

Jon whistled shrilly as people began arguing. "Let's go people. Argue as you walk. Make sure your partner is with you and move out down the beach. Kirk won't be providing food or water, so while you're welcome to stay here, or go wherever the hell you want, we're leaving."

He gestured to Kirk with his chin, and still holding Dillion with an arm around Kendra, he began to walk down the beach.

Kendra pulled away and whistled. A gray

horse coalesced from blue mist in an instant.

"Diva." Kendra reached up and patted the nose, then leaped into the saddle with magical ease.

Despite her misery, Jen grinned and looked away. Kendra looked ridiculous in her paladin armor. The red mailed mini-skirt she normally wore while playing solo revealed fat thighs. Her belly protruded alarmingly from the bikini top. Bright red pauldrons, resembling flower petals, covered her shoulders and matched her greaves and the armor on her shins. Jen took a second to thank God she hadn't chosen that outfit.

On Kendra's video game character, it looked good, sexy and feminine. The crown held the video games character's black curly hair off a beautiful face. In real life, the helm resembled a gold crown with red glass on the ends of the sharp points and revealed Kendra's bumpy skull. She did admire the thick white fur cloak with red trim. It looked soft and inviting and was likely the reason Kendra had donned the outfit despite how ridiculous she looked in it.

Jon drew her aside. "Jen, I was thinking, you, one of the druids, and a rogue maybe, should head to the village Maria found while we set up a camp. Kirk can make you supplies, and we'll have stones to summon you back here."

"Okay, but let's plan this. No more rushing off. Kirk, can you make us a couple cauldrons? Give us each five summoning stones, a translator, and as much food as we can carry."

Kirk stopped walking and held his wand out. Jen watched fascinated as he summoned the cauldron.

A blue mist turned into a green glow that solidified into a metal cauldron. It took a minute to form just like in the game. He waved his wand above it, and green runes appeared. Small symbols resembling hieroglyphics raced around the cauldron, the light settling into grooves in the metal and forming bigger symbols.

"Jen, call the wielders. I can only do this once every three days. Every wielder takes a translation stone, then group one."

"Return to the cauldron if you're in group one or a magic wielder!" Her shout traveled across the beach, and people turned. "Maria, Ethan, and Cass will be coming with me." Jen reached into the pot when the sigils on the side glowed steadily and withdrew a clear ball the size of an egg.

A faint glimmer of blue shone from it. In the game, translation stones lasted until you logged out. A vanity item, they were used to speak to members of the opposing faction and were needed to complete some of the quests for vanity gear and spells. Translation stones let you understand the computer-generated insults and yells of ogres and trolls, translating in both directions flawlessly, and were a major source of income for warlocks because of the timer to conjure them.

She dropped it on the ground and stomped on it. It sank into the sand. She glared and summoned her sword and shield, placed the ball on the shield, and used the pommel of her sword to try to break it. Satisfied it wouldn't easily break, she picked it back up.

"We need packs." She rose her voice. "We need to borrow backpacks or purses or anything we can use to carry supplies! If you have anything like that, return to the cauldron or give it to a druid, please."

"Please return your trays and seats into an upright position," Sam mumbled and giggled.

Jen rolled her eyes.

"Why take Cass and not me?"

"Because Cass can really hunt, and you've never killed a thing. Stay with Kirk and Kuan. You won't go hungry with them." She didn't mention Sam was hopeless as a ranger. She'd played the game, but not well.

"Idiot," Kirk snapped, startling her. He glared at a man holding two clear balls. "Only the person who picks them up can use them. Two is pointless." He sighed heavily and waved his wand over the cauldron again. "Jen, tell them all again. These knuckleheads can't grasp the concept of one each."

"Treat it like a beginner walkthrough. Tell everyone." Jon gestured to the backs of the people walking away down the beach. "When we get to the water I'll make sure every raid leader speaks to their party leaders, and we'll go over it again. Most of these people never played a video game and don't understand the rules. We need to be patient."

Kirk's lips tightened as he glanced from Jon to Sam, but he said nothing.

"Summon stones next. Each of you takes four, and the druids can split the rest."

Jen placed her four at her feet.

Sam and Kendra headed into the woods. Jen thought they went for a bathroom break, but they returned a few minutes later with thin green branches. Sam sat beside Kirk and began stripping the leaves and weaving the limbs together. In a few minutes she had a crude pouch.

Kendra returned to the forest with Jamal and Brandon.

They returned ten minutes later with more vines and thin limbs.

"This is bullshit, that no one is willing to let us use their backpacks and crap." Kirk stared after the disappearing crowd with angry eyes.

Jen had to agree.

"You're right. I'll speak to everyone about that too," Jon said. "We all have to contribute what we can. I wish a mage had made it through the portal to form us packs, but I guess it's good none did or they'd insist we try a portal again, and I for one, never want to step through another one. It's just luck we wound up in the air and not beneath the earth.

Jen laid a hand on his arm, trying to comfort him. The thought of being trapped in the earth horrified her too.

Kirk said, "We don't need them. Let them find their own help."

Sam glanced up frowning.

Kirk sighed. "Sorry, it just makes me so mad. They're all, 'give me, give me' like I owe them or something." He smiled down at Sam when she patted his knee.

It was all Jen could to do not to make retching noises.

"These should do." Sam stood and handed Jen the twig basket. "Tie the bread to it with the vines. I'd let you use a shirt or something" – she gestured to her suitcase in the sand behind her— "but if these are the last designer clothes on Earth, I'd rather not."

Jen stuffed two summon stones in her jean pocket, then dropped the other two small red spheres beside the clear one in the makeshift pouch.

"This is new. What one is this?" Sam pointed to the blue glyphs swirling around the cauldron.

"Health potions," Tony said as he leaned over and peered into the cauldron.

The blue runes on the side of the cauldron darkened.

"Look." Kendra pointed to a pine tree behind Kirk.

The needles on the tree turned brown and began to fall. Green mist boiled from the mouth of the cauldron.

"I'm stealing its life." Kirk waved his hand

through the green mist traveling from the tree to the cauldron. "This is so cool. I have no idea how I'm doing it."

"Did you pick that tree on purpose?" Jon asked.

"Yeah, I can sense the life in things and call it to me. It's creepy but cool."

The mist dissipated, leaving green glass vials in the pot. Silver filigree decorated the sides of each three-inch vial, connecting to a silver stopper.

"If you have your own heal, just take one. Ethan, take four. Cass, take three. The rest of us take two."

In moments, the pot was empty. Jen added her green vial to the collection in her crude basket. Kirk filled his cauldron with bread next. The familiar rectangular loaves poked from the cauldron and smelled delicious. She took four and tied them awkwardly to her basket with vines.

"Hope this isn't poison ivy," she mumbled as she tied the greenish red vine around her last loaf.

Sam said, "Shouldn't matter; you can cure poison."

"Is that a poison?"

Sam shrugged.

Jen sighed and made another long loop of vine to hang the entire thing over her back. She whistled and Gallant appeared. He pranced in place, neck arched and hooves flashing in the sun.

"He's really beautiful," Sam said admiringly.

Jen had to agree. Tufts of silky, white hair

adorned his fetlocks. His snow-white coat shone, and his mane flowed freely. Not a speck marred him from head to tail. Bright-blue eyes glowed with intelligence, and silver tack glittered in the sun. A blue leather intricately-tooled saddle sat atop a silver saddle blanket formed of delicate, silver chainmail like her cloak and was soft like her cloak. An empty scabbard dangled from the saddle on the right and a hook for her shield on the left. Both were silver edged with gold and glittered brightly in the sun. She draped her basket over the hook for the shield.

"Cass and Ethan can take turns riding with me. If Maria doesn't return in twenty-four hours, summon us."

Sam kissed her cheek. "Be careful. If you need help, summon us."

"You too. I love you, Sam."

Saying the words embarrassed her, but she wished she'd said them on parting with her brother. Later, squirt— didn't carry quite the same weight. Tears burned her eyes, and she squeezed them closed a moment.

"I love you too." Sam stepped back and took Kirk's hand.

Kirk smiled at Jen. "I'll take good care of her."

Jen nodded. He would. She didn't think he cared about anything else in the world except Sam… and maybe money. Cass mounted behind her, and she followed Ethan who ran down the beach. Gallant kept up easily. Maria soared overhead, casting an enormous shadow with her eagle wings.

Good thing they had Sam to keep Kirk in line, Jen mused to herself.

"Which bird shape do you like better?" Cass asked, pulling her from thoughts of Kirk and Sam.

"Kuan. Although all are beautiful."

"Yeah, I wish I rolled a druid. That must be so amazing, and they're getting better at it."

"Kuan is a natural. He was born for this," Jen said.

"You think he caused it somehow?"

"No. Maybe sensed it coming, but no, how could he have?"

Cass shrugged and tighten his hold on her, his arm around her bare midriff. A blush climbed her cheeks, and she was glad he couldn't see her. Her blush deepened as she eyed Ethan's muscled back. He ran shirtless before her, booted feet kicking up sand.

What the hell was wrong with her? Neither of these men would be the slightest bit interested in her.

Her thoughts screeched to a halt brought up on the wall of reality. *Actually, now with only five women with magic for competition, she might be able to take her pick. Too bad her pick was married...*"

She groaned and coughed to cover it. "Swallowed a bug," she lied. She wanted to smack herself for even contemplating it. This wasn't the time or place. Everyone was reeling from Maria's revelation. They'd all lost loved ones. It was hard to remember though with the sun beating and the beauty of the beach. This felt like a vacation. Like the time she and Sam went to Mexico and flirted with the man who took them horseback riding on the beach.

She closed her eyes and smiled, lost in a memory of fruity drinks and boys desperate for Sam's attention at the pool. It was hard having a friend as beautiful as Sam. Her plainness glared beside her gorgeous friend. Her brown hair looked dull and limp compared to Sam's curling blond mass of hair. Brown eyes couldn't compare to the sparkling blue of Sam's.

A deep sigh escaped her. Even Kuan had more beautiful eyes, totally unfair for a boy. Bright-blue with a purple tinge and framed in black lashes, Kuan's eyes startled in his Vietnamese face.

Compared to them, she was average. Too tall and thin without curves to soften the angular line of her body, she always felt gawky next to Sam. Whenever a man looked right past her to Sam, it hurt. But Sam was the best friend she'd ever had. And she knew how much it hurt her when other girls were mean to her. She understood why Sam had so few woman friends, but Sam couldn't help being beautiful any more than Jen could help being plain.

Maria cawed above them, interrupting Jen's train of thought, and dove to the sand, landing as a bird before becoming a woman again. "Cut through the trees here and be careful; we don't want to run into anyone."

Harsh Realities

Jen laid beneath a hemlock and gazed over the village. Rutted dirt fronted a row of wooden shacks. Three rough, wooden row boats were tied to a dock to the left of her.

Docks in varying stages of decay lined the shore to the tree line to her left. Most held wooden racks for drying fish. Seagulls swooped and shrieked overhead. Their shrill calls competed with yelling men and shrieking children. Nets hung from posts covering the racks, to which small rafts and boats tied off.

"They have metal tools," Cass murmured.

He lay beside her, staring with a mixture of awe and horror on his face.

Jen felt sick. She didn't want to live like this, in this noise and stink. The smell of rotten fish competed with another odor she didn't have a word for. The closest she could get was outhouse but so much worse. A donkey brayed, sheep baaed and somewhere close someone banged metal against metal hard and repetitively.

"I don't think they have druids. Look at the sickly, stunted shade trees." Cass pointed to a line of trees bordering the dirt road.

Dirty, barefoot women carried lumpy baskets woven from thin strips of wood down the street. Children shrieked and ran unsupervised, from toddlers barely able to walk to ten-year-olds pulling goats along.

"This is a nightmare. Am I being punked? Is this entire thing an elaborate hoax?"

"God, I wish," Cass said. "See any signs of magic?"

"No, but what does that prove? We all don't have it either. Maybe this is a group of regular humans. Maybe their wielders live somewhere nice."

"Yeah, that worries me too. How the hell will we do this?

Jen rose an eyebrow.

"Mix with regular folk. I, for sure as shit, would hate me if I didn't have magic. I'd be jealous as hell. And you…"

"Me?"

"You, the druids, Kirk. You stand out. Your differences are glaring. I forgot you even had jeans and sneakers." He gestured with his chin to her clothing. You seem underdressed. I'm used to the fancy armor already, but for someone not used to it, with no experience of nicer things" —he stabbed a finger at a man passing three hundred yards away wearing a ragged brown tunic belted with rope— "someone like that dude, you'll be as impressive as hell."

"So, what do we do?"

"Accept the things we cannot change."

He said it like a prayer; as if he tried to convince or comfort himself.

"If this is the past, these folks will be greedy bastards. England was in a constant state of war over land and serfs. We need to find out what year it is."

"Does it matter?"

"Yes, are these Romans, Saxons, or Franks?"

"What's the difference?"

Cass snorted. "Language and law. Didn't you ever take a history class?"

"In grammar school, but who remembers…"

"I thought you were in college."

"I am. Was. I study computer science."

"Yeah, that'll be helpful."

"Don't be a dick. It isn't like I knew this could happen and should be prepared for it."

"Sorry." Cass squeezed her shoulder. "I'm just worried is all. We have a lot of power, which means we could do a lot of harm. We better get our shit together, and fast, before we start something we can't finish."

The muted clip-clop of hooves in dirt drew

Jen's eyes. A gray pony pulled a wooden cart filled with sacks down the narrow dirt lane. In the cart, a man sat holding the reins with one hand, eating an apple with the other. A scar crossed his face diagonally from temple to chin, missing his nose by a hair, but splitting his lip.

"Local royalty," whispered Cass. "See the sword? and look how everyone bows. You ride in there on Gallant, and everyone will fall at your feet.

Jen giggled.

"It isn't funny. It's sad and scary. They'll either revile you and try to kill you, or treat you like that?" He jerked a thumb toward a man bowing repeatedly on the side of the narrow lane. "I for one don't want to live like that, bowing and scrapping."

Jen nodded thoughtfully.

"It's going to be a fine line between respect but not subservience. And not just with this crowd. The people we brought with us will have to work and live with these people. Obviously, our people should be in charge, our knowledge gives us power, but how do we enforce it?"

Cass trailed off, looking grim.

Jen turned back to the village, her thoughts whirling.

Two hours later, Maria crawled through the brush and swatted Jen's foot. Even knowing it was Maria she was still terrifying when confronted suddenly.

Now a mountain lion, her teeth glinted wickedly sharp when she yawned. Jen tapped Cass's shoulder and began to eel her way through the underbrush after Maria.

Half a mile away, at their camp beside a stream, Maria stopped and resumed her form.

"Well?" Cass asked.

"I'm going to head back to check in and see about summoning Miguel, Rob, and Matt." She glanced at the watch on her arm. Will you be okay without me overnight?"

"Yep. Will you be able to find us again?"

"I think so. If I can't, can you find your way back?"

"Yes." Jen hugged her hard. "Be careful. We saw bows."

"I will, but I doubt one shot could kill me. Injure me— sure, but I can heal myself and hide."

"Don't get cocky. We don't know what would happen. I worry about you flying around. What if the magic wears off?"

Maria laughed so hard she grabbed her stomach. "Holy crap, I never considered that. Kuan was so convincing, but it's all BS, isn't it?"

"Who knows but be careful."

Maria peered into the sky. "I might be fated to die from falling. The crash should've killed me. It didn't and look at me now." Maria leaped upwards, transforming as she did so into her eagle form. Wide black and white wings blocked the sun as she flew straight up.

"No natural bird can fly like that." Cass shaded his eyes and stared after her.

Jen shrugged. "She isn't a bird, she's magic."

Both watched her out of sight.

"Let's catch us a rabbit. One's thata way." He pointed into thick brush beside them.

"How's that work?"

"I think to myself, where are the animals, and I know where they are." Cass pushed through the brush. "I wish I had a bow, but my trap should work. We'll need your sword to kill it though. All my spells that could kill it would leave it to mangled to eat."

Jen summoned her sword into her hand. Its shape and weight reassured her. A moment's thought transformed her jeans and sweatshirt into her white armor. She followed Cass, wincing as he mumbled complaints about the sharp brush that she didn't feel at all. To the naked eye it appeared as if her skin showed, but to her, it felt as if heavy canvas encased her. She felt the branches, but their sharpness didn't penetrate. Fire felt hot but didn't burn. A cold hand felt cold, but her own never chilled.

"Wait," Cass murmured.

A moment later, he held a gray rabbit aloft and grinned at her triumphantly. He held out his hand for her sword.

"No, let me. I need to get used to this," she said.

Cass nodded slowly, his smile fled. He placed

the rabbit at his feet and twitched his fingers. The rabbit appeared to fall asleep.

Jen bit her lip, took a deep breath, and stabbed. The rabbit jerked and squealed before falling limp.

Tears trailed down Jen's cheek. She wiped them away, ignoring Cass's comforting smile.

"Next time try to behead it. If you nick the intestines, we can't eat it. Well, Tony could purify it, but it would make us sick without that. Maybe you could heal that, maybe not. Easier to just be careful." Cass flipped the rabbit onto its back. "Normally, you use a skinning knife and cut along here." He traced a line across the animal's abdomen. "Remove the stomach and intestines. All the parts can be used, but let's worry about that later. For now, just cut off the legs and breast meat. The sword is too big to skin or butcher it properly."

"How do you know all this?"

"I hunt. Well, I used to when my dad was still alive. I haven't in years, but I remember."

"Sorry, about your dad, I mean."

"Thanks, you too; we're all orphans now."

Jen's eyes filled with tears.

"Sorry," Cass said again softly and put an arm around her shoulder.

"Don't be, it's true. You think we'll all go crazy?"

Cass snickered darkly. "Maybe." He grabbed the meat and headed back the way they came.

"Let's get this to the brook and clean it, and I'll show you how to make a fire."

She summoned Gallant, and the two rode through the woods until they hit the stream. They went downstream for five minutes before Cass led them unerringly toward the camp."

Gallant picked up speed as the brush thinned.

"How's that work? Communicating with him, I mean," Cass asked.

"I think go back or picture what I want, and he does it. I have no idea how it works. I never sense anything from him."

"He never eats or sleeps?"

"Not that I've seen. I feel kind of bad, using him with no return."

"If Sam is right, Gallant is you, so you're feeling bad for yourself. And he doesn't seem to mind it."

"What do you think the magic—"

She broke off and stopped Gallant. "Sam is calling me."

"Go, I'm fine."

Yes, she said in her mind and appeared before Sam. A dirty, tear-streaked face greeted her. Jen hugged her, then checked for injuries. She casted a heal just to be sure. The weak yellow light of her Lesser Heal made Sam glow for a moment.

"Things are out of control here. Kendra is worse than useless, and Brandon is out with Jamal and Jon."

"What's going on?"

A group of twenty or so are demanding Kirk make them bread and more summoning balls. He stalked off in a huff, and they began demanding I take them to town."

"Right, lead on."

Sam took her hand and began leading her through the trees.

"Why are we in the forest anyway?"

"I ran. They scared me, and I didn't know what else to do."

"Scared you?" Jen stopped and examined Sam again.

"Insults, nothing physical, but I didn't want it to escalate, so I left.

Sudden loud shouts in the distance changed to a scream. Both quickly died away.

"Stop it!" Kendra yelled.

Jen began running. The sound of metal on metal was distinctive and chilling.

I'm a Free Woman

"What the hell is going on here?"

Birds rose in a whirling mass and exited the trees Jen yelled so loudly.

A clearing had been made beside the brook, the slope smoothed and covered with a thick carpet of grass.

Druids, Jen thought in awe. They'd moved trees and flattened earth.

Kuan in bear form stood on his hind legs beside Kendra. Six-inch claws tipped with metal gleamed on his paws. Jen hadn't seen him in bear form yet. Bigger than any grizzly she'd ever seen pictures of, he towered over Kendra. A dark, dull-gray, metal helm covered his head with matching gray armor on his sides and legs. The edges shone silver interspersed with rough-cut gems. Their guild symbol of a lightning bolt crossing a world triad glittered in silver on the chest plate, clearly visible in his upright position. Beside him, Kendra rode Diva and carried her sword and shield.

Tony stood beside her, his face grim. Louis stood in front of them, his posture showing his willingness to fight.

"Where's Cami and the wizards?' Sam asked.

"Headed back to the village with Maria; they decided to walk back and save stones."

"Stones your fucking wasting!" a man yelled.

Jen whirled. "Stop, we aren't savages yelling insults in the dark. Come forward and speak like a civilized man.

Dillion ran up and grabbed her. She kissed the top of his head absently as a large man pushed through the crowd and stood glaring at her with his hands on his hips. Unshaven, his ragged beard gave him a wild appearance. Messy, sandy-blond hair contributed to the effect as did the ragged, dirty clothes he wore.

"Stop ordering us around. Who the fuck do you think you are?"

Jen narrowed her eyes.

"I'm Genevieve Frey. Who are you?"

"Stan Bosko, and I'm sick of this shit."

Jen peered closer, the man's ragged beard and hard expression combined with his ragged clothing changed his appearance drastically from the man she remembered from their small isle.

"Well, Stan, you're free to go wherever you like. What you're not free to do is insult or threaten anyone here."

"See, telling us what to do again."

"Oh please; asking for common curtsey." She scanned the growing crowd. Only a few people remained beside the fires, sitting with their backs turned, clearly not willing to take a side. Jen winced. It was clear there were sides. All the wielders stood behind her. A woman carrying a little girl approached, the same woman Jen had grabbed as they were falling, and took Dillion's hand, leading him away. He glanced back but followed her willingly. Jen gave her a quick, grateful smile before turning to glare at Stan.

"What's the problem here, Stan, specifically?"

"We want bread, water and summon stones. It isn't fair that you hog them all."

"Did you ask Kirk?"

"He said no. And ran off like a coward."

Jen held up a hand. "Let's not have name calling. If Kirk said no, then the answer is no. He's neither slave nor servant, but a free man. Before you go screaming about rights, consider his."

"Fuck that. We have a right to food."

Jen sat cross-legged on the ground. "I thought we'd have more time for this. I didn't even realize it'd be a problem until today when Cass mentioned it. We're different from you. We have skills you don't. It doesn't make us better or worse, just different."

"Oh, here we go with the politically correct bull crap." Stan strode forward until he was within touching distance, looming over her. "All the yammering in the world won't change the fact you're trying to make us second-class citizens."

"How am I doing that? And you can sit and talk. We can all talk and clear the air."

"Fuck that manipulative bullshit. You'll make us beg for food and want us to thank you for it."

"I only have the food Kirk gave me, and I left it with Cass. Oh, and we caught a rabbit. I have no food to give you."

"Cut the shit; you know what I mean."

"I do. You think Kirk owes you food." Jen shrugged. "I have no idea if he owes you anything or not. That's between you and him. If you're asking me to force him to work for you —I won't. I won't force you to work for him either."

"Yeah, we're free. Your girlfriend has been preaching that all day. Free to starve if we don't bend the knee."

"Now you're just being stupid. Listen up, all of you, and really think about our situation. The village I saw was primitive— real primitive. Our knowledge will bring these people out of the stone age. By Cass's best estimate we're around the year five hundred AD or so. The Dark Ages."

Jen scanned the restless crowd, letting that sink in.

"England has been at war for a majority of its history. In this era, mostly being invaded. First the Romans, then Saxons, then Franks. Add in some Vikings, and who the hell knows, and you can see we'll need to be able to defend what we build here. But before we build, we need to agree. Are we all free people? I think we should be. I think everyone within our lands is free. Free to come and go and trade honestly. We can't force people to give up the labor of their hands or minds because we covet it.

"I won't go to that village and kill the populace and steal their homes because I have none. I'll build my own."

"Easy for you to say; you have magic," Stan scoffed to mumbled agreements from the crowd.

"Yes. Magic does make it easier for me. My friends make it easier yet. I propose we all think about what kind of society we want to live in. What laws will we live under? How we'll treat the less fortunate than ourselves—"

"And if you don't like our answers, you'll leave us stranded and defenseless."

Jen rose and dusted off her spotless cape. "Yes. I won't be a slave. I'm free to come and go. I won't agree to be a party to any group that espouses slavery. My sword and shield are mine. I fight at no mans' command to steal from another."

"Me either," Sam said and put an arm around Jen's shoulder.

"Dikes!" someone called out.

Jen's ears burned. Sam kissed her cheek.

"Bigots." Sam whirled and stood with her back turned beside Louis.

"I won't be a slave either. I choose who and

when I fight." Louis put an arm around Sam's shoulder, turning his back on the growing mutters.

Tony stepped up and waved a glowing hand. "The talk today of going to the village and taking what we want— it would be easy— sickened me. I'm not pointing fingers— you know who you are. And yes, I'm aware wielders were involved. That's why we need rules. If we're going to be stuck here, I want a nice place to live, not some medieval nightmare of serfs and lords."

Stan glanced behind him and dropped his hands from his hips. "None of us want that. That's the point, but you make yourself lords if we have to beg for your assistance."

Jen shrugged. "There's no answer for that which will satisfy you. If you want something I have, you have to ask me for it, and I have the right to say no."

Jen walked away, ignoring the grumbling behind her. Sam followed. Jen waved a hand at the cleared land.

"This is a nice spot. I assume the druids moved the trees?"

"Kuan." Sam gave her a half smile. "He's scary. He lifted his arms and the trees flowed away from him. The ground rippled underfoot smoothing out and grass sprung up in minutes. I think we need to make sure he doesn't spend too much time in animal form. Keep him human."

"Where is he?"

"That way." Sam's half-grin widened. "It's so

cool knowing where everything within range of me is."

"And Kirk?"

Sam jerked a thumb to the south. "He got mad when I wouldn't go with him." Sam bit her lip and blushed. "I sort of wanted to but was afraid to leave this lot unsupervised. Tony wasn't the only one who heard the talk. I think Stan waited until Jon left to try to push the others into forcing Kirk."

"I wouldn't worry about it. No one makes Kirk do anything he doesn't want to."

Sam sat with her back against a tree and idly picked a long stem of grass, which she chewed. "He would've reacted violently if I weren't there. I know that sounds conceited, but it's true."

On her elbows beside her, Jen peered up into the darkening sky. "I wondered how much you noticed and, err, manipulated."

"Yeah, I feel like a shit doing it too. Leading him on like that."

"Are you? Don't take this wrong but it feels real to me. Him too. He seems likes he's sincerely trying. He's cut way back on the snark, and not just for us."

Sam laughed. "He is trying." Abruptly she started crying and curled into Jen's side.

Jen said nothing, quiet tears tracked her own cheeks for all they'd lost.

Jon returned two hours later. Jen left Sam sleeping

in the grass covered with her cloak and pulled Jon aside.

"What are you doing back?"

"Sam summoned me. We have a problem brewing."

"Stan and his cronies?"

Jen drew back and examined his expression in the weak light.

"I'm not stupid." Jon laughed bitterly and turned away, gesturing at the campfire beside the stream bank. "It's sinking in we're going to be here awhile, and Stan's worried he'll be a nobody working for the man. He's the kind of guy that has to tread on someone to feel important."

"And you left him here... unsupervised?"

Jon shrugged and turned back. "Why try to hold back the tide. People are who they are, Jen. We can't stop them from doing what they're going to do. Decide who you are and be that person."

"You make it sound so easy."

"It is."

"Aren't you afraid of what they might do?"

"Afraid...Not really. I think most are decent people. There'll always be people who try to steal. That was true where we came from too. Now we have the power to stop them. The rangers can track any thief. You and I can fight intruders. This is a big land. We can make a nice place to live. A safe place."

"Yeah, that's fine for you and me. Our magic protects us, but the some of the others are defenseless."

"The wielders will have to protect them too."

"Some of the wielders are afraid too."

Jon snorted. "Kendra."

Jen nodded. "And Sam."

"Sam?" Jon said in surprise.

"That's why she summoned me; she was afraid. She said they scared her."

"They scared her?" Jon repeated slowly as if he didn't understand the words. He grabbed her shoulder. "What did they do?"

"She said insults. She ran away and summoned me."

"She ran away. She was so scared she ran away?" Jon's eyes flared blue with shocking suddenness.

Jen stepped backward. "Jon, your eyes."

He lifted a hand to his face.

"They're blue, like glowing blue. Are you okay?"

"No, I don't think I am. I'm really angry." He spun away and leaped, landing running thirty feet away. Jen followed.

She was right behind him when he grabbed Stan, picked him up with one hand, shook him, then threw him to the ground.

"Go near Sam again, say one fucking word to her, and I'll kill you. You want anarchy— you got it. Go be in charge wherever the fuck you want, but I'm in charge here."

Stan pushed himself to his feet and glared at

Jen. "It wasn't me who called your girlfriend names."

Jon stepped forward. "Shut up. It's all I can do to not kill you right here. You're really pushing your luck."

Jen jumped forward, putting herself between them, and held out her hands. "Let's everyone calm down."

Five of Stan's friends stood back staring. Two ran off yelling. In moments, more people gathered until a crowd surrounded them.

Jon glared around. "Good. I won't have to say this again. Pay attention because I won't warn you twice. Any of you assholes bother any of the women here, and you'll answer to me. We aren't fucking reverting to third-world chauvinist pigs. Women here have equal rights."

"Who died and made you king?" one of the men called.

"I fucking made myself king! This land is mine. I claim it. If you want me off, or to set the rules, you'll have to move me off. Right here" — Jon pointed to the ground at his feet —"this is England, and I rule it. In England, we have equal rights, and no one forms a mob to scare anyone. If you want to talk, talk— no violence or threats. We're going to have law and order in my England."

"Your England," Stan scoffed. He turned to his friends. "See, I told you they were going to take over, and we'd be their servants."

"Idiot, go make your own kingdom. No one

here cares, but this one is mine."

A bear roared. Jen jerked and spun. Kuan stood on his hind legs in bear form behind her. He towered over her, claws glinting in the firelight. He roared again, showing two-inch-long, sharp, white teeth. Before Jen could blink, he leapt forward, over her head, landing before Stan.

Stan fell on his ass and scrambled across the ground, using his hands to pull himself backward.

"Kuan!" Sam called.

Jen hadn't seen her arrive, too intent on the men before her.

The bear roared again.

Cami soared overhead and screeched.

Kuan shifted forms, becoming a man. "Jon is the king and we his knights. Leave his lands."

"Look, son, I'm sorry. We didn't mean to upset you, but you can't just declare yourself king."

"Jon was fated to become king. It's his destiny, as it was ours to become his knights."

"Kuan," Sam called again softly.

Jen bit her lip. A blue mist surrounded Kuan lit with sparks of static.

Kuan peered over his shoulder and smiled. "I know it. The same way I knew what the lightning meant."

Jen stepped up and put an arm around him. The glowing blue eyes he peered through disconcerted her. His calm demeanor reassured her. He was so certain she could feel his certainty.

"You aren't my king," Stan said

Jon laid his hand on Kuan's shoulder. "Then go. Visitors to my land must abide my rules."

"This is ridiculous—"

"He is King Arthur, and you will respect him!" Kuan held out his hands.

The blue surrounding him surged and pulsed, covering Jen too. A shiver traveled her, both awe and fear.

"Oh, this is precious. The retard thinks he's in a fairytale." Stan smirked at Kuan and turned to his cronies laughing.

Storm clouds gathered above, flickering with lightning.

Jon turned Kuan to face him and took his hands. "Let me handle this."

Kuan nodded and let the storm dissipate.

Jon released Kuan to glare at Stan. "Stan, change your fucking attitude or get the hell off my land. If you think I can't make you go, your sadly mistaken."

Stan's angry gaze traveled Jon, then Kuan and Jen. He surprised Jen by laughing.

"Fine." He turned and bellowed. "Who wants to stay here with King Arthur and his fairy men? You can live in the woods and eat nuts and berries and kiss his fucking ass with his retard and dikes. Or, we can go to the nearby town and live like people!"

The crowd milled uncomfortably.

"Steve, you going to bow to Jon here or come with us? What about you, Tony? Kendra, are you going to be a farmer and live off the land in the dirt, or do you want a house and servants?"

"Listen to yourself! How the hell will you get those things? Go steal them? Force the people there to work for you? We can build houses. Here we can be free, all of us can be free," Jen yelled as loudly as she could.

"Some of us don't have your magical skank clothes to keep us warm. We need houses. What's wrong with going there to ask for help? We have skills to offer in trade."

Jon grabbed Jen's shoulder and squeezed. "Fine, then go. No one is stopping you. Tomorrow, I'll lead those who wish to accompany me up the coast to Margate where we'll settle and make our home. We'll live on the coast as equals under modern law. You're free to settle near us as friendly neighbors for trade and live however you like, but we won't tolerate criminals on our land."

Jon grinned and ruffled Kuan's hair. "Sleep on it. Tomorrow we go to build Camelot." He led Kuan away, talking quietly.

"Holy crap, you think he really is King Arthur?" Sam asked as she stared after Jon. "Does that make you Guinevere?"

"Don't be retarded.

"No seriously. We even have a Lancelot." Sam rubbed her arms. "I'm freaking out. What if we're the reason there are rumors of magic and shit."

"First, and I can't stress this enough, Camelot was never real. King Arthur is a fairytale."

"Jon is real."

Jen rolled her eyes. "And second, unless we all die tomorrow, I guarantee there'll be more than rumors about us. Not because we have magic and people will remember, but because we can read and write. We'll leave records."

"Kuan seems pretty sure."

"You know how he is. He isn't retarded, but he isn't all there either." Jen rubbed her forehead. "Go keep an eye on him. Make sure he eats and rests. Ask Jon to recall everyone."

Sam started away, then turned back. "What are you going to do?"

Jen grinned at her. "First, I'm going to go pee. Then I'm going to call Kirk."

Sam rose two fingers to pinch her bottom lip, then nodded decisively, ran her hands over her bald head, and scurried after Jon.

The Man She Needs

Jen headed into the woods. A simple thought removed her armor, leaving her in jeans and a sweatshirt. The summon stone was still in her pocket. Eyes closed, she pictured Kirk and the steps she'd have taken in the game to summon him, imagining a drop-down list and his name, then clicking it with a computer mouse.

Kirk appeared before her. "You okay?"

"Yeah, fine. Some shit went down you need to hear about."

Kirk's eyes narrowed, then widened. "Is Sam okay?"

"She is, but never do that again. Don't leave her alone."

Kirk spun as if to leave, then stopped.

"Where the fuck are we?"

Jen grabbed his arm. "Kirk, Sam's been my

best friend for years now, and I know her really well. I'm telling you this as a friend. If you go in there all angry and possessive, she won't like it. Honestly, I never thought you had a shot with her, but now… Well, she likes you, but if you rush her, there's no way."

"Why are you helping me all of a sudden? For years you've been warning her off."

"Kirk— you were a drug dealer…" Jen laughed at his surprised expression. "Everyone fucking knew. And she had Randy, and they were in love. Really in love. She'll need time to get over that. Here you get a clean slate. You can be the kind of man she can love, or you can be an asshole who takes advantage, and she'll choose another."

"So, you're on my side now?"

"Hell, no! I'm on Sam's side. I'd rather not have to choose a side though. We've been friends for years now too. You're a good guy when you want to be." Jen grimaced ruefully. "You can be a real dick too. Sam always hated when you were rude to others, calling them names or whatever when they couldn't keep up in the game. Do that in real life and you won't have a shot with her."

Kirk crossed his arms and leaned back. "And what's in it for you?"

"Sam has magic, but she's never going to be a fighter. I don't want to say she's defenseless, but we're living in an era where women have little worth. She'll need someone to protect her. I'll do it with my life, but next to Kuan, you're the strongest of us. If the world knows she's under your protection…"

"So, some shit went down and now you want to use me?"

Jen sighed. "No. I wanted to talk to you before you talked to her. She's upset and scared and needs her friends. Is it so much to ask for you to be a friend?"

"What exactly happened?"

"Stan was being an asshole, and Jon declared himself king. Kuan is backing him up. He's convinced its destiny. That Jon is King Arthur."

Kirk's eyes widened. "No way! Is he?"

"Don't be stupid. There was no King Arthur. Not like you mean anyway. But we're leaving here tomorrow for Margate. Stan wants to go to the town instead. He thinks they can just walk in there and the peasants will fall all over themselves to help them, or they'll be able to just take what they like."

"How many are in the town?"

About a thousand, I think, maybe more. Maria surveyed it from the air. There were outlying farms, but most of the people appeared to live by the shore as fishermen. The men carried daggers; we only saw one man with a sword.

"If your asking could we take it over, then yes, but why? It's a stinking hovel. With the druids help we can have a nicer place in no time. We can plant our own gardens and catch fish ourselves."

Kirk leaned his back against a tree and closed

his eyes, rubbing them with his fingertips. "This fucking sucks. I hate camping."

Jen sat and crossed her legs. "I've been thinking. Cass really opened my eyes. Seeing that town myself… it isn't a picturesque tourist town; it's smelly and gross. And I hated how they lived. I think it'll be better to build a nice place. One where others will want to live. We can offer them protection and law. They can offer the skills we need. None of us know how to store food or do any of the things these people can, but we know about hygiene and electricity. If we had laborers, we could really make a good place."

"We have no money. Stan is right, if we want servants, we'll have to force them."

"No. We have no money, but we have trade goods. How much do you think you can sell a summon stone for or a health potion or an enchant? You don't have to force anyone, you can hire them fair and square. But to do that you need a safe place to live, or you'll constantly be fighting off thieves. Not that it would be hard, but who wants to live like that?"

Kirk slid down his tree and sat beside her. "I hear what you're saying, and I agree. I want to live in a town with laws too, but Jon as king?"

"Why not Jon? Someone has to run it. If you don't like his kingdom, you can make your own, but do you really want to spend your days in meetings running shit?

Kirk laughed." Fuck no. That's why you were

guild leader. But I do want a say in how it's run."

"Me too. I'm going to talk to Kuan. It'll be easy to convince him we need a round table. In fact, I bet he already thought of it."

"Okay, I can see that working, but who decides who sits at the table?"

"We do. There's time to work out how later. Everyone will want to be heard and have an opinion, but most are like us and don't want to do that for a living. If they feel they're being represented, they'll be happy. Or happy enough anyway. And if we hate it, we can always leave. I'm going to push for at least one of each type of wielder at the table. In Jon's kingdom no one will be forced to work for anyone else. If they want me to guard, they'll have to ask, and I can turn them down."

Kirk rose and offered her a hand. "Right, let's go build Camelot."

Jen accepted the hand to rise and hugged him. "Please, be nice to Sam. Be the man she needs," she whispered.

She released him and led him back to the brook.

While she was gone, two more fires had been started. Meat roasted on four fires, the smell making her mouth water. Ethan, Cass, the druids, and warlocks had returned and sat by the far fire with Jon.

Almost all the rest of the wielders sat beside them.

Steve, Miguel, and Kendra sat with Stan at the closest fire.

Stan rose when they approached, smiling at Kirk. "Kirk—"

"Save it. I'm not buying."

"You sure? We've been talking, and we think you'll make a better king than Jon."

"Really? With Kendra as my queen?"

Kendra flushed.

Stan put a hand on her arm.

"There's plenty of beautiful women. You don't need to suck up to Jon and a fag to get one. We can make you a king, man.

"How exactly are you going to do that?"

"We'll go and take that town over. We can have it ship-shape in no time."

"Sure, you do that." Kirk laughed when Stan frowned. "Say what you fucking mean. You want me to go and terrorize the peasants, and for that, you'll graciously let me have my pick of the local women first. Well, I have news for you. I could do that without your help, but I'm not interested in rape or murder. Get yourself another scapegoat. If I want to be a king, I can do it myself."

Kirk stalked away and joined Jon.

Jen couldn't help her smirk.

"Fine, go be one of Jon's peasants!" Stan called after him.

"As opposed to one of yours?" Jen added will to her voice. "You're a thug, wanting to steal from strangers! Kendra, you coming?"

"No. We're special and deserve to be treated with respect. I want to live in a house, not a field."

"It isn't' your house to just take. How do you think you'll get this house? Ask the owner politely? Use your brain." Jen threw her hands up and left them at their fire. She was glad to see Ramiro, Warren, and Nina, at Jon's fire.

Ethan handed her the basket containing her conjured items she'd left behind. She stuffed the balls into her pockets and summoned her armor. No lumps appeared under her skirt. She ran her hands over it, feeling nothing except her skin and the deceptively soft material of her skirt. She canceled the spell and withdrew the green health potion from her front pocket to examine it.

"Seems fine, and my summon stone worked earlier." She shrugged and donned her armor again.

Sam patted the ground beside her. Kuan sat to Sam's right, poking the fire with a long stick. Kirk stood across the fire staring at them. Jen sat.

Jon said, "We were just discussing our move. Brandon got Ed to carry four of the children. Do you think you can get Gallant too?"

"Ed," Jen said with laughter in her voice.

Jon grinned. "Mr. Ed. We don't have much to move, but it'll be a long walk for the children."

"Sure, too bad we couldn't make a cart."

"We have the floating disks. Matt and Rob will stack the luggage on them, and if you and Brandon can carry the eight youngest kids, we should be fine. There's no rush after all."

"Do we know where we're going?"

"Along the coast where the Stour river meets the sea." Jon laughed ruefully. "We debated going more inland and building right on the Thames, but if we want to attract traders, we need to stay on the coast. The druids are going to go ahead of us and scout it out. Assuming nobody else is already there, we'll make our home somewhere between where Margate will be and Herne Bay."

"You plan on being a port town then," Ramiro asked.

"Yep. We'll need supplies to get started. The channel is only thirty miles or so; we can send people to France to trade."

"What do we have to trade?" Nina asked.

"At the moment, not much, but we will have furs and fancy woodwork. Kuan can get the trees to grow in fanciful shapes that we can cut and sell."

"I can hire out as a guard or bandit hunter or something," Brandon offered.

Jon slapped him on the shoulder. "You could, but that would be your pay, not ours. What I propose is we build homes together. Everyone pitches in. The rangers can hunt, and we can skin and prepare foods. We'll all be trying to think of trade items and send a small group to the nearest big town to sell them or trade them for seeds and metal. Once we get seed, our druids can make it grow."

"How do we split the profits?"

"I think at first everyone will need to work a certain amount of time in the fields, unless, as a group, we deem their work time is more valuable spent elsewhere like for the rangers and druids. At first, there won't be profit. We need too much. Our traders will have to be careful they aren't followed back here until we're established. Then we can trade our surplus food and split the profit equally between everyone. If we choose, we can pool our money. Say you wanted to buy a boat or something you could find someone who wanted that too."

"And the casters and paladins? What will they do?" Warren asked.

"Work like the rest of us. Or go out in the world and sell their services, but that would be dangerous. They burn witches now. No one here is equipped to believe a video game explanation."

Warren nodded. "Seems reasonable. Who decides our laws?"

"We do. We'll have a council. There aren't that many of us; it shouldn't be too hard."

Warren glanced over at Stan's group and lowered his voice. "What are we going to do about them?"

Jon shrugged. "Nothing. There's nothing we can do."

"He's going to go attack those people," Nina said, sounding outraged.

"I agree he shouldn't, but I'm not willing to babysit him to ensure it. We can't afford to worry about who's attacking other towns. We need to concentrate on ours. If he attacks ours, we fight him off. Otherwise, he's free to go where he wishes."

"It isn't right."

"What should we do, Nina? Kill him?"

"No, but…" She trailed off unhappily.

"Nina, this world is full of injustice. We can't force others to be like us, or we become tyrants too."

"Yeah, but he's going to kill people and steal," she lowered her voice to a whisper, "and rape."

"But he hasn't done any of those things. We'll live a peaceful life and protect those in our care. That village is none of our business. If Stan, or a stranger, attacks them and they come to us as the nearest neighbor for help, we can decide then as a group if we'll help them."

Nina closed her eyes and laid her head on her knees. "I wish I'd followed my husband through the portal."

"Then you'd be dead," Kirk said. "Philip's portal likely came out over the ocean again. I've been thinking about this, but we should've known it wasn't working right when we didn't see the people passing through in the picture."

"You don't in the game though," Sam said.

Kirk shrugged. "Just a theory, and one we'll never prove."

Jon nodded to Brandon. "How's the meat coming? I'm starved."

Brandon summoned his sword and sliced a long sliver from the half of deer on the spit hanging over the fire. He offered it to Jon on the tip of his sword.

Accepting Her Fate

Jen glanced behind her at the line of people trudging through the sand. Stan had watched them go, calling derisive comments after them. Twenty-six people had chosen to stay with Stan, including Kendra, Steve, and Miguel. Jamal and Matt were heading out on their own.

"You sure about heading out now?" Jon asked.

"Yeah, we want to explore and see the world." Matt grinned at Kirk. "Thanks for the bread, mate."

"Matt, if you need to speak to us, send your bird with a note. If your running low on summon stones, take turns coming back for more, assuming Kirk agrees of course," Jon said.

"Jamal, you need help, summon me," Kirk said and slapped Matt's shoulder.

"If you need healing, summon me." Jen hugged him, then Matt. "Be careful. We have no way to find your dead bodies."

"Thanks, this is more than I expected," Matt said. "Jen and Kuan already know the true name of my familiar. Please keep his full name secret, but if you need to contact me, or need his help, Flynn's full name is Finnian Lior Neil."

Rob held up his arm and his firebird appeared. "Joash's full name is Jupiter Astor Shani. If you need to contact us, call him."

Joash preened, fluttering his feathers and bobbing his head as if he agreed. Darker red than Flynn, he cooed softly to the other bird. Flynn shook out his orange-red feathers, revealing the bright gold underside.

Jen put out her hand to catch the white sparks that drifted from him, but they evaporated on contact.

"Split the pot of health stones," Kirk said. "In fact, wait a sec and I'll conjure you a pot of summon stones. Jon, we should assign someone to stay in camp we'll notice missing. Anyone can summon if they need to speak to someone in camp. If that person disappears, we know to summon them and whoever summoned them back."

Jon nodded and cupped his mouth with his hands. "Rosa, Archie, can I get the rest of the cooks here, and let's see, get Mr. Henry too."

The people Jon called stepped forward.

"Kirk had a good idea. We can keep in contact with our group no matter where they are with summons. To be sure we notice, we want a volunteer, someone who'd normally be in camp. There is a bit of danger to it. They might summon you because they need help. We'll summon you back here as soon as we notice, but…"

"I'll do it," Adam Henry said. "I may be old, but that I can do."

"Great, thanks.

"We're a guild," Kuan said unexpectedly. "We stick together and help each other out just like in the game. You're getting ganked, call for support."

Matt laughed and hugged him. "Man, I been trying to get accepted into Genesis forever."

"We aren't Genesis anymore; we're the Knights of the Round Table."

"Of course, we are." Jamal heaved a disgusted sigh, then laughed and hugged Kuan. "You take care, buddy.

Jamal bundled the conjured balls into his T-shirt and tied it to his belt with a length of vine. He used more vines to tie the conjured bread together and threw them over his shoulder. "Man, we're lucky you were along," he said to Kirk.

"And willing to help." Matt gave Kirk a quick hug and slung his conjured bread over his shoulder. He lifted a hand and the two men headed into the forest.

Accustomed to a conjured pot of bread now, everyone took turns removing a loaf until the pot emptied.

"Mr. Henry, can you ride Gallant and carry Sophia?" Jen summoned her horse with a whistle, not because she needed to whistle, but because she thought it sounded cool.

"I appreciate the thought, Missy, but these old bones can't climb that mountain of yours."

Gallant laid in the sand.

"He'll go nice and easy." Jen helped Mr. Henry mount. "No squirming around or you'll fall off," she said to the four-year-old she set on Gallant's back.

She placed Dillion before them and handed him Gallant's reins. Every time Dillion saw her, his hopeful expression changed to deep sadness. He expected her to find his family somehow and it was breaking her heart.

A woman approached and held out a laughing toddler.

"Can Sophia pet the horse?" she asked.

"Sure."

Clearly a horse lover, Sophia cooed to Gallant as she stoked his nose.

"How about a ride, sweety?" Jen took the girl and handed her to Mr. Henry. "She'll be perfectly fine with Gallant. Not a thing to worry about," Jen assured Sophia's mother. "He just looks like a real horse, but I'm in total control of him."

Jen knelt before the two Miller boys who grinned at her. To them, this was a vacation and an adventure. They had no concept of what they were missing, how much their lives had changed. Their bright smiles eased her heart.

"Hold on and no fooling around. If you fall or make them fall, they can be hurt."

"We'll be careful, Jen," Frank, the older one, said.

Jen ruffled his brown hair and lifted him on behind Mr. Henry. She placed his brother Ben behind him and stepped back. A mental command made the horse stand. The boy's anxious mother stood to the side.

"Gallant will follow us, but if it makes you feel better, you can lead him," Jen offered.

"My name is Ines and thanks. I know I'm being silly; you can heal them and rez them, but" – She leaned over and whispered in Jen's ear— "It's truly horrifying to see your child dead. I never got a chance to thank you for bringing him back for me."

"You're welcome." A blush heated Jen's cheeks, and she turned away, pretending to adjust the stirrups.

"Okay, people, let's move out!" Jon waved his arms and pointed west. He grabbed a stack of tied suitcases and threw them over his shoulder.

Jen picked up a stack and awkwardly adjusted it on her back.

"Um, gimme that," Rob said and held out his hand.

Jen shrugged and grinned ruefully. "I know I make it look light, but it's too heavy for you.

Thanks though."

"I'm not a man. I'm a wizard." He turned to the pile of luggage waiting to be loaded onto his flying disk and twitched his fingers. The pile shrunk to half its size. He twitched his fingers again while a crowd gathered and gasped. The pile shrunk again. Jen laughed and let her luggage thump to the sand.

Jon snatched it up and set it by the pile Rob was shrinking.

"I forget we have magic," Jon said sheepishly. "I need to remember and take it into account. Building will be a breeze with your help if we can get some tools."

"It will take us all a long time to become used to it," Jen said as she watched Rob shrink the pile to postage size and carefully gather them up. "You know, I could ride ahead and just summon us there."

"Yeah, but everyone needs to really feel how much effort summon stones save, and this is a safe, easy walk along the beach. Let them walk at least a day. We don't want people feeling entitled."

The three druids leapt into the air, becoming birds and soaring away.

Jen stared after them with one hand shading her eyes. "Beautiful. I could watch them all day.

"They are beautiful, and we're lucky we have them." Jon pointed at the eagle that was Maria. "Cami told me Stan cornered her and offered to make her a queen. I'm sure he tried with Maria too, but she hasn't said anything."

Jen grabbed his arm and tugged him forward. "As if she'd agree to that…"

Jon smiled down at her. "It always surprises me what people will do. Take me for instance. I bet half my co-workers will be shocked to find out I play video games. I'm too old, and I work. Most people think it's just you young kids."

Jen snorted. "Thirty-eight isn't old."

"It's old for games. At least most people will think so. I'm sure I'm water cooler gossip." Jon made his voice high pitched and whiny. "Did you know he was into video games? Really into them, he ran a guild and everything. He must be some kind of pervert hanging out with all those little kids."

Jen giggled. "On campus, no one ever believed I played until I showed them pictures of Genesis in Gamer magazine. Everyone is sure girls don't game, never mind be guild leaders of a successful guild. They never believed Sam played; she's way to pretty."

Ethan spoke, making her jump, she hadn't heard him arrive.

"Why do you always do that?"

"Do what?"

"Act like Sam is the only pretty one. You're pretty too."

Jen glared as a flush covered her cheeks.

"I thought that was an act, you being all inferior to Sam, but now I realize it isn't."

"I'm not inferior to her." Mortification made her voice higher than she'd intended.

"No." Ethan held up a hand and waved an apology. "That isn't the right word. You put yourself down though. I thought you did it so she'd like you, but I see it bothers her too."

"What are you talking about? You barely know us." The blush on her cheeks burned it felt so hot.

"Your right, sorry. I just hate hearing you do it. My wife was like that. She was a beautiful woman convinced she was the ugly one in the group. Her sister was a real bitch. One of those people who try to make others feel bad about themselves. She always had a mean comment for my wife, real passive aggressive— insults phrased as flattery. But the real kicker was my wife would do it too, a habit to get her sister's approval."

Jen laid a hand on Ethan's arm. The pain in his voice hurt.

He didn't seem to notice and continued speaking, his eyes on the distance caught on a memory. "She bought a new dress for Thanksgiving dinner and showed me. The very last conversation we had, in fact. So, she tries it on, and she's just gorgeous, and she frowns at the mirror. 'Good enough, I guess. I'll never have Dee's figure,' she says all sad and embarrassed. And I tell her she's beautiful, but I can see she doesn't believe it. In her eyes, only women like Dee with big boobs and teased hair are beautiful. Personally, I thought

Dee was ugly and not just because of what a bitch she was. I swear to God, I never saw that woman smile, only sneer."

Ethan trailed off.

Jen exchanged worried glances with Jon.

"I'm so sorry," she finally whispered.

"Yeah, me too. And now my daughter will grow up like that…"

Jen put an arm around him and squeezed. He accepted her embrace for a moment, then pulled away. "I'll go make sure everyone is keeping up."

He turned and jogged back the way they'd come.

Jon stared sadly after Ethan. "Wow, that's brutal. I lost family, but… I see my parent's holidays and call once in a blue moon. I love them, but we weren't super close."

"It really hasn't sunk in that I'll never see my family again. I tell myself at least they're alive. It's not like I lost them in a car accident or something. If I could contact them, and tell them I'm okay, and they didn't need to mourn…"

Jon put an arm around her, and they walked in silence.

"We need grief counselors," he finally said.

"Maybe we should hold a wake or something, give us closure."

"Yeah, and we need to stay busy, move forward, not wallow." The two walked quietly for a while.

"Think we can make a modern town?" Jen

finally asked.

"Modernish. I have some ideas to get us electricity and running water. We'll never have computers or dishwashers, but we can make it clean and safe."

"A castle?"

"Yes, we need one place that can fit everyone to make it easier to defend." He dropped his arm and gestured at the people walking up the beach. "Once word gets out we have something worth taking, we'll need to defend it."

Jen bit her lip and peered over her shoulder at Gallant and the children.

"Don't worry, we'll be a tough nut to crack. What we need to do is have an explanation of our magic that doesn't freak out the populous. Something they can believe and accept without wanting to burn us as witches."

"You don't think they'll believe regular people struck by lightning and transformed by a crazy man?"

Jon threw his head back and laughed. "For the rest of my life I'll remember the feeling of awe I had when Kuan transformed. I thought I was having a fever dream and it was still the most beautiful thing I've ever seen. He glowed with power."

Jen closed her eyes, remembering Kuan becoming a raven, impossibly large and beautiful, and such was his intensity she'd listen when he'd said she could become her true self.

"I thought I was delirious too, but I felt his sincerity. His strength of will is impressive. I could barely moan the pain was so bad."

Jon shuddered and rubbed his arms. "The cost was high that's for damn sure. At the time, I thought he wasn't as sick as us, sitting between you and Sam and holding your hands, but now I think he was embracing the change." Jon ran a hand over Jen's bald head. "As sick as he was, he was still your healer. We all knew he was a bit tweaked. The most amazing druid I'd ever seen play though."

"He was the druid; it wasn't a game for him. He played every day waking until sleep. UBM was a real place for him."

Jon nodded and put his arm around Jen's shoulder again. "Thank God it was or we'd all be dead now, every single one of us. We'd have died writhing in agony, and the rest drowned."

"Not just him, we have Ramiro to thank too. If he hadn't made them take us all from the plane, or stopped them from killing us while we were so ill…"

"He's a good guy. Most of them are. Thankfully most of the bad ones went with Stan."

"We have some left?" Jen gazed behind her again, then thoughtfully examined the people in front of them. She hadn't made the acquaintance of many yet unlike Jon who seemed to know everyone.

"More lazy or stupid than bad," Jon continued. "I bet Kendra returns soon with Steve.

They'll take one look at a real medieval town and come running back with their tails between their legs."

"Will we take them back?"

"If they agree to live by our rules."

"Speaking of rules, I think we should form a council or whatever and have one of each class on it— regular people too, of course."

Jon chuckled. "Already promised Kuan. We're going to have a round table and take the oath of chivalry.

"Which is?"

"From what I can recall, we promise not to murder, rape, or pillage, and help those who ask if their cause is just."

"Sounds okay, but you better limit the last or Kuan will be flying all over the world, and we'll spend all our time helping him.

"We can add in our realm to that. You know Kuan pretty good. Keep an eye on him; make sure no one, including me, takes advantage of him."

"I will. Sam will too."

Jon sighed, his gaze traveling to Sam and Kirk who walked with Rob beside the floating disk that held one suitcase, in which all the rest of the shrunken luggage and supplies had been stuffed, and two giggling girls.

"Sam's going to be a problem." Jon threw a hand in the air as Jen started to speak. "Not her beauty. Ethan's right, by the way, your unhealthily obsessed with that. Sure, Sam's beautiful, but so are you. There's more than one type of beautiful." He waved his hand and shook his head. "That isn't the problem. Her weakness is."

"She isn't weak," Jen said indignantly. Her pulse pounded and palms sweat. She was angry, and not because he'd called Sam weak but because he'd called her beautiful. "And don't try to manipulate me. If we're going to be friends, be fucking honest. I'm not in Sam's league and know it. It just pisses me off when guys do that."

Jon snorted. "Whatever. I wasn't hitting on you or anything just saying what I thought." He jabbed a thumb at Sam. "She's weak because her spells are almost all violent and she isn't violent at all. She could easily be overpowered and held against her will. I'm worried Stan will think of that too."

"Kidnap her?" A cold sweat broke out on Jen's brow, and she thought she might vomit. She stopped walking and leaned forward, taking deep breaths.

"You okay?'

"Why would he do that?"

"Her buffs."

Jen straightened and clenched her fists. Without her willing it, her armor turned black. "I'll fucking kill him."

Without warning, colors brightened and sounds grew clear and distinct, and she knew without looking where everyone around her stood. The feeling was so disconcerting she almost missed Jon's next words.

Jon stepped away from her and held his hands to his sides." Calm down. No one hurt her." He waved the people past who stopped and stared. "We'll have to take precautions though."

Jen's heart thudded, and she swung back the way they'd come. She wanted to charge back there and slay the threat. Jon grabbed her shoulder. Without meaning to, she held her sword at his throat.

"Take a breath here, Jen. Your eyes are all blue and freaky. I'm on your side, remember?" Jon swallowed hard and slowly stepped back. "Keep going, we're just talking. She's showing me something," he said to the gawkers.

Jen squeezed her eyes closed and listened to her pulse pound. This sudden violence was completely out of character for her. She remembered Jon's surge of anger and blue eyes.

"Anger triggers it, I think, and maybe protectiveness. Gimme a sec." Eyes still closed, she breathed deeply, telling herself Sam was fine. When she opened her eyes, her clothing was once again white, and color and sound had reverted to normal. She released her sword and shield, letting them return to mist.

"Good now?"

"Yeah, but I really wanted to kill him."

Just saying the words caused colors to flicker and she wondered if her eyes flickered too from blue to brown.

"I mean, I really did. I'd have killed him…" she trailed off, horrified by her reaction. "Sam's defenseless," Jen said slowly, thinking aloud, trying to justify her response to herself. "She wouldn't have the heart to hurt anyone. She needs our protection." The thought steadied her. She wasn't looking for a fight, but if Stan or anyone tried anything, they'd be sorry. She had a right to defend herself, she told herself firmly.

"We need to get her a pet. A nice, vicious wolf or something."

"That's an awesome idea. Hey, Cass!" Jon called, waving his hand.

"Cass!" Jen shouted and grinned at Jon when Cass turned.

"I wish I had that."

"Meh, what you have is better. I can make them hear me; you can make them listen."

Jon jerked as if startled. "Jesus, I never thought of that. You think that's why they agreed to let me be king— Commanding Presence?"

"No, no one else wants the job."

Jon snorted.

"You rang my liege?" Cass said and bowed with a flourish.

Jen laughed.

Cass grinned at her.

"You and Sam need pets. Are any suitable ones near?"

"Probably, I was tempted to tame a boar yesterday but wasn't sure it was safe. Gimme Tony to heal us just in case, and we can go see."

Jen frowned. "Get her a wolf or something. She won't like a boar. They can't be too far if we can hear them howling. And take Louis, a shaman is better for animal tracking.

"But don't bring back a dangerous animal unless you're sure of your control," Jon added.

Camelot

Jen leaned back on her elbows in the sand. Tony thumped down beside her and handed her a slightly charred slab of meat.

"I still think it tastes funny, but maybe with salt it won't be too bad," he said.

"Thanks." Jen sniffed it, then took a bite. "Not too bad."

Tony leaned toward her and lowered his voice. "I've been thinking, and we need to change the names of some of mine and Kirk's spells, and we need to do it subtly. Most of these guys have no idea what the true name is for a familiar, so if we call it a companion, they'll accept it. We can call Kirk's demon a shadow or something. Every spell that could have an evil connotation, we should call something else."

"Okay, but why the whispers?"

"Because, if we tell them, then in their hearts they'll be like, no— it's a familiar, but if they come to think of it naturally, on their own, it'll be a companion. So, we need to call it the name we choose loudly and often."

Jen grinned at him. "Worried about being burned at the stake?"

"It isn't funny. You're fine, a paladin able to escape anything, but me… I can be held, and I can burn."

Jen laid a hand on his arm. "Sorry, man, you're right."

"From now on, I'm just a priest. I no longer have a shadow form; I have a defensive form."

"Got it. Shadow form isn't too bad though…"

"Wizards and warlocks are going to be a hard sell. I'm torn between recommending Kirk always has a minion out or never shows one."

"Don't worry about it. No matter what we do there'll be gossip and haters. We need to make ourselves strong enough to withstand them is all."

Tony glanced at her from the corner of his eye. "I was in a riot once, after a game. Fighting broke out all over. People got trampled and really hurt, and they weren't involved, just trying to get away like me. A mob is terrifying with a life of its own. And sure, we could fight free, but we'd have to hurt them to do it, maybe friends and neighbors swept up in the crowd."

"We'll just have to make laws against it. What else can we do?"

"Try really hard to give the people no reason to riot. Stan is an idiot who's destined to be murdered. He thinks he can just walk in and take over... that's crazy, these people are way more violent than us. They burn witches and whip people in public. They're used to living under the sword. We're using to calling a bobby."

"We can be civilized though."

"I hope so, Jen."

Jen woke up screaming. A nightmare of Sam's dead eyes gripped her, awful in its intensity. Sam leaned over her, her face concerned.

"You okay?"

Jen grabbed her and hugged her tightly. "A bad dream. Sorry I woke you." She pushed away to see her better. "Hey, when did you get back?"

"A few hours ago; meet Elaine." The grin in Sam's voice was clear.

Ethan crouched beside Sam, watching with worried eyes.

"You okay?"

Jen's gaze flitted from him to Sam, and she winced. Of course, he was by Sam's side. Irritated with her jealousy, she nodded briskly.

Jen released Sam and rubbed her eyes, trying to banish images of a dead Sam from her mind. She'd never had such a vivid dream before. It felt like a memory, not an imagining. But then again, she'd never seen a dead body before either, she told herself firmly. A warm breath caressed her thigh, and she jerked back. "Holy crap!"

"Beautiful, isn't she?" Sam asked proudly.

"That isn't a normal wolf."

"Yep, there were twelve more just like her. Cass caught one he's calling Thor. His is a bit darker and a hair bigger than Elaine. And his wolf's fur doesn't glint like Elain's does. He never bought the vanity spell." Sam patted the wolf's head. Blue eyes drifted to half-closed slits, and a gray tail wagged.

"You sure that's safe?" Jen gestured to the hand rubbing the wolf's flank.

"Yep. Her eyes used to be golden. Cass says our magic traps her, but she's happy, I can tell." Sam closed her eyes and smiled. "She likes me. We fed them right away, and they bonded. At first it was a struggle to hold her back. But once she ate, she calmed right down."

"Don't let her get hungry." Jen reached out and tentatively rubbed the silky ears. Elaine cocked her head and stretched her head out like a dog begging for petting.

"There's plenty for her to eat. All the bones and scrap we throw away. And she can catch her own."

"She listens to you?"

"Yep, just like in the game." Sam giggled and flicked her fingers, and Elaine stood on her hind legs and hopped forward.

Jen laughed, recognizing the trick, another

vanity spell.

"She'll do any of my fun spells, play-dead, roll over— Sam grinned as she rubbed her wolf's head— "I want to tame a bird and a cat and see if those spells work too. I'm so glad I got all the vanity spells."

Elaine sat and scratched energetically behind her ear. Jen dropped her hand and wiped it on her jeans, making Sam laugh.

"Don't worry, Cass and I had them submerge in the ocean to kill their fleas. They didn't like it but didn't resist us at all. You would've gagged at the number of fleas on them."

Jen made a face and pulled away. "Did you submerse yourself?"

"Yep, flea free." She giggled and reached behind her back. "Cass made us real crude bows. It works though." She held out a stick bent and held by thin strips of untanned deer hide. "Watch."

She held it to her ear and pulled back as if she had an arrow notched. When she released, a black bolt with a glowing green head soared from the bow and sailed into the air where it exploded into brilliant sparks of green. A thirty-yard-wide circle of green motes swirled overhead, changing to white as they fell. White light suffused the ground bright enough to cast shadows.

"What the hell," Jon exclaimed.

"Sorry, just testing a spell, go back to sleep," Sam said sheepishly and flicked her fingers. The light disappeared.

"No arrows needed. So far, all my spells work. The light only appears where I set it, but the effect works in a three-hundred-yard radius. Even when you stand in the dark area you can still see like your standing in daylight. I can also make daylight pitch black. Cass sends up white sparks when he casts Day-to-Night; he never bothered to get the vanity spell, thanks for that by the way. Mine is way prettier than his."

Jon rose, stretched, and joined them, giving Elaine a wide berth. Jen waved off Sam's thanks. Most of Sam's vanity spells she'd gotten her while farming for her own. Sam hadn't raided, but she'd loved farming spells together. Tears filled her eyes, and she turned away to hide them. Some of the best times in her life had been with Sam, playing UBM for fun.

"Glad you're back all safe and sound. I see you were successful," Jon said.

Jen straightened and wiped her face. Sam was alive and well. They could have other fun times.

"Yep, Elaine is awesome. And useful. She can't be summoned though unless I'm holding her. Kirk and I tested summons while we were out too. Once called, you feel the call for three minutes exactly unless the caller cancels it. The sphere dissipates after three minutes. It also dissipates when you cancel the call."

"Just like in the game. Damn, I was hoping we could reuse the stones to notify people we wanted them without actually summoning." Jon crouched and offered his hand for Elaine to sniff, then scratched behind her ears.

"Kendra come back yet?" Cass asked as he sat beside them.

Sam snickered. "You mean Queen Kendra? How can anyone be that gullible? Stan offered to make both Maria and Cami queens too. Can't she see he'll toss her aside like an old shoe as soon as he doesn't need her anymore?"

Jon rose and stretched. "Her problem. I'm surprised she lasted this long with them and what— two other women?" He walked away to add more wood to the fire and stopped to speak quietly to the two men awake beside it.

"Want to tell me about your dream?" Sam whispered.

"Nope. What time is it anyway?"

"Almost dawn. No, it wasn't magic." Sam grinned at her. Cass has a watch."

"You get any sleep?'

"Yes. We wanted to make sure the pets didn't release while we slept. Have Kuan or the other druids returned yet?"

"Maria to show us where to turn inland to skirt a beachless section of shore, but since then, no. She told us she found a nice spot along the shore to build Camelot and there's another town about fifteen miles or so away where Canterbury was." Jen loosed a small laugh. "It's hard to believe ten miles is far now. Most of us will stay within five miles of Camelot for the rest of our lives. I used to drive farther than that for a coffee."

Sam heaved an unhappy sigh.

Three and a half hours later, Jen stopped and stared. It had taken them three and a half days to walk from Dover. Margate didn't exist in the now. Instead, a swampy island separated from the mainland by a shallow channel stood where Margate would be. They'd cut through the woods to avoid the swampy land and followed the coast to where Herne Bay would be.

Cami waited atop a rough, rock wall that curved three hundred feet out to sea, rising about five feet above the waves. A pristine white beach stretched before her, ending in a lumpy rock jetty. Unlike the beach they'd walked up, which had bordered tall, rock cliffs, this beach sloped gently to a green meadow. A meadow so perfect Jen knew it wasn't natural. Kuan and Maria stood at the tree line on a wide, rock path. Both wore proud grins.

"Come see what we made," Cami called excitedly.

"Real impressive." Jon shaded his eyes and peered out to sea.

"That isn't finished yet." Kuan ran lightly down the path and hugged Jen, then Sam. He patted Elaine on the head absently as he spoke. "We plan to add perches where we can stand to summon storms if enemy ships approach. We're just learning how to move and shape the earth and rock. But come see what we did."

"More? You guys have been busy." Jon slung an arm around Kuan's shoulder and let him lead him up the path. At the top, he stopped dead, then took a hesitant step forward.

"Holy… Kuan, that's amazing."

"Thank you, Your Majesty."

Jen ran a few steps forward, her hands flying to her cheeks. "Kuan," –words failed her.

"Welcome to Camelot." Grinning ear-to-ear, Kuan ran to Sam and put an arm around her.

"It's so beautiful. And huge. And alive," Sam said in awe.

Jen was awed too. Before her, a half a mile of emerald-green lawn dotted with flowers spread around a towering edifice. Maple trees shaded a rock road leading to the building. Twenty feet wide, the road curved from where they stood at the top of the path, leading to a two-story doorway ample enough to drive two wagons through side-by-side. Prickly bushes clumped on either side of the doorway. It was obvious they would form the door.

Elm trees of varying heights grew so closely together their trunks and entwined branches formed solid walls. Tall turrets and round towers sprouted through the roofline, seemingly at random, but somehow appearing balanced. Branches flowed unnaturally, twining together to form leafy roofs. The tallest roofs stood over two hundred feet from the ground. Gracefully arched windows and doors made of living wood lined the exterior. Rails formed of leafy limbs in intricate patterns edged wooden balconies. Ivy, holly, and plants Jen didn't know the names of, wound around railings and climbed up walls.

To the left, a low rock wall abutted shaggy cedars growing so closely only a child could fit through the gaps. A family of pigs rutted happily in a large mud puddle beside a bulbous and misshapen tree with a hollow core Jen could see daylight through. The tree was clearly meant to be a shelter for the animals.

Kuan followed her gaze and grinned. "That was our first attempt. We'd thought to make a few big trees have hollowed centers we could use as rooms. And that works, but it was so easy to manipulate the trees we designed the castle instead."

Jen nodded absently, still scanning the vista before her.

To her right, a rock wall enclosed a small pond. A brook traveled from the pond to the main house. Barely glimpsed to the back right, a row of elms grew closely together, their branches forming a tree house. The sides dipped and bowed oddly in long sinuous curves giving the house a fairytale gracefulness.

A corner of wooden steps leading to another tree house and the edge of a wooden walkway peeked from behind the main building, hinting of other projects in progress. A twisted, vine-covered, wooden rail edged the walkway hanging between the tree branches.

"Cool, isn't it?" Kuan said enthusiastically. "We just started really. Kirk, you'll need to be careful not to suck the life out of it. We only have the two tree houses, but we plan to make more and some smaller homes on the ground. You can't see it from here, but we made a deer park behind the castle, so even if the rangers are busy, we can get fresh food.

"It's alive?" Kirk stopped beside Sam, his amazed gaze traveling the length of the building.

Kuan nodded. "And growing. We convinced the trees they're all one organism and that this is their correct shape. If it gets too big, or needs too much maintenance from us, you can suck the life out of it, but we're still tweaking it inside and its more fire proof this way. We'll grow some houses when we decide where the town will be. Kirk can suck the life out of them, and we can add chimneys for the people without an Endure Elements buff."

Maria swooped down, landing beside Jon and greeting him with a hug. "People used to live here. We found abandon buildings and some real rough rock walls that we left by the pond. Our closest neighbors are fifteen or so miles away in Canterbury. Another smaller settlement is across the bay down the coast."

Kuan turned to Kirk, his blue eyes alight with eagerness. "We've just started moving the rock in the water here. There's a nice ledge right on the edge of our water break we can turn into a tower for you so you don't need to worry about accidentally killing your house. That way, when visitors arrive to buy your potions and stones, you'll be nice and close to the docks."

"Matt and Jamal need to see this," Rob said as he removed a red summoning ball from his pocket.

Maria took Jon's arm. "You'll love this. Cami had a great idea to reroute the river in two branches. It flows under the castle and exits half a mile out at sea. One branch will be drinking water, the other sewer water. We made a crude reservoir on the roof for rainwater so we'll have indoor plumbing. We were thinking to build a stone bathhouse so we can have hot water too."

"Guys, I don't know what to say. This is amazing. More than I imagined possible." Jon sounded choked up.

Jen realized they stood on the path alone and peered over her shoulder to where everyone waited. Spread out on the edge of the grass, the survivors of flight four-fourteen stared with eyes wide in amazement; no one said a word.

Jen ran back and grabbed Nina's arm. "Isn't this great?"

"It's beautiful— a fairytale come true. Is it safe?"

"Let's go and see." Jen linked her arm with Nina's and pulled her forward. "Come see!" She infused her voice with will, making herself louder. A mental command brought Gallant to her. She swung Ben and Frank Miller down and set them on their feet. "Go explore your new home."

Shrieking with laughter, the two ran to the open doorway. Dillion stared after them with sad eyes. Before Jen could comfort him, Sophia's mother took his hand, leaning close to whisper in his ear. When she released him, he flashed her a smile and ran after the Miller boys.

The three kids on Brandon's black charger, Ed, jumped to the ground and followed, calling for Ben and Frank to wait up. In minutes, all the children under eighteen ran forward, laughing and calling to each other. Jen had Gallant lay so Mr. Henry could ease off. She took Sophia from him and gave her a quick kiss on the forehead before handing her back to her mother.

Awed comments and laughter grew as they drew closer and could more clearly see the detail in the design. Everywhere Jen looked she noticed a new element. Flowers grew along the edges of windows and doors and lined the road they walked upon, perfuming the air with a delicate fragrance. Trees formed a dense leafy canopy overhead that blocked the light, leaving the road shady and cool. They were so dense, Jen assumed they'd block most rain too.

She'd be glad to sleep undercover. Nightly rainfall had made sleeping miserable. Jon had rearranged the groups, putting the rangers in with the elderly and children but even when the cold wasn't bothersome water trickling across your face and soaking your clothing was annoying.

"I never imagined something like this," Jen said to Nina who walked beside her.

"Who could have— I knew the druids went ahead to make a camp and looked forward to smooth soft ground but this…"

The two women continued to gaze about in awe until they reached the main steps. Formed of stone, slightly uneven wide steps sprouted from the earth before the main door.

Two firebirds swooped past Jen and circled overhead, dripping sparks and cooing. They landed on a rail of a balcony above the main entrance. Jen halted and glanced back. Matt and Jamal had returned. Both stared dumbfounded. The firebirds sang in joyous welcome, the sound unlike anything Jen had ever heard before. Impossibly high notes trilled and chirped between chitters that sounded like bird laughter to Jen. The two tamed wolves rose their heads and howled. The small hairs on Jen's arms lifted at the eerie sound and she absently rubbed them. Kuan assumed his raven form and flew to the balcony where he became human once again.

"Long live King Jon! Hail King Arthur!" Kuan called as they approached; he glowed blue and his eyes shone.

"King Jon," Nina cried and clapped.

Soon everyone clapped and yelled hail to the king.

Kuan waved his hands. "Let us who have

magic gather and make a pact. No longer separate guilds but Knights of the Round Table. We'll swear to be honorable knights, to neither murder, rape, nor steal. We'll do our best to help those in our realm who seek our help with just cause. When we sit at the Round Table, we'll give honest council for the betterment of the realm, not ourselves. Do you swear?"

The blue glow billowed from Kuan and covered them, making the crowd exclaim and draw back. Arcs of static flickered over the magic weilders. The smell of ozone filled the air, and the air itself felt weighted as if a storm approached although the day remained sunny. Jen glanced at Sam who rubbed her arms and shivered as though she were cold. Jen turned to stare at her fellow wielders; she could feel their awed amazement.

"Do you swear?" Kuan repeated and rose his arms in the air.

"I swear," Jon called. "And further, I swear to be a good, honest king, putting the welfare of my people before my own."

Jen felt his sincerity. The blue cloud seemed to be transmitting it. The sparks in the blue glow grew bigger and flitted between them faster.

"I swear." Sam reached up to Kuan.

"I swear." Jen grabbed Sam's hand as one-by-one they made their oaths. She felt their awe and wonder, and the power in her oath, and wasn't surprised when lightning struck Kuan.

It hit her with a sizzling crash, knocking her

to her knees. Saint Elmo's fire sprang up as the crowd behind them screamed. A wave of purplish blue flame that didn't burn covered them, then flowed to the castle, coating it in blue phosphorescence.

Electricity hummed across Jen's skin a degree below painful. Just like when her eyes flared blue, color and sound grew clearer. Emotion buffeted her, and she could almost hear the thoughts behind it, but it was hard to differentiate who felt what. Most still felt awe although fear and pain had joined it.

The lightning coated them for two minutes before dissipating. The Saint Elmo's fire crawled over the roof and disappeared. Jen pushed herself to her feet and casted a group heal. A small ball of yellow light jumped between them and was joined by the bright sparks of Tony's group heal. The ground gave off a green radiance from Cami's group heal. Pale green sparks flitted from Cami's fingertips and soared between them, alighting on bare skin and being absorbed.

"Look," Nina called, sounding both awed and scared.

Jen turned to her.

"Your cloak, look." Nina pointed.

Jen removed her cloak and held it up. A white iron cross with a lightning bolt bisecting it had replaced her guild symbol.

"Mine too," Brandon said.

The three druids transformed to bears. The

same symbol now covered their chests.

"Are you okay?" Ramiro called.

"Fine. Magic takes vows seriously," Jen said, making her voice loud enough for all to hear.

"I wish I knew if Kuan were doing it on purpose or not," Jon muttered.

Ben Miller appeared on the balcony beside Kuan. "You've got to see this place." He leaned over and beckoned to his father. "Dad, you got to see this."

Frank Miller Senior grinned at his wife, then bowed to Jon. "After you, my liege."

Jon smiled and entered the building.

A round, stone table big enough to sit at least thirty rose from the ground to the right of the door. Behind the table, three broad, slightly crooked, stone steps led to a dais where a half-grown wooden throne sat flanked by two trees with trunks so wide it would take three people holding hands to circle them.

An arched doorway behind the half-finished throne led to another dimly lit room. To the left of the door, long, narrow, wooden tables sprouted from the rock floor. The trunks spread unnaturally to shape the tables while the limbs entwined to form the floor thirty-foot above them. Vines hung from the ceilings wrapped around thick branches that peeped from the thick leaves lining the ceiling and arched across the span of the room. Jen wondered what the intent was as most ended way above head height although some dangled from the misshapen branches obviously fashioned to be used as swings. That they were intentional she had no doubt.

"Light fixtures," Kuan said and frowned. "We plan on talking the chestnut trees we found to be oilier but haven't had time."

Jen smiled and took his hand, nodding absently as she continued to examine the room.

Arched doorways lined the wall on either side of the biggest staircase Jen had ever seen. It wound and curved in a sinuous manner fifteen feet above their heads to the second floor where a railed balcony overlooked the first floor.

Everywhere she looked she noticed something new; patterns in the leafy walls and rails, purposeful designs in the railings and floors. The entire room smelled of fresh-cut wood and grass.

"We're still working on the bedrooms and bathrooms upstairs and the roof leaks in spots, but we can fix them when we notice them," Cami said. "There's plenty of room for us to sleep down here though until we finish it. The room behind this has a soft grass floor that should work fine to camp in until the bedrooms are done."

"We'll do a cookhouse as soon as we decide the best place for it." Maria turned to Kirk. "I've been growing silverware, plates, trays— stuff like that out back, if you could suck the life from them, we can break them off, and we might be able to eat like civilized people."

"Can you grow me a better bow?" Cass asked

eagerly.

"How about instruments?" Warren called.

"And chairs? Or stools or something?" Nina asked.

Jon clapped his hands to gain their attention. "This is amazing and really pushes our timetable up. Tomorrow, we'll gather salt and ash to tan hides. If we can get seeds before spring, we'll be in great shape.

"We don't need to wait for spring. Get us seeds, and we can grow it," Maria said.

"Then that's our priority. An all meat diet will get old quick. Everyone work on trade goods. Think small and easily transportable. Yes, Rob and Matt can shrink things, but we need to be subtle. Also, pick eight people to sit at the Round Table with my knights. Choose wisely as we'll be the ones making our laws.

Paris

Jon stood on the pier and frowned at the boat bobbing in the gentle swell. "You guys sure you're okay doing this?"

"Yep, we'll back in a week or so. I have our list in my pants pocket." Jen jingled the bag of shrunken change. It didn't have value as metal but with Rob's enlarge they hoped to sell the coins for the engravings on them as jewelry. She removed her armor with a thought and stuffed the bag in her shirt.

Sam giggled. You're a lumpy mess."

"True, but I don't feel it with my armor on." She winked at Sam and reapplied her white armor.

Kirk had supplied them with as many conjured items as they could carry. He stood with an arm around Sam's shoulders.

"Don't forget to get a cat if you can," Kirk

said, scowling at the holes a rat had left in his sweatshirt.

"We'll do our best to meet everyone's requests," Jamal said and slapped him on the shoulder. He and Matt had decided to accompany them to Paris instead of exploring England. They'd discovered summon stones only worked inside the zone and they planned to get more gear before venturing too far. He kissed Sam's cheek and shook Jon's hand.

"No visible magic. You'll be strange enough as you are. Keep the swords sheathed unless you need to use them. Keep answers vague, no lies, but let's keep the rumors down if we can." Jon frowned and eye Jen unhappily. "Your armor makes me nervous."

"It's not like we have anything better for me to wear."

"I know, but maybe you and Brandon should stay here."

"I'll hang back in the boat unless we need the horses." She didn't add or unless her group needed protection, that went without saying. She, Ethan, Maria, Jamal, Matt, and Brandon got in the boat. They'd been preparing for this trip for two months. Heaped high with skins of all types, wooden and rock sculptures and jewelry, there was barely room for them to sit at the oars.

The druids had grown the boat in three days. They could've finished in minutes, but Kuan wasn't happy without decorating it. A glorified rowboat, it had a curved bottom, three seats, and a bird figurehead. Birds in all stages of flight covered the wood, grown right into it as if the druids couldn't help but put a piece of themselves into everything they crafted. Animal figures of all sorts showed up on everything they made. A coiled vine rope with a crude harness for Maria sat in the prow.

None of them had ever boated the channel before. Maria was backup in case they needed more strength to cross the current than they could produce. She could pull the boat in dolphin form or cause the water to flow where she willed it. They planned to cross and head down the coast to where Port Le Havre would be and up the river Seine to Paris.

"Don't forget to look around to see what other things they might want we could make," Sam called after them. "And be careful!"

"You too. I love you." Jen called back and waved.

She and Brandon shared a bench. She leaned forward as he did, and they pulled the oars hard. The boat shot forward.

"I'm guiding it," Maria said. She sat with her eyes closed, leaning over the prow with one arm wrapped around the wooden neck of the bird figurehead.

The shore dwindled from sight within minutes. In less than an hour they were across, floating down the coast, searching for the entrance to the river.

Cool, February sunshine caressed Jen's face as she sat, clutching her cape closed with one hand and gazed around her. Gawain, Jamal's pet wolf, rested his head in her lap content to sleep despite the noise and bustle of the wharf.

Tethered by their vine rope to the front of a rickety wooden pier, a much bigger boat beside them intermittently bumped their smaller craft. Men and women, both afoot and driving carts pulled by ponies, scurried across the dock carrying cloth wrapped bundles, burlap sacks, and wooden chests. Most wore tunics, simple garments stained and frayed and tied with rope. All carried a pouch and dagger tied to their waists.

She'd seen two women in long gowns with flowing veil-like streamers floating from pointy hats, and unable to help herself, had burst into laughter. Both women were attended by armed men in chainmail vests, and both times the others on the dock had bowed and stepped back, clearing the road.

A group of oriental men, wearing long black robes, escorted a woman cloaked and veiled in deep red along the wharf. Simply dressed women in ragged brown tunics with kerchief covered heads walked unescorted among the men but kept their eyes downcast.

Shifts in the wind brought the odor of the city

to her, making her eyes water. People shouted, laughed and cursed as they went about their work. At first, she'd heard a babble of sound, but now the words came to her clearly and accented.

A grin crossed her face at the cockney accent of a man berating a boy for staying out all night. Beside him, a man in much finer clothing spoke to his equally well-dressed companion in a rich, French accent. Both paused to stare at Jen before moving on.

She ran a hand over her head. Her hair had begun growing back, for which she was grateful. Now, a half inch of brown fuzz shadowed her skull. Her helm sat at her feet under a pile of skins. She'd been here four hours and hadn't seen anything resembling the quality of her cloak or the hilt of her silver sword jutting from the furs beside her hand. The diamonds on the pommel flashed in the weak sunlight.

Because no one went unarmed here, they'd decide she should show she had a weapon handy. She nervously ran a hand over her nearly bald head again. No one here wore their hair cut so short. But, she supposed, it was just one thing in a sea of oddities about them. She sniffed in disdain at herself for worrying over her appearance when she had so many other things to worry over.

The smell of freshly baked bread made her stomach rumble. She eyed the conjured bread stacked inside a fancy wooden box with disfavor. While nutritious and filling, she was sick of it. She wanted a salad and soda.

Tears filled her eyes, and she hid her face in Gawain's ruff. She'd never have soda again, never share a pizza with her little brother or eat her mom's chocolate cake. No more Christmas cookies or candy bars or family dinners. Grief assaulted her without warning over the oddest things. A sound, a scent, a memory, all could turn her day dark and depress her for hours. Everyone seemed to suffer from mood swings, but it was getting easier. Or maybe she was getting better at denying it.

But they're alive, she told herself firmly and straightened. "And I'm alive," she whispered to Gawain. Heavy booted feet approached, the tread echoing on the wooden pier. Since ninety percent of the populous went barefoot or wore soft leather shoes, it grabbed the attention.

She smiled at Brandon. His black plate-mail stood out in this crowd. Sharp black spikes covered the rounded pauldrons and the backs of his gauntlets. Rough-cut chunks of black glass or maybe gems, she wasn't sure which, edged his chest piece. A darker black iron cross with a bisecting lightning bolt of slightly shinier metal appeared to be inlaid into the front and back of his chest piece.

He didn't wear his helm or the blood-red cloak with the matching design. A black scabbard hung from a thick silver chain over his back, revealing the hilt of his broadsword. Much bigger than her sword, his was matte-black with a thin, barely-seen tracing of silver runes and chunky black gems on the hilt.

"I brought us guards to watch the boat. Come eat and take a break." He offered his hand.

She bit her lip and examined the men he'd brought with him. Only one carried a sword, the other five carried daggers. Scarred and weathered, they appeared capable of stopping petty thieves.

Not that she was worried about thieves. Rob had locked the trunk containing the shrunken items and no one besides themselves could open it. The packs they used for their personal belongings were also locked by Rob. Even trying to cut one open wouldn't work. Jen wished they had a mage for mage packs but with Rob's shrink, Jen could fit everything she owned into a pocket. Not that she owned much, only a rough leather vest and underwear made from donated cloth Rob had enlarged that had been painstakingly resewn with thread the druids formed from plant fibers.

Wizards could only enlarge an item to twice its original size and cloth was one of the priority items they'd been sent to get.

"Can we afford that?"

"Yep, I won a few bouts. Entertainment is really scarce here; they're willing to bet on anything."

She glanced doubtfully down at her cloak.

"There are lots of women dressed different ways."

"Gawain, guard," she said as she sheathed her sword behind her back in one smooth move. Her magic encased it with a thought. Holding her cloak closed with one hand, she gave her other to Brandon who pulled her effortlessly to the deck.

The men with him bowed. The man carrying the sword mumbled, "My lady," as she passed.

Jen blushed.

"Get used to it," Brandon whispered. "Here, we're knights, and they address us as such. Ethan made a killing on our coins and jewelry. He's lining up buyers now for the bigger items. Tomorrow we'll hold an auction. He's spreading the word on what types of items we'll accept in trade."

Passerbys stared as they strode down the dirt road. Jen avoided their eyes, staring at the road before her. Deep ruts made for treacherous footing. They passed a group of men laying stones and stepped onto a smoother cobbled surface. Two-story stone homes flanked the street, putting them in artificial twilight. Shallow gutters filled with nameless filth lay on either side of the road.

Jen resisted covering her nose with her hands, but it was hard.

Brandon laughed and put an arm around her. "You'll get used to it."

She grimaced, making him laugh again.

Jamal leaned against a rough wooden wall eating an apple. The tip of his bow was visible behind his head. His quiver held arrows for show and his conjured spheres and health potions from

Kirk. Grown to match his bow with wooden feathers lining the wood in fanciful swirls, his quiver hung on his back by two, thin, leather straps against his black UBM sweatshirt that Kirk had enchanted, making the cotton shirt repel a strike as easily as an iron chest piece.

"How are they taking him and Ethan?" Jen whispered as they approached.

"Not turning a hair. This is a cosmopolitan city. We've seen Orientals and a group of the blondest men I've ever seen. They were the ones who challenged me. Vikings, I think. In some ways, this is so cool."

Jen snorted. "Do they have a bathroom?'

"Not one you'll like." Brandon laughed and slapped her shoulder before reaching out to bump fists with Jamal.

"Matt's inside securing us a room for the night and a meal. Ethan will be along in a minute; he's exploring." Jamal winked and grinned. "By the way, the stones work pretty literally. They think we're language experts. Everyone hears us in their own language when we speak to them. When we speak amongst ourselves, they don't understand us. They speak French, but not our French, it's vaguely understandable without a stone."

Jamal grabbed the door and held it open. "The beer and wine taste like crap but it's better than the water. Sanitation is truly appalling."

A wave of warm air smelling of turnips and sweat gusted past them.

"We're assured this is the best inn in the area."

"Jeez…" Jen scanned the room, trying not to appear as horrified as she felt.

Cracks gaped in the uneven, wooden floors. Crooked tables sat before equally crooked benches. Splotches of wax and hardened food covered the tables. The talk died down when they entered, then picked up louder. Every man stared as they crossed the room. Men wearing tunics and leather pants, holding wooden cups, stood before a long bar that divided an eating area from a set of wooden stairs and a cloth-covered doorway.

A fat man in a dirty, brown tunic approached. A wide smile covered his face, and he gestured to an empty table. "Sit, my lady. Your man has run to your ship to fetch plates and cups for your use. My good wife is preparing a feast of roasted vegetables as he requested. Anise!" he called and peered over his shoulder.

A girl of fifteen or so appeared in the doorway. Her light brown hair was braided and wrapped around her head. She rose a hand to a pock-marked cheek marring what would otherwise be a non-objectionable face. Not beautiful, but average. Her nose was a hair too long, the chin a bit too receded to be pretty, but her youth and health gave her an attractive air. Big brown eyes stared at them as if she'd never seen their like, and Jen had to clamp her lips hard to keep from laughing.

"My daughter would be honored to serve

whatever you require." He clapped his hands and made a come here gesture.

A blush covered the girl's cheeks as she gathered her thin skirt and curtsied, then ran over. Crooked white teeth flashed in a nervous smile as she curtsied again before them.

"My Lady," she mumbled. Her gaze flicked to Brandon and her flush deepened, "Sir." She clasped her hands together and stared down at them.

"Our companion Sir Lyon wonders if you might know of any archery contests?" Brandon asked.

The barkeep eyed Jamal and pursed his lips.

"And did Sir Mathew secure us rooms? I'd like to take off my armor."

"Anise can lead you to them."

The girl bowed again and gestured to the stairs.

Brandon winked at Jen and followed the girl.

Jamal sat and held a hand to Jen. She took his hand and stepped over the bench, letting her cloak fall open as she took her seat.

The barkeep inhaled sharply and cleared his throat. Jen followed his gaze.

Her silver belt glittered in the candlelight while the diamonds adorning it gave off sparks of blue. The fine, silver chainmail that edged the white shone. To him, she must be a vision of unbelievable wealth and strangeness. Bare shoulders, midriff, and thighs marked her as outside the bounds of propriety, but the sword warned she was a soldier, not a whore. And in a world where people wore their wealth, her garments proclaimed she was very rich indeed.

"He's going to expect an amazing tip," she murmured to Jamal.

Jamal snickered.

Brandon returned sans armor and sword, dressed like Jamal in his black UBM sweatshirt, jeans, and sneakers, and sat across from them. Without his armor, he appeared smaller but was still bigger than most of the men present. Unlike them, no scars marred his six-one frame. Since the lightning, he'd lost weight. With no junk food and having to exercise, he was down a good fifty pounds.

Jamal was an inch shorter and more muscular. Both men kept clean shaven, borrowing a sword daily to scrap their faces. Razor sharp, both paladin swords gave a close shave.

The barkeep's eyes widened and he glanced fearfully at Jamal, obviously regretting not being as obsequious as he might.

"I bet he thinks you have armor and a sword just like his," she said.

"Likely."

"Borrow mine tomorrow and walk around near me," Brandon offered.

"Nah, what if I get challenged? I'm better off with this." He touched his fingertips to the wooden bow.

Maria had crafted his bow from a yew tree, forming it to her best recollection of fancy bows she'd seen in movies and unable to resist adding a feathered effect to the wood so it appeared a thin wooden wing peeping over his shoulder.

"We should bet on Jen; we'd make a killing," he continued and winked at her.

Jen's eyes widened.

"Relax, we won't."

She leaned her elbows on the table and rested her chin on them. "Actually, that isn't a bad idea, but we should promote it, rent a spot, and sell tickets. Maybe even offer a purse to attract contestants and charge them to fight me, and you can bet too."

Jamal pursed his lips and examined her. "Jen, these men fight all the time and fight dirty. You could get hurt. Sure, your spells could defeat them, but a fight?"

"I can fight. I mean, I could before this. I kickbox and have a brown belt in karate and started studying jiu-jitsu." Jen giggled at Jamal's surprised expression. "Sam worked at the gym and got me free classes."

"Sam knows karate?"

"No, she was a dancer. She studied dance since she could walk and taught it part-time. When we were kids, our parents brought us to the gym. I sucked at dance, so took other things. I did gymnastics for a few years, but I'm too tall and felt dumb next to the short, graceful girls so— I took karate. Since I will never be graceful, I embraced my tomboyish nature."

Jen sighed hard, frowning at her outfit. "I feel stupid as hell in this, but I bet we could sell tickets, and we need money.

"You don't look stupid," Ethan said unexpectedly

To Jen's surprise he kissed her temple before taking a seat beside her.

"I only caught that last bit. What are we selling tickets for?"

"A fight. Jen versus all-comers."

Ethan half stood and glared at Jamal. "No fucking way; she could get hurt."

"Relax, between her training and buffs, she'll be fine. Besides, she'll be wearing her armor. Wear the prot armor and really give them a thrill."

Jen rolled her eyes.

Brandon laughed.

Jamal waved the bartender over. "Excuse me, good sir."

"Really? Good sir? What are we— in a bad movie?" Jen murmured, making Brandon and Ethan laugh and Jamal blush.

"Could you recommend a building to rent to host a fighting exhibition?"

The barkeep rubbed his chin.

"Hob's barn would do," Anise offered meekly.

She'd been so quiet Jen had forgotten she stood behind them.

"Or my cousin Eustace's warehouse."

"Capital idea, girl. That's just the thing. Spacious and well lit. Will you be fighting, Sirs?"

"Maybe," Jamal said thoughtfully. "Lady Frey will be the main contender. Can you send word to your cousin that we'll visit to see if the warehouse is suitable and discuss terms?"

"At once." The barkeep nodded and backed away, grinning and rubbing his hands.

Enter the Fray

Three days later, Jen stood behind a makeshift counter trying not to feel horribly exposed and ridiculous. Wooden crates formed a row before her. Stacks of crates teetered to the forty-foot roof ten feet behind her. To her right, bales and bundles lay in haphazard piles. A blond man carrying a sword leaned against them staring at Jen.

A blush heated her cheeks as she turned away. She was glad they had no mirrors so she couldn't see how ridiculous she looked. "They don't know me," she whispered to herself.

"Hmm." Matt turned to her and grinned, making her blush deepen. "Sorry, it's just so cool seeing that set in real life. Your armor, I mean," he added hastily.

Jen snickered and glanced down at her boobs.

In the game, her character's double D's filled this outfit and then some. In real life, her B cup just looked silly confined in the black bustier. Thin silver chains crisscrossed, holding her top closed. Silver buckles cinched the black leather shoulder straps while another set crisscrossed her back. If she carried a sword, her sheath would appear on her back attached by silver buckles, but she hadn't summoned it. She'd removed her boots, not wanting to kill someone accidentally with her heels, and stood barefoot on the dirt floor.

Silver buckles held black leather with thin tracings of silver swirls to her calves and covered her knees. Normally, her thigh-high boots covered her leg protection. Bare skin showed from her thighs to the black bikini edged in silver and glittery black gems.

Black gems or glass or something, she wasn't sure what they were actually made of, covered her gauntlets, gloves, and vambraces, catching the light and sparkling brilliantly. Invisible armor covered every inch of her. Her bare skin would repel a strike as well as her black gauntlets, and she spent a moment being thankful she'd had such good armor in the game. The very first spell she'd ever bought was the upgraded fortitude and even naked she could withstand a strike that would kill a normal man.

Her helm and cloak rested on the counter. She tucked them beside her boots on the floor, not at all worried about thieves. If she went over six hundred yards from them, they would disappear as quickly and completely as popped soap bubbles.

Ethan and Jamal waited outside the door with Brandon. He wore his protective armor too. Much fancier than his plate mail, the flowing, tarnished-silver links formed a tunic that belted with a wide, diamond-studded, silver belt over a black silk tunic emblazoned with the iron cross and lightning bolt emblem. The thin links of his armor appeared delicate and fragile, each one so tiny no space remained between them.

The same chainmail covered his legs, what you could see of them. High, black-metal boots curved around his leg formed to resemble a raven's wing. Matching bracers surround his arms to the elbow. His pauldrons also resembled the wings of a bird. Each black metal feather ended in a sharp point. Every two feathers a flat one made of sparkling black glass-like gems nestled, glittering whenever he moved.

He didn't wear the matching black helm formed of a raven's head, not because it was heavy or restricted sight, but because it was so outlandish. His magic let him see perfectly through the thin eye slits. The tiered metal feathers and glittering gem feathers didn't irritate his neck; he didn't feel it.

The hilt of his broadsword stuck up behind his head beneath his cloak, gems glittering in the candlelight. He walked the streets calling for customers and directing them to the warehouse.

Already, a crowd had gathered. Inside, Matt and Anise served beer at the makeshift counter.

Wooden crates and rough rope formed a ring in the center of the room.

Ethan brought in another cage of chickens and winked at her.

She stifled a laugh behind her fist. They were accepting trade goods as well as coins and had already amassed far more than their boat could carry, but it had taken them less than a day to get here. What they couldn't fit, they could return for.

Her gaze turned to the men who'd paid to fight her, wagering one gold piece for the chance at ten. So far, sixteen men had offered their gold. Local noble's sons mostly, wearing nicer clothes than the crowd behind the rope, but young and untried without scars. Three older men more than made up for their lack of scars. One, in particular, was much larger than she and muscular. He wore loose trousers belted at the waist with his chest, head, and feet bare, and used the dagger he carried to clean his nails.

The man beside him wore mismatched pieces of armor and carried a sword sheathed at his side. He sipped from his wooden mug and laughed with the man beside him.

Probably at her, Jen thought ruefully.

Every contestant had been promised a refund plus one gold if she quit the field. She eyed the boys sourly, knowing they hoped the bigger men would defeat her and they'd get a gold without a fight.

"Do we have enough gold to cover it if I lose a fight?"

"One fight, so don't lose," Matt said.

Jamal led a goat and ten men into the warehouse. "They get a free beer too," he called to Matt.

Matt nodded and poured the beers.

"So, you're her," one said doubtfully as he sipped his beer. "You don't look so tough. Kind of scrawny actually.

"Care to wager on it?" Matt asked. "We're offering two to one odds." He gestured with his chin to the waiting men. "Pick your champion."

"I got a penny I can spare on Sture winning his fight."

"Name, Sir?"

"Randall."

Matt took his penny and turned and wrote Randall/Sture- one, on the wooden crate behind him in chalk. Names covered the crate.

"You be a knight too, then?" Randall asked.

"Yes." A wide smiled covered Matt's face, and he began to laugh. "We're King Arthur's knights. The Knights of the Round Table."

"Ner heard of him. Where you be from?" Randall's companion asked.

"Camelot." Matt grinned at Jen, making her laugh.

"A rich country by your dress. Odd as it may be, the cloth is fine and well dyed. And your shoes— I've never seen such."

Matt gazed at his Nikes unhappily. "I'm going to miss them, that's for sure," he said to Jen.

Jen laid a hand on his arm. "Me too," she said sadly.

"Your shoemaker died then?" Randall said with real sympathy in his voice.

"I suppose he has," Matt said.

Ethan entered, carrying a bundle of cloth, which he set behind the counter. "Start anytime now. The crowd outside is thinning. Remember, Jen, give them a show, but don't get hurt."

"Randall, mind giving me a hand?" Jen asked.

Randall flushed and nodded agreement.

Jen grabbed her helm and handed it to Randall. A small sack of plastic beads taken from Sophia's toy abacus in hand, she approached the waiting fighters.

The crowd quieted to hear her.

"Choose a color and drop it in my helm. Randall will pick one randomly, and that person will fight me first."

A man wearing a chainmail tunic took her hand. He wore his brown hair pulled back in a tight ponytail and a neatly trimmed beard. "I would pay you not to fight. Such beautiful skin shouldn't be bruised."

Ethan pulled his hand away. "She fights, that's it! Lady Frey is a knight."

Jen glanced at him, she hadn't seen him arrive, but she was glad he had, not sure how to handle that. "He means well, but eww."

Ethan smiled, then sighed hard, a frown appearing on his face. "Be careful." He gestured to the ring with his chin.

She hopped lightly over the rope and stretched her arms and rotated her neck, then jogged in place a second.

"Who's our first contestant?" Matt called.

"It be the green ball!" Randall called back and held up the small bead to show the audience.

One of the timid boys, Jen stepped back, clasped her hands and bowed. The boy stood nervously, obviously unsure how to proceed.

Jen stepped forward and swung at his face, not meaning to connect, to get him to react. He swung back and tried to grab her. To her, he moved sluggishly slow, and she wondered if his slowness was the wizard buff, her enhanced relaxes, or if he were just slow.

She let every hit almost connect.

"Oh aye, she's playing with him, she is," Randall said loud and approvingly.

Is that all you got, boy!"

"Let's see some real action."

The crowd began yelling comments and advice. The boy's eyes narrowed, and his cheeks flushed. On his next punch she grabbed his arm and threw him, following him down to kneel on his back with his arm twisted and an arm around his throat.

The crowd roared its approval.

"She be the winner!" Randall bellowed. He reached into her helm and withdrew another ball.

The crowd roared and groaned as she defeated the next four contestants as easily. The fifth carried a dagger into the ring.

"Eh, what you about there, boy? This be a friendly match," Randall said heatedly.

Jen grinned at him. He'd taken a shine to her; her simple request to hold her helm and call the fights making him her champion.

"Daggers are fine if he feels he needs it. No swords though, unless I can use mine."

The crowd laughed and yelled insults.

"Well, Jorge it's for sure you be no gentleman." Randall sniffed as Jorge climbed into the ring.

Jen turned her back. The strike Jorge aimed for her neck skittered over her invisible armor. His hand passed her face as he stumbled forward. She dropped and kicked a leg out, knocking him to the ground, turning with the swing to face him. With one hand, she grabbed the wrist above the dagger, with the other, she punched him twice in the side, quick jabs, being careful to hit lightly, then twisted the wrist in her grasp. The dagger fell to the dirt. She kicked his feet out from under him again, then did a backflip away to let him stand.

The crowd stamped their feet.

"Bitch."

She held a hand out and beckoned him. He ran forward. She let him get close before kicking him in the face twice with a front snap kick, knocking him down again. Back in the future, she'd just started learning these moves and hadn't been able to kick that high. She turned and grinned at Jamal who laughed.

She was having fun now. It felt good to fight. She felt strong and graceful unlike in the future where she'd struggled to master these moves. Energy practically fizzed in her blood. She felt as if she could fight for a year; she wanted to fight for a year. The thought surprised her. She shook her head to clear it then stepped back and lowered her hands, reigning in her eagerness.

This time her opponent rose slowly, wiping his bloody nose on his sleeve. He rose his hands before his face and approached to jab at her. She easily ducked each jab. With a wordless yell, he charged her, arms wide, hoping to grapple her.

She let him connect and turned, throwing him hard over her shoulder with a body drop and rested her bare foot lightly on his balls.

"I yield," he bit out.

She stepped back and grabbed the knife, spinning and throwing, leaving it quivering in the dirt between his legs.

"Lady Frey, Lady Frey," the men chanted and stomped. Laughter and insults flew.

Her next opponent was the man in chainmail. He returned her bow with a deeper one. "You're skilled, my lady."

They spared a moment, feeling each other

out.

"Fast too, but not as strong as a man, alas." So saying, he rushed her.

To her, he moved so slow she could've circled him twice before he reached her. She let him take her to the ground, using his momentum to roll them over. Kneeling astride him, she forced his hands to the side.

"I'm stronger than I look and nobody's paid companion," she said softly. She released him and backflipped away.

"Oh, she's a wily one, I bet she could take you with her arms tied behind her back," Randall said.

Her opponent pursed his lips and tilted his head. "Can you?"

"Yes."

The crowd began hollering bets to Matt.

"You sound sure."

Jen shrugged. "Are you going to be a sore loser?"

He grinned and threw his head back, laughing as if she'd said something funny. "I'll take you to dinner. Will you accept if I defeat you? Just dinner," he added hurriedly when she frowned.

"Yes." She held her hand out. "We shake on deals where I come from."

He took her hand and kissed it. "Bind her, Randall. Let's see if she can beat me." He lowered his voice and whispered. "I really hope you can't, think of my reputation."

He grinned so happily Jen had to laugh.

"What's your name, Sir?"

"Galahad."

Jen paled and swayed.

"Holy shit!" Ethan vaulted into the ring and stepped between them. "Is that a common name here about?"

Randall glanced between Ethan and Jen, a frown furrowing his brow. "Common enough, I suppose," he said

At the same time, Galahad stepped away and said, "Yes, do you seek a man named so?"

"No, no, you just surprised us. Carry on."

"I'm Galahad too!" another man yelled out.

His friends laughed drunkenly.

"I can be Galahad if you're looking for one," another called to loud peals of laughter.

"It means nothing, Jen," Ethan said and ran a hand over her head.

"It gave me the willies," Matt said and shivered.

Jen gave them a wan smile.

"It's just a name, Jen," Ethan said and squeezed her shoulder.

Jen nodded and wriggled her shoulders and neck, trying to relieve the tension. Ethan hugged her before leaving the ring.

Galahad took the rope from Randall and approached, looking troubled. "My lady?"

"Yes, sorry, I'm fine. It's nothing. Go ahead and tie me."

Jen turned and placed her arms behind her,

hoping the ropes would stay put if she wasn't trying to get free of them.

"I will forfeit if this fears you," he whispered.

"I'm not afraid. Your name startled me is all. It isn't a common one where I'm from and made me think of someone else."

"Someone you dislike?"

"Not at all. Someone very like you." Jen grinned at him over her shoulder.

"Will you dine with me? Win or lose, I desire your company. I wish to hear of your travels and homeland."

"This fight gonna start anytime soon?" someone yelled.

Galahad sighed, stepped away, and bowed deeply. She nodded her head. She'd kicked him three times, denting his chest armor, before he could grab her foot. The crowd roared its approval. Her left foot caught in his hands, she hopped forward and kicked with her right, connecting under his chin. She landed on her back and jumped to her feet without using her hands. Winded and woozy, he lay spread-eagled on the floor. She placed her bare foot on his neck.

"Lady Frey wins!" Randall screamed into the cheering throng.

"You okay?" Jen leaned closer, concerned that Galahad hadn't risen.

"You kick like a mule," Galahad gasped. He pushed himself up by his hands and rubbed his chin. "You're the most magnificent creature I've ever seen. I'd love to see you fight, really fight. Your enemies must tremble before you."

He sounded so thrilled she laughed.

He smiled ruefully and, still rubbing his chin, left the ring.

"Before I remove these ropes, anyone else want to up the stakes and try me tied?"

Getting no takers, Matt untied her. "No one wants their chest crushed. Easy there, sport."

"Two fights later she faced Sture, the crowd favorite. Silence descended when he entered the ring.

"Hold back, and you'll get hurt," he warned and stepped forward, surprisingly fast and graceful for his size.

She blocked his punch with her arm, grabbed it and tried to throw him. He countered with the correct move. A fast flurry of blows followed, him punching and her dodging. He was almost fast enough to be a challenge. The crowd chanted his name.

He caught her in the side, let out a surprised oof, and shook out his hand. She took advantage of his distraction and karate chopped his collarbone. If she'd been fighting for real, she'd have hit his neck and killed him.

His eyes widened and he tried to grab and throw her. She landed hard on her back then used both feet to kick him back.

He screamed, making her wince.

"Sorry, got carried away." She offered Sture a

hand to rise.

"I yield." Clutching his ribs, he eyed her in amazement. "I've never met a woman trained in the oriental art of fighting before. Not even in the Orient.'

"Yeah, I'm an odd one alright,

He laughed and rubbed his ribs.

Jen rose her voice. "We'll hold a shooting contest here tomorrow. We'll be paying three to one odds on Sir Lyon's ability with his bow. My comrades will fight, you can choose which of us you wish to fight for a small entry fee and the chance to win ten gold. Sir Brandon and I will spar with swords, a short bout to first blood."

Jen approached Randall. "Thanks for the assistance."

"You're an impressive fighter, my lady. I've never seen Sture defeated. And you beat Galahad in his armor with no hands. No one is going to believe this. It was worth the half-copper for entry and then some," he finished happily.

Jen eyed him thoughtfully. "Will more come to challenge or have I scared them away?"

"Word of your prowess will spread. The boys won't come again though, well, not the smart ones, maybe drunken fools, but serious fighters will show. They'll be harder to beat— skilled, hardened men."

"Would the people here pay good money to see an exotic dancing girl or fancy riding?"

"You dance?"

"Not me, Lady Quinn. Never mind that, would they pay?"

If she were as beautiful as you and as skilled, yes."

"Is there a spot that could hold a much bigger crowd?"

"A few. Most would require the king's permission."

She turned to Ethan and grinned. "I have a great idea."

He continued to accept bets and cross names from the wall. "I'm almost afraid to ask. That's a scary grin."

"A circus, with dancing bears, tame wolves, trick riding, and a sword show. We could rent some instruments and Sam could teach our woman a Vegas style dance. We could sell food and drink and charge them to enter."

"Dancing bears?" Ethan burst out laughing.

"Think about it, we advertise and steal every trick from Barnum and Baily, including a trapeze and high-wire. I bet the rangers could even tame some other animals, something scary like an alligator or something. Or maybe cute like kittens. I always loved the birds on bicycles."

"No clowns though, I hate clowns."

She laughed and jumped over the counter to hug him.

His eyes lit, making her heart pound.

Matt cleared his throat.

A hot blush on her cheeks, she released Ethan

and spun away, reaching for her stored armor.

Stupid, she told herself, resisting the urge to smack herself in the forehead. He was way out of her league. He was Sam's league with his muscular build and beautiful smile. Besides, he was married, widowed, whatever… She shook her head trying to clear her thoughts.

"So, how'd we do tonight?" Matt asked.

Ethen let a sack of coins thump to the counter. "Not enough to buy a manor house, but it's a good start."

Brandon hefted the small bag of coin in his mailed fist. "I've been thinking, and we need a fancy sword for Jon. It's going to look odd as hell if ours are nicer."

"And armor," Matt said thoughtfully. "For all of us. I wish Brandon's was a bit plainer, something we could copy."

"You could always illusion it."

Matt nodded, but a frown creased his brow. "For Jon that would work, we could make him appear magnificently garbed sitting on a throne, but for walking around town— not so much."

"Let's visit an armory and see what's available. I don't think anyone can duplicate Brandon's armor, but maybe all different types would work.

Matt flicked Brandon's armor with his fingernail. "Remember, we have to actually wear it, hot, heavy, and uncomfortable."

"Light chain like his prot set wouldn't be too bad to wear. And the tabard shouldn't be hard to have made," Ethan said.

"Light chain wouldn't do much for protection."

Ethan shrugged. "We don't need it for protection."

"Let's get Jon fitted out first. And tabards for the rest of you, then worry about it," Jen said

"And daggers, I feel naked with this little thing." Ethan waggled the wooden knife at her.

"It works for buffs and spells so hold onto it."

Eustace approached, smiling.

"Thank you, sir." Ethan handed him a sack of coin.

"Just the one more night then, Sirs?"

"For now. Who's the best blacksmith here?"

"No one here can make armor like Sir Homes wears. You have truly great artisans in Camelot. Danyau makes a decent blade and has a few fancy pieces."

Jen laid a hand on his arm as he started to turn away. "Eustace, you wouldn't happen to know the date, would you?"

"The date, my lady?"

Jen nodded.

"Februarius twelfth."

"The year and day?"

He peered at her as if she were crazy. "Thursday, my lady." Five hundred and fifty-one years after our savior's death. Pope Vigilius is still incarcerated by the heathens, and King Childebert still reigns in Paris."

He said the last as if proud to remember his history lessons. Jen bit back her smile as her stone translated his indecipherable words to the familiar dates.

"Is he a good king?"

Eustace glanced around the emptying room and lowered his voice. "He's no Clovis, but he'll do."

"His father, right?" Matt perched on the edge of a crate. "He had two daughters and no son's, if I remember right, and a very scary mother."

Eustace laughed. "She is that. Best to keep far from them. He has a son though. Someone better left alone." He cleared his throat and turned away, red climbing his cheeks.

"He just remembered you're one of them." She turned to Eustace. "Thank you. I'm going to go change."

The filthy outhouse out back gave her the willies. She used it as fast as she could and emerged in her jeans and sweatshirt.

"Where'd Ethan go?" Neither he nor Eustace were inside when she returned.

"For a walk. Jamal went to get Gawain; they'll stay here tonight to guard our stuff. Tomorrow, we'll go see the armorer."

Matt held the door for her. "There's so many kings and battles, it's amazing they can rem—"

He broke off as Galahad hailed them. "You have an admirer."

Jen rolled her eyes.

"I must say I prefer you in your armor," Galahad said.

"It chaffs," Jen said shortly.

Matt snickered

Galahad laughed until tears filled his eyes. "Let me escort you to your lodgings."

Jen sighed and gestured.

"We need a gift for our king. Where are the finest swords made?"

"Locally, Danyau. If you can travel, then Quiros for fine decorative work. For a monstrous sword, like Sir Brandon carries, the Goths are known for their size and power.

"What's a weapon like mine go for?"

"I can't imagine, never having seen such before, but upwards of a thousand gold pieces. How much did you pay for that and where?"

"It was a gift."

"From your king?"

"No, from his..." Brandon shrugged— "healer, I guess."

"You guess?"

"We call him a druid."

"Ah, your pagan, then? I thought you Christian by your device."

"In our kingdom, we're free to practice whatever religion we wish. I'm a Christian, but I have no idea if Jen is."

Jen said, "Technically, I'm a Catholic, but I haven't attended church since I was nine."

Galahad looked horrified. "And you?"

Matt shrugged. "No religion."

"You must attend a service with me—"

Matt held up a hand. "Thanks, but no thanks. We don't generally speak of religion."

"It's forbidden where you're from?"

"No, just bad manners. We can worship however we like, but it's considered rude to try to sway others. A friendly invitation does no harm but pushing will make people avoid you."

"Point taken. How far is your home from here?"

"Impossibly far," Brandon said sadly.

Jen linked her arm with his. "Not far anymore. We have a new home."

Mondred

Jen examined the daggers on display with a critical gaze. Ethan leaned over her shoulder and picked one up. The proprietor eyed them hopefully. Drifts of dark gray smoke wafted past them, bringing the scent of molten metal.

Danyau retreated to the back room where he berated someone for wasting the heat.

"Serviceable, but plain, I was hoping for something a bit fancier," Matt murmured.

"This won't do at all for Jon," Jamal added.

Jen picked up the chainmail and shook it out, surprised by its weight. "Uneven and too big. This must be hot as hell to wear."

"We could make a press easily enough and form our own links." Ethan took it from her and held it to his chest.

She eyed him appreciatively. He grinned at her when he dropped the mail back on the counter.

Flustered, she spun away to examine the swords on the wall again.

Danyau returned. "See anything that interests you?"

"How much for the entire lot?" Ethan asked.

Ethan wouldn't cast Sweet Talk unless he thought he was being cheated. It could take them hours to settle on a price. Jen stepped outside as they began to dicker. Galahad joined her there.

The stone building that encased the smithy sat on the edge of town. A low, dirt berm, supporting a wooden palisade consisting of round posts sharpened to spikes, surrounded the entire town. Two men dressed in brown tunics and leggings, and carrying swords, lounged beside an open gate through which wagons and people passed.

"I'd kill for a Coke." She shook her head at his inquiring noise. "Does anyone here sell chocolate?"

He shrugged, clearly not recognizing the word.

"Candy? Sugar?"

"Yes, sugar can be had, but it's expensive. There's a spice shop not far. Shall I show you?"

She stuck her head back inside the shop. "I'm going to a spice shop with Galahad."

Ethan turned and frowned.

"Have fun," Jamal said and winked.

"As if."

Matt laughed.

She and Galahad meandered through the

crowd, taking their time, stopping to peer in windows and stare at oddly dressed men and woman walking the street.

A bell above the door tinkled as they entered and a man wearing a yellow tunic and a dirty, white turban emerged from a curtained doorway. Glass vials lined wooden shelves filled with unrecognizable liquids. Small wooden boxes sat beside cloth pouches. Overhead, plants hung from the rafters drying. The room smelled overwhelming of garlic and something sweet she didn't have a name for.

Galahad pointed to large barrels behind the wooden counter.

The shelves drew her eye. Chalk labels written on the wood identified the contents of the various boxes and bags. Most of the names she didn't recognize.

"Matt has got to see this. Are these really marigold seeds?"

She pointed to a small, white sack.

The proprietor bowed low and rose smiling. "Flower seeds, yes, you read?"

"Just a few words," she said truthfully. Most of the letters remained indecipherable to her, and she didn't know if it were even intended as French. "What other types of seed do you have?"

"Many types, Lady Frey. If you tell me what you desire, I will seek it out."

She smiled at the use of her name. Already she and her companions were famous. "Chocolate and coffee beans, sugarcane seedlings, pepper, tomato, poppies, and cinnamon. Any spice or fruit plant really."

"Most of those won't grow in this climate."

"Can you get them?" Jen asked eagerly.

"Maybe— for a price."

"If the price is fair, we'll pay it. What types of seeds do you have in stock?"

Jen left an hour later clutching a small sack of mixed seeds. The proprietor had been horrified she'd only wanted ten of each and mixed them in the bag, but he accepted her gold easily enough and promised to search out cuttings and other exotic seeds.

Galahad had bought her a taste of sugar and laughed when she made a face.

It tasted burnt and smelled acrid. "Not like ours at all," she murmured, wiping her lips.

By the time they returned to the smithy the others had left.

"I can see myself back to the inn if you have things to do."

"Nothing so interesting as this. Besides, it's dangerous for a lady to travel alone."

She laughed.

His smiling gaze traveled her. "You're fearless. Is crime so rare where you come from or are you that certain of your skill."

"We had crime same as you. Women could walk alone though, although smart ones avoided certain areas. My skills will keep me safe, and my friends avenge me. In a lot of ways, I'm safer here than home.

"Are all as skilled as you there?"

"No. We have different skills. What about you? How do you make your living, or is that rude to ask?"

"My sword. I'm a knight, a lowly unlanded one, but I'm young yet."

"How old are you?"

"Twenty and two."

"Me too."

"Really? I would've thought younger. Let me buy you supper or come to my home. I rent rooms three streets away from the inn."

Jen paused unsure how to handle this. Normally, a glance at Sam was all it took; she would step in, flirt, and make excuses, leaving the men smiling behind her.

"Just dinner," he added softly.

She was surprised he looked embarrassed. "Where I come from men and woman are equal. I have many male friends who I share meals with. I see it's different here, and I don't want to give the wrong impression. I'm a lady, not a… concubine." Warmth scalded her cheeks.

"I'm sorry, I shouldn't invite you alone to my home; I meant no disrespect. How much longer will you be here?"

"I'm not sure. Matt and Jamal might stay a while. Both love to travel."

"You miss your home?"

"So much." Her voice caught and she cleared her throat.

"Are your people banished?" Galahad asked hesitantly. "You seem so sad as if it's lost for good.'

"Not banished, lost, and can't return. We hadn't expected to be gone long at all. A storm caught us, and now we have no way back."

Galahad laid a hand on her arm. "Seaworthy boats can be bought."

"None of us know how to find the way home. Let's talk of other things. Tell me about the laws here and how a soldier can earn enough to retire."

Jen offered a hand to her defeated opponent who lay wheezing at her feet. The laughing crowd stilled. She glanced at the door and straightened, expecting to see another group of men escorting a veiled woman into the room. The turnout for tonight's bout had been bigger than Jen had expected. Men and woman both had jammed into the cavernous space, pressing up against the rope that marked the arena, leaving just a small cleared patch in the center. The better dressed women stood behind their men but called out wagers just as eagerly. Matt, Ethan and Jamal were busy taking and collecting bets from the excited spectators.

Men in red tunics belted with golden cord stood in the doorway. Behind them, two men in full, mail armor strode into the room. The crowd quieted and bowed their heads.

Another man followed, this one wore rich, blue velvet beneath a chainmail vest. A red gem the size of her fist dangled from a gold chain around his neck. A thin gold circlet held long dark-brown hair from a bearded face. The people in the front knelt. Behind them, pressed too close to kneel, they hunched.

The man waved his hand, and the kneelers rose. He strode forward as if no one else was in the room. "You must be Lady Frey."

His brown-eyed gaze traveled her, then Brandon who stood on the edge of the ring behind her. He turned to stare at Matt and Jamal before turning back to her.

"I'm Prince Mondred."

"You have got to be shitting me," Brandon murmured.

Jen choked back a hysterical laugh.

"Lady Genevieve Frey, Your Highness." She curtsied slightly.

His gaze traveled her again, lingering on her breasts and changing to a leer. She blushed, glad she'd worn her white outfit this time.

"My companions— Sir Brandon Homes."

Brandon stepped forward and bowed a bare nod of his head.

"Sir Ethan Lance."

Ethan inclined his head in acknowledgment.

"Sir Jamal Lyon."

Jamal bowed deeply with an extravagant flourish, and Jen had to stifle another laugh at his flamboyant sarcasm.

"And Sir Mathew Biddle."

Matt nodded.

"What king do you serve?"

"King Arthur, Your Highness." She couldn't help the sharp bark of laughter and nervously cleared her throat.

"I've heard rumors of your prowess and beauty and wished to meet you for myself. Will you fight my knight?"

"Yes, sir."

"Dante, will you—"

"Of course, sire."

The man so addressed cut through the rope with his long sword and strode into the ring.

The prince rose an eyebrow.

"Jen," Ethan said in a worried tone and dropped his hand to the pouch on his waist that held his health potions.

She winked at him, not worried at all, almost looking forward to a real challenge. He frowned and released his pouch, sliding his hand to his dagger and glaring at Dante.

Jen stepped back, clasped her hands and bowed.

Dante lowered his visor and swung. She ducked under the blade and kicked him hard in the knee. As he lurched, she grabbed his sword arm and swung over it, getting to the right of him and kicked his knee again, this time from the back. He staggered forward hard and tried to hit her with the shield in his left hand. She grasped it with both hands and flipped over it, landing on his left. Her weight had pushed him forward.

He used the momentum to turn and slash again. If he'd connected, he'd have killed her. Instead, she fell into a backbend and kicked out, being careful not to use her full strength.

Dante flew back, landing on his ass in a crash of metal. The crowd remained silent as he pushed himself to his feet.

Jen waited for him to come to her. This time, he dropped the shield and tried to grab her as she bent away from his slash. He tried to pull her close with one hand, unable to get an angle with his sword.

With her elbow, she hit his chin, then grabbed his sword arm, twisting as she used her feet to trip him. He landed hard again. She didn't release the sword, kicking a leg over the arm holding it and turning, using her body mass to force him to drop it or break his arm.

She snatched it from the ground, put the tip to his throat, and one foot lightly on his chest.

"I yield."

She offered him a hand to stand.

"Most impressive," Mondred said unhappily. "There was to be an exhibition between you and Sir Homes was there not?"

"Yes, Your Highness."

"Do you wish a rest first?"

"No, I'm fine."

Jamal handed over her sword and shield. The crowd gasped at its glittering brightness.

Brandon stepped forward and unsheathed his. The crowd exhaled as one, a long, drawn-out sound of envy. Matt handed him his shield then placed his helm on him. Again, the crowd exclaimed.

Brandon's shield was round and black with a silver inlay of the iron cross bisected by a brighter lightning bolt. Rough chunks of onyx interspersed the tarnished silver studs that encircled the edge, catching and reflecting the light. The same silver designs decorated her shield, but hers was white and shield shaped with a pointed tip and straight edged top with no embellishments. Brandon's sword and shield dwarfed hers.

He grinned at her and saluted with his sword. She bowed and stepped back on her left leg, letting her sword point behind her. They'd fought before for fun, using spells and their enhanced reflexes in impossibly fast moves. Now, they rushed each other, smashing their swords together. Sparks flew the length of her sword as he forced her back. Their shields collided with a hard, metallic bang. Her sword screeched across his armored shoulder and thigh before he knocked her back again. For a minute, they exchange blows on sword and shield. Sparks flew, and metal rang.

Mondred clapped sharply once. "Pretty toys. Dante, spar with the lady until first blood."

His patronizing tone angered her. Brandon

slid his helm up and glared. With his sword, he pointed at the other knight and beckoned him forward. The two knights approached, exchanging uneasy glances through their slitted helms.

"Don't kill them," Brandon murmured.

He needn't have, she'd no intention of killing anyone. She wanted to knock the sword from Dante's hand and the smug smile off Mondred's face.

As soon as Dante stepped forward, she spun and swung hard. Metal ripped with a sharp squeal. The top half of Dante's shield tumbled to the dirt floor with a dull thud. His severed sword followed it. She kicked him hard in the chest and pressed her sword tip through the metal of his chest piece.

"I yield." He held up his empty hands and gazed sadly at his ruined sword.

"Better move if you don't want to get trampled." She didn't offer him a hand to rise this time.

Her sword slid into the sheath on her back with a sibilant hiss. The crowd hummed, repressing their excitement with effort, casting uneasy glances at Mondred.

A few men slipped through the doorway, others looked as if they'd like to but didn't wish to press forward from the crowd and draw Mondred's attention.

Brandon used the point of his sword to draw a line in the dirt, then stood back and waited.

His competitor stepped forward. Brandon

swung as his opponent's toe crossed the line. He connected with the flat of his blade and knocked the other knight to the ground. He let him rise and swung again. This time, he swung as his opponent rose, shearing the top of his shield off in both the first swing and the back swing.

"I yield," his opponent said and dropped his sword.

Brandon removed his helm and offered his gauntleted hand.

"Impressive. May I see your sword?" Mondred held out his hand as if it didn't occur to him Brandon might say no.

Brandon offered the hilt over the crook of his arm.

The prince examined it closely and waved it before suddenly lunging for Brandon's neck. Metal rang on metal as Brandon slapped his gauntleted hands together, stopping the thrust. The two men stared at each other.

Mondred released the blade. Brandon gripped the blade in one hand and flipped the sword in the air; it tumbled once above him. He caught it by the hilt and slid it into the sheath on his back in one smooth move.

Mondred stalked by him and nudged the metal scraps on the dirt with his booted foot. Dante stooped and picked them up. Mondred left without a word. The crowd erupted into loud talk as soon as the door closed behind him.

"We meet a Merlin, and I might go crazy,"

Matt said into the silence.

Jen burst into laughter.

"They're just names. Be careful you don't judge them with preconceived notions. Galahad could be a real a-hole and Mondred the good guy," Ethan said

Jamal snorted.

"I said could."

Behind her, the crowd began to exit. The talk swelled in a mix of angry mutters and excited comments.

"What's an a-hole?" Galahad asked.

Jen jerked around in surprise, she hadn't realized he'd gotten so close.

"A swear."

He frowned at Ethan. "He swore at me?"

"No, your name, not you."

"I never saw a sword that could cut through metal like that. Can I see it?"

She unsheathed her blade and handed it to him.

"What do the markings say?"

"No idea. I think it's just decoration. I'll ask Kirk when we get home. If anyone can read it, he can."

"Does it have a name?"

Jen startled and paled. "It does, and I'd forgotten." She took it from him and held it up to the light. "Alonis Lightning Strike. His blade is Black Howl. Both are legendary weapons although mine is a lower level."

Ethan took her blade and spun it in his hand. "My blade was Time Ripper."

"I carried Immortal Despair," Matt said.

"My bow was called Justice Flight," Jamal said. "What was Jon's?"

"King Maker." Ethan handed Jen back her blade. "It's just names. They mean nothing."

Jen put a hand on his arm. He clasped it in both of his and pulled her to his side.

"They mean nothing, Jen." He rose a hand to frame her face, his brown eyes serious. "This isn't fate or a plan. We weren't chosen. It's just an accident."

Tears filled Jen's eyes and trailed down her cheeks. "Kuan carried a staff called Bringer of Destiny."

"Just words, Jen, made up by geeks." Ethan hugged her, resting his chin on the top of her head.

"I want to go home." Suddenly she was crying hard and clinging to him. He picked her up and carried her from the building. Ignoring the whispers and glances, he sat against the wall in the back with her in his lap.

"No, cry if you need to." He pulled her closer when she began to rise.

"I'm being stupid, you lost more than me."

"No, we both lost everything."

She began crying again, deep wracking sobs that shook her body. He said nothing, just stroked her head and back. Eventually, she realized he cried too and gripped him tighter.

Attending the King

Matt handed her a bale of cloth wrapped in burlap and tied with string. She placed it atop the other bales and tied it down. Beneath the bales, twenty-five shrunken daggers, three cheap swords, and assorted metal tools sat atop an assortment of shrunken scraps of cloth, all of which had been offered in trade to attend the fights. Empty space waited in the prow for the animals they'd bought and received as payment. The raw, unworked metal they'd bought they would return for. The quality of the offered goods was so low they'd decided their funds were better spent on supplies. With wizards to enlarge and shrink it would be easier and less expensive to form their own tools and weapons.

"Joash delivered a note from Maria. She'll meet you at the mouth of the river. You'll be home by tomorrow."

Jen took the last bale and stacked it with the others. "You're sure you and Jamal will be okay here?"

"If not, my bird will come get you. Don't worry about us. Get home safe. We'll line up a spot for our circus and see about renting a bigger boat to get our loot home. It's such a pain in the ass we can't just shrink things openly."

Gawain turned to the shore and perked his ears.

"Jamal must be coming," Matt said and peered over his shoulder.

The jingle of mail and men shouting, "Make way!" floated over the water.

Jen jumped to the dock and stood beside Matt, knowing whoever came, came for them. The surrounding citizens knew it too and disappeared onto their ships or into the nearby buildings although a few braver or more curious souls lingered.

Twelve men wearing red tabards and carting lances surrounded four mailed knights astride horses. Two of the knights dismounted and laid their helms over leather protuberances on their saddles clearly made for that purpose. Neither grabbed their swords or shields. They talked quietly for a minute with the other two knights, then both approached.

"Sir Dante." Jen inclined her head.

"Lady Frey— "

"The king demands." The other knight stopped speaking and let out a sharp oof as Dante elbowed him in the side.

"The king requests the honor of your presence and sent us to escort you to him," Dante said, giving his companion a pointed look.

"Just me or my companions?"

"All are invited to attend the king, my lady."

"Some of my companions aren't here."

"Are they expected back?"

"By noon. We'd planned to leave today."

Matt stepped forward. "If we're going to visit the king, we'll need to arrange guards for our goods."

Dante turned and snapped his fingers. One of the lance-carrying men ran up and bowed. "Take two men and guard this boat until Lady Frey returns." Dante indicated Jen with his chin, and the man bowed again.

"Shall we wait at the inn?" Dante offered her his arm.

Jen laid her hand lightly on his forearm and stepped forward. "How long will this take?"

Dante appeared startled as if it had never occurred to him to wonder.

It probably hadn't, she thought wryly. His king commanded, and he did it.

"I ask because arrangements must be made for Gawain." She pointed at the wolf.

"You can tie him to the dock here, and my men can see he has food and drink."

"He'll accept nothing from another's hand," Matt said and scratched behind the wolf's ears, earning a tail wag.

Dante shrugged, clearly uninterested in the wolf's fate. "Bring him then; he can wait outside."

Jen allowed Dante to lead her to a nearby inn. The patrons quieted when they entered and stared surreptitiously. The odor of rotten fish and feces made her gag. Both hands over her mouth, she pretended to cough to cover it,

"You fight well. Have you been in many battles?"

Jen laughed, then frowned thoughtfully. She dropped her hands and tried to breathe through her mouth. "I'm not sure how to answer that. As a paladin, I've been in many. As myself, only these here." She ignored his confused, questioning glance. "How about you?"

"A fair amount. For five years I battled the Goths with the late king in Germania before King Childebert ascended the throne. I was with him when he went to rescue Princess Chrotilda, his sister in Hispainia. We joined his brother King Clotaire and besieged Zaragoza. Before that, as a squire, I attended my lord at the battle of Gottar with the Danes. The men there are tall and strong. They carry giant axes and swing as if cutting wood. Never have I seen such a magnificent sword as yours though. May I see it?"

Jen lay her sword on the table. Candlelight flickered over the silver runes embedded in the silver blade and glittered on the diamonds in the hilt and crosspiece.

"Truly beautiful. Wherever did you get her?"

"A gift. I don't know who made it."

Dante grinned at her. "What did you do to deserve such a magnificent gift?"

"I survived."

He leaned back and nodded slowly. "Yes, sometimes that's a very difficult thing to do. My court is abuzz with speculation about your court. Does your king rule a large kingdom?" He gestured about the room with a proud smile on his face. "Do you have magnificent cities like this?"

"Not large, but surely magnificent."

"Your king must be an amazing warrior."

Jen laughed, tried to stop and couldn't. She waved her hands apologetically and wiped the tears of laughter from her cheeks. "Jon is, without a doubt, the best warrior on Earth," she finally gasped out.

"Why is that funny?" Dante frowned, appearing insulted.

Jen shrugged apologetically. "Too hard to explain. Jon is a good king."

"Is he a relative?"

"Just a friend. Are you related to your king?"

"A distant cousin so far back it hardly counts," he said it airily but beamed proudly.

One of the pikemen entered and bowed. "My lord, the others have arrived, except for one of the Nubians. Sir Homes informed us Sir Lance won't return until nightfall."

Dante rose and offered her a hand to stand. "Can you ride, my lady?"

"I have a marvelous war horse at home. We plan to bring them here and offer a show."

"Yes, I'd heard of the show and am intrigued. I hadn't heard you were to be in it though."

"Will we need royal permission?"

Dante shrugged. "Ii isn't my place to say. It's an unusual situation. A lady generally doesn't perform."

"We're in an unusual situation." She stopped speaking as they exited.

Matt, Jamal, and Brandon held rope halters on the sorriest looking horses she'd ever seen. All the horses she'd seen so far had been smaller than those she was used to, but these three were barely larger than ponies. Sway-backed and knock-kneed, their ribs showed through their dusty coats. Ethan stood to the right of the door, invisible to all except them. He carried a dagger and looked pissed.

The pikemen surrounded the three knights, their attention riveted to Brandon who wore his protection armor.

"The king awaits," Dante said happily as if he couldn't sense the tension.

Maybe he can't, Jen thought, staring after him as one of the pikemen gave him a boost to his charger's back. Maybe this was his usual state, dealing with unhappy, scared people. The knight's chargers jittered and sidestepped, clearly uneasy from Gawain's presence at the rear. The three new nags stood placidly, controlled by Jamal's magic.

"These horses are pathetic. I feel like I should carry it instead," Jamal said and rubbed the brown nose of his steed.

Hands on his hips, Brandon surveyed his offered mount. "Is this horse fit enough to carry me?"

Jamal left his horse and ran a hand along the flank and forelock of Brandon's mount. "Old and tired, but sound enough. I wish Lou was here; he could fix him right up."

Heaving a heavy sigh, Brandon mounted without assistance. Jen accepted the hand Jamal offered and swung up behind him. Matt awkwardly scrambled onto his horse.

The populous made way, bowing as they passed.

Grander stone homes replaced the low wooden shacks of the docks as they rode through the city. Jen hadn't been to this section of the city yet. Two and three-story homes faced narrow cobbled streets. Red tile roofs topped rough-cut stone walls. The narrow windows closed with wooden shutters on the bottom levels and latticed glass windows on the top. If you ignored the stench it might even be considered quaint, Jen thought and snorted as she turned her gaze from a fly covered pile of refuse.

The farther east they traveled, homes became

shorter and squatter and stood on their own plots of land, boosting wooden outbuildings.

"Is that Rue De Montmorency?" Brandon asked, sounding surprised. He paused before a gray stone building and admired it.

"No, a predecessor perhaps. It's nowhere near as large." Matt turned to the nearest knight.

"Excuse me, sir, but that building— what is it called?" Matt gestured to the three-story stone building with the rounded roofs and stone gables. Decorative carved rock trim adorned the windows and doors.

"Saint Peter's Cathedral and the Priory of Saint Michael. The king has ordered a new construction for the church so the good fathers can contemplate and pray in peace."

"It's beautiful," Jen said.

"Do you have such in your city?"

"No churches… not yet, anyway."

The knight turned and pulled away, his shoulders tight and body ridged.

"Thinks we're heathens and bound for hell," Brandon said with a breath of laughter in his voice.

"Wait until he really knows us," Matt said sourly. "These people will hate us with a fanatical hatred."

"It is what is. I for one am not going to pretend what I'm not." Jen nodded at the woman in the street curtsying deeply as the knights passed. A man grabbed her arm and yanked her away. "No way are women going back to that."

Eight men wearing red tabards and carrying swords stood before a wooden gate set into a wooden palisade. Sharpened stakes set at angles stuck from a dirt berm before the wall. Behind it, a red tiled roof peeked from towering pines. Elms and maples lined the cobblestone street leading to the castle. Jen eyed the stone crenulations topping two stories of dark-gray stone dotted with thin slitted windows, her gaze lingering on the armed men who paced a narrow path atop it. Wider windows covered the side of the third story topped with the red tile roof.

Two boys followed a flock of mixed color sheep across the short-cropped grass beside the castle. Men and woman bustled about busily. Most paused to stare after them.

Wide, shallow steps led to the wooden doors held open by two men in gray tunics. An older man with a gray beard and hunched back waited with a group of boys before the wide, stone steps. The pikemen who'd escorted them lined the stairs as the boys helped the knights dismount and took their horses.

Ethan glided up the stairs and disappeared inside. Jen's gaze traveled the armed men waiting on the stairs. She and Brandon had stepped forward, placing themselves between the armed men and Matt and Jamal by instinct. Her job as a tank was to protect her group, and she felt the need to protect them in her soul.

The sensation disconcerted her. The lightning

had changed them more than she'd thought. In the past, she'd have stepped back and let one of the men speak for her, or Sam. Now, it was all she could do to not summon her sword into her hand.

The four knights joined them and escorted them up the stairs. The pikemen bowed as they passed into the hall.

Right inside the doorway, a long, narrow, wooden table ran down the center aisle of a brightly lit room stretching the length of the castle. Wax-caked, wooden chandeliers lit with hundreds of candles dangled above the table. Chains connected to the lights dangling from the balcony's overhead, allowing the light fixtures to be lowered. Torches flickered every few feet along the walls about four feet over the heads of the men and woman crowded against them.

Bowmen lined the balcony, their faces hidden in shadow. No candles or torches lined the four-foot-wide balcony that encircled the main hall. Metal helms and arrows glinted in the dim light.

Jammed together behind the table, a crowd of richly dressed people spoke in hushed tones. The room smelled of smoke, sweat, and burnt meat, *but it was better than sewer and turnips,* Jen thought as she led the way inside.

Armed men lined the closest side of the table, leaving a wide path leading to a dais on which a man with long, graying hair and a long beard sat on a tall, iron chair. He wore discolored chainmail over a dark-blue tunic with a sword resting beside his right knee. A gold crown with five points and gems the size of ping-pong balls rested atop his graying hair. A man wearing a red robe and white conical hat stood beside him. Before him, one step down, two women and Mondred sat in smaller, less fancy, wooden chairs.

Tapestries, depicting men on horseback in battle, hung on the wall behind the throne.

A woman entered from a hidden door behind the tapestries and stood behind the king. Elaborately braided, graying black hair held back by a wide, gold circlet, framed a wrinkled face. She wore a gown of dark blue cinched at the waist with gold chains. The crowd bowed, the front row dropping to one knee.

"Rise," the woman said, her voice carrying into the stillness.

The kneelers rose. Soft tittering laughter and oohs and ahhs followed Jen and her companions as they paced down the aisle between armed men and the wooden table to a cleared area before the stone steps. Brandon's metal-shod feet clanked against the rock floor. Her heels clacked with a ringing ting. She didn't know what her armor was made of, but it didn't sound like metal.

The knights accompanying them dropped to one knee and bowed.

"Rise." The king gestured with a be-ringed hand.

The knights rose and stepped back, leather-booted feet shuffling on the rock floor.

"You don't bow to a king?" the king asked.

The crowd inhaled. Jen imagined she could feel them holding their breath.

"We bow to no man," Brandon said. His voice echoed in the room.

Fair Warning

Jen bit back her smile, Brandon had put will behind his words to ensure all could hear him.

Gnarled fingers drummed against the arm of the gilded chair.

The man beside the king stepped forward. "Lady Frey." He held out his hand as if he expected her to take it— or kiss it. "The church welcomes you. We've heard you've been a neglectful daughter, but forgiveness is yours. You may kiss my ring."

"No, thank you. I don't seek forgiveness, and I'm not a member of your church."

The crowd gasped and murmured. Above them, the bowmen rustled and whispered.

"As a Catholic, you *are* a member of the church and subject to its laws. I can order you confined for your insolence."

"I renounce the church. You have no authority over me. You or any man. *I* am a free woman."

"Bishop," the king said softly.

The bishop stepped back, his face red and hands clenched.

The king appeared to take no notice. He said, "You're strangers here so allowances will be made and time given to accustom yourselves to us. We've been told you're shipwrecked far from your homeland."

"Galahad," Jen murmured, disappointed he'd betrayed her trust. She wanted to smack herself for trusting because of his name.

"Your prowess as knights is undeniable and your weaponry fierce, yet you buy simple daggers in quantity. You carry blades that any knight would envy, yet there are few of you and your boat, although finely crafted, small."

The king leaned back in his chair and examined them. "Only two of your legendary weapons remain?"

Brandon glanced at her and shrugged.

"There are only three such swords in the world. That we know of anyway," Jen said. For all she knew, the missing passengers of flight Four Fourteen had fallen into the portal and emerged on the other side of the Earth, including the magic wielders. It comforted her to think of them alive somewhere.

Again, the king examined them. Behind them,

the crowd stirred and murmured.

"Let us speak frankly. You are few and far from your home. I would welcome you to my army, grant you lands, and reward you well for your service."

"Thank you, but we have a king."

"Your King Arthur would be welcome as an ally."

"If you wish to deal with our king, you'd need to speak to him directly, but I can promise you, we will never be a vassal to any man," Brandon said.

"Bold words. Can you afford to be so bold with so few of you? As I understand it, one ship survived the storm. I respect that you stand by your king, yet you travel here to seek supplies and maybe recruit more men?" He lifted an eyebrow.

"No. We seek supplies, but not men."

"All kings seek out knights and soldiers. Else their kingdoms can fall to another. And, you, no matter how skilled a knight or good the weapon, are only two," King Childebert said as he steepled his fingers and smiled at them.

Mondred rose from his seat before the king. "Take them and be done with it. As you say, they are only two. No matter how strong or skilled, we are many and stronger."

"Sit!" the king barked.

Mondred sat and glared.

"My son is ambitious but lacks wisdom. I would that you joined me as willing allies."

Jen stepped forward and rose her empty

hands. "Your Majesty, we are not two, and while it's true we have fewer men, we are far stronger. Jonathan Arthur is not a greedy man. We are content in our kingdom, following our ways."

Brandon pulled her back. "If you attack us here, we'll kill everyone in this room, starting with you."

Jen's glance flicked to Ethan who stood with his dagger in hand behind the bishop. Ethan could kill both men in seconds. He smiled at her, and her heart leaped. She smiled back, then cleared her throat and looked away. She was a fool, easily distracted by daydreams. His smile meant nothing. Angry with herself, she glared at the king.

"You threaten the king? The bishop sounded outraged and horrified.

Brandon spoke, the sound fluttering the candles. "Not a threat, the truth."

Matt stepped forward. "We're not like you. We believe all men and women are equal. There will be no special treatment for nobles or bishops or anyone at all. If you raise a hand to us, or order it done, we'll fight back."

"Why fight and die when you can join us and live well in peace?"

Matt sighed. "You think your knights can overpower us, they can't. I'm not bragging, just stating a fact."

Mondred stood and faced his father. "Father, there are only two. Their archer doesn't even have an arrow."

Brandon snickered. "Shoot me. Have your best archer shoot me." He placed his helm at his feet.

The crowd muttered, the rustling of their clothing sounding like bat wings.

"Percival, stand forward!" Mondred called. He lowered his voice and spoke to Brandon. "You're a fool. Your archer isn't the only good shot. Percival can shoot an apple from a tree at a hundred paces. He'll shot your eye out before you can blink." His covetous gaze traveled Brandon's armor. "Then your sword will be mine."

On the balcony, a man stepped forward with an arrow knocked. "My liege?"

"Shoot him." The king waved his hand.

"A killing blow, my liege?"

"Yes!" Mondred snapped.

The sharp twang of an arrow was followed immediately by the sound of metal crashing. Brandon handed the arrow he'd plucked from the air to Jamal. The spectators exclaimed loudly. Brandon replaced his helm and turned his back on Percival.

"There, now he has an arrow, although he won't need one with me here. You can try again, a back shot if you like. Jamal could use another souvenir." Brandon shrugged and turned further to face the crowd. "If I were you, I'd leave before real violence breaks out."

The crowd stirred uneasily.

The twang of an arrow leaving the string

ended in a plink as it hit Brandon's back and tumbled broken to the floor.

"Didn't even feel it," Brandon said as he turned back to the king.

"Impressive armor and speed of hand, but your comrades are unarmed." Mondred waved his hand, and the archers stepped forward.

Gawain hunkered and growled, raising his ruff and baring his teeth. Blue eyes focused on the king, and the growl rose in pitch.

"No, my comrades appear unarmed, there's a difference. And I assure you, if you shoot one of them, I won't stand idly by."

"Enough," the king said and clapped his hands once sharply. "We have no intention of making enemies of our future allies. Let us be friends."

He waved his hand, and the archers stepped back. He rose. The crowd bowed, the first row kneeling.

"Come, we'll retire to my chambers where a meal awaits and speak as friends."

Those on the dais followed them behind the tapestry through an arched doorway and up a steep flight of stairs. In the room at the top, wide windows overlooked a courtyard filled with mulched flower beds and small shrubs. Jen stopped at the window to gaze out.

"The queen's garden," the king said as he paused beside her. "We hear you have an interest in botanical things." He clapped sharply, and a man in a black tunic entered, carrying a large basket. "Cuttings and seeds from her garden."

"Thank you, that's very kind." Jen took the basket and stood awkwardly. "We have no gifts fit for a king."

Jamal offered his bow. "You may have this. The wood is supple and strong with no weak spots."

"The carving is marvelous." The king held the bow to the light and admired the feathered pattern. "Your craftsmen are skilled. Where do you hail from?"

"I'm from America, but I think you mean where is our kingdom now?"

The king nodded and gestured to the table. Silver cups filled with wine sat beside thin wooden plates. Bowls of vegetables and bread covered the table. Small bowls of salt sat beside each plate. A man entered, carrying a platter of roast meat and set it on the table, then bowed and retreated.

"You've heard of our fondness for vegetables, I see," Jen said as she sat on a low stool. "You must have spoken with Sir Galahad, so you know we come from Camelot."

"Yes, we've spoken." The king waved Jamal to a seat. "And yes, I meant in what country does Camelot reside."

"I believe you'd call it Britannica," Matt said. "We call it Great Britain or England."

The king leaned back in his seat, looking pleased. "Ahh, not far at all and barely populated.

I haven't been in ages. Quite an uncivilized place with not much anyone would want."

"We're content there," Matt assured him. "We'd planned to return here in a month or so and hold a show to raise money to buy supplies, but we have no wish to make enemies. We can go somewhere else if you like."

"By all means, return. We welcome trade. Follow our laws, and there will be no problems."

"We have every intention of being law-abiding visitors, but your laws and customs are strange to us."

"They need a native guide, my lord." The woman who'd stood behind the king said.

"Ahh, how remiss of me. My wife, Ultragotha."

Jen bit back her laugh at the queen's name. The queen's attire could be mistaken for modern goth wear. Ethan clapped a hand to his mouth, his eyes sparkling at her, and she had to pretend a coughing fit to cover her mirth.

Childebert introduced his two daughters and sipped his wine. As if it were a signal those gathered began to eat. "My lady is correct. We shall have one of our good knights accompany you."

"Maybe a visit to Camelot could be arranged?" Ultragotha asked.

Brandon nodded and reached for the rolls as he spoke. "All are welcome, but while there, our laws are to be followed. Everyone there is treated equally. No one bows or makes way. Insults and violence are forbidden. Threats or intimidation aren't allowed. No man may enter another's home unless invited, including the king.

"There are exceptions, if you're a criminal for instance, and wanted for questioning, a police officer would come to retrieve you. They can enter unbidden but must treat you with respect."

The king rose an eyebrow. "And if the criminal refuses to go?"

"We make them." Matt shrugged. "Our laws protect those accused of crimes until they're proven guilty. Here, if a woman is pawed by a man in a tavern it isn't a crime. There it is and punished. Our women are always treated with respect. They can dress as they wish, hold jobs, and chose who to marry."

"Sounds like anarchy," Mondred said sourly.

"We like it." Matt helped himself to a slice of turnip and hunk of meat.

"And your priests don't mind there are no churches?"

"We only have one priest and not the type you have," Brandon said, making Jen laugh.

Behind the king, Ethen grinned and turned away. Jen pulled her eyes away from him and turned to her plate.

"Anyone who wishes could build a church, but we've been busy erecting homes. We've only recently arrived," Matt said.

"How recently?" Ultragotha asked.

"Seventy-two days."

"And already you venture from the land you claim?"

"We needed supplies."

"And yet you didn't come here and try to take Paris for your own."

"And we never will. We're not interested in conquest, but we will defend ourselves. We're perfectly willing to work for money to buy what we need. We aren't thieves."

"Ahh" – the king turned to Brandon—"I could offer you gold, Sir Homes. Our northern border is hard pressed. I'll give you a thousand men to lead and a gold for each. The Goths have taken the duchy of De Lion and press forward. If you successfully recapture it. I'll triple the gold."

"It's a generous offer, but I'm too new to this area to choose sides. Besides, my king might need me."

"Will your king attend your show?" Ultragotha asked.

Brandon shrugged. "No idea; we haven't spoken to him about it."

"So, he might forbid it?"

"He could ask us not to, but we're free people, he can't forbid it. We go where we will."

"He sounds powerless," Mondred said.

"He isn't." Matt shrugged and leaned back in his seat. "Our ways are different is all. We have law we all follow. We can go wherever we want to, whenever we want to. The people of Camelot choose what they'll do with their time."

Ultragotha refilled the king's cup and offered more to Matt who declined as she asked, "But, how does he command if you all do whatever you like?"

When we fight, we listen to our leaders. We listen to our bosses. Say for instance I worked as a cook. I would agree to come in and cook for certain hours, and you would pay me. If the quality of my food lacked, you would fire me. If I thought you were a lousy boss, I could quit and look elsewhere for a job. If I stole food, you could have me arrested; if you stole wages, I could have you arrested." Matt shrugged. "It's pretty simple actually if everyone does what they say they will."

"But how can the king count on your support?" Mondred asked.

"We are his knights and made a vow to protect the people of Camelot and serve him as king."

"So, your word is your bond?"

"Yes."

"And visitors are welcome in Camelot?"

"Yes."

The king leaned back and rubbed his chin.

Matt laid his two-pronged silver fork on the tabletop. "We should warn you, we aren't at all like you. We're so different that your priests would call us heretics or worse."

"Because you have druids?" A half-smile on his face, the king rose an eyebrow.

Matt hesitated then squared his shoulders.

Before he could speak, Brandon did.

"Let's not beat around the bush here," Brandon said. "We aren't devil-worshiping demons. But we do have magic."

Ultragotha laid her goblet back on the surface of the table and stared with wide eyes. "You admit to being witches?"

"No. I admit I have magic. By your definition, a witch has made a deal with the devil for power of some sort. We've made no deals."

"Nonsense," Mondred said.

Matt held up his hand and Flynn appeared.

Ultragotha exclaimed and jumped to her feet.

Mondred rose slowly. "What devilishness is this?"

Flynn flew to the ceiling, leaving a trail of sparks behind, and perched on a crossbeam.

"What is he?" The king stared upwards, then turned to his wife. "Calm yourself, woman. You've seen rabbits pulled from hats before."

"Flynn is a firebird and my companion."

"Where did you get him?"

"He was a gift."

"A gift," the king repeated thoughtfully and turned to examine Matt. "You've received many impressive gifts."

Matt shrugged.

Childebert rapped his knuckles on the table. "Leave us."

Without complaint, those eating rose and left the room. Mondred paused at the door, then continued when his father flicked his fingers at him.

"So, you're sorcerers with enchanted armor and swords."

"We have magic. It isn't evil, and neither are we."

"My church will not agree. Claiming magic is dangerous." The king leaned forward, bracing his hands on the table top. "The might of the church is great. You doom yourselves with this. Maybe where you're from such isn't true, but here… having a druid would eventually bring the attention of the church to you. Some of my citizens still practice the old ways but know better than to do so in public."

"We're allowed freedom of religion."

The king waved his hand irritably. "Yes, yes, but you're here now, with what? A hundred men? The church can raise an army of a hundred thousand, and it will, to destroy a nest of sorcerers."

"Then they'll die."

Childebert pressed his lips together and rubbed the bridge of his nose. "If you won't see reason and repent this claim, then you're doomed."

"Your Majesty, we cannot be different than we are. Anyone traveling to Camelot will see our differences. For your sake, don't attack us."

"The church will demand it."

Matt stood and conjured his wand. A flick of his fingers placed an explosive rune in the fireplace, another flick detonated it. The building rumbled, and a crack appeared in the wall. Dust billowed, leaving the odor of scorched stone in the air.

Guards rushed into the room with drawn swords.

"Out!" the king bellowed. Pale of face, he stood and backed from Matt.

The guards bowed and walked backward from the room.

"That was the weakest explosive rune I have." Matt held up his hand, and Flynn hovered over him, dropping a small glowing orange marble into his hand. He turned and threw it into the fireplace. Smoke and flame leaped, catching the wooden floor. He waved his hand, and the fire disappeared as if it never was, leaving a black scorch mark on the floor and a smoky haze in the air. Another flick of his fingers placed a rune on the floor behind the king. He placed another at his feet and stepped on it.

"As you can see," he said, making the king whirl to face him. "Our magic is very strong."

The king crossed himself. "A nest of demons."

"No, just men and woman with magic."

"Go and never return. I'll be cursed for a coward for letting the devil's spawn leave, but I see you're powerful. Stay on your isle and leave men alone." The king's hand trembled when he pointed to the door. "Guards!"

The same two guards entered nervously.

"Escort them outside and let them leave.

"Well, that went well," Ethan whispered in Jen's ear, making her laugh.

The king glared.

Matt sent Flynn away. The bird disappeared, and the king flinched.

Two quiet guards escorted them downstairs and through the hushed crowd. Outside the door, people crossed the grounds and walked to their destinations, not paying any particular attention to them.

Jen paused and stared back at the castle. Sun glare hid Childebert's expression as he peered down at them from the window. She whistled and summoned Gallant. Beside her, Brandon called Ed. Gallant's silver hooves flashed in the sunlight as he reared. With a thought, she cast Sword-of-Truth and held the glowing blue blade aloft.

Jamal vaulted to Gallant's back behind her. She pointed her sword at the figure in the window then sheathed it, and whirled, galloping down the cobbled road. Ed, carrying Matt and Brandon followed, his hooves like thunder on the rocks.

Once out of sight of the castle she slowed, and they made their way to the docks. The entire way there, people bowed and scraped, their gazes and awed exclamations following the two war horses. Bigger, than any horse they'd seen thus far, and glowing with health, the horses attracted quite a bit of attention.

The pikemen left to guard the boat bowed at their approach. They crossed themselves and ran when the horses turned to mist.

"Since we aren't being subtle anymore, how about Brandon and I go back for the rest of our gear?" Matt turned to the boat and twitched his fingers. The stacked bales of clothes shrunk. He twitched them again until they were tiny, inch-long bales. Each figure twitch had caused the onlookers to exclaim. Men hollered to each other and those in the boats closest began to gather on the dock.

"Yes, get every animal we can fit." Jen picked up the scattered bales and stuffed them into a sack containing shrunken daggers.

Brandon resummoned Ed, causing more exclamations and a renewed surge of movement and he and Matt headed to the warehouse.

"This is reckless." Jamal shaded his eyes and stared after them. "Jon's going to have a fit."

Jen shrugged. "Yes, but it's the truth. Let them see and know we're strong before coming and attacking us. We can't change their ideology, but we can warn them."

"Yeah, the fucking church will come though, and we'll have to kill them."

"Maybe they'll be smart. See our defenses and go?"

"Ha!"

Jen grimaced ruefully at Jamal. "It's not like we could keep it a secret. Camelot screams magic."

"I'm not disagreeing, but…"

Jen glanced at Ethan who remained invisible. A black shadow of his former self, he sat on the edge of the dock dangling his legs over the water. He shrugged and became visible. A woman screamed, and man exclaimed. He didn't turn to look.

"Matt was right to warn the king. I feel bad for him. He knows we're his doom one way or another."

Ethan jumped to his feet as the clatter of running hooves approached. The boat rocked as he landed in it and disappeared.

A red-faced knight halted on the edge of the dock. His horse blew hard beneath him. "The king has ordered two of his knights to accompany you and asks you to delay so they might follow. He sends a message for King Jon or, err, Arthur, and wishes you to deliver it." The man held out a scroll coated in wax tied with a gold cord and sealed with an imprint of a lion in red wax.

Jamal accepted it and tucked it beneath his sweatshirt.

"We'll wait and depart tomorrow at dawn."

The delivery man nodded and galloped away, peering over his shoulder as he turned the corner.

"A trap?" Jamal asked as he turned to the boat.

Ethan became visible. "What can they do?"

Jamal grimaced. "Die horribly."

Return To Camelot

A grinning Galahad joined them two hours later. His grin faded when Jen glared at him.

"Are you unhappy I'm to accompany you?"

"I'm unhappy you reported a private conversation. You're a spy."

"Childebert is my king and asked what we spoke of. Was it supposed to be secret? I won't plot behind my king's back. Would you not do the same if your king asks what we spoke of?"

Lips pursed, Jen nodded slowly and offered her hand. "Yes."

He took it and kissed it, making Jen blush. "You were supposed to shake it."

"I prefer our custom." He kissed her hand again.

"Is this all your bringing?" Jamal eyed Galahad dubiously.

"No. My household is packing. I quite look forward to this. The king is supplying fine accommodations. I'm instructed to make friends and report everything I see."

"No one will believe you," Jamal muttered, then louder. "I hope you have a boat. Ours will be full of livestock."

"Yes. The king has ordered a boat to be stocked with goods he believes I can use as trade for food and accommodations. I've been ordered to be generous." He leaned forward, lowered his voice and winked at Jen. "I believe he wishes to give gifts to your king without seeming to.

"You're the sacrificial goat," Ethen said becoming visible behind him.

Galahad whirled.

"Did he tell you your church will likely vilify us?"

"I've been ordered to observe and report, that's all."

"Will reporting things they don't wish to hear get you killed?"

"If so, it's my sire's privilege."

Ethan shrugged.

"You could stay in Camelot. If he'll kill you for reporting, stay with us," Jen said.

Ethan frowned at her and turned away.

Galahad smiled and shrugged slightly. "Would you desert your king as easily as that?"

Jen sighed.

"His choice, Jen." Ethan jumped into the boat

and hugged her. She hugged him back, wanting to press her lips to his neck. For a moment, she let herself enjoy his embrace, imagining it was personal before forcing herself back to reality.

Tromping feet and loud shouts of, 'Way, make way,' echoed over the water.

A boy of about eight with blond hair and an urchins grin darted up to Galahad. "My lord, my mother asks if you'll want the bed and if so who shall fetch it?"

"Tell her yes and send Royce to hire a wagon." Galahad drew a coin from his purse and handed it to the boy.

"Your son?" Jamal asked.

"My youngest squire. I am unwed as of yet." He winked at Jen again, making her blush. "This is Fredrick. I acquired he and his mother in the siege of Zaragoza." He ruffled the boy's hair and the child's grin widen.

"He's a slave," Jen said appalled.

"My servant, who one day, if he works hard, could become a knight."

"But he can't leave and do something else?"

"Like what?" Galahad frowned at her, then the boy.

Jamal held his hand out to Fredrick.

"You shake it," Galahad, whispered loudly when Fredrick drew back with a grimace.

He showed the boy, who copied him hesitantly. Men wearing the king's livery passed in the street leading ponies pulling loaded wagons.

They headed to a nearby dock and began loading a sailboat.

Jamal turned to Jen. "Leave it alone, Jen, their ways are different." Then he turned back to Galahad. "On our land, he'll be a free person able to choose who he serves. His mother also. No one is forced to do anything they don't wish too."

"Good Lord, your city must be filthy." Galahad sounded horrified. "Who'd choose to clean night-soil?"

Jen giggled.

Jamal shrugged. "Generally, we clean our own messes, but I suppose you could pay someone to do it for you. Oh, we also have a rule that all children under thirteen, who live in town, must attend our school."

"Then Fredrick shall attend."

Fredrick didn't look at all happy about that. Galahad grabbed his arm to stop him from darting away.

"What type of school is it?"

"We'll teach him to read, write, and do math. The druids, rangers and our shaman teach woodcraft. I think he'll like it. If your visit is short, he needn't go."

"I've been ordered to stay until summer and follow your laws." Galahad released Fredrick. "Tell your mother to ensure you have enough clean clothing and shoes that fit." He handed the boy another coin. "If there's time before we go, get yourself a treat." He gave the child a penny and pushed him away.

"How many squires do you have?" Jen asked.

"Just the two. Royce is my sister's son. He's sixteen and full of himself, eager to win his spurs. He nearly swooned with excitement when I told him we'd be accompanying you. Would you care to go to the inn for dinner?"

"Nope," Ethan said before she could reply. "We're all staying right here tonight.

Galahad bowed. "Very well. I'll join you in the morn. You're welcome to travel aboard my ship if you wish, or store some of your gear."

"Thanks, we're good." Ethan waved him away.

Galahad bowed again and strode off, chainmail clinking, and sheathed sword slapping his thigh.

Jen huddled beside the unhappy goats. Rain sleeted down in sharp stinging pellets further darkening the dull gray of the dawn sky. Chickens stacked in flimsy wooden cages in the rear of the boat sputtered and cawed. They'd removed the middle seat to make room for four sheep and three goats. Three cats cowered under the seat Jen sat on. Jamal sat between her and Brandon and kept all the animals calm and stationary.

Matt and Ethan shared the second seat. A mound of ducks and geese tied by their feet and covered with canvas muttered irritably in the prow.

Kuan and Maria flew in lazy circles over the mouth of the river, both diving and transforming into dolphins when their boat appeared.

Jen wondered what the men on the boat following thought or if they'd even noticed through the sleeting rain. Her boat picked up speed as the druids directed the water flow. Three-foot waves rippled the surface of the sea, but they floated on smooth ocean with just a gentle ripple showing the water sped against the tide.

Jen peered over her shoulder, the sailboat followed and gained until it floated a car-length behind. Men lined the rail and stared into the sea uneasily as the ships traveled without sail or oars against the tide on the smooth ocean.

The ship from Paris followed so closely she heard the sailors exclaim when Maria and Kuan leaped from the water as fish, became birds, and soared to a much-changed port.

No longer a low rock wave break, now a twenty-foot-wide rock road encircled the beach with only a small gap allowing access to the ocean. A wooden grate covered the gap flanked on each side by stone buttresses. A wooden rail extended the entire length of the shore side. On the ocean side, stone piers jutted into the water. By the fineness of the construction, Jen knew Rob had helped craft it.

Druids could form rock and soil crudely, but Wizards could shrink rocks and dead wood to work with it then dispel and enlarge it. Building methods were constantly being refined and reworked as they tried to figure out the best methods for their building projects. It had grown into a favorite past time. Ethan had worked hard to get the best deals he could on wood and stone working tools. Jen hefted the small bag of shrunken chisels and hammers and tucked it into her jeans pocket, then resumed her righteous armor.

Maria dove and landed, becoming a woman and waved as Jen and Brandon rowed them to the pier.

Jen leapt to her, traveling the thirty-feet in a blink of an eye and gave her a hard hug. "You've been busy." God, it's good to see you. We brought seeds, cuttings, and vegetables. How's everyone?"

"Good, some minor accidents and one death. Fred fell from a walkway atop Camelot while fitting a new chimney, but Tony fixed it right up." She nodded toward the sailboat hanging back. "You brought guests."

"Direct from Paris and wearing the latest fashions."

Maria snorted. "We moved Camelot. It was the coolest thing I ever saw. The trees flowed through the ground and settled into their new home. I wish you could've seen it."

"Where'd you move it to? This could be awkward if the city moves all the time."

Maria laughed and linked arms with her, leading her down the rock quay. "We decided it was too close. See those tall trees there?" She pointed. "That's it. We built a hill and a castle wall and expanded it. The hardest part was getting the stone here. We didn't want to take too much from the ground and get below sea level."

"How'd you do it?"

"Blasted chunks from the cliffs to the north, then Rob shrunk them, and we brought them here where we formed them small, then he enlarged them. We made the ocean much deeper before our rock jetty to use the rock for that. We still have a lot left to build, but all the couples have their own places now with fireplaces and everything built right into the wall. We have two stone barrack type buildings for the single men. Kuan wants to finish the wall, encircle the entire castle, but that much rock will eat up the cliff, we need to go farther for it, so we put it on hold. We're building fast now using Rob's shrink and enlarge. He just shrinks the materials until we can build a small model home then dispels it on site."

Maria turned back and gazed out to sea. "If we had television and computers, this would be an awesome place to live."

"Don't forget fast food, candy, movies, and cell phones."

"And books. There's like nothing to do here except work."

"Well, I appreciate all your hard work; this is awesome." Jen waved at the docks and road disappearing into the trees lining the beach. "I especially like the beach umbrella trees."

Maria giggled. "Kuan worked on the castle while I did the houses and Cami laid out the town. Kuan is much more artistic than either of us. She put in roads with sanitation. The river is rerouted under us in a bunch of different branches now. If people come to live here, we'll be ready for them.

Cami soared over them and circled the sailboat before landing beside Jen and transforming back into a woman. "Welcome home." She gave her a hug and kissed her cheek. "Kuan is dying to show off the castle. Go hurry our guests up. They seem scared as shit of me. Didn't you warn them about us?"

"Sort of, it's a long story."

"Rob is arranging transport for everything. Tell them they can leave their gear and we'll bring it to the castle if they like."

Jen ran back to her ship where Jamal was handing Brandon animals to place on the stone dock. Brandon whistled to summon Ed and began hanging sacks on him. Jen summoned Gallant.

"You guys load up. I'll go talk to our guests." A simple leap brought her to the dock twenty-five feet away where the sailboat had come to rest.

Sword in hand, Galahad stared at her with a shocked expression.

"You're a fae?"

"I don't think so." She grinned and held out her hand. "Scared of me?"

He ignored her offered hand, clutching his

sword so hard his knuckles whitened. "Are you a devil— A demon?"

The sailors behind Galahad crossed themselves.

"I'm a woman, a paladin, and a knight of the Round Table. Welcome to Camelot."

Galahad glanced at her, then turned to Kuan who soared over them.

"That's Kuan, and he's a druid.

"A druid," Galahad repeated faintly. Kuan soared to the dock, dropping the last few yards to land on his human feet and rose his arms. The rain trickled to a halt, falling around the dock but not on it.

The sailors exclaimed and crossed themselves. Some began to pray while others exclaimed loudly.

Dante stepped up to the rail and bowed. "My lady, your beauty should have told me you were of the fair folk. Forgive me if I've offended."

Jen snorted and rolled her eyes. "I'm not. Offended or a fair folk," she clarified when he nervously stepped back. "Come meet our king as yours commands. Leave your luggage; my people will transport it for you."

Dante placed his hand on Galahad's shoulder as he hesitantly stepped forward.

"If we enter, may we leave again?" Dante asked suspiciously.

"Any may come and go freely. Our food won't entrap you, I swear it. Time will pass at the same rate, and you'll age. Am I forgetting anything?"

Galahad threw back his head and laughed. "Faint heart wins fair maiden not." So saying, he clambered over the side, landing hard on the stones. "Fredrick, Royce, attend!"

A boy of sixteen with jet-black hair and green eyes leaned over the rail. "Fredrick is sick, my lord."

"Heave him onto the dock. Oft times the first voyage will make one ill."

Royce disappeared back into the ship. Two men placed planks to the dock, which Dante descended, followed by three women and two boys. Two of the women appeared older, late fifties with gray hair covered by kerchiefs and stooped backs. The third was younger, large breasted and plump with fine, blond hair worn in a single, long braid. All three wore long tunics belted at the waist with rope and thick woven shawls. Despite the chill in the February air none wore shoes.

Royce appeared, carrying Fredrick who he dropped on the dock. Fredrick looked miserable, pale and shaky.

Jen crouched before him and felt his forehead, then stood and removed her armor with a thought. In her jeans pocket, she carried one of the green vials Kirk made. The group shuffled nervously, and the woman exclaimed.

She held it up to the light. "This is a healing potion. It does nothing except heal. It won't enslave him or change him in any way."

"May I see it?" Galahad held out a hand.

"Yes, but only the person who takes it from its creator can open it." Jen handed him the small, glass vial.

Galahad held it up to examine, running a finger across the silver scrollwork on the top before giving it back. She flicked it open with her thumb and knelt beside Fredrick again.

"Swallow this, and you'll be all better."

Fredrick looked to Galahad who nodded. The boy opened his mouth, closed his eyes, and scrunched up his face. Jen poured the liquid in.

"Tastes good," Fredrick said and jumped to his feet.

"How do you feel?" Galahad asked.

The boy grinned up at him. "Fine, better than normal actually. My knee doesn't hurt anymore." He lifted his tunic and held out his leg. "Hey, it's gone, and that was gonna be a great scar."

Galahad knelt and ran his hand over the boy's knee. "You cured it," he said awed. "I was worried rot had set in, but the wound is completely gone. Your healers make a wondrous potion."

"Kirk is a warlock, not a healer. The druids are healers but can only heal us."

"A warlock? Is that the same as a wizard?"

"No. But let's go to the castle so Kuan can release the rain."

Reminded Galahad and his party rose their eyes to the sky. Rain fell around the two boats, but none touched them, falling to the sides instead.

Rob appeared on the top of the path, then the beach, then the docks, flitting from rune-to-rune before appearing by her side and giving her a hug. "I'm luggage transport," he said cheerfully.

"Sir Galahad, Sir Dante, this is Sir Miller. He's a wizard."

"Call me Rob." Rob offered his hand.

"Galahad," Galahad said faintly as he shook the proffered hand.

"Did you bring us a Merlin too?" Rob asked and grinned.

"Kirk is Merlin."

Rob laughed. "Well, show me what you wish to bring ashore."

"Royce, Belgin, attend the knight."

One of the boys standing behind Dante reboarded the ship. The other boy bit his lip nervously. Both boys appeared to be in their mid-teens with light-brown hair, and freckles.

Rob slapped her shoulder and followed the boys. The rain slowed, becoming a drizzle.

Jen gestured the rest of them to the shore. Brandon joined her, leading Ed and Gallant. The geese and ducks hung from Gallant's saddle. The rest of the animals followed with Jamal trailing.

Matt carried the cages containing the chickens balanced on his floating disk. "Meet you there," he called and began placing runes, transporting instantly from one to the next.

Transported to a Tale

'I feel as if I've been transported to a tale," Dante said as Maria landed and held the drizzle off as they walked to the beach.

The druids took turns, leapfrogging along the path to supply clear weather as they walked.

"Us too sometimes. We weren't born like this," Jen said reassuringly.

At the top of the path, the party halted.

"Camelot," Galahad said awed.

Jen was awed too. Ethan took her hand and squeezed. The castle now sat about a mile and a half away atop a small hill. A twenty-foot-tall, turreted wall stood between them. Towering pine trees, bigger than any Jen had ever seen framed the opening of the wall. Two open, wooden lattice gates connected to the pine trees. Smoke rose intermittently along the wall.

"We built houses into the back of it," Maria said.

Jen was so busy gawking she hadn't seen her arrive.

"This will be the inner wall. The outer will join the docks."

"'Tis amazing," Galahad said.

Jen followed his gaze to Camelot. Distance blurred the detail, leaving the outline. Soft yellow light shone across the front of the building's main entrance. Flickering torches lit the balconies lining the front of the magnificent edifice and the path leading to the door.

The building appeared massive in the gloom. Round turrets jutted hundreds of yards into the sky. Angles and squares connected to curves and circles in a wild, beautiful mishmash. Ramps, stairs, and hanging pathways, grown from the trees themselves, connected the differing sections of the building. Flowering vines and smaller fruit trees framed open windows and doorways.

The party moved forward joined by the druids as the rain stopped. Ethan kept her hand in his, fluttering her stomach. She told herself it meant nothing, a friendly gesture he'd make to any of the women, but her heart wanted it to mean more.

"Are you a man?" Fredrick asked Kuan

"Sometimes, but sometimes I'm a bear." Kuan transformed again, standing on his hind legs then dropping to all fours and roaring.

Fredrick shrieked and ran.

Jen laughed, released Ethan's hand, and snatched him up. "Kuan is kind in all his forms. Only to our enemies is he fearsome."

"Can I touch him?"

"Ask him. He retains a man's understanding."

"May I touch you?"

The bear nodded.

Hesitantly, Fredrick reached out and stroked Kuan's head.

Kuan let him a moment then resumed his shape. "Sometimes, I'm a tree." He became a towering cedar with shaggy bark and drooping limbs.

Fredrick ran his hands along the rough bark. "He feels real."

Kuan became himself again. "It is real. My claws can shred, my wings fly."

"Can I learn to do that?"

"No, I'm afraid not. It isn't something you can learn; it's a gift."

Jen laughed at Fredrick's disappointed scowl.

Ethan ruffled his hair. "There's other things we can teach you, like how to make light and fire."

Fredrick brightened and darted ahead after Kuan who sprinted forward in his panther shape.

Jen took Ethan's arm. He smiled at her and tucked it close to his side, making her pulse pound.

"We don't allow hunting inside the walls," Maria said. "If you wish to hunt, leave the cleared area."

"How many of you are druids?" Dante asked.

"Three, but the rangers have pets inside the walls, and while they could resurrect them, it's a traumatic experience for the pet, so please don't injure animals inside the walls.

Dante paused mid-step and turned to her with his mouth hanging open. "You can raise the dead?"

The women crossed themselves and mumbled prayers.

"Our dead, yes."

"Holy Mary Mother of God." Galahad crossed himself and pulled out a rosary from under his tunic. "How is that possible? Even the fae can't raise the dead. Are you gods?"

"No. Men with gifts," Ethan said firmly.

"Does our king know of you?"

"We told him, not specifics, but he knows we have magic," Jen said.

"Magic is from the devil," one of the women said and fell to her knees. Eyes squeezed shut, she mumbled prayers.

Dante pulled the woman to her feet. "No. Magic is a force of nature. Before Christ, there were druids and gods threw lightning bolts. They walked among men and sired children. The church reviles witches who deal with the devil."

"No devils here," Brandon said cheerfully.

"Kirk has a spell that summons a shadow, and it's scary as hell looking, but it isn't a devil it's a magical construct meant to incite fear in men," Jen said.

Ethan placed a hand over hers on his arm and

patted it. "Kirk has a few spells that are meant to incite fear. Because you fear demons, his spells resemble them. His armor is meant to terrify. But he also has spells that give life." Ethan gestured to the castle on the hill. "We've been here less than half a year. Your king has been told we're powerful and we aren't looking to conquer. Make it clear to him attacking would be foolish."

Kuan returned, a hundred and forty-pound black raven soaring overhead chased by a panting Fredrick.

Both knights paused to examine the gate. "The druids grow these?" Galahad rapped the enormous tree trunk with his knuckles.

Ethan released Jen and ran a hand over the smooth wood of the gate. "Druids can command plants like the rangers can animals. Earth, air, and water responded to their thoughts. They fashion the plants as they will them, using magic to make them grow. A seed can become a flower in moments. To form this gate, they place a seed or cutting on the ground and think at it, envisioning in their minds how they wish it to become. You can see the magic surround the plant and infuse it. It's both beautiful and amazing to see."

"Will they show us?" Dante asked.

"Likely, if you ask. Rangers and Druids like to sit in the woods alone; please don't disturb them if you see them like that."

Galahad fixed his squires with a gimlet stare.

"Yes, my lord, we'll leave them be." Royce

bobbed his head. He glanced at Fredrick and sighed heavily. "I'll see that he behaves.

"Merrithew, Belin, I expect you to abide by their rules. No sneaking off to spy on rangers in the woods," Dante said.

Jen laughed. "They won't be able to sneak up on them, but it will annoy them to be disturbed. If you ask nicely, I'm sure they'll take you hunting or exploring."

Jen paused inside the wall and glanced around. The wall was new to her and continued to the tree-line where it ended. Stone houses, she assumed Rob had made because of the squared blocks cemented together, also new, bordered the wall, each with their own yards set well back from a wide road that paralleled the wall. Some of the stone homes were rounded although a few were square and a few a combination of shapes. It looked like they'd been practicing different techniques, but the overall effect was charming

Treehouses interspersed the rock homes with hanging pathways between them. Flowering trees or bushes of some sort decorated every yard. Swings hung from vines beside front doors, and tree trunks formed seating beside wooden tables before resuming their natural shape.

An empty field separated the road before the wall from another road equally as wide. Wooden homes grown in place then killed by Kirk's magic lined the street to the tree line. Those had been here when she'd left. Two and three-stories, each home had a grassy roof, rock chimneys and was bordered by thick hedges. Small rock sheds with chimneys formed of rough stone sat in almost every backyard. She thought they might be the kitchens that Cami and Kuan had been designing. The hedges and sheds were all new as were the trees lining the roads and the roads themselves. Trees shaded the winding drives and manicured lawns.

Flowering trees formed arched openings in the hedges, separating the yards from the road. It looked to Jen like a fairytale come true. Their guests gaped in amazement.

Every fifth tree that lined the wide road to the castle possessed a platform accessible by either wooden stairs grown from the tree's trunk, or a vine ladder that connected to wooded walkways formed by tree limbs. Golden eyes peered down at them, lesser ranger pets lounging in the trees.

The women with them stopped and exclaimed, pointing fearfully at the three weasels that peered down at them. The animals bared their tiny teeth and hissed in an unnatural way.

"They're tame pets. Nothing to worry about," Jen said and made a shooing motion. The weasels chittered and leaped to a higher branch. "You'll see lots of animals within the walls, but they won't bother you."

Kuan said, "The animals are under a ranger's control just like the trees are controlled by the druids. We made them flower for you today, but we'll let them return to normal after this fruit."

"What kinds are they?" Beside her, Ethan scanned the castle grounds with a hand shading his eyes.

"We've found wild cherry, plum, and apple so far. The hedges beside the moat are raspberry. Behind the castle, a damson field abuts the deer park.

"Lou found mulberry, currants, boysenberry, and strawberries. These trees are kept small for decoration. The orchards are behind the hill."

"Who lives here?" Galahad gestured to the large, wooden homes.

Jen said, "Families. Most of the single people prefer the stone cottages or living in the castle. A few picked tree houses. Kuan was so disappointed most of them wanted to live on the ground." She laughed when Kuan snorted.

"Do we have electricity?" Ethan nodded at the evenly spaced trees along the road.

"No, those are for shade. If we get wire, we can embed it in the ground." Maria gestured, and a fissure opened at their feet. Another gesture closed it. Grass crawled, covering the bare patch of earth in seconds.

"Holy Mother of God." Galahad crossed himself.

Maria laughed and rose her arms. Her eyes flared blue, and the closest bushes began to flow through the ground toward them. She was an elemental druid and could manipulate the water and earth in ways the healing druids couldn't. She halted the bushes at the edge of the road and lowered her arms. "I can force them across rock, but they don't like it." The blue receded from her eyes as the shrubs rejoined their fellows.

The two knights exchanged nervous glances. "You'd be formidable foes. How can we defeat you if you could swallow our army in the ground?"

"You can't. But it's nothing to worry about. I'm not going to go to you looking for a fight."

"What are we doing for sanitation?" Ethan asked.

"Running water still sucks, but sewers are good. Waste water flows two miles out to sea three miles south of us. Cami is still rerouting water, but gravity feed or the hand water pumps are our strongest water pressure right now. Jon is already planning for a waste processing plant, but our sewers are good enough for right now. If we can get wire, we'll have lights and electric pumps. Half a mile behind the castle we've raised a hill for a waterfall and built a stone building just waiting to become a water turbine. We have a building set aside there for a smithy. The manufacturing district will be south of us outside the walls to keep fumes and waste downwind."

Maria turned to the knights. "We'll accommodate any housing requests if we can, or you're free to use any of the empty buildings. We have about twenty empty ones right now, some nicer than others. We're getting better at building though, and we'll try to accommodate any requests. You can stay in the castle, but we don't heat it, so you might find it uncomfortable."

"Fire would be a problem for you, wouldn't it?" Dante sounded relieved.

"Not really. An inconvenience, but the castle is live wood and hard to burn, and we can control fire and water."

She rose a hand and a storm cloud appeared accompanied by the smell of ozone. A white-hot flash of lightning struck the road before them, making the women shriek and men exclaim. Water rose from the ground and swirled in a mini tornado, hovering beneath the storm cloud a moment before splashing to the stones. The cloud disappeared as if it'd never been.

"Warlocks and wizards can control fire like I do water."

"What do paladins do?" Dante asked with a thoughtful glance at Jen.

"They fight," Ethan said, grinning at Jen.

Jen drew her sword. "Alonis Lightning Strike, my Sword-of-Truth." The sword began to glow blue. She spun and pointed. "Evil is that way. My sword can guide me to evil or my enemies." With a finger flick, she casted Sanctuary and strode onto the glowing earth. "Here, no one may harm another. It's a safe place to rest. No arrow or thrown dagger will harm you here, no knife can cut you nor fire burn you. Your wounds will stop bleeding and you'll feel no pain until you leave my sanctuary."

Jen tilted her head back and yelled, "Charge!"

The group flinched back, making Ethan laugh.

"My voice can be heard across a battlefield giving orders, and if my command is followed, you'll be twice as strong. Your speed will double in retreat if I call for it and your swings hit harder if I yell attack."

"Is your king a paladin as well?"

Ethan took Jen's hand again, rubbing his thumb along her knuckles. "Jon is a warrior. Where Jen commands he can compel. His enemies will cower from him, and if he wills it, they'll run in fear. The angrier he becomes, the greater his strength. Wounds will heal him and injure his enemy."

Ethan released Jen and threw an arm around Galahad's shoulders. He strode forward, taking Galahad with him. "Come meet the king."

Mr. and Mrs. Ethan Frey

Her guild crowded the doorway and hugged them as if they'd been gone a year instead of a week. The rest of the residents of Camelot hung back, sitting at the round tables that filled the other half of the room, except for Dillion who ran up and threw his arms around Jen's legs.

Their boisterous greeting saddened her a moment as she wondered if they'd always be haunted by the fear that small separations would lead to longer, permanent ones. She shook off her melancholy, swung Dillion into her arms and hugged Sam.

The inside of the castle had changed in the week they'd been gone. The dais had been raised and thirty chairs placed before it. Green vines grew across each wooden chair spelling a name of a council member. A stone table sat beside the chair closest to the steps leading to the dais. Green flames roiled beneath Kirk's cauldron on the stone table. A smaller throne sat beside the first with a sign proclaiming, 'For the once and future queen.' On a smaller paper it said, "If her name is Guinevere, I resign."

Jen laughed and gestured to the thrones. "Beautiful, Rob's work?" The once wooden throne was now carved, polished stone gilded in patches of silver and gold. Behind the throne, trees and shrubs formed a living tapestry depicting their guild sigil in shades of green and white.

Maria nodded. "Yeah, he carved then enlarged them."

"Where'd we get gold and silver?"

"Jewelry and a couple computers Rob enlarged."

"Who is the once and future queen?" Galahad asked.

"Ahh, you can read, and Kirk wrote it." Jen giggled and hugged Sam again so happy to see her it hurt. "We don't know who his queen will be."

Dillion squirmed to be released, so she set him down. He hugged Ethan and Brandon then took Jon's hand.

"Guinevere is a myth," Ethan said pulling Sam from Jen's grasp and hugging Sam tightly.

A hot wave of jealousy scorched Jen followed by a bigger wave of sadness. Then Jon hugged her, his presence comforting. She hugged him back hard and didn't want to let go. Tears filled her eyes when she released him. Without thought, she grabbed his hand, needing to touch him and know he was well. He turned from Brandon, his eyes wide in surprise.

Brandon grasped his other hand. "You're well?"

Brandon sounded scared and confused. He yanked Jon to him and embraced him. Sparkling motes condensed into a blue mist that surrounded Jon.

"Get back!" Ramiro called and scooped Dillion up, then pulled Galahad backward.

Jen had no attention to spare for anyone except Jon and her crazy need to touch him.

"What is it?" Jon called and grabbed her hard. He threw an arm around Brandon and squeezed his shoulder. "I feel your fear," he said in awe. He released Jen and waved a hand through the blue cloud. It suddenly became larger.

"What's happening?" Dante asked.

"They're greeting the king, and their magic wishes to greet him too," Ramiro said.

Yes, Jen thought and eased. It wasn't her need to know Jon was well, but her magic's.

"The vow we made." She took Ethan's hand and placed it on Jon's. Ethan inhaled sharply and stepped forward.

Jon kissed his cheek then reached to Matt. Sparks shimmered as the blue grew in density. The others crowded closer and soon stood in a swirling vortex of magic.

"I'm well, and glad my knights have returned to me."

Jen laughed and clapped her hands. Clear and sharp Jon's sincerity washed over her. "I love you, Sam."

Sam kissed her cheek. "I love you too."

Eyes closed and head tipped back, Jen stood surrounded by magic, feeling Sam's love and cried. Jen took Kuan's hand in hers. "Kuan, I love you."

"And I you." Tears filled Kuan's eyes when he kissed her cheek.

"I love you all," Jon said.

The magic surrounding them pulsed.

"And I you," Jen said as the others did.

Thunder crashed and lightning flickered through the magic.

Laughing and crying they embraced. Jen closed her eyes and savored each embrace, the friendship and respect they felt came to her clearly as each touched her. Still holding Sam's hand in hers, she embraced Kirk. His eyes glowed when he released her and reached for Sam. Sam cried out and fell to her knees.

"Why fear, Sam?" Kirk sounded heartbroken but worse, he felt heartbroken.

Jen hugged him again, releasing Sam's hand. Sam covered her face with both hands and cried. She understood Sam's fear and wanted to comfort Kirk.

Ethan grasped Jen's shoulder to pull her back. "Let them…" he trailed off and frowned. "Was that for him?

A hot flicker of jealousy flickered over her skin. Kirk and Sam forgotten, she rose her hands as if to brush the magic off her. A blush burned across her cheeks, and she yanked away from Ethan, praying he hadn't felt or understood her desire for him. The blush built as her embarrassment became apparent to all. The magic made her feelings a neon sign.

Head cocked to the side, he regarded her. Without warning, he kissed her.

A corner of her mind noted they were making a spectacle of themselves but his feelings when he kissed her were intoxicating. She moaned and deepened the kiss.

"Everyone, get away from them," Jon said. "Kirk, take Sam a few feet away. Good idea, Maria."

Jen heard them but couldn't break from Ethan's embrace. Sound grew muffled, and the light dimmed against her closed eyelids.

Ethan's desire overwhelmed her. He slid his hand over her breast and moaned loudly at her answering spike of desire. Every fiber of her being wanted to embrace him, to feel his skin against hers, but they stood in public.

At that moment, she didn't care that he loved her lust and sought comfort for the deep loneliness he felt. More than anything she wanted to kiss him again and revel in his desire for her. She pulled back from him breathing hard. Her skin felt flushed as if she were feverish. Seeing they stood alone with the hedge tapestry surrounding them, she relaxed.

"Sorry, are you okay?" He traced her face with his fingertips, making her breath catch.

"Jesus, when you feel like that." He did it again and closed his eyes. "I want you too, so much," he murmured. "Yes, be happy I do. God, your happiness feels so good. I love you."

Her heart leapt with joy. He fell to his knees crying. Blue magic swirled around them in a frenzy. Sparks of static covered them, so large they stung where they touched her bare skin.

"We're in love," he said wonderingly. "Why doubt it when you can feel me?" He grasped her hand and placed it under his T-shirt on his heart. "I love you. No fear, accept it, and let me feel your love."

Terrified and excited, so filled with hope she'd thought she burst, she kissed him. His love surrounded her, stronger than his desire. Hers fed it, making it grow until his love felt white hot, a passion which she'd never experienced before.

"I love you." Crying, she rested her cheek against his.

He sat on the floor and pulled her into his arms. "This is the most amazing thing that's ever happened to me." For a moment, he felt sad with a feeling of deep loss.

"You miss your wife and child."

"My daughter. If she were here, I'd be

perfectly content."

"And your wife?" She couldn't help the dread and jealousy.

"I loved her until I realized she was incapable of love. Maybe if we'd had time we could've reached each other again." Ethan sighed hard and ran a hand over his head. "Not incapable, she loves our daughter, and we shared passion."

A scalding wave of jealousy flushed her skin.

"I love you," he murmured.

His words soothed, but the feeling when he said them salved the heat.

"Charisse was unable to trust, always doubting my affections. I think she held back from fear, but the constant need to reassure her grew wearing. She'd go home to see her family and return the same day convinced I was an unfaithful asshole. When I left for the tourney, she threatened to divorce me, sure I was going to be with Maria."

A blush crawled across his cheeks as his grip tightened. "My gaming became a war in our home and embarrassing. If I used headphones to talk privately, she'd shriek and rant. I was almost glad she wanted a divorce although I doubt she'd have gone through with it. She was the queen of indecision.

"I quit playing for four months, hoping that would help but it made it worse. Where was I going, what was I doing, who was there, and she never believed the answers even though I'd never lied to her. Jon called when he needed a rogue, and

I returned just in time to make the cut-off for the tourney."

Ethan kissed her temple and breathed deeply. Sad and confused, he kissed her temple again and felt joy. Jen's happiness grew as he quietly enjoyed holding her.

"In a lot of ways you remind me of her, but in most your nothing alike. She never saw herself clearly either, always doubting her beauty, just like you. But she was never strong or loyal, two things you are to the bone."

His eyes grew sad. "I knew she lied to me. She lied to herself too. I told myself she did it out of fear. " He shrugged irritably. "I wanted her to be the woman she pretended to be when we met. Not the woman she was, so I lied to myself too. I doubt we'd have been married much longer. I was determined to not be a deadbeat dad like our fathers and stayed when I should've left. Becoming a father was the greatest joy in my life."

Sadness again infused him, overpowering the joy he felt when he spoke of his child.

He framed her face with his hands. "You can trust me, Jen." He smiled, and his eyes closed. "Trust me, and I'll trust you. Will you marry me?"

He inhaled sharply and jerked back as if she'd slapped him.

She cringed at her embarrassed dismay, wishing she could hide it from him.

"What? Whatever it is we can work it out."

She laughed and hugged him. "No need to be

jealous. It isn't another man or woman; in case you think I secretly want Sam like half the people here do. I love her, but…"

He frowned now.

"There's no birth control here. We could end up with a zillion kids."

He laughed relieved and then worried.

"I'm seriously unlikely to die having a baby, and I could be resurrected, but the danger to them living here in this era… We both know the church will come. An army of a hundred thousand men and me with children to protect? How could I go and fight?"

She leaned her head on his shoulder. "And is it fair to bring them into this world, not their rightful one?"

"Both good points and we can wait to make love…" He moaned softly. "Your desire kills me. Yeah, we aren't waiting, not long anyway." He glanced around and laughed. "And not on the dais. God, we're making a scene."

She giggled, then sighed when he kissed her. For minutes they kissed in a soft blue cloud of magic.

"First things first. Genevieve Frey, will you marry me?"

"Ethan Lance, I will." She giggled again. "Everyone thinks I'll end up with Jon, not Lancelot."

"Just names, sheer coincidence," he said it assuredly but felt nervous and jealous.

"I swear I'll be a faithful wife, for better or worse, in sickness and in health, through riots, wars, and time itself, till death do us part." The magic surrounding them swirled harder, and thunder rumbled.

Jen waved a hand through the thick cloud of magic. Full of potential it sparked against her skin. "Ethan, the magic is gathering for an oath, be sure you mean what you say."

Thunder rumbled again, and Saint Elmo's fire appeared. The crowd beyond the tapestry quieted.

"You two okay?" Jon called.

"Fine, we just need privacy, we're getting married!" Ethan grinned and hugged her, laughing in delight at their shared joy.

His happy excitement became hers.

"Genevieve, I swear to be a good and faithful husband. I'll be the father of your children and protect and support you all until my dying breath. You will be my beloved wife through whatever this crazy world throws at us until the day I die."

He leaned forward and touched his lips to hers. Thunder sounded again, and lightning flowed through the trees of the wall nearest them.

The lightning burned along her skin a degree below painful, pulsing and weaving around them. She shut out the screaming crowd and concentrated on her love for him. Let loose from her control, her love bloomed.

A soft, phosphorescent glow lit the magic around them. Each emotion felt magnified tenfold. The freedom to let herself love him, and accept his love, exhilarated her. With all her soul, she thanked the magic, embracing it, and welcoming the vow, knowing he felt the same.

When it passed three minutes later, he slumped to the floor holding her tightly to his chest. His heart thudded against her ear. The magic had dissipate and she no longer felt him.

"Everyone okay?"

"Yes!" Ethan yelled back. "We sealed a vow. Give us a minute."

Outside, in the main hall, strange music began to play. Drums and a stringed instrument joined the soft sounds of a flute.

"Is that Aero Smith on a cello?" Ethan's chest rumbled when he laughed.

"This is embarrassing; they think we're in here having sex."

"I'm willing if you are," he said in a deep, low voice and kissed her. Her magic sprang from her, surrounding him. He groaned as his joined it. Blue magic swirled madly about them as they kissed, intensifying their feelings.

"Okay, yeah, this is awkward. Don't let anyone walk through it while you feel like this," he murmured and kissed her neck, his warm palm on the bare skin of her waist. He pulled away breathing hard.

"I love you." The joy she felt filled the words.

He laid beside her on the wood floor and cuddle her close. For minutes, they basked in their love. Finally, reluctantly, he pulled away. Their magic dissipated as they parted until she no longer felt his reluctance.

She kissed him again and laughed in delight as their magic collided. This time when she withdrew, she consciously called to her magic the same way she called her armor and sword to her and smiled when the magic dissipated into her skin. She kissed him again, willing her magic to not appear. In minutes, they were both able to call it and dispel it at will.

"Okay, we can face them now, I guess."

He snickered and stood, offering her a hand to rise.

The crowd cheered when they appeared, and she blushed to her toes.

Ethan strode to the edge of the dais. "Jen and I have married. The magic came and sealed a vow." He waved a glowing, blue hand. "We can call out our magic with a thought and make it go the same way. I feel what she does when we touch in our magic. We'll need to be careful if we wish to keep our feelings private."

Jon leapt to the dais to hug them both.

"Congratulations. The druids have gone to the stone cottage on the far right to prepare your room. Knowing them, it'll be filled with flowers and fruit.

Jen scanned the crowd, searching for Sam, surprised she hadn't joined Jon.

Jon followed her glance and lowered his

voice. "She and Kirk left a while ago." He turned and rose his voice. "Next time we're apart, we'll greet each other privately. The magic makes our feelings clear and can be overwhelming. Please know it isn't a slight, or that your unwelcome, it's just a private, intimate experience."

"I bet!" someone called out.

Raucous laughter and jests met that.

"Is all we did was kiss." Ethan kissed her again to loud cheers, and swung her into his arms, then leapt forward, landing on the Round Table. "I'm taking my wife's name. We are Mr. and Mrs. Frey. There is no Lancelot!"

"I know a Lancelot," Dante said.

The crowd laughed and booed.

"Never bring him here," Brandon laughed and slapped Dante's shoulder.

Ethan swung her around and kissed her to applause and good-natured jests, and Jen noticed the heaping bowls of perfect fruit on the table when she almost stepped in one. Flushed and laughing, she pulled Ethan to a seat. Platters of roasted vegetables and venison arrived, the servers sitting to eat with them.

Jon rose and lifted a wooden goblet embossed with leaves and flowers. "I'd like to propose a toast to Lord and Lady Frey, may they have many happy years together."

"To the Frey's!" Brandon shouted, making his voice loud and commanding.

"The Frey's," the knights echoed and lifted

their glasses.

The power and sincerity of their well-wishing shivered across Jen's skin.

Arden rose and climbed on her bench, tapping her wooden spoon against her wooden goblet. "This seems like a good time to make my announcement. For those of you who don't know me, I'm Doctor Arden Long, previously an OB-GYN. With Maria's help, I've developed an IUD. For those interested, I'll be holding office hours" – she paused and winked at Jen— "tonight in my workspace on the second floor above the library." She paused again for the applause. "While I can't guarantee complete effectiveness yet— the trial has been too short and too few— it seems very likely to be effective. Complications that might arrive, the druids can heal, including ingrown and infection."

The men clapped wildly and stamped their feet.

"It's going to take you hours." Ethan grabbed Jen again and leaped to the stairs. "We go first."

Doctor Long followed them up the stairs laughing.

A Conversation on Magic

Arden gestured to a table separated from ten others by a vine screen. Jen took a moment to examine the shelves lining the wall beside the door. Different sizes and shapes of bottles and bowls filled them. Some were open, but most closed with cork stoppers. Green health potions brimmed over a large wooden chest on the floor.

"The druids are making me a new lab space by the main gate." Arden picked up a wooden bottle and brought it to the table. "Some of my chemicals can get explosive. This is ether. It'll knock you cold for a good ten minutes. You'll wake sick as a dog, but a heal or potion fixes it." She handed Jen a small, flexible stick. "I can implant this in about three minutes, but the tenser you are, the more uncomfortable the procedure."

"So, ether to knock me out?"

"Yep, you shouldn't feel a thing when you wake. If you experience pain or cramping, come see me. Have you been sexually active in the past?"

A hot blush rose in Jen's cheeks. "No."

"Then I definitely recommend the sedative. I wish we had heals in the future and could sedate for these simple procedures."

Jen nodded and turned to Ethan. "Wait outside, please."

"I love you," he murmured and kissed her cheek. His blush heightened hers. She breathed deep welcoming the ether.

Fifteen minutes later she awoke. Nausea roiled her stomach and burned her throat, but she felt overwhelming relief. A flick of her fingers made her glow for a moment.

Doctor Long pulled back the curtain of her cubicle. "How do you feel?"

"Perfectly fine."

"Great, if that changes, come see me. Please don't remove the IUD yourself. I need to study it. It's such a shame we didn't have heals available back in the future. I'm learning so much because I can afford to make huge mistakes when you guys can heal them. I'd literally kill for a microscope."

"They have glass; we can make you one— no killing necessary."

"I spoke facetiously. I thank God every day we have a king like Jon and not Stan."

"God, me too. Have we heard from them?"

"Not as far as I know. They're going to be

kicking themselves when they see—"

A knock on the door interrupted her. "Your free to go, and congratulations," she said over her shoulder as she approached the door. "I was careful, and you're still a virgin." She opened the door and gestured Nina inside. "Good timing, a table just freed up."

Jen smiled and blushed at Nina as she scurried from the room. Music greeted her in the hallway. *Something by the Eagles*, she thought in amusement, wondering how the knights from Paris were taking the festivities. So far, they'd reacted better than she had when exposed to a druid and herself for the first time. The memory made her smile.

Ethan jumped to his feet. A few men she didn't know glanced up and grinned.

"How'd it go?" Ethan asked.

"No problems, piece of cake really." She rubbed her arms as a sudden wave of uneasiness shivered her. "Maybe too easy."

Ethan laid his palm against her hot cheek. "No birth control is foolproof, and while I agree waiting until we're more settled would be best, I can't wait to be a family with you." Tears made his eyes sparkle. "Just imagining you pregnant with my child..." His voice roughened, and he cleared his throat. "I love you. We can keep our children safe."

Another shiver shook her, and her unease deepened. He smiled and ran his hand over her head. "Stop worrying so hard. You're a protection paladin, and we've all seen how that triggers your protective instincts. It makes sense children would trigger it strongly."

Her unease lessened, and she lowered her voice as they walked away. "I need to make time to meet more people. I should know all their names, and I don't."

"Me too. I think we've all been trapped in our little bubbles of misery. A party is just what we needed."

"Have Sam and Kirk returned?"

"No."

"I'm a little worried."

"Me too, but we'll be there for her if she needs a friend, him too."

Jen bit her lip.

"You want to go look for them?"

"Yes, but I'm not sure I should."

"Does she love him?"

"Part of him. His darkness scares her. I know she's afraid he's only nice on the surface, that if she lets him in, he'll be cruel and cold."

"He's neither. His friendship was genuine. I felt his respect when he took my hand."

"She was deeply in love, and I'm sure she feels guilty too. It's a mess."

"They'll work it out." He stopped on the stairs and kissed her.

The crowd applauded and cheered, making Jen laugh and blush.

"Let's dance at our wedding." He grabbed her and leaped over the rail, landing on the floor before the gathered musicians. "Play us something romantic."

The three men and two women conferred a moment, then one of the women stepped forward and lifted a flute to her lips. The familiar melody of "You Light Up My Life," filled the room. At first softly, but then loudly, the crowd sang along and clapped hard when the song ended. Jen placed her glowing hand on Ethan's cheek so he could feel her happiness.

"I have a song I'd like to sing for them, and while I'm nowhere close to the original performer, my heart will be in it."

Jen spun in surprise and grinned at Sam. Sam leaped forward and hugged them both before returning to the musicians.

Jen scanned the room and found Kirk sitting with Jon and Kuan at the Round Table. He nodded and smiled, but his eyes remained sad. Haunting strains played on a flute and the room quieted as Sam sang in a soft, clear voice. Everyone stood and clapped when Sam finished the song. Blushing and laughing, she waved off calls for another and sat beside Kirk. He kissed her temple and put an arm around her.

The musicians played a polka, and the dance floor became crowded. Flushed and sweating from the crowd and happiness Jen sat beside Sir Galahad. "So, what do you think of our music?"

"I think Lady Quinn could make her fortune singing that one song. Your people are so amazingly different my mind boggles."

It feels fun and friendly, and the priests would faint," Dante said. "I imagine my family was much like this once. For years we practiced the old ways in secret until my grandfather really converted to Christianity. Still, my father would forget and occasionally call on the old gods. Mother would leave milk on the back step and rise early to hide it from our neighbors."

"Milk?" Jen rose an eyebrow.

"For the fae, the wee ones who dance in the moonlight."

"Have you ever seen one?"

"Never, but I've heard stories from those who have."

Galahad laughed. "Stories told by drunkards?"

"Are you sure? Look around you. If this isn't an Elven Hall, what is?"

Galahad pursed his lips and nodded slightly.

The music stopped, and Rob and Matt's firebirds flew to the dance floor and placed two glowing balls. The walls behind the dancefloor transformed with a wave of Rob's hand. A Christmas tree appeared surrounded by wrapped presents with a life-sized nutcracker beside it.

Brandon rose and waved his arms. "Sam has agreed to dance for us to music from her iPod. As she has almost zero charge left; this might be the last any of us will ever hear Tchaikovsky.

Jen cried when Sam leapt to the floor to the strains of the "Sugar Plum Fairy." She'd just gotten the part in a small ballet and would've performed for the first time before a paying audience when they returned from the tourney.

Her skin color leotard had a small skirt that flared as she bounded across the stage in impossible leaps and whirls. She'd brought her practice outfit and ballet shoes with her, unwilling to go five days without practice.

Her love of the dance shone in every graceful movement. It broke Jen's heart that she would never dance this again.

Before the song came to an end, the battery on her iPod died. Tears glittering in the light, she sank to her knees and covered her face with her hands. Kirk rushed to her. Beside Jen, Galahad cried.

"You are truly fairies banished from your lands. She could mesmerize and make you dance a million years," Dante said in awe.

"She's the most beautiful person," Jen said sadly and leaped forward to her friend.

Dante ran his hand over the smooth surface of the Round Table. He glanced at Jon then took a sip from the wooden goblet before him. "If I hadn't seen this with my own eyes, I wouldn't believe."

"The table?" Jon placed his palms on the table and considered it with pursed lips.

Dante laughed his deep, happy chuckle. "No, My Lord, the ease with which you share your privileges." He nodded with his chin at Ramiro and Nina who sat across from him. Nina held Sophia in her lap and feed her pieces of strawberry.

Sophia's mother entered and set down a pizza before Jen. "Goat cheese and bacon pizza. Better than it was, but still not great."

Dillion followed her in, lugging a stone bottle that he hefted onto the table.

Jen took a slice and slid the platter to Galahad.

"It doesn't even bother you that you're not served first," Dante said in amazement. "It doesn't even occur to them."

Jon shrugged. "Jen ordered the pizza. And I despise goat cheese."

"We're making you a red sauce and bacon pizza." Sophia's mother paused to kiss her daughter's forehead and smile at Jon. She winked at Jen and curtsied deeply as she added, "Your Majesty," making Jon laugh.

Dillion followed her from the room.

Jen smiled after them, glad Dillion had a stable, kind, foster mother.

Dante's gaze followed her from the room before swinging back to examine Jon. "There's no doubt you're the king, and I can't put my finger on how I know it. You dress the same, and they treat you casually, but something…"

"It's Commanding Presence, his aura," Jen said then blew on the piece of pizza before taking a bite. "Oh, so good. Much better than last time." She took another big bite. "Her restaurant must have been amazing."

"Jon has always had that," Ramiro disagreed. "On the plane he commanded and you listened, and he had no magic then."

Jen stared thoughtfully at Jon. "That's true. Maybe the magic picked him purposefully."

"Your tale is fantastical, but the evidence supports it," Dante took a bite of the pizza and grinned, then took another big bite. Your conclusion is wrong," he continued with his mouth full. "It's obvious you're the fae returned."

"We aren't."

"You think you aren't, but you are. Magic is a force of nature— Danu, Mother Earth. You say there's no magic in the future and the Earth itself is sick. The fae lived thousands of years ago in cities made of plants. They laughed and drank and sang to glorious music and had few children. Their lives were wondrous and deeds mighty. But humans envied, so they retreated into the mist, hoping the humans would cease bickering and live in peace."

Dante gazed at his rapt audience and smiled. "We didn't live in peace. Wars, sickness, and famine followed, so Danu recalled her fae. She picked as she could from the humans available to her."

Goosebumps rose on Jen's arms and she absently rubbed them. "That might be true. There's no doubt Kuan was the best druid in the game." She paused thoughtfully. "His eyes have always been magical blue."

Jon leaned forward with his elbows on the table. "Sara Mitchel had the same blue eyes. Barlow-blue like her mother. She was the best priest I've ever played with."

"Charlie Hayes was an amazing warrior, had you ever dueled him?" Jen asked.

"Yes, the fight went on a ridiculously long time. I won, but it was close. I think he got bored and gave up." Jon took a sip from his cup. "A very good warrior. His team would've been the top competition if they'd lived."

"Maybe they did live." Jen glanced at Dante, her skin goose-bumped from awe. "Maybe the magic chose them as the best. Kuan has always been a druid in his soul. So much so that he couldn't function well back in the future. Jon, you're the best warrior in the game because you are that. A fierce protector; a natural leader. Look at Cass, he was born to be a ranger. He practically was one before the lightning. And he was an amazing one in the game."

"But it was just a game."

"Yes, but if the magic wanted to reenter the world wouldn't it pick people that could use it? If Nina awoke as a druid how would she know what to do? For us, it was second nature. Maybe it gave the future Team Valor to save them and the past the Knights of the Round Table."

Jon stared at her with wide eyes. "So, you're saying we're destined to fight our battles and disappear, becoming a fable?"

"No," Ramiro said. "You're destined to change the course of history. Danu"— he bowed slightly at Dante— "has realized her mistake. Magic and mortal must find a way to coexist, or the Earth itself is doomed, and both species will die. The future has changed with the arrival of Team Valor— and I'm seriously happy that isn't my responsibly. I can't imagine how difficult it will be for them to survive and change the world we knew for the better."

Sophia's mother and Dillion returned with two more pizzas, one of which she placed before Jon.

Jon nodded his thanks for the pizza and waved a hand over it to cool it. "How do you explain the similarities between us and a fable?" He took a bite and hissed through his teeth, snatching his cup and chugging the contents.

"No idea. Maybe, back in our real past, there were small rifts in time, and magic eased through them bringing dreams of us?"

A thoughtful frown on his face Dante leaned forward. "Perhaps man subconsciously craved your return and told themselves stories. Danu saw and guided you to become what you are. She had to wait until man was able to use magic again. As Lady Frey says, how would someone know how to without your training?"

Galahad tapped the table top. "The God of man, creator of the Heavens and the Earth, created angels as well, so why not fae? He gave us his son; then saw we still did not live in peace, despite his sacrifice, so he returned to us his fae with the power over the Earth because he loves the Earth, not just the humans on it."

"It's a good theory," Ramiro said. "Your right about the magic choosing the best it could. Even with magic, I'd never be the paladin Jen is. The plane crash with all its strangeness still wouldn't have been enough for me to accept and embrace the change like you all did."

"Believe me, it wasn't easy. If it looked easy, you're mistaken," Jon said wryly.

Jen shuddered, the memory of those days clear in her mind, filled with more pain and fear than she'd ever known.

"Although that theory also explains why the magic feels alive sometimes. It is alive." Jon leaned back in his seat. "When we gather and let our magic mingle, we're closer to Danu. The magic is her essence, which she shares, and she rejoices when we gather in happiness. She worries when we're apart."

Jen nodded. "I feel her push me to go and check that the others in my party are well."

"Does that happen often?" Ramiro asked.

"No. It's only happened twice. Once when I heard Kuan scream and the other when we arrived home from Paris. Touching them eased the need. The need was fierce though. I would've dropped anything to see them."

"I felt it too. A sudden intense need to know you were well," Jon said.

"Have you felt it since?"

"A few times. When Brandon fell from the roof. The same day Kuan came in screaming that upset Jen. I think it pushed all of us."

"What caused Kuan to scream?" Dante asked.

"A shark in the bay. He formed a gate to keep them out now, but then it was just an opening. I think it shocked him how upset we all were when all he wanted was to warn us."

Dante rose an eyebrow. "Couldn't he kill it?"

"Easily, but he didn't want to kill it. Kuan is a healer in his soul. He doesn't hunt."

"Don't take that to mean he wouldn't attack fiercely, he would for us," Jen added. "If one of us had been in the water, he'd have attacked."

"I'm pretty sure if anyone— no matter who it was— was in the water, he'd attack.," Galahad said. "He's the absolute soul of patience with my squire. Fredrick hounds him mercilessly. He'll be heartbroken when we go."

"He's welcome to stay," Ramiro said. "I'd take him as my ward in your absence."

Galahad looked troubled. "I'm unsure what is best for the boy and myself. My position as a knight requires squires, and Fredrick is a good one. The only way to knighthood for most is to be a squire. It's a position of great honor. But here he could live a good life on his own land without needing to fight. Until the church comes, and then what? Then he'll be without the skills to fight, and if they catch him, he'll be killed and likely in a gruesome manner, not honorably with a sword in his hand. But that fate might await him if he returns with me too."

"I'll leave my youngest squire here and the women from my household. With your permission, of course." Dante bowed his head to Jon.

"They're welcome. Will you return?" Jon asked.

"If I'm able, but my king will likely have need of me for a good long while." He eyed his plate sadly. "The legends of fairy food being addicting are true. I know you add no magic to them to make them so, but your cooks are divine."

"Your priest is very powerful," Galahad said. "I've seen his blessing restore rotted food to perfect condition. I think I've put on two stone." He rubbed his stomach and grinned.

"Wait until you see what we can make if we get some cows," Sophia's mother said.

"I'm sorry, I forgot your name, ma'am," Galahad stumbled a bit on the polite phrasing, not yet using it naturally.

"Gwen." She winked at Jon and laughed when he stood and moved two seats away. "Happily married to Garret who works with Doctor Long."

"Mrs. Russo, you're truly an artist in the kitchen. I'm sad for your sake but happy for mine you were on flight Four-Fourteen," Jon said.

"I'm glad I was aboard. My husband and I love it here. Granted, if we'd left Sophia behind as we'd considered doing that would be different, but neither of us miss our old lives in our stuffy apartment trying to save enough to open my own restaurant. His work took him all over for long stretches. The money was good, but Sophia… we wanted to ensure her care." Tears filled her eyes as she smiled at Jen. "I would've given up anything to restore her to health, and you did it with a wave of your hand." Her gaze flicked to Dillion, and her smile deepened. "And I have a new son to love. My husband and I are happy here."

A pink blush covered Dillion's cheeks. He stared down at the tabletop with and odd expression Jen realized was guilty happiness.

Jon seemed to notice too. He leaned over and kissed Dillion's forehead. "We'll always miss our loved ones, but they'd be happy we're recovering. It's okay to be happy here." He laid his hand on Dillion's shoulder a moment before picking up his glass and turning it absently. "The majority of us are settling in now. Mostly because of the druids. Our farm labor is ridiculously easy, and we have plenty of free time to do what we wish. There's a surprising number of hobbyist from winemakers to painters."

"It isn't surprising," Dante said. "The fae are known for their love of art and beauty. Their artisans were legendary. You are all fae; the Knights of the Round Table are your nobles, but you are all fairy."

Ramiro let loose a sharp bark of laughter that billowed into a full-grown laugh. "Calling someone a fairy where we're from is a great insult, and here it's an honor. Oh, how my life has changed. Wait until I tell Rob."

"Will you two marry?" Jen asked.

Ramiro saddened. "He hasn't asked."

"Why not ask him?"

"I don't want to ruin what we have."

"If you do marry, be prepared for the lightning. I'm not sure what it will do but…"

Ramiro nodded.

Dante dropped his fork. "You wish to marry a man?"

Galahad stared horrified.

Jen laughed at Ramiro's blushing face. "Here, any adults may marry."

The two knights exchanged disgusted glances and pushed back from the table. Without a word, they strode out.

"Well, good. Let them stew on that," Jon said and slapped Ramiro's shoulder. "It's good they know."

"Homosexuality might be the straw that breaks the camel's back church wise." Ramiro stared down at his clasped hands. "They might be able to accept magic as a return of the fae by God's will, but this… I'll leave and live elsewhere before causing a war."

"No. We'll be a free people if it kills us," Jon

said forcefully.

"It might kill us," Ramiro said unhappily.

Jen rose and hugged him. "It'll be a hell of a fight."

Jon leaned back in his seat and stretched. "Tomorrow, take the knights to the docks and have the casters put on a display."

Jen grinned and ruffled Ramiro's hair before heading to the door. "Save my pizza," she called back over her shoulder.

Crafts and Magic

Jen gazed up at the wave that towered over her. Weak sunlight shone dimly through it lit by the ranger's flares. The wave changed directions and rolled out to sea where it crashed into the ocean with a mighty roar. White droplets of water flew hundreds of yards into the sky. Black clouds formed and lightning forked, sending up sizzling streamers of steam. Meteors appeared in the sky and slammed into the water where they sputtered and sank. Smaller, burning balls sleeted through the lightning as the firebirds began to cast.

A line of neon green at their feet raced out to sea, becoming a twelve-foot wall of green flames. A fire imp capered by Kirk's feet. Bright red with glowing yellow eyes, it carried a glowing yellow orb the appeared to shimmer with heat. A lesser demon, it could cast fire or augment Kirk's fire spell as it was doing now. The smell of sulfur reached them on the wind.

Yellow-orange balls sped from Tony's fingertips growing in size until the waves swallowed them. Tony slammed his staff, formed of spiraling black oak and topped with the image of the sun with wavy rays, onto the dock. A black wave rippled over the water. Smaller black balls flowed from the sun on his staff, bouncing over the ocean and exploding into black flames tipped in blue.

Fredrick and Dillion stood entranced before Jen. "Cool."

Jen laughed at Fredrick's mimicry. He used their slang naturally now. Dillion flicked his fingers and made casting motions. Fredrick copied him. Jen grinned at them. Fredrick tapped the air randomly, but Dillion used a pretend keyboard hitting the correct keys for fireball.

Thunder and lightning continued to boom as the water swirled and slammed together. The casters kept up the display for forty minutes. As one, they let the water settle back to smooth, rolling waves.

Rob kissed Romero lightly on the lips, then turned and spread his arms. "We'll have a fairy wedding May first. The druids have graciously agreed to supply flowers and seating for an outdoor wedding, and we'd like you all to attend."

Jen clapped. Beside her, Ethan laughed.

"We'll have a feast!" Jon yelled.

"A feast!" Jen bellowed.

Laughing, Brandon echoed her.

Jon leaned over and said something too low to hear to Rob. Rob nodded. Jon rose his hands and faced the gathered crowd. "Any wishing to wed that day are welcome."

Jen linked her arm with Ethan's and rested her head on his shoulder as they walked along the rock quay back to the shore. "Are you happy here?"

"I've never been happier," he assured her and kissed the top of her head, laying his glowing blue hand along her cheek so she could feel his sincerity.

Me either." Jen glanced over her shoulder at the thin strip of ocean separating them from France and shivered.

Dust puffed up from the bag of granite chunks she dropped to the ground. She and Rob dismounted and cut the other six bags loose, letting them fall atop the first bag before checking to make sure Gallant was unhurt.

"No matter how much it weighs he seems to run the same speed," Rob said as he patted the horse's nose.

"Sometimes Danu makes no sense to me. How come you can shrink things to postage size yet only enlarge them to twice their original size?" She grunted as she picked up two of the bags.

A row of stone buildings now lined the

outside of the wall. She headed to the one on the left and dropped her bag on the wooden table in the center of the room.

"Rob, do you have time to dispel some of these chunks today?" Nina asked.

The other woman in the room stopped tapping with her hammer and chisel and nodded a hello.

"Sure, what's this one?" He lifted the cloth covering the model on a stone table beside the door.

Jen peered over his shoulder at the miniature art-deco house.

"Oh, I love this one!" he exclaimed.

Nina snatched the cloth from his hand and covered it again. "That's supposed to be a surprise. Jen, can you bring the bags outside to the rock pit?"

Jen nodded assent but went to the back wall to examine the drawings tacked there. A cork wall lined the back of the building between the windows. Tacked to the wall, thick paper hung two deep. A wooden crate on the floor held files bearing names.

Each table in the room held tools for chiseling; some held small containers of paint and brushes. A few held clamps and woodworking tools. The metal tools hung on the wall in a place of honor. Bins underneath the shelving lining the walls contained an assortment of materials different types of rock, wood, and cloth. Chalk labels on the bins stated the amount the item was shrunk. She paused beside a new table set before the windows open now to the soft April breeze.

"What's all this, Nina?" Jen leaned closer to examine the miniatures on the table.

"Some of the crafters are trading, some donating. If you see a piece you like, these are for sale. Nancy is making a store now where she plans to sell full-sized items." Nina smiled at the woman behind them sitting alone at the table, then picked up a small, stone tub with clawed feet. "These all need to be enlarged. The little tag tells the buyer how big the item will be when dispelled. The base material has to have been shrunken the same amounts or dispel ruins the project but were figuring ways around it. We've learned to keep careful track."

"You can't just make everything the same size? Jen asked Rob.

"I can but it's hard to work with some things like tiny cloth. So that's generally shrunken three times at most while stone and wood is easier to form when it's small so that might be shrunken quite a bit depending on the size of the original chunk and ultimate goal."

Nina rested a hip on the table and gestured to a stack of loose-leafed books tied with vines on her desk in the corner. "Now that we have some metals we've begun experimenting on adding wiring, but our methods of extraction are still too imprecise and we end up with too much breakage.

Its's better to run a conduit that matches the dispel size-wise through the walls and then add enlarged wire when the home is full-sized, but the process is still much faster then what we used in the future. When we get some real supplies... I can't wait to see what we can do. This is an architect's dream job."

She grinned at Rob. You're going to be rich."

Rob rose an eyebrow.

"Ten percent goes to you," she clarified.

He frowned. "That's too much for a wave of my hand."

"Without you, it isn't possible at all. Mr. Henry is designing money for us. Trading is fine, but it's hard to pay you guys like that, so we're deciding the worth of these things by man hours and material, then say I trade a tub for a decorative planter I know I owe Rob two cents. If there's something he wants, we can trade instead, like say he wanted these goblets. They're priced at twenty-five cents. I could just take his two cents off the cost, and he'd owe twenty-three."

"How the hell will you remember who owes what?" Rob held up one of the carved stone cups. "These are real cute."

"I write it down. Lisbeth, the woman who arrived with Dante, is learning to read and write. Once I'm sure of her skill, she's agreed to be my bookkeeper." Nina sighed, and a ran a finger over a six-inch statue of a naked woman. "She's half convinced she's going to hell for living here. It's going to be really hard to convince people we aren't devils if the church prosecutes us. The only thing convincing her otherwise is Dante's Danu stories. That, and we aren't cruel."

"I'm okay with people being unwilling to join us as long as they stay away," Rob said as he handed Nina the tiny goblet. "Put these down as mine. I'll pick them up when they're all paid off."

Nina smiled and placed them on the table beside the door with the sheet-covered model home.

"Man, I need a job," Jen said in dismay, reluctantly placing the tub back on the table. She'd barely the skill to chisel anything except big hunks.

"You get paid for rock delivery in our system. Also for the training you do with the militia. Both you and Brandon will be paid for the use of your horses. We're still working rates out for that. Those who live inside the second wall won't pay tax, but we'll always have mandatory farm hours. Of course, you could pay someone else to do them…"

Nina peered out the window and frowned. "The druids are hardest to pay. What they do is so indispensable that even giving them half doesn't seem like enough, but we need to be able to pay the others who deliver and prepare the food, and we want to keep food prices low."

"Their food should cost more because it's perfect," Rob said.

Nina turned back to the room and sat on the edge of the table. "Everyone has been helpful and understanding, and I hope it continues as we shake out these money issues. Mr. Henry is our only trained banker, so we're bound to have problems."

"Have people complained?" Jen asked.

"Not at all. As far as I know, everyone is doing whatever is needed without complaint or expecting payment, but we need to be ready for that to change. We can't expect the druids to supply the products and get no recompense. The shops here on Broadway will be available to anyone, which is why we built them outside the wall."

"What are you doing about Kirk?" Jen asked.

"Totally up to him. What he does requires nobody's help, so he can set the prices however he likes. You guys should come to the town meetings; they're really interesting."

Jen made a face and Rob laughed.

"I'm with you, Jen. Let them work it out. The twice-monthly meetings at the Round Table are enough for me."

Jen grabbed the bags of rocks and brought them outside to one of the thirty-foot rings behind the building. Red flags encircled an inner ring and white ones were set twenty-feet back.

She paused to admire a much bigger building being constructed within a circle connected to a grid of other circles, most still empty. They were learning how to manufacture larger buildings in smaller chunks and connect them using dispel and enlarge.

A group of men had gathered around the farthest circle where a rock building had partially collapsed and lay half on its side in the next circle. Lou glanced over and waved but didn't approach.

All the men carried thick notebooks made of thin bark the druids convinced the trees to shed.

A woman Jen didn't know clambered from a window carrying a measuring tape in one hand and lugging a thick roll of paper.

The men gathered around, breaking out rulers and gesticulating. They spoke in excited voices.

Rob joined her, and both observed the gathered builders a moment.

"That could collapse any second," Jen said.

Rob shrugged. "Lou can rez them, and I'm sure he gives the people entering a pain dulling ankh in case the building collapses on them. OSHA wouldn't approve, but standard safety precautions are silly for us, and this way is much faster.

Jen grinned and left them to it.

Rob dispelled the rock chunks Jen carried, returning them to their natural size. Those who wished to use them would mark them with chalk, noting how small they wished the piece to be shrunken, making them much easier to chisel and form.

Rob headed to a nearby building that flew an orange banner. Jen glanced around but seeing no pink ones, headed back to the castle. Without telephones, a system had sprung up of colored banners. If someone wanted Rob's help or company, they rose an orange one. The rangers used different shades of green and Tony white.

Tony was always busy. Five white banners, two green ones, and a periwinkle blue flew from the houses on her way to the castle. A red banner with a black dagger crossing a lightning bolt bordered in pink, her husband's banner, waved from the castle.

As she entered, Fredrick rose the pink banner edged with red to signify she was in residence. One of the children had that duty all day. The knights signed themselves in and out at night. She thanked him and glanced at the display thoughtfully; she needed to decide on a device soon.

Jen liked the custom and hoped they kept it even when they got the phones working. She loved to glance at the castle from a distance and see her husband's banner flying.

Ethan's smile when he saw her was her favorite thing in the world, she thought as he leapt to her side and kissed her.

He slung an arm around her shoulder and led her back to the Round Table. A round model of Camelot and its environs sat in the center of the paper-strewn table.

"How goes the rock collecting?" Ethan asked as he pulled out a chair for her.

"Fun. It's so cool watching the casters assault the cliffs. They're getting better at blasting out standard size chunks. The druids rise columns of rock from the ground and they just blast it free. What are you guys up too?"

"Deciding where to go for a cow. The druids are building a cattle barge right now." Jon stood before the plant tapestry growing on the wall beside the stairs. Kuan had copied it from Frank Miller Juniors beginner's world atlas. One of six books they owned, it was kept in a locked chest in the library along with their eight magazines, twenty-seven laptops, sixty-five cell phones and assorted cameras.

One of the suitcase's they'd retrieved had belonged to a woman they'd never found. They'd hung a pair of her jeans on the wall with a pair of sneakers. A pink 'Hello Kitty' T-shirt and purple bra hung above it. Gradually, other items appeared— a Yankee's ball cap, a broken wristwatch, the wrapper of a Babe Ruth Bar, an empty birth control dispenser.

The wall became a shrine for things lost they'd never have again. Everything from iPods to Gameboys had found their way to the library. Art had begun to appear. First, famous city skylines, then icons of their lost lives. The golden arches of a McDonald's sign sat beside a painting of John Wayne. The Google logo had made Jen laugh, then cry.

Jon had hung a painting of a ballerina dressed as Princess Odette from Swan Lake on the wall over the musician's dais and had Rob enlarge it. The loss and fear in the fairy's face is clear as she leaps from an unseen assailant across a dark wood. The picture made Jen tear up, and she hoped he moved it soon. She took a seat with her back to the painting.

"Germany is likely the best place." Jon traced his finger along the coastline. "This time, we'll go in dressed as natives, buy, and get out. Lou will go with you and pick the cattle. I'm tempted to recall Jamal, but don't want to leave Matt alone. Cass will have to handle it. So, Cass, Lou, Tony, Rob, and Brandon."

What are we using to trade?" Jen asked.

"Trunks of paper, fancy bows, leather work, stone and wooden jewelry, and boots." Hopefully, that's enough for two cows and a bull. As much I want to buy metal to make wire, we need cows."

"Too bad the druids can't take it from the ground like rock," Ethan said.

"Maybe they could if they could find some, but it's just rock here." Jon shrugged and turned back to the map.

Certain Danger

Dante and his squires followed Jen into the field behind the castle. Despite the chilly spring air, the plants thrived. Kuan sat in the field between a row of walnut trees with his eyes closed and head tipped back. Jen smiled at Dillion who sat beside him the same way,.

"You could feed all of Paris." Dante gestured to the straight rows of plants covered with plump, ripe fruit. In the field across from them, workers picked the produce and stacked the baskets. "One druid can ensure healthy crops that produce as needed," Dante said in awe, his gaze on Kuan.

"He' isn't making the plants grow right now. He's convincing the trees to make the walnuts oiler for our lamps." She picked a walnut and cracked it in her hand. "These don't taste that good anymore. They're kind of greasy tasting now. We have limited means of food storage, and while we could load a ship and send it back, they might burn you for it when they found out it was from us."

Dante removed the healing potion from his pouch and rolled it between his fingers. "How can health be from the devil?"

Jen shrugged. "You're welcome to stay or return here after reporting to your king."

I have two thousand of these health potions, not to mention the summoning stones and loaves of bread that don't rot. When word reaches the mainland, pilgrims will come in droves to seek Sir Moreland."

"And they'll find him in his tower. If they pay him enough, he'll give them what they seek, unless they annoy him, of course."

"And dirty peasants will overrun your beautiful city."

"No. The wizards will lock the gates, and only those they wish will be able to pass. Cami is laying out streets where we expect a town to spring up, and we have more empty homes all the time. All law-abiding citizens will be welcome. Taxes will be cheap, and the price for food fair or you could hire a druid to oversee your crop."

"And you? What will you do?"

"Eventually, Ethan and I'd like to travel and see the world, but for now, I'll train our militia with Brandon and Jon."

Dante glanced at her from the corner of his eye. "You once told us there were three swords like yours, yet your king doesn't carry one. Where is the third?"

"When we arrived here, not all agreed to live a peaceful life. Some wanted to travel to a nearby town to steal instead of earn. They left days after we arrived." Jen plucked a walnut from the tree and cracked it in her hand. Oil dripped between her fingers.

"How many?" Dante asked grimly.

"Three," she said softly and let the pieces of nut fall. "A paladin, a warrior, and a rogue accompanied by twenty-three lesser fae. The paladin carries Luminous Revenge, a long sword, but can only fight with magic. She doesn't possess the training or disposition to make war."

"And you haven't seen them since?"

"No. We've been busy, but I think we're avoiding it too. If we go, and they're being horrid, what shall we do? Kill our once friends? There's no way to contain them. The only way to stop them is death."

"Could you? I mean do you possess the capability?"

"Yes, Kuan and I were the top player-verses-player team on our realm. But that was a game, and they were our friends. Miguel would be hard to kill, but not impossible. Brandon and I could track him, but he's faster than us. We'd have to exhaust him, harry him until he slowed and faced us. One-on-one he might defeat Brandon. They've dueled in the past and Miguel won about half the time.

He's never beaten me," she finished softly and turned away, saddened by the thought of fighting Miguel for real.

Her heart lifted when Ethan approached. He wore his guild tabard over a new linen shirt and tan, drawstring pants. The belt he'd worn on the plane carried two sheathed daggers now. Knee-high, brown leather boots laced to his knees completed his ensemble. She wore the exact same thing except her pants belted with a woven, cloth belt and she only carried one dagger.

Gallant galloped after him, frisking and kicking up his heels. As long as she stayed between the inner walls, her horse remained solid. If she ventured further, he returned to mist. He seemed to enjoy wandering, so she let him be.

Ethan leapt forward, traveling the last thirty feet in an eye blink and swung her around, then kissed her.

Dante cleared his throat and turned away, making Jen giggle. "Sorry, we're used to public displays of affection."

"I'm well aware. It's harder to get used to that, then Kuan or Kirk."

"Is it illegal to kiss your wife in public in Paris?"

"Not illegal, at least I don't think so. It's just never done. Once in a great while, one of the, uh, lower classes will kiss their spouse in public but usually because they've just been run down or something. The only women who kiss men in public are paid to do so, and still, they do it in taverns, not under the sky before God."

Dante sounded so indignant Jen laughed again. Unable to resist, she wrapped her arms around Ethan's neck and really kissed him. Pressed so tightly against him, she could feel his heart beat harder. The soft aroused sigh he loosed made her pulse quicken.

"Your eyes are glowing, my beautiful wife," he murmured, then kissed her ear.

"Yours are too."

He slid his hands down her back and pressed her harder against his arousal. He moaned when she touched his face with her glowing hand. "Dante's with Kuan; let's go home," Ethan said.

For answer, she jumped astride her horse and offered him her hand. Gallant turned and ran. Silver hooves flew across the ground, sparking off the rock road. She leaned forward and urged him faster until it felt like they flew. In moments, they'd reached the cobbled driveway before their home. Blue magic surrounded her.

Her magic wanted him desperately too, she thought as it coated him. He leapt to the doorway from the back of her horse while Gallant still ran.

"I can't decide if I love your emotions or your body more when we make love," he said as he brushed the tear from her cheek with his thumb.

Her palm traced the curve of his shoulder and skimmed across his back. "You're so beautiful. I don't think I would've ever believed you really loved me if I didn't have magic. Someone as beautiful as you wouldn't love a girl like me." She kissed him when he frowned. "I believe you think I'm beautiful too. I wasn't fishing for compliments; I'm just saying I love how I can feel your sincerity.

"If we didn't have magic and dated, I think a part of me would've held back." Tears of happiness trailed across her cheek. "What we have is so amazing. If Danu did nothing except this, it would be enough. It was worth every second of suffering to share your emotions. You mean everything to me, Ethan."

He let his weight rest lightly across her naked breasts and kissed her a long time. "I love it too. This" – he said as he slid inside her- "is the most amazing sensation. Your pleasure and my pleasure— sometimes it's so much I feel like I'll burn with passion."

"Make me burn," she moaned and pulled him close for a kiss. Each thrust fanned the flames inside her until she writhed against him unable to contain the heat he generated. She screamed his name with her climax and jerked hard against him when she felt his. Trembling and panting, he collapsed across her.

"Well, that was some show," Miguel said. "Almost makes me want to take Kendra for a ride."

Ethan leapt, but Miguel had already disappeared. Jen sat in her Sanctuary shocked. She grabbed the sheet and huddle under it, feeling violated and exposed. A thought summoned her armor, another her sword. Ethan followed, tugging on his pants as she ran from the room.

Arden spun to face her as she galloped past. "Miguel is here," she yelled and followed her glowing sword to the forest.

"Coward," she screamed as loud as she could. "Come face me like a man!"

The dense trees surrounding Camelot slowed Gallant. Ethan caught up and jumped behind her, hugging her tightly against his bare chest.

"Are you okay?"

"No, he's going to fucking pay, the pervert."

"We'll ask Rob to lock our doors. He should pay, but it isn't a killing offense."

In the distance, the wooden horn warning of danger blew.

She turned in the saddle, riding backward so she could hug her husband. The warmth and smell of his skin comforted her. His steady heartbeat under her hand comforted her more. Gallant turned and headed back to the castle at a walk. Kuan appeared, changing in mid-leap from a panther to a man.

"Are you hurt?"

"Angry. Miguel spied on us making love. We've been too lax. Have Rob lock all the doors and the gate."

"I will, but that won't make you safe, he could follow you in."

"He won't attack me." A flutter of unease

morphed into fear. She scrambled for the summoning ball in her pouch and realized she'd left without it. "Kuan, summon Sam— hurry!"

"I have no stone." He shifted into the panther and raced away. Ethan leapt from Gallant and followed.

Crying now, Jen urged Gallant as fast as she could through the trees. Miguel wouldn't have come to her first, and Sam would be easy for him to subdue. Sweat beaded her brow and her hands shook by the time she cleared the trees. Kuan flew across the castle grounds in raven form, cawing ahead of her.

"Sam!" she bellowed, then, "Help, summon Sam!"

Kuan continued to caw as he dove at Kirk's tower. Gallant galloped through the field, clods of dirt flying from his hooves. She bounded over Nina and the Miller boys working in the field. Brandon approached on Ed, he carried his sword and galloped toward her. In the distance, Kuan still screeched. Her heart beat so fast she thought she might faint. Surely, he'd stop if Sam were there and well.

Cami and Maria soared over her head. Gallant hit the road and kept pace with the druids. The wind of her passage dried the tears on her cheek. She tried to tell herself they could resurrect her anyway, but it didn't comfort her. He'd know that and hid her body.

"Why would he kill her? He wouldn't, he

wouldn't," she repeated over and over to the pounding of Gallant's hooves. Her soul knew differently. Beyond a shadow of a doubt, she knew Sam was in mortal danger.

Neither Sam nor Kirk were in his tower. Ethan jumped to the ground from the balcony on the second floor. No doors or windows allowed access from the first floor. To enter you took his portal, climbed, or flew.

"He was here," Ethan said grimly. "Get home and get a stone; I'm going for Jon."

Maria plummeted to the ground and transformed. She snatched a red summon stone from a cord around her neck and held it out. "Sam," she said and closed her eyes. "Samantha Quinn," she whispered with tears in her voice.

Cami landed beside her. "What's going on?"

"Miguel was here, and Sam isn't."

"Don't panic, he has no reason to hurt her." Cami plucked a summoning ball from the cord around her neck. "Kirk."

Jen screamed and fell to her knees when Kirk appeared. Black spots swam before her eyes and her heart pounded. She didn't realize she'd fallen to her face until Ethan hauled her up. A red haze coated her vision.

"We'll find her. Kirk, summon everyone." Cami grabbed another stone from the woven cord. "Jon."

Clenching his sword in a white-knuckled grip, Brandon swore, "Fuck, I'll never go without stones again. I'm making a necklace like theirs."

"What's going on," Kirk said as he summoned his cauldron.

"Sam is missing."

"No, I was just with her; she's taming a white wolf."

"Where?"

Kirk pointed east, and Jen collapsed against Ethan's neck crying. "She's okay, just busy. Thank God, thank God."

Kirk patted her back awkwardly as she cried in Ethan's arms.

"What happened?" Jon asked as soon as he appeared.

"Miguel was here. At first, I was angry he'd spied on us, but then I realized he'd never come to me first. And Sam would be easy for him to subdue."

"But why would he?" Cami asked.

"I panicked. Logically, he wouldn't, but I felt her danger. She's in danger, I feel it in my soul."

Ethan kissed her brow. "You weren't wrong, he came here. Your bedroom is trashed, Kirk."

Kirk turned toward the woods where Sam was.

"We'll go," Kuan said and soared into the sky. Maria followed him.

Jon laid his hand on Kirk's shoulder. "We'll handle him." His gaze traveled them. "We've been avoiding this too long. Tomorrow, we'll go see what they're up too and do whatever needs doing."

I'm a Fairy Knight

Stiff and sore from sleeping on the floor across Sam's doorway, Jen casted a heal on herself then stretched. Ethan had gone home angry with her for staying. He'd returned an hour later with a pillow and blanket and laid beside her. They waited now by the main door with the other fae as Jon gave directions for their absence. She healed Ethan too, earning a small smile.

"Sorry, I know you're worried." He kissed her brow and hugged her.

She shivered and tried to get closer.

"Give me your hand." He gasped and pulled her tighter against him when he touched her glowing blue hand. "You're more than worried, you're terrified. There's no need. We can protect her."

"I was certain he'd killed her and hid her body. I was certain of it. Why do I think he'd do that? Is my magic telling me?"

Ethan turned to Jon who shrugged uncomfortably. "I don't know why either, Jen, but we won't take any chances with her. Brandon, Cami, Tony, and Cass will stay to guard her. She's in the castle with all doors and windows locked by the wizards. Her floor is sanded. If he enters, prints will show."

Jon fingered his new belt. Woven of thin vines to make breaking them easier, pockets containing summoning stones lined the front and sides; the dangling end reached mid-thigh. All of them wore similar belts with a pouch holding health potions.

"We should take more women," Jen said as her gaze landed on the people gathered to see them off.

"We can handle this," Ethan said.

"Yes, but how will the women there take a horde of armed men descending after being at Miguel's mercy for months. You saw what a pervert he was."

Jon turned to the steps where the citizens of Camelot had gathered. "Can I have ten volunteers, preferably those who do well in militia training, and at least five women please?"

Thirty women rose their hands.

"You pick, Jen." Jon gestured to the volunteers.

"Ling, Vicky, Alysa, Shelia, Nina." She turned to Jon and frowned. "We should have tabards for everyone. Similar enough to ours they're clearly marked as our citizens."

"I'll get right on it," Ramiro said.

Jon eyed the men on the stairs. "Emilio, Conner, Sota, Jase, Wayne go grab your weapons and whatever's handy in the kitchen food wise. We'll summon you last."

The men he named ran off.

"The rest of you stay alert. I admit, Kuan being so concerned worries me. I'm also worried that this was intentional to produce just this response, taking us all from our castle. I don't like splitting up like this, and I hate that Maria and Kuan are flying there alone." Jon paced in a small circle and shrugged his shoulders irritably. He carried a sword and shield Galahad had traded for health stones. In his hands, they became unbreakable weapons capable of stopping both Jen and Brandon's sword.

Everyone wore their tabards over white, linen shirts and tan, drawstring pants tucked into leather boots. Translation stones dangled from thin, leather cords tied about their necks. Jen wore the same, but hers was hidden under her black armor.

"Not that I don't love the view but try this." Ethan handed her his tabard.

She put it on and glanced down at herself, shrugged and gave it back. She removed her tabard and resummoned her armor then put her tabard on over it. "Needs a belt, but it'll do."

"Use your summon stone belt." Ethan tucked a strand of hair behind her ear.

Now about two inches long the wind caught the ends and tossed it every which way.

"I'm afraid it'll disappear if I dispel my armor because they're summoned items too. I'll experiment later."

He nodded and kissed her.

Jon reached into the pack at his feet and withdrew a length of vine, cut a section off, and handed it to her. She nodded her thanks absently. Every muscle in her body felt tight. The druids were headed into danger unprotected, and it was killing her.

Ethan stepped back and pursed his lips as his gaze traveled them. "You three better relax before you burst a blood vessel. Your eyes are glowing, and sparks are beginning to fly from your magic."

Jon rotated his neck then rubbed it. "Danu doesn't like this. We should be with them." He turned to Brandon and frowned. "I'm sorry, but you have to stay here to protect all of them."

Ed stamped his hooves and whinnied. Astride him, Brandon held his naked blade across his armored lap. His eyes glowed blue from his slitted helm.

"Have you ever tried to make him fly? Wasn't he a flying mount?"

Before the words left Jon's lips, Jen had summoned Gallant. In the game, Gallant grew wings when she wished to travel by air. She did it rarely. Usually, Kuan or Kirk summoned her or Philip had portaled her. She'd preferred to gallop across the ground when playing for fun. Ed was already in the air, silver hooves giving of gray clouds.

Gallant leaped upward, and white wings sprouted from his shoulders

"Don't you dare. Come back and get me!" Ethan called.

She circled them and landed, holding her hand to her husband.

"Bring my pack," Jon said to Lou and jumped on behind them.

Gallant's wings flapped slowly, and his body moved as if he galloped.

"It never occurred to me to try. He amazed me as a regular horse. This…" She shook her head and leaned forward. Ethan lay against her back, the solidness of him comforting.

They'd barely cleared the castle grounds when Jon said, "Maria calls," and disappeared.

Jen guided Gallant to the ground searching for a clear enough spot to land him.

"Kuan is calling me." The need to accept made sweat break on her brow, but she couldn't disappear and let Ethan fall. She turned Gallant back toward the castle.

"Go, I can leap." Ethan kissed her and jumped.

She hesitated. His passive ability to jump from

great heights should help him, but he could still break a leg or knock himself out on a branch. Tears filled her eyes as she accepted the summon. The conflicting needs made her feel sick.

As soon as she arrived, she broke a red ball from her belt and summoned her husband. Yellow light flickered from her fingertips in a heal that bounced between everyone present. She kissed Ethan quickly then hugged Kuan. She did the same to Jon and Maria before taking a second to check her surroundings.

Her tabard hadn't disappeared when she dispelled her armor to reach her summon stones, she noted. It remained under her armor when she reapplied the armor. She removed it and her belt, reapplied her armor, and the tabard and then her belt. She kissed her husband again and hugged him tightly, placing both hands on his chest.

"That bad, huh," he murmured and brought her hands to his mouth to kiss them.

"I'm okay. Conflicting needs suck."

His breath misted her hands as he chuckled quietly. A sigh of relief escaped her. "Do that again."

He rose an eyebrow.

"Blow on my hands."

He kissed her fingertips, then blew on them.

"That's so much better." She made a face when he laughed. She glanced at Jon who glowed with magic.

"Maria, try kissing his fingers and blowing on

them. Let's see if we can make his magic calm down." By the time everyone was summoned Jon was much calmer.

"Yeah, feeling them breathe works better than hugging them. We should experiment latter. Rob, give Jen an invisibility ball and use a cloak, Ethan, Rob, Jen, and I will scout. The rest of you hang back."

The druids had summoned them to the shore on the edge of the Dover cliffs, which was as far as they could go and still be in their zone. The village was only a mile away and an easy walk. No one spoke until they could see the roofs of the buildings in the distance.

Rob conjured and donned a black cloak that would make him appear as someone you expected to see. Joash appeared and dropped a small, clear marble at Jen's feet. With that, she'd be invisible as long as she remained quiet, but it only lasted an hour.

"Thanks, Joash." The bird bobbed its head and headed to a branch above them to roost.

Jen followed her husband through the trees. The odor of the village grew with each step.

"It wasn't this bad before," she whispered, gagging on the stench.

"Something big died, and it's rotting. More than one somethings. Probably people. Jen, go back to the others," Jon said.

"No, let's go."

Jon sighed hard but didn't try again for which

she was grateful. She didn't want to pit her magic against his— ever.

They appeared from the trees on the outskirts of the town. To their left, a narrow dirt path led to a cleared field. To their right, lay the sea. Desiccated corpses hung from wooden poles sunk into the sand of the beach. None looked fresh. The smell came from the left where three corpses rotted in a cage beside a path leading to a planted field.

Decay made the remains unidentifiable.

"Not likely them." Jon beckoned them forward.

The village was eerily quiet. No one walked along the street or docks. A loud clang as if someone close beat against a piece of metal made Jen jump. As if it'd been a signal, a group of men exited a nearby building and headed to the dock.

Four, older women wearing dirty tunics sidled up the road, casting nervous glances behind them. They entered the building the men had just left.

On the docks, one of the men peered back and shook his head then got in a small boat. Another man entered a boat, and they spread a net between them.

"Trawling, but doing it wrong," Ethan said.

The four of them headed down the street. The street curved and split. One section continued along the beach, the other wove through wooden houses. They headed inland. Each intersection sported a decaying corpse impaled on a sharpened stake.

"Last time I was here lots of people were about of all ages," Jen said.

"They're still here," Ethan said as a girl darted from a house and ran down the street, her bare feet kicking up dust as she ran.

A dirty cloth covered her head, and she hunched, gazing around as if she expected a monster to leap out. They followed her to her destination, a similar house two blocks away where she knocked on a door, biting her lip and peering over her shoulder.

"Fool," the woman who answered the door said. "They catch you, and it's the ax or worse." She yanked the girl into the house.

Ethan jumped and swung himself into a second-story window. He returned five minutes later looking grim.

"Her mother is sick, and they have no water left. She isn't allowed to go to the well for two more days."

They continued forward. Another loud clank of metal on metal and doors opened. People emerged carrying buckets. They didn't speak to each other, walking with their heads down, staring at their feet. The sound of hammering and men calling orders came to them. They passed a group of men dismantling a house, overseen by a man carrying a whip, and followed the men carrying the pieces to the edge of town.

"Holy Christ." Jon stopped dead.

Jen thought she might vomit. "We should've come sooner." Trembling and nauseated, she clutched her husband's hand in her sweaty one. Chained men swung hammers and laid stone adding onto a stone manor house. A pile of rotting skulls stood beside the door. Corpses dangled by their tied wrists between other men who labored on the house. Flies buzzed about, coating the live and dead men in swarms.

"This isn't our fault, sweetheart."

"We could've stopped them." Jen's reply was muffled by her husband's chest. Unable to face the horror, she hid her face against him and tried to still the wild beating of her heart.

Ethan rubbed her back in small circles. "Bad people are everywhere; we can't stop them all. We protect our own."

"These were our own." Her words caught on a sob.

As she cried, Steve strode from the house the men worked on. Instantly, every man fell to their knees. He laughed and snapped his fingers. One of the few untied men rose. Hardly more than a boy, he stood uncertainly, peering from Steve to the tied men.

"You there, the queen desires company. Go to the harems and fetch someone young who can sing or tell stories. Make the queen happy and you'll be rewarded."

The young man ran back the way they'd come.

Steve sauntered down the street whistling.

"Let's go see what Queen Kendra has to say for herself." Jon strode past the piled skulls into the manor house and up the stairs to the second floor where a woman cried.

A wooden cup banged against the wall as Rob opened the door.

"Oh, Tilas, it's you." Kendra sat beside the window in an upholstered chair with her feet on an ottoman. A tray holding a glass decanter, glass cup, and gold goblet sat on a marble table beside her. Tapestries hung on the wall, curtains enclosed the bed, and woven rugs lay on the floors. A fine coating of dust covered everything and shimmered in the air.

"Send the maid upstairs to sweep before the king arrives."

"Do you require lunch?"

"No, you may go. Wait, how is your daughter?"

"She died, your majesty," Rob said without inflection.

"You may go." Kendra waved at the door and turned back to the window. Rob returned to the door and cast an illusion of the room before him. As long as he remained still, he'd be invisible behind it.

The men outside yelled commands, lifting the stone blocks while others chipped them.

"I hate this place," Kendra said. "I hate this place!" she screamed and threw the book on her lap at the door, then covered her face with her hands and cried.

"Then why do you stay?" Jon asked, becoming visible.

Kendra screamed, then slapped her hands over her mouth.

A man ran through the door his face white and eyes wide, "You cal—"

"OUT!" Kendra bellowed.

The man turned and ran.

"Jon, oh God, you have to get me out of here!"

"You're a paladin. No one can hold you against your will."

"If I go, Miguel and Steve will kill me." Kendra heaved herself to her feet and clutched Jon. "Please, I'm so sorry I went with them. I can't fight them both. I did try. What they do…"

"You're a liar," Jen snapped and became visible.

"No, I did try…"

"Diva could outrun them. You could've come to us, and told us, and we could've stopped them. What's stopping you from leaving right this second and running away?"

"Where would I go? I don't know where you are. When they caught me, they'd hurt me. I considered killing myself, but I don't want to die. I don't want to live here either."

"Where is Miguel?"

"I don't know. I haven't seen him in weeks. I see no one except Steve and the servants."

Is he the king?"

A red flush crossed Kendra's cheeks. "Stan is the king. Please, can we go?"

"Really? Just like that?" Jen strode to the window and gazed out, then pointed to the pile of skulls. "How many did you kill?"

"None, I swear." Kendra bit her lips and licked them. "Please, Jen? We were friends once. How can you leave me here? " Her gaze traveled the room, and she brightened. "I can pay for your help."

"How?" Jon asked in a soft, dangerous voice.

Her smile wilted. "This is all mine. I'll give it to you. Or…" She licked her lips again and looked away, ringing her hands. "I can send for food. You must be sick of bread."

"How about a harem girl?"

She nodded eagerly and smiled again. "They'll bring one to me if I ask."

Jon grabbed the decanter and threw it against the wall. Red wine stained the tapestry as glass shards flew.

"Idiot, it was the only glass jar in this town!" She snatched the glass cup as if afraid he'd grab and throw it.

"None of this is yours!" Jon bellowed.

The man ran back into the room and froze. He fell to his knees, his expression terrified.

"Gather your townspeople!" Jon snapped.

"No, we must sneak away." Kendra grabbed Jon's arm "Tilas, stay there; I command you."

"You are queen of nothing!" Jen yelled. She grabbed Kendra by her red gown and yanked her forward. Touching her made Danu pulse hard and Jen was suddenly furiously angry.

Kendra summoned her armor and pulled away. "Let me go."

"See how easy it is to get away, you fucking liar!" Jen drew her sword. "Go outside right now, or I'll kill you where you stand."

Kendra's wide-eyed gazed darted between them.

"Tilas, go summon your people." Jon reached forward as if to lift Tilas to his feet.

Tilas fell to his face.

"Go gather the people!" Jen bellowed and grabbed Kendra's arm. Kendra let herself be pulled from the room.

"Steve Wallace!" Jen screamed when she exited. She released Kendra and drew her sword. Without her willing it a blue glow coated it. She swung and severed the chain holding the men. Screaming in fury, she swung again, cutting loose the chained corpses. The men cowered from her.

She grabbed one at random. "You, what's your name?"

"I be called Graham."

"Graham, has Steve Wallace wronged you?"

His gaze darted to the men beside him. She flicked her fingers and casted Sanctuary. "No harm will come to you while you stand on this spot. I'll be your champion against Steve Wallace. I'm strongest when fighting evil. Has he done evil?"

Graham straightened. "Oh yes, murder, so many murders, and rape."

Her magic rushed from her and surrounded the men. Their fear and rage became hers.

"He's stolen!" another man yelled.

"He's destroyed my house!"

"He killed my sheep!"

"He killed my father!"

In moments, all yelled crimes. The sword in Jen's hand blazed with blue fire. She felt the sword's need as if it were a living being. It pulled at her, trying to make its need hers.

"Steve, face me in single combat, or we'll hunt you down like a dog!" Her voice echoed from the buildings.

With a thought, she summoned her mount and galloped in the direction he'd gone whistling his jaunty tune. Blue flame licked along the length of her blade, she and Danu were in accord, both wanted to stop the evil.

She screamed her charge and leapt, landing in a group of men. To her eyes, they pulsed, outlined in red, the evil so thick on them she could practically smell it. She killed them in seconds. A corner of her mind was horrified, but mostly she felt relief from the pressing need to slay evil.

"Jen!" Ethan called.

She heard, but Danu had her and she couldn't stop. She followed her sword.

Steve stood on the edge of a field. He turned

as she approached and grabbed up his sword.

"This is my kingdom!" he yelled. "You chose to stay with Jon and make your own. You have no right here."

"Not anymore it's not. Your kingdom is Hell!" She swung. Her sword clanged against his with a harsh metallic screech. Their shields crashed like thunder. Gallant screamed in rage and pawed the air.

"Jen!" Ethan called, sounding terrified.

She glanced back, and Steve's sword caught her on the side of the head. She rolled with it and jumped to her feet.

"I got this, stay back."

Steve said, "I'll kill you, Jen. Go home."

"If I die, I'll be rezed; will you?" She swung again, laughing as he ran from her. "Where will you go, Steve? How will you hide from me?"

He stopped and turned. His angry gaze traveled them. Jen glanced back in time to see Kuan appear at Ethan's side.

Steve's expression tightened to fear as Jon appeared summoned by Ethan.

"This is none of your business. Mess with me and Miguel will kill you in your sleep!"

"Really? Hiding behind Miguel, you piece of shit! Let him fucking try. You think I can't find him?" Jen held her sword aloft. It blazed so brightly it casted shadows. "I feel the evil here. Once I clean this shithole up. I'll find and kill him."

Jen waved her empty hand at the manacled

men behind her. "Why, Steve? Why do that when you could live in peace with us?"

Behind her, the townsfolk muttered, casting nervous glances at the gathered knights.

"I'm a god here. We can all be gods—"

"Go to Hell!" She rushed forward.

Steve's head rolled from his body. She wiped her sword on his corpse and sheathed it with shaking hands, turning back to Ethan, wanting the comfort of his embrace. Without the sword's push the horror of her act overcame her.

She remembered Steve laughing and dancing with Sam at a bar in Japan and playing the game with his friends. He'd joked and been one of the guys. A normal man, not a monster who raped and murdered. It scared her to think she'd never seen this darkness in him. It made her sick to think she might've been able to help him if she'd come before he'd grown this corrupt. And as much as she'd like to blame Danu for his death, she'd wanted him dead too.

Silence broken by whimpers brought her gaze over her shoulder to the groveling field workers.

A blue mist rose from Steve's body and rushed her. She screamed. The magic was terrified, it wanted to live. Without her will, her arm rose, holding her sword aloft. Lightning struck, knocking her to her knees. Ozone filled the air as the lighting lingered. Her arm sagged, and the lightning jumped and impacted Emilio who screamed and fell to the ground.

"Back away," Jon called, his words dim in Jen's ears.

Fire coursed over her, waves of white-hot agony she remembered from the plane, but this time she didn't pass out. She felt every excruciating second.

Ethan sobbed and called her name, held back by Kuan's embrace. He leapt and landed beside her, kneeling, but not touching her. "Let it go," Jen.

"I can't; Danu wants another."

Tears trailed across her cheeks, feeling like molten metal. Etan released his magic and screamed when it touched hers. "Let it go, Jen, please."

"Help me."

Kuan stood beside her now, surrounding her with his magic. A ball of greenish-yellow light flew from his fingers and she fell to the ground. Maria joined him. Ethan grabbed Jen and screamed when the lightning coated him too but didn't let go.

Maria cried out and stepped back, pulling her magic from Jen. Then biting her lip, and face scrunched with anticipation of pain, she stepped forward and began to cast heals. For five minutes and thirty-six seconds, Jen shook in her husband's arms. When Danu dissipated, she lay limply and cried. Ethan lay in the dirt beside her, trying to offer comfort.

The pain had vanished, but the memory would haunt her forever.

"Emilio?" She pushed herself to her feet. Emilio lay in Maria's arms unconscious.

"Becoming fae, I think," she said and laid him gently on the ground.

Jen's sword appeared in her hand with a thought and she turned back to Steve's corpse. The field hands had gathered beside the townfolk on the edge of the field. Most watched silently although a few cried.

"Burn the body and scatter the ashes!" Jen yelled.

"Jen?"

A shudder rippled her skin at the sound of Ethan's voice.

"Genevieve Frey!" Kuan called, sounding pissed.

It made her laugh despite herself. She put will in her voice and bellowed, "Burn the body and scatter the ash! Tell me who has wronged you and I will be your champion!" The field workers had gathered on the edge of the field as far as the ropes holding them would let them get.

"Is that a good idea, Jen?" Ethan grabbed her arm and examined her face. "You're freaking me out a bit. Calm down please."

"So much evil here." She shivered and flicked her fingers. A soft, red glow tinged with yellow surrounded the corpse. The woman cowering over their half-filled baskets began to cry.

"She isn't resurrecting him, she's laying evil spirits!" Ethan yelled.

Rob stepped closer. A wave of fire covered the corpse. Black smoke billowed in choking clouds, smelling of burnt pork. When all that remained was a charred spot and ashes, the druids rose their hands. A tornado sucked up the ash and lifted it into the air. Over the treetops, it dissipated, releasing the ash and small debris it carried. The ash drifted in the wind and was lost from sight.

On the edge of the field, Kirk stood beside his cauldron, glaring at the gathered men with his hands on his hips.

"On my honor, it will heal, not harm," Jon was saying as Jen approached.

Her magic flowed across the gathered men. Jon's and Kuan's magic joined it. Sparks jumped along it. The men moaned and fell to their knees. Some ran, casting terrified glances over their shoulders.

"You," Jen pointed with her sword to a man who wore dangling metal manacles and a dirty breechcloth. "Hold out your hand." Using the tip of her sword, she sliced the metal. "The green potion can only be used by the recipient. It will heal. A major illness or injury might take a few potions spaced out over an hour. Use them or not, it's your choice, but I swear they won't harm you."

Thunder rumbled although the sky was clear.

Her magic returned to her, and she jerked back and cried out. Danu was afraid and angry. Jen's fear and disgust of what had been done with the magic combined with the villager's righteous fury in a seething mass she could actually see. The magic within her felt bloated. Pressure built, a tingling pain in her arms and fingers. "Tell me the name of who has harmed you, and I will be your champion." The pressure eased as she spoke, letting her take a deep, gasping breath.

Ethan grabbed her arm and tried to pull her away. "Jen, stop."

"I have to. I'm sorry, but I must. It's who I am." The magic surrounding her roiled and gusted in agitation. The urge to mount Gallant and charge away in search of evil doers competed with her desire to stay with Jon and Ethan, leaving her feeling dizzy and sick.

Ethan laid a hand on her shoulder.

"Let us help. Tell us the name," he said softly to the man in the breechcloth.

Another man pushed forward and offered his bound hands to Jen. She recognized him as the scared man from her first visit months ago. Now much thinner in just a dirty breechcloth she saw scars marred his entire body not just his face.

"Please, Lady? Silas chained us, but not by his choice. If you're looking for evil, then look to our queen." He spat on the ground, then rubbed his freed wrists. "Might I, Sir?" He nodded to the cauldron.

"Help yourself." Kirk made an expansive gesture at the cauldron and stepped back.

The scarred man took one, popped the top with a thumb and drank the contents. The flask returned to mist and dissipated. The lesions on his wrists disappeared. Crusty red bruises on his chest began to fade.

"You need another," Kirk said and waved at the pot.

"Obliged," the man said and took another. The scar across his face faded.

The people watching gasped. Suddenly men pressed forward eagerly, offering their chained hands. Jen cut them free. Each sword strike inflamed her desire to seek out the evil and destroy it.

Jon laid a hand on her shoulder. "Be still."

The need to run off and find the evil in the town lessened and she sighed gratefully.

"I am Jon Arthur, King of Camelot. Nothing can repair the harm you've suffered, but we'll help set things right. Miguel will be hard to catch, and until he's caught, something must be done for your protection. How many are you?"

"About five hundred, your majesty." The man paled and bowed.

"No need to bow; I'm not your king. We offer sanctuary in our castle. Any may come and leave when they wish. My wizards can lock your doors so only you may enter, but Miguel could follow you in. He can do the same at the castle, but we'll be there. If he comes there, we'll chase and catch him."

While Jon spoke, a few men ran off. More arrived. The man who'd drunk the potion grabbed another handful.

"Will you come free my fellows and the women, Lady?"

"Yes."

Jon pulled her back as she strode forward.

"Lady Frey is a protection paladin. Your pain will incite her. Think carefully before telling her the names of evil doers, she'll kill them without mercy or warning. It is her nature." Jon grabbed Ethan's arm. "Stay with your wife. Lou, you and Rob go with her and try to keep up.

"I'm going to," Kuan said.

Jon hugged him, then pushed away to stare into his eyes. "Be careful. Jen is more than she was. Danu will push her. Hold her back, don't encourage her. We don't want Danu to take her completely.

Kuan smiled sadly. "I'll be careful. I don't want her to go into the mists either."

Jon searched his face another moment before releasing him.

"Maria, go to Kendra and bring her as far as you can from this place."

The men exclaimed angrily.

"No, we don't wish to save her, but if Jen sees her, she'll likely kill her, and I'll spare my knight from that." Jon kissed Jen's brow. "Try to stay away from her. I felt their sincerity too." He gestured at the gathered people who mumbled complaints about Kendra. "You'll have justice, just not right this second. Go and free the captives while we organize help."

The now scar free man stepped forward. "I am Sir Alberic, and this was my town gifted to me from King Irminric of Caer Gwinntguic. Your evil knight thought it good sport to see me suffer unable to help my fellows. Will you really free them and go?"

The townsfolk stared with suspicious eyes.

"Let me borrow your magic so he can feel my honesty," Jen said.

She waited until a dense, blue cloud surrounded Sir Alberic. He rubbed his arms but stood his ground.

Jen strode into the whirling blue magic and took his hand. "I will free them, and our people will help as they are able. We can't go until we catch Miguel though. To do so would leave you defenseless. It would be much safer for your people to come to Camelot. We can't afford to leave our people defenseless either. Most of us will return and soon."

"I feel your sincerity," he said amazed. Then he narrowed his eyes. "Are you a demon? How can I trust this..." he trailed off not certain what to call the blue mist surrounding him.

"I am a woman with magic. You call my kind fae." She gestured at the whirling cloud of blue mist surrounding them. "Danu is here." She smiled at his start of amazement. "We're not evil by nature, but from choice, the same as you."

"Thank you for your help." Sir Alberic bowed

deeply his expression caught between terror and wonder and his eyes trying to track the flickering static through the mist. He turned from her and rose his voice. "I feel the truth of her words. Go to your homes and gather your families. We'll go to their castle until Miguel is caught."

Jon stepped forward. "He could be here now. Be quick. There's too much evil here for Lady Frey to pick him from the rest. Get to the beach so my knights can guard you." He hugged Jen again. "Take your party and free the chained ones."

Jen nodded and motioned for Sir Alberic to lead the way.

Rob gestured to houses they passed. "Point out homes with no occupants and I can lock them until you decide what to do with them. The fewer places we leave Miguel to hide, the better."

The men eagerly pointed out buildings, sometimes arguing amongst themselves over the fate of the inhabitants. Each word they spoke incited Danu until Jen walked in a glowing blue cloud.

"What are you?" The man walking beside Alberic asked.

"Mrs. Genevieve Frey, this is my husband, Ethan. What's your name?"

"Amos, but that isn't what I meant. Our queen was an evil witch. What are you?"

"A fairy."

His eyes bugged out. "A fairy queen?"

"Not a queen, just a knight. I'm Lady Frey,

wife of Sir Ethen Frey. I'm a protection paladin and Knight of the Round Table. My title keeps getting longer and longer," she said in aside to her husband.

"Likely they be witches and liars too," someone mumbled

Jen whistled and vaulted to Gallant's back and had him hover above them. She drew her sword and called loudly, "On my honor, I am no witch but a fairy with magic. Good magic from the Earth itself. Kendra was corrupt; I am not she." Dust flew from the sweep of Gallant's wings as she landed. The crowd exclaimed as he melted into mist.

A man wearing a ragged tunic belted with a withered vine nodded sagely. "Aye, they canno lie, but they be triksy buggers. I remember stories from me grandmum. She be tellin' to ner accept food nor drink. Favors done came steep."

"Then she be tellin' about Kendra," Ethan said and turned twinkling eyes to Jen. "The food we offer is just food with no hidden properties. We won't trap you in our castle, you can go whenever you wish. Time will pass same as ever. What else…" he tapped his chin, then snapped his fingers. "We won't steal babies or entrap you with music. And I hate to tell you this, but we can lie if we choose. What we can't do is break oaths made with magic."

"When the king and queen arrived, they were all sweetness and light too!" someone shouted.

"Where is the king?" Jen called.

"The harems probably. That's where he is most days. He takes who he wants and does what he wishes."

Red hot rage scorched her.

"Oh, now you did it," Ethan said angrily.

Her arm slipped from his grasp. An overwhelming need possessed her. She wanted to stay but couldn't stop herself from mounting Gallant and charging away. The sound of his hooves striking the dirt was deeply satisfying. The sword she waved in the air glowed with blue fire.

I must look like an idiot, she thought as she skidded to a halt. The effort to do so left her sweating. Blue magic covered her in a swirling cloud lit with bright sparks.

"Wait, please wait," her husband begged, and she wanted to.

The conflicting needs made her tremble.

"Help me."

Kuan and Ethan reached her at the same time.

"Let her go," Kuan said. The magic surrounding her thickened. "Feel her need, Ethan. You're hurting her. Let her be what she is."

"Go free the men. I'll go with my wife."

Jen rushed forward as soon as Ethan jumped on behind her. Their magic continued to writhe in a maelstrom about them. He was very angry and disgusted. Spikes of sadness and horror flickered with love and worry.

"I'm not angry with you, I'm worried. Your

eyes are glowing white, and the magic is so thick about you I'm afraid you'll go like Gallant and be gone for good. Hold onto me, Jen. I feel the need, but don't let me go. You're terrifying me."

His terror hurt, burning along her nerves like fire. His lips on the back of her neck quenched the burn. He kept them there until Gallant skidded to a halt before a ramshackle inn. A sagging, shingled roof topped two stories of graying planks. Windows closed with shutters lined the front. The man that had been leaning against the closed front door ran when he saw her appear at the end of the street.

Ethen leapt and cut him down.

"I recognize him. One of Stan's toadies."

Gallant screamed and reared as she dismounted. Together, she and Ethan kicked the door in.

"Take one step, and I'll run you through." The men resumed their seats, exchanging nervous glances. "You," she pointed at the naked woman serving drinks. "Go upstairs with my husband and bring every woman down."

"I can't, my lady, most are chained."

"I'll watch them here. You go get them," Ethan said as he jumped and landed on the center table. "I'm a rogue just like Miguel," he was saying as Jen ran up the stairs.

Four men rushed her when she reached the top-floor hallway. She killed them all in seconds then began kicking in doors. She'd killed fifteen more men and freed twenty women in under ten minutes. So furious her hands shook, she bellowed for the women to follow.

"Which ones of these filthy swine are rapists?" Jen pointed her glowing sword at the men cowering before Ethan.

"All of them, my lady," the sobbing barmaid said.

A red haze clouded her vision. When it cleared, she stood among corpses awash in blood. Her skin tingled as if recovering from pins-needles.

"Help is coming," Ethan said, sounding far away. "Dress as best you can. My wife is a fairy, but a good one." He laughed. The laugh cut off abruptly. "Are there more such houses?"

Without willing it, Jen had a hold of the barmaid's arm and pulled her screaming into the street. She released her arm and vaulted to Gallant's back, following her glowing sword.

Keep Your Vows

Jen woke with a blinding headache and a throat so dry she couldn't speak. And she wanted to speak. Her husband lay crying with his head on her breast. He jerked upright when she stroked his hair.

"Jen, thank God. Are you okay?"

"Water," she managed to croak.

"Kuan, bring water!" Ethan shouted. He ran his hands over her and pressed his lips to hers, mumbling his words. "Never do that again. I love you so much."

Kuan entered and handed Ethan a pitcher that glistened with water droplets. Ethen drew back and poured water across her lips. In a moment, she was able to heal herself. In another, she could sit and take the glass. She drank five before her raging thirst dwindled.

Kuan retreated after throwing a heal and kissing her brow, leaving she and Ethan alone in the room.

"What happened?"

"You don't remember?"

"I remember the harem and the woman screaming. God, I'm sorry I scared her like that." Jen winced and rubbed her head.

Straw crinkled under her hands as she pushed herself up. Ethan sat beside her, his worried gaze traveling her. She winced when his magic engulfed her. He withdrew it quickly with a wince of his own.

"Sorry." Tears filled his eyes as he leaned forward and hugged her hard. "God, Jen, I thought I'd lost you. You scared me to death."

"How many did I kill?"

He hesitated before mumbling," Sixty-seven. But they were all bad."

"Jesus." Acid burned her throat, and she thought she might vomit.

"It wasn't you, Jen."

"That doesn't make it better." She began to tremble. "Danu can make me murder people, Ethan. I'm a murderer. No trials, no mercy…" She pushed him away and scrambled from the bed. In the bathroom, she vomited until dry heaves racked her.

He knelt beside her, smoothing her hair with trembling hands.

"Jen…" his voice broke, and he gathered her

in his lap. "It wasn't you. I stood in your magic and felt nothing of you. Danu felt fear, sorrow, and a powerful need. There was no recognition of me or Kuan, no love. You didn't hate them. While I can't say for sure what the feelings were for, I believe Danu was sad it needed to kill and afraid for the wronged villagers there."

Jen closed her eyes and breathed against her husband's neck; the smell of his skin comforted her. The warm solidness of his body made her feel safe but she knew now it was an illusion.

"I couldn't stop it though, Ethan. What if it makes me kill an innocent person? Hell, for all we know I did kill innocent people."

"No. I stood in the magic with Kuan and Rob. We felt the truth when the villagers spoke. Those men were evil. What you did was necessary. Miguel allowed them to be as evil as they wished without fear of reappraisal. Don't think for one minute the citizens of Limenware let that happen. They tried to fight back and paid horribly. Miguel found those responsible, and Steve killed the families in a gruesome manner. A manner Kendra devised."

"Jesus, I forgot about Kendra."

"She's here. I think the change made her kind of crazy. I really hate to think she was this evil and I never noticed."

Jen snorted.

"No seriously. Miguel was always a bad guy, trying to cause problems but also not wanting to get blamed for it. This just let him be more himself like Kuan. But Kuan is a good person, a healer at heart. Miguel is a psychopath. Kendra… she's a combination of lazy and greedy mixed with a level of disregard for other's feelings boarding on psychopathic."

"What are we going to do with her?"

"Execute her."

Jen's breath caught on a sob.

"Jen, the things she ordered done… crazy or not, the villagers from Limenware deserve justice. We can't lock her up and hope to 'cure' her, and if we let her go, she'll be a real danger. Whoever gets a hold of her could easily manipulate her. She doesn't seem to know right from wrong. She ordered the deaths of hundreds of people, laughing over the gruesome ways she devised. I'm sorry, Jen, but she deserves what she gets. In fact, I think Jon is being too lenient. If it were up to me, I'd give her to them and let them punish her."

"They couldn't kill her."

"She isn't you. Kendra never dueled because she couldn't. Scripted fights she did well, but her teams never won because she couldn't handle the unexpected. Faced with a new situation, she freezes. Without Stan telling her what to do and Miguel's protection, the townsfolk could've killed her."

"Stan. What happened to him?"

"You killed him. One quick thrust." Ethan laid his face against hers. "I'm glad you don't remember it."

"I don't want to remember; I just don't want to lose control like that again. And if Kendra is a murderer for ordering deaths, I surely am for swinging that sword."

"We'll be careful of people touching you standing in magic. Kuan thinks if you didn't fight it, but cooperated, you could retain control."

She shuddered and tightened her grasp on Ethan.

"I'm not me anymore. I died. Genevieve Frey doesn't exist anymore. The lightning killed her."

He kissed her temple. "No, Jen, it changed you, but your still you. We're all changed. Mostly in good ways."

"This isn't good." Tears trailed down her cheeks.

"I admit it's scary, but justice by the sword is expected in the world we live in now. There are no prisons. Murderers are killed. Crime is punished harshly. I'm so sorry you're the conduit for Danu's justice, but I'm glad she wants justice for her magic misused."

Jen said nothing. The warmth of her husband's love soothed her soul. She'd speak to Jon and make sure they had a plan to stop her if she lost control again.

"What if it takes me and never lets me go?"

Ethan started crying.

"Please, I can't help it." She began to cry too and her headache returned. His distress hurt her soul. "I swear I'll come back if I'm able."

Tears glittered on his cheek as he framed her face with his hand. "Yes, swear. Take me with you if you go."

Jen reached to her magic and put will behind her words as she whispered, "I swear I'll return to you. That I'll fight to be with you. I'll do everything in my power to keep my magic from taking me from you."

Ethan's eyes flared blue, and he grasped her hands so tightly it hurt. "We'll share everything. Every call you feel, I'll feel. Your needs will become my needs and mine yours."

The magic gathered. Jen felt it tingle along her skin like lightning about to strike. She spoke eagerly, willing her words to be true. "Our magic will bring us together, not apart. Where you go, I go. Where I go, you go. I'll help you slay our enemies. Nothing will separate us, not death, or time; we belong together." Lightning flowed through the window and slammed into them with shocking suddenness.

Jen closed her eyes and imagined herself running and Ethan keeping pace. She pictured him leaping to Gallant's back and holding his hand on her glowing, blue sword. She relived the fight in the harem in her mind and pictured Ethan fighting with her, a shadow knowing exactly where she would be and what she would do. A vision of the karate studio appeared in her mind, she and Ethan copying each other in the mirrored wall.

"Yes," she said with as much will as she could.

When she woke again, Ethan handed her a glass of water and stroked her hair as she drank. "Rest, sweetheart. We can worry about the town later. Sleep and rest easy. You tried very hard. Too hard. Rest now." His pants settle to the floor with a whisper of sound, and he climbed in beside her.

"I'm naked, she murmured, just realizing it as she lay against him.

"Yeah, I like you that way. I'll show you how much when you wake."

She laughed and drifted to sleep in his arms.

Ethan's arm pinned her to his side. She eased it aside and tiptoed to the bathroom. Their gravity feed shower felt like heaven. Before returning to the bedroom, she opened the front door to check the castle to see who else was home. Her gaze halted on a row of new houses. She recognized most as miniatures from Nina's shop that had lined a shelf above her desk.

"Everything is handled and everyone safe. Come back to bed." Ethan reached over her head to close the door

Smiling, she turned in his arms and let him.

A commotion drew Jen from her bed an hour later. Wrapped in the light sheet, which was the only covering on their fur-covered bed, she went to the

door to peer out. Ethan followed and pressed against her back to see over her shoulder.

She turned to smile at him, loving how his presence filled her with joy. Maria and Cami flew overhead screaming. A glance at the castle showed no one in residence except Sam. Instantly, she was overtaken by a wave of despair. Goosebumps appeared on her arms. She dropped the sheet and ran for her clothes.

"Miguel," Ethan said and scrambled for his clothing.

Gallant waited outside the door, pawing the grass and snorting. He bolted into the air in one smooth move as soon as Ethan vaulted on behind her.

"There." Ethan pointed unnecessarily; she'd already seen the druids headed outside the walls toward the east to the stadium they'd made for the wedding. Her sword flared blue. She followed it. People ran along the tree lined path both toward and away from the stadium. Most carried weapons.

The shallow bowl ringed with rock tiers for seating would fit thousands when it was finished. Staggered tiers formed the western side, covered with leafy bowers that provided privacy and shade. Thick green grass lined the meadow, empty now of decorations but full of milling people.

The druids had moved the oak tree they'd used as the maypole, leaving it beside the south entrance. Jen peered at the king's pavilion to the north, but no one stood on any of its many levels.

As she drew closer, the indistinct mummers became clear calls of, 'Murderer.'

Ethan tightened his grip on her. "Keep your magic contained."

They flew over the crowd that encircled Kendra who stood on her Sanctuary. Jon and his knights surrounded the glowing patch of ground.

Jen nodded and brought Gallant in for a landing behind the swarming mass of people. The crowd made way for her.

Calls of, 'The Frey, The Frey,' echoed as she pushed through the townspeople from Limenware. Most wore ragged clothing, although some wore new tunics and a few even wore jeans and T-shirts.

"Don't touch her," Ethan shouted, appearing beside a man reaching for Jen's arm and pulling him away.

"I'm okay," Jen said, but she was glad when they broke through the crowd and into the circle of knights. The citizens of Camelot stood behind Jon. Outnumbered by the new townspeople from Limenware, they stood quietly.

"You're the selfish one," Kendra stood on the edge of her Sanctuary and yelled in Jon's face as Jen arrived.

Despite the seriousness of the situation, Jen winced, and half laughed. Kendra looked ridiculous in her protection armor. A thin black band crossed her chest barely hiding her nipples. Plump ass cheeks swallowed the black, G-string.

The only attractive pieces were the diamond tiara and glittery silver pauldrons, greaves, and gloves. Small chips of diamond and onyx caught and reflected the light. Kendra wore the same exact boots as Jen did in her prot set. Jen spent a moment hoping they didn't look as ridiculous on her.

Gallant returned to mist, leaving Jen and Ethan standing behind Kendra.

Kendra waved her arms. "You had all this, and you left me to rot in that filthy place. And now you'll murder me for being afraid to leave."

Jon swept his hand out, indicating the angry people behind her. "What about them, Kendra? Don't they deserve justice for the murders you committed?"

"I killed no one! They're not real anyway."

"Kendra," Jon spoke slowly as if to a small child with limited understanding. "Your threats and support of Steven and Miguel allowed them to murder with no fear of reprisal. You helped cause that nightmare. You owe recompense."

"Fine, they can have their stinking hovel back! You happy?"

"Their homes are yours to neither take nor give." Jon's gaze flicked to Jen, and he motioned her back. "Her death will be on my hands."

"You can't just kill me, Jon." Kendra whirled to face Jen. "This is crazy. Jen, you can't just let him kill me. It's my magic. You can't steal it from me."

"How do you not see how wrong what you did was?" Jen stepped back from her beseeching hand.

"They mean nothing. Look at them; they don't even really exist. We're special. I didn't make Steven or Miguel do anything. Why should I be punished for other's actions?'

"What about my daughter?" Tilas shouted and pushed himself to the front of the crowd, dragging a girl of about twelve with him. She cried and tried to pull away.

Sanctuary flickered and reappeared further north. Kendra pushed through the surrounding people to the farthest northern edge. The crowd adjusted until they encircled her again.

"This is pointless," Jon said.

"You are such a lying hypocrite." Jen strode onto the Sanctuary and stamped her feet. "You could have easily done this all the way to us, assuming they caught up to you. You choose to stay there."

"I didn't know where the fuck you were!" Kendra shrieked.

Ethan pulled Jen back. "Cowardice doesn't excuse murder. You might not have known exactly, but you didn't even try. I'm willing to bet if Jen reaches out to that girl, you wronged her horribly."

Kendra pressed her lips together and glared at the girl who whimpered and hid her face on her father's chest.

"Not just her, Lady Frey. She had my sister killed because she coveted her belongings." A man pushed forward and spat at Kendra. "You laughed when Miguel struck her down. And for what? A glass jar and some glasses?"

"If you'd just handed them over like you were told, she'd still be alive. It isn't my fault she was a liar. We warned you nothing could be hidden from Miguel."

The man reached to Jen and grasped her arm.

"Enough!" Jon bellowed. "Tony, Lou, silence her. All of you, off the field." Jon waved his hand shooing them away. "Don't make me ask twice," he said in a low, dangerous growl.

The townspeople backed away. By the time all had reached the rock bleachers, Kendra had moved Sanctuary twice more.

"I'm sorry, Kendra, but you brought this on yourself," Lou said as he dropped a silencing totem in the circle of light.

Kendra opened her mouth in a soundless scream and summoned her sword. The swing passed through Tony and whirled her around, leaving her off balance. She stepped outside the edge of light. Instantly, an arrow thudded into her foot,

She screamed soundlessly again and yanked it back, landing on her ass.

The rest of the knights stepped forward, crowding the yellow space, leaving her nowhere to go. All carried drawn weapons. Their grim, angry faces stared without pity.

"We've heard too many tales told in our magic. Tales we know are true. Ordering a death is murder, Kendra. The gruesomeness of those deaths…" Lou lifted his sword, one of the ones they'd brought back from Paris.

Jen turned to survey the crowd who now stood silently ringing the right side of the amphitheater. Behind Jon, a group of Camelot's citizens remained. Jen's gaze traveled them.

"Did Emilio recover?"

Cami turned to her. "Kuan is with him now and assures us Emilio will be a warrior. Jon is teaching him his spells. We wanted to wait until his transformation was complete but we're getting tired of chasing Kendra down and listening to her rants. The women there" – she pointed to the women behind Jon— "have agreed to the change. We asked some men as well to give Danu a choice."

Kendra swung again at Lou. Jen winced, if she'd thought to swing at the totem instead, she could destroy it. Her sword passed through Lou doing no damage. Sanctuary flickered, and Jon rose his sword.

The crowd cheered.

Ethan pulled Jen further away as the lightning hit Jon's upraised, bloody sword. The smell of burning meat and black smoke billowed from the ground. Everyone stepped back. Jen closed her eyes, laying her head on Ethan's shoulders.

"She was so stupid; why couldn't she see?"

Ethan rubbed her back and kissed her temple. Before them, Jon stood alone in the lightning. The lightning jumped to Victoria who screamed and fell to her face. The two druids began healing Jon. The crowd watched in silence. Jen strode forward and casted rest evil spirits on the charred remains of Kendra.

One of the watchers screamed. Jen whirled and staggered back. A cloud of magic rippled over the crowd and raced to Jon. Her magic leaped from her and engulfed the approaching cloud. She fell to her knees sobbing.

"Sam. It's Sam's magic."

The cloud hit Jon who staggered and fell to his knees. The lightning pulsed and flickered, flaring into another strand that slammed into Ling, knocking her to the ground. Her husband screamed and reached for her. The lightning coated him too.

"Back away!" Warren called, gesturing the crowd back. "Some of you get to the castle."

Jen summoned Gallant with a thought. Her hands trembled she was so angry with herself for stopping and wasting time with Kendra.

"No need," Miguel said.

The crowd screamed as the lightning pulsed again and hit Warren.

"Wow, that's quite a show. Almost better than your nightly acts. You're a bitch in heat, Jen. Good thing you trapped Ethan with that oath before he gets tired of your desperation." He placed a fingertip against the glowing sword descending for his neck and smiled. "Kill me, and you'll never find her corpse."

Kirk shrieked and grabbed him.

Miguel disappeared, reappearing behind Jen. "Temper, temper. Piss me off, and I'll just go."

Ethan laid his hand on Jen's shoulder. "What do you want?"

"A vow. I saw you two make one. You guys are great entertainment by the way. Better than any porn I've ever watched." He laughed as Ethan straightened and grabbed his daggers.

"What kind of vow?" Jen called, surprised at the calmness of her voice.

"You and Brandon promise to neither hunt nor harm me."

"While you pick off the rest of us one-by-one? Why would I promise that?"

"For Sam's head?" he laughed again when she fell to her knees. "I'll lead you to her head. Maybe you can find her corpse— maybe not. I hope you do. She was fun to kill." He disappeared and reappeared further way, laughing at Kirk. "Next time, maybe I won't just kill her."

"Stop!" Jen bellowed. She pulled away from her husband and held her hands out as she walked slowly to Miguel. "Fine, Brandon and I will swear."

"Not so fast, swear on your life."

"No, Jen, Sam wouldn't want you too."

Jen turned to her husband who sounded

terrified, then turned back to Miguel and straightened her shoulders. "If Brandon will swear, I will too."

Brandon strode to her, his booted feet stomping the ground. "Jen, if we swear, he'll escape and be free to kill again."

"And if we don't, Sam will remain dead."

"Swear, damn it! We'll catch his sorry ass. He can't avoid all of us." Kirk grabbed Brandon and shook him. "SWEAR!"

Miguel laughed and said, "I swear I'll give Jen Frey Sam's head." He continued to laugh as Kirk swore.

"I swear I won't harm or hunt Miguel," Brandon said angrily and closed his eyes.

"I swear to neither hunt or harm Miguel if he gives me Samantha Quinn's head within three hours," Jen said as her husband screamed no. Lightning manifested and coated her in a scintillating wave. The pain of a vow made to Danu didn't dent the pain of Sam's death. She swore vengeance to herself and the burn intensified.

Ethan glared. He knew as well as she, she'd be forsworn, unable to let an evil like Miguel loose on the world.

"Guess we'll see who she loves more." Miguel said as he rose. He winked at Ethan and slapped his shoulder.

Ethan grabbed his dagger and stabbed at his throat.

Miguel disappeared, reappearing fifty-feet away.

"Tsk, tsk, kill me and where will Sam be? Sure, you might get lucky and find her head but in three hours before her spirit releases?" He shook his head, an overdone sad expression changing to a manic grin. "Looks like I'm holding all the cards."

"Stop fucking around and take me to her," Kirk screamed so angrily spittle flew from his lips.

"Not you. I'll take Jen."

Ethan leaped forward, putting himself between Miguel and Jen. "The fuck you will. She's defenseless against you now. You'll take us both."

Miguel laughed. "Like you could take me? Sure, come along. Drop the summon stone belts first though." He turned and blew kisses to the crowd observing from the stone bleachers. "See ya soon." He waved and turned away.

Jen peered over her shoulder at Jon who now lay face down on the grass. The lightning disappeared in a final shower of sparks, and the druids leaned over the fallen men and woman.

She added will to her voice so it would carry as she vaulted to Gallant's back. "Kirk, summon Jamal and take Cass and Rob east to the forest where her magic came from! Leave Jon some guards but check on Kuan and Emilio."

"Jen…" Kirk stared after Miguel and clenched his fists.

"I know— she'll be safe, I swear it."

Tears filled Kirk's eyes, and he said her name

again, this time sadly. Ethan grabbed her ankle and glared at her. "Honor your vows, all of them."

She offered her husband her hand, and he vaulted onto Gallant's back.

Miguel grinned at Kirk. "Anyone follows us, and I'll disappear, and we'll find out how many of your people I can kill before Jen can find me. Leave me alone, and you'll never see me again." He smirked at them a moment before turning away.

Jen followed astride Gallant.

"If you don't keep your end up, I'll hunt you to the ends of the Earth!" she yelled at Miguel as he sprinted away inhumanly fast.

Jen led her horse away at a gallop, wanting Miguel as far from Jon and her lightning-struck friends as she could get him.

"Aren't you two so sweet." Miguel appeared by the horse's head and jumped back when Gallant snapped at his face. "Thought you could control this beast," he said peevishly as he straightened his stolen tunic.

Jen simmered with rage. He wore Sam's blood-splattered clothing.

"Don't think I can't see you planning to break your vow. I'll be ready when you do and strike you dead while the lightning has you. Ethan here won't be able to save you, and then I'll kill him and behead you both."

Ethan swatted at Miguel. "Shut up and take us to her. Jen will keep her vows, all her vows." Gallant reared and crow-hopped forward.

"Control your fucking horse, Jen. Sam means shit to me. I'm not afraid of you either, it just seemed simpler to not have to worry about you, but if you want to play it that way, I'm game."

Jen half-turned in the saddle to stare at her husband who smiled and laid his hand on her face.

"Keep your vows, sweetheart, all of them."

He kissed her quickly, then straightened. Gallant followed Miguel without her will, and her hope grew. If Ethan could control her horse, maybe he could control her sword too. She peered over her shoulder but could no longer see the stadium through the trees. For an hour, they followed Miguel through the forest in a meandering, crisscrossing loop.

"Wait here," Miguel finally said and sprinted away.

"Can yo—"

Ethan silenced her with a kiss. "Surround us in your Sanctuary. He might think he can kill us alone like this." The yellow glow of her Sanctuary infused the ground beneath them. Gallant stamped his feet and circled, first to the left than the right before going to the center and rearing on his hind legs.

Jen turned in the saddle to hug him, breathing in the scent of his skin and resting in his embrace.

Miguel returned thirty minutes later. "Nobody followed." He led them down a bank to a stream, kicking at rocks as he passed.

"How about we make another deal," Ethan

said. "You and I fight to the death right here. I'll swear not to run away if you will."

"Right, like Jen won't heal your ass."

"She'll swear on her life to not interfere in the fight."

"You're a good rogue, but not as good as me," Miguel said.

"I think I am."

Miguel turned away, frowning. He kicked another rock in the water then swooped down. "Ah ha, just like I promised.

"Stay here. Give me your tabard." Ethan jumped from Gallant and held his hand out for her tabard.

Nausea roiled her stomach, and a cold sweat dotted her brow. She leaned over Gallant's side and vomited when Ethan lifted Sam's dripping head from the water.

Miguel laughed. "You should see your face." His laughter died as she summoned her sword.

"It glows blue, and I'll kill you before the lightning dissipates."

Ethan wrapped Sam's head in Jen's tabard and handed it to her.

"He's too much of a coward to fight me. We're safe from him. A simple stab at doorways as we go through them will ensure he doesn't sneak into our rooms. We're about a thirty-minute run from the castle, so I figure Sam's body is twenty minutes from the castle at most."

Ethan laughed when Miguel grunted. "Sure,

you won't take me up on my offer of a fair duel?"

"Sure, I'll kill you if you're just dying for it." Miguel laughed at his pun. "Swear you won't run like a coward, and I'll do the same if she swears she won't heal you."

Ethan, no!" Panic made her voice breathless.

"Jen, sweetheart, trust me. We need to stop him. I can stop him."

"Please" – Jen licked her dry lips and slid from Gallant's back to clutch Ethan's shirt in both sweaty hands— "I need you. Please, you can't fight him."

Miguel laughed and placed his hands on his hips. "She knows I'll kill your sorry ass." He turned a leering gaze on Jen. "Don't worry, I can scratch your itch—"

"Shut your filthy mouth!" Ethan shouted and pried Jen's hands from his shirt. He rose them to his lips and kissed them. "Jen, I swear to you, we'll be together forever. Don't listen to him. He's too much of a coward to fight me anyway."

Miguel glared. "I'd fight you, but two on one isn't fair. She has to swear she won't heal you. And you know she will. You'll kill both of you," he said cheerfully, the glare gone and a sunny smile replacing it.

"Jen trusts me."

Jen had clutched his shirt again, turning to bury her face in Ethan's chest. The thought of him dueling Miguel made her nauseous, but he wasn't wrong, they did need to stop Miguel. And he could control Gallant. She straightened and glared at Miguel who leered at her again, his gaze traveling her bare thighs and lingering on the silver chains holding her bustier closed. A sudden thought almost made her smile. He thought she was naked.

"For this fight only," Jen said.

"Fine, for this fight only, but he won't have another one. I'm going to take his fucking head, Jen. You're a fool for letting him try to fight me. When he's dead, maybe I'll come keep you company. Without your magic, you'll be defenseless against me, and with it, the lightning will kill you." He grinned and buffed his nails on his bloody tunic.

"Or, you guys could join me. I'll even lead you to her body." Miguel leaned against a tree and crossed his arms. "Stan was fucking crazy and had no intention of really staying there. They were just learning the ropes, seeing how people reacted and shit and planned to find a nicer place to take over. Me— who needs that shit, I can take whatever I like, but it'd be nice to have company. We could bring Sam too if you want. The four of us—"

"You make me want to vomit," Ethan said and strode forward with his daggers out. "I'm attacking either way, but if you don't want me to disappear if you're about to win, then you swear not to as well.

Miguel sighed and pushed away from the tree.

"Fine, you dumb fuck. I swear to fight Ethan Frey to the death without retreating beyond six hundred yards as long as he does the same with no healing from his wife."

The familiar tingle of a building vow rippled across Jen's skin.

"I swear I won't heal Ethan Frey in this duel," Jen said and held up her sword.

Ethan placed his hand on the hilt and smiled at her. "I swear to fight Miguel Garcia to the death without retreating six hundred yards."

The lightning arrived and covered them. When it passed, Miguel pulled himself to his feet, shaking his head.

"Powerful shit. I don't think you can break that vow and live, Jen. Are you sure you wouldn't rather just come with me? What do those strangers mean to you anyway? They're already dead. Nothing we do here matters."

"They're people, and they matter." Ethan leapt forward with her sword in his hand.

Miguel shrieked and ducked. "How the fuck… you're fucking cheating."

"The fae be triksy devils," Jen said softly as her sword flared blue in her husband's hand. "Everything I have is his. We've bound ourselves with oaths and love. Please, by all means, run from him."

Miguel stopped running, and turned back, a snarl on his face.

"I can still kill him."

Jen slid to the ground. Gallant ran forward with his ears back and teeth bared.

Miguel cursed and dodged the striking hooves and snapping jaws. He disappeared, reappearing behind Ethan, but the sword in Ethan's hand spun him to face the danger. Ethan connected with a solid cut to Miguel's shoulder, leaving new blood stains on the tunic. Jen dispelled her armor and grabbed a summoning ball from her jeans pocket.

"Kirk." She whispered the names of the two firebirds who appeared and dove at Miguel shrieking and spitting flame.

Miguel screamed in fury. "You fucking cheater."

Kirk appeared right as Miguel stabbed at her back. The blow rocked her but did no damage.

Kirk held out his arms and flaming rocks began sleeting to the ground. Miguel shrieked as he tried to dodge them, and Ethan disappeared, reappearing a moment later and casting his Knock Out Punch, leaving Miguel dazed on the ground.

Kirk snarled in triumph and a wave of green flames poured over Miguel.

Cursing, Miguel tried to rise but the two firebirds dropped flaming balls atop him. The resulting explosions knocked him back down and set him afire. Ethan attacked in a flurry of blows, the flames cast by the birds and Kirk doing no harm to him but making Miguel scream and writhe. A meaty odor rose into the air and he stopped moving.

"Get Tony to dispel his magic, quick," Ethan said. He wiped his blood splattered face and stepped away.

Kirk ripped a summoning stone from his belt. "Tony." A tendril of neon green traveled from a nearby tree to Miguel's body. Kirk was trying to keep him alive until Tony arrived, but it was too late. Blue magic leaked from the burning corpse. Jen jumped back and casted her dispel.

Tony appeared before Kirk.

"Dispel his magic," Kirk said and casted waves of green fire again until all that remained was a pile of ash. He kicked the ash into the brook while Jen casted Lay Evil Spirits. Glittering blue motes from Tony's fingers encased the magic and both dissipated. More glittering motes covered the ground around them as Tony continued to cast his biggest dispels.

"Did you find her corpse?" Jen asked.

"Not yet. Did he cut—"

Kirk began crying as Jen handed him the balled-up tunic.

"We'll find her, man." Ethan hugged him, then kissed Jen. "Take them on Gallant. Miguel brought us this far trying to leave the zone so your minion couldn't locate her. I'm betting she's across the narrowest part of the river. He probably thinks that's a different zone too and used the water to break his trail. Make your demon look for her sneaker."

Jen stepped back as a black shadow pulled itself from the ground. It resembled Kirk but with snout-like features, spiraling horns and a forked tail. Black bat wings with a faint red tracing of glowing veins fluttered from its back. Unable to find or carry live things, it could be sent for inanimate objects if Kirk pictured them clearly.

"Follow it," Kirk said excitedly.

He needn't have; Gallant already crashed through the trees in pursuit. The two firebirds followed, shrieking and trailing flames.

Galloping into The Future

Kirk unwrapped the severed head and placed it atop the neck. Tony had removed his tabard and covered the body. Sam's naked torso lay beneath a pile of blood-soaked leaves.

"Summon Kuan." Jen began crying and hid her face in her husband's neck. Magic oozed from his skin. He was as sickened as she.

"Can't you?" Kirk said in a voice thick with tears.

"Kuan's magic is strongest. Please summon him."

Tony held out a red summon stone. "Kuan."

Kirk leaned over Sam's corpse, crying.

Kuan appeared.

"Sam," he cried out in anguish, and a blindingly white glow covered the corpse.

A ripple traveled her body.

Eyes closed, and strained face tipped to the sky, Kuan called for more magic.

Jen casted her resurrection spell.

Ethan knelt beside Sam and placed his glowing blue hands on her heart. "She has none, give her some of yours."

Kirk knelt beside him and placed his glowing hands on her head as Tony casted resurrection. Light shimmered across Sam's corpse in waves of green, yellow and white. The light grew so bright it seared Jen's eyes.

The head reconnected. Another ripple traveled Sam's skin, and she sat and screamed, peering about wildly as the light faded, leaving dancing afterimages in Jen's eyes.

"He's dead," Kirk said with vicious satisfaction.

Sam grabbed him and began crying. The magic surrounding her pulsed. Jen let her magic join theirs.

"Danu is terrified. Sam, are you okay?"

"What happened? Did he kill me?" Horror laced her voice, and she trembled in Kirk's arms.

"You're okay." Crying, Kirk sat and pulled her into his lap. "You're okay," he said again as if trying to convince himself.

Ethan laid his hand on Sam's head. "Summon Rob, Tony. He can send Joash with a note to summon Sam back to the castle and inform the others they can stop searching."

"I'm not okay, I'm naked and bloody. What

happened?" Sam's voice rose shrilly, and she pushed away from Kirk to Jen.

"Miguel killed you, but we resurrected you. Do you remember any of it?" Jen asked.

Sam shook her head wildly. Sweat trickled down her face and Jen could see the pulse in her neck jump but it was the fear and horror she felt that made Jen moan.

Kirk kissed her lips and wiped her face. "Don't try too. He's dead, and you're not. That's all that matters."

Tears filled Sam's blue eyes, and she began sobbing. Rob appeared and sent Joash to the castle with a note while Jen cried and tried to comfort Sam.

"Get her clean and warm," Jen said to Kirk, then to Sam, "You're safe now, Sam." She sat as closely as she could, surrounding Sam in her magic and stroking her hair until she disappeared, summoned to the castle.

Jen slumped in the bloody leaves. "Thank God."

"Except now everyone knows how to kill us and that doing so will incapacitate the rest of us," Rob said.

"I'm being summoned." Kuan disappeared.

Ethan pulled her into his arms, glaring over her head at Rob. "And they also know we can make more of us. We'll make it clear that for every one of us they kill, they'll be two more."

Tony laid a hand on his shoulder and kissed

Jen's temple. "It's clear we kill our enemies. That's our best defense. Make it real clear to Galahad and Dante that you'll seek out whoever sends men against us— that distance won't save them."

"We will." Ethan kissed Jen's brow. "God, you're exhausted and sick with grief."

"I need Jon and the others. I need to know they're all well."

Tony and Rob disappeared.

"You go first," Ethan murmured and kissed her brow again.

She nodded tiredly and accepted her summons.

Warm balmy air and the smell of soap greeted her. Maria had summoned her directly to the baths. She waded into the warm pool with her clothing on. A dense cloud of blue magic surrounded Sam as she cried on Kirk's shoulder. Jen's magic joined it, and her tense shoulders eased as she felt their love and concern.

Ethan also stepped into the water clothed.

Jon entered, followed by Kuan. "I put Ramiro in charge and told him to spread the word Miguel is dead. He is dead, isn't he?"

"Deader than a doornail." Jen reached her hand to Jon and smiled wryly when he kissed her fingers and blew across them. Beside her, Ethan relaxed as she did. The magic about them was so dense she could almost hear thoughts in it and with a slight shock she realized Danu was present and she was sensing her emotions.

"It isn't magic we carry inside us but Danu," she said and ran her hand through the swirling cloud.

"It's both, I think," Kuan said. "We each carry a part of her. Her essence, which is raw magic. She's much too powerful for any human to contain. When we gather, she can manifest. Her separate parts rejoin, and it feels like she grows more aware of us. Or maybe we grow more aware of her…"

He trailed off, obviously deep in thought.

Ethan shrugged and said, "Well, I'll feel better once I'm clean. Maybe she will too." He waded through the chest-high water and grabbed a bar of gray soap from the ledge, stripped of his clothes and threw them on the rock floor, leaving only his boxers on.

Jon did the same before jumping into the pool and kissing Sam's brow. She turned to him crying. The tears eased as Jon held her against his chest.

The knights huddled together in the water until Danu floated about them in lazy swirls.

Jon's worried gaze traveled them. "We're more connected now. More connected than I think was possible when we were human. Keep that in mind; when you risk yourself— you risk us all. We need each other. Sam's unhappiness is breaking my heart."

"Jon, what I did— murdering all those

people...." Jen glanced at Ethan and bit her bottom lip so hard it bled.

"No, Jen, it wasn't murder." Jon sat forward and took her hand. "Executions aren't murder."

Jen clasped Jon's hand hard and continued, "It isn't right that I can kill with no punishment."

Ethan's surge of terror made the gathered knights moan.

"Jen, it wasn't you. It wasn't her, Jon." Ethan pulled her from Jon and clutched her.

His gaze darted about the room as if he planned their escape.

"I love you more than anything, but it's only right that I pay for my murders too." Jen kissed him. She'd withdrawn her magic, but so much surrounded her she felt his despair clearly.

Jon took Ethan's hand. "Stop. Ethan, there's no need to be afraid. We aren't going to hold Danu's actions against Jen. I'm sorry, Jen, but you have a hard job in Camelot. You are The Frey, Danu's hand on Earth. It's a great burden and one I wish I could take from you, but Danu chose you, Brandon, and Victoria."

"Who's to say though, Jon? What makes my kills right and others wrong?"

"Danu says. Can you cause your sword to glow?" Jon placed his hand on her shoulder. "It's a valid worry, Jen. No one should be able to kill indiscriminately. Trust Danu. If we doubt, we'll question you in our magic. If the power corrupts you, we'll stop you."

"You promise?"

"I swear it."

Thunder rumbled, making Jon wince. "Shit. I've had too much lightning today."

Kuan laid his hand over Jon's. "We swear to do our best to help each other use our power for good."

"I swear," Sam said.

"Me too." Kirk kissed Sam's brow and took Jen's hand. "It'll be hard, but you aren't alone. We'll all help you."

Thunder rumbled but lightning didn't appear. Emotions flickered through the magic, mutating and overlapping, making it hard to pinpoint the source

Jon closed his eyes and waved his hand through the blue mist of magic. "Everyone is so sad and worried." He laughed when Jen kissed Ethan. "Danu likes that a lot better, but I feel like a voyeur."

Jen grinned and kissed her husband again, sliding her hand along the damp skin of his back. Laughing, she released him and grabbed the soap. Her gaze traveled to Sam who dozed on Kirk's shoulder and her laughter faded.

"Kendra was right in a way."

Jon rose an eyebrow.

"If we'd gone earlier, we could've saved a lot of people and maybe her. I think we need to police ourselves. While we're all here, and together, this is fine, but we should check regularly on wielders who choose to live apart. We're too powerful, our gifts are too great for us to let them become so corrupted."

"You're right, and we will." Jon gestured to the soap in her hand. "Going to use that?'

With a thought, she wore her protection armor and soaped herself before handing the bar to Jon.

"Will that work or are you just washing your clothes?"

"No idea." Jen shrugged and submerged to rinse her hair.

"— oath," Kuan was saying when she surfaced.

"You can administer it when the transformations are complete." Jon grinned at Kuan.

"Emilio will be a fury warrior, and he'll need to be careful that anger doesn't make him do anything he regrets."

"We'll all help him. The rangers can hang out with him until he gets a handle on it. It should help keep him calm."

Cas and Jamal nodded agreement.

Kuan said, "I think Vicky will be a paladin and the other three rangers. Cass has agreed to teach them so Jamal can return to Matt."

"If Matt would like to come home, Gallant and I will take you wherever you wish," Jen offered.

"That's kind of you to offer, Jen, but we're

trying to map the coast. If we fly over it…" Jamal laughed and shrugged.

Have you found any other villages?" Jon asked.

"One so far where Southend-on–Sea will be. It's about the same as Limenware was."

"How is Limenware?" Ethan asked.

Jon sighed and looked troubled. "Empty, but they can return now or stay if they'll follow our laws. Either way, we'll help them recover as best we can. It won't be easy. Over half their populace is dead, and some real anger remains for the survivors."

"They should be angry," Jen said.

"They're angry with each other. Some families were decimated, some not. The finger pointing has started." Jon smiled grimly. "Your rampage actually helped with that. Whenever someone starts complaining, someone else points out how you tore through the town slaying evil as you found it."

"I don't recall that at all. I could've missed some."

"I doubt it. You were pretty thorough. I was there and saw how'd they'd touch your hand and you'd follow your glowing sword to the evil doer."

"Never do that again," Ethan murmured in her ear.

"Not like I did on purpose."

"I know, but you were gone." Tears filled Ethan's eye. He closed them and rested his forehead against hers. "Standing in your magic, there was nothing of you. No love, anger, fear, nothing."

"She was Danu, the spirit of the Earth," Kuan said.

Jen's gaze flicked to Kuan where he reclined beside Kirk with a hand on Sam's shoulder.

"Danu was sickened by the corruption of her gifts that allowed evil to flourish."

"How do you know?"

"I just do." Kuan shrugged and closed his eyes.

"Can't argue with that," Ethan said and pulled himself from the pool. "I'm pruning and starving. Kirk, call us if she wakes and needs us, or if you do. Whatever she needs, we'll do."

Kirk nodded his thanks.

Ethan left and returned fifteen minutes later with a basket of food followed by Gwen and Dillion both carrying baskets.

Jen waded from the water and kissed Ethan's cheek, then Dillion's. His pale, tear-streaked face brightened when he saw Sam.

"See, told you Sam was fine." Gwen placed a hand on his shoulder and turned him toward the door. "Let the magic users rest. We can visit later."

"I'm a mage. My mom said I was a good one and when I was older I could go to tourneys with her."

Jon glanced at Jen and winced. Dillion didn't speak of his family often. She debated what to say, but Kuan beat her to it.

"Your mother was an amazing healer." He climbed from the pool and crouched before the boy. Thunder rumbled as he laid his hand on Dillion's arm. Kuan jerked back as if struck. "You are a mage," he said in wonder.

Lightning flowed through the open window and rolled Dillion over.

Gwen screamed. Jen pulled her away.

On all fours, Kuan hovered over Dillion, the lightning surrounding both and pulsing.

"Stop! He's just a boy. Kuan don't!" Gwen struggled in Jen's grip.

"I'm not doing it." Kuan lifted a strained face to Jen.

"Everyone, give them space." Jon jumped from the pool and crouched beside them. A grimace on his face, he placed his hand on Kuan's. "Fuck, this fucking hurts," he gasped and slid to his knees. "Not as bad though. For me at least." His lips tightened, and his head lowered.

"What are we going to do…" Gwen began crying and clutched Jen, no longer trying to reach Dillion. "He's only eight. Can he survive this?"

"Get Arden." Ethan pulled Jen into an embrace. His worry matched hers exactly. A sick fear for the suffering of the child. "Maybe she can knock him out or something."

"I can try to dispel him," Tony offered.

"No point. If Danu wants him, it's going to take him. Let's dope him up or knock him out or something. We can always heal him afterward. All the newly chosen should go to Arden. There must be something she can do."

The lightning continued to flicker and pulse. Saint Elmo's fire appeared and coated the silent watchers. Five minutes later, the lighting retreated from the open window. Gwen scooped Dillion into her arms. Kuan and Jon remained on the floor where they'd fallen. Gwen hurried from the room, clutching the still unconscious Dillion.

Pale and shaken, Jen began healing everyone. Tony and Cami added their heals to the mix until everyone in the room glowed softly. The room remained quiet, the knights waiting anxiously for the king to rise. Jen straightened Kuan, making him as comfortable as she could before doing the same to Jon. Forty minutes later he sat. Within minutes Kuan stirred.

Jon rose and pulled Kuan up.

"You okay?"

"Yeah. I swear, I didn't do it on purpose."

Jon nodded and slumped against the wall. "It didn't hurt me as much; I think because it hit you first, so we were sharing damage. I wish I could share all of yours, not just my healers." He paused, then said thoughtfully, "Can you do it on purpose?"

"Maybe." Kuan shrugged and looked thoughtful.

Jon grabbed his discarded clothing from the floor. "Let's all rest and recover and worry about that later. We'll have a feast and welcome our new knights. I have no idea what to do about Dillion."

Ramiro stuck his head in the door. "You better come quick, three ships are headed to the port."

"Brandon and I will go. The rest of you dress." Jen pushed her wet hair off her face and kissed Ethan's cheek. In a nearby changing room, she stripped off her wet clothing and emerged in her white armor feeling naked.

Maria handed over her summoning stone belt and a new tabard. The bathing room was already half empty. Brandon waited outside the baths astride Ed. His eyes glittered blue from the slots of his helm. He wore his protection armor and carried his Sword-of-Truth unsheathed in his right hand.

Midnight-black, armored in tarnished silver with only his blue eyes showing Ed floated ten feet from the ground with his silver hooves kicking off small gray clouds. Brandon appeared imposing and on the edge of violence. The thought steadied Jen, together they'd be more than a match for three boats of sailors.

A thought summoned Gallant, and the two bounded into the air. They landed to pick up Galahad and Dante who hurried toward the docks followed by their squires.

"The ship sails the prince's banner," Galahad said as he swung on behind Jen and clutched her hard.

"What shit timing," Brandon complained, his voice carrying to her easily.

"You've killed your evil knight then," Galahad asked.

"Yes." She wanted to add, 'but not yours,' and bit it back.

She had to remind herself that just because she didn't like Mondred that didn't make him evil. His name was only a coincidence.

On the top of the path leading to the harbor she paused and glanced back. Camelot appeared tranquil, distance hiding the people scurrying for their homes to change. Airy and graceful, the castle towered over the countryside. Formed by magic as the druids willed, it's otherworldliness suddenly struck her. Already she'd begun to take such things for granted.

The last few months had changed her more than she'd thought possible and she suspected the future would mold her into a someone she wouldn't recognize. Magic and circumstances had formed stronger bonds with these people than those she'd left behind. Bonds she cherished even though the strength of her need for the other wielders scared her sometimes. Love for Ethan was a fire in her soul. Life without him didn't bear thinking of.

Just considering Mondred had come to harm the people under her care caused Danu to flare from her, and she faced the truth of what she was. Genevieve Frey, computer geek, had died. She was no longer a simple girl with modest aspirations, but a protection paladin— a fae bound by magic and oaths to be a creature of violence to protect those in her care.

Jen's gaze flicked to the smoke rising from the chimneys along the outer wall. Without magic, and few in number, the citizens of Camelot would be easy prey. And the loss of their knowledge would be a tragedy for all mankind. They were worth protecting.

If she had no magic at all, she'd still fight to live in a world with equal rights for everyone. The magic within her settled, at ease with her desire to protect those in her care.

Eyes hard and determined, she turned back to the boats approaching her shore. She hoped she proved strong enough for what lie ahead. With a thought, she urged her horse on, galloping into her future.

The End

About the Author

S. M. Savoy lives and works on the family farm in Connecticut. Married with two grown children, she spends her free time writing. A lover of fantasy books since childhood, and at one time an avid gamer, she likes to think her two loves merge in this book where magic takes on a life of its own. Her two series, Valor and Return of the Fae were a labor of love as she explored the different beliefs her characters hold about the same phenomenon.

Enter the Frey

Jen Frey is a modern woman plunked without warning into a medieval world. Gifted with magic, but cursed to live in a time where magic is reviled and women of little worth, Jen finds herself at odds with the church.

Her modern ideals threaten the very existence of the priesthood, and they'll stop at nothing to eradicate the threat the fae represent.

But Jen is also a protection paladin who's made vows to the Earth itself, and she's willing to shed her pacifist ways if that's what it takes to keep those in her care safe.

www.ingramcontent.com/pod-product-compliance
Lightning Source LLC
Chambersburg PA
CBHW071431190726
48292CB00001B/189